ALSO BY JACK STEWART

<u>**The Battle Born Series**</u>
Unknown Rider
Outlaw
Bogey Spades
Declared Hostile

To find out more about Jack Stewart and his books, visit
severnriverbooks.com

For Sarah,
Who encouraged me to fly.

OUTLAW

JACK STEWART

SEVERN RIVER
PUBLISHING

Severn River Publishing
SevernRiverBooks.com

This is a work of fiction. Names, characters, businesses, places, events and incidents are either the products of the author's imagination or used in a fictitious manner. Any resemblance to actual persons, living or dead, or actual events is purely coincidental.

ISBN: 978-1-64875-495-1 (Paperback)

1

Diamond 100
Navy FA-18F Super Hornet
East China Sea

Lieutenant Sierra "Doc" Crowe reached across the cockpit with her right hand and twisted in her seat to watch the Chinese fishing trawler go down their port side. It was little more than a blur as the Super Hornet hummed through the humid air a scant one hundred feet above the water. She glanced back at the large moving map display in front of her and noted their position in the East China Sea—well outside Chinese territorial waters.

"Did you see the name?" her pilot asked over the intercom.

"Was I supposed to?" Doc looked forward and saw the pilot's grin in one of the three mirrors along his forward canopy bow. "Quit busting my balls, Colt."

To outsiders, a comment like that coming from a woman would have seemed odd. More than odd, even. But, to Colt Bancroft, Sierra was just one of the guys. He abruptly banked right and climbed away from the water. "Tiger, Diamond one hundred."

The E-2D Hawkeye controller replied immediately. "Go ahead."

"The vessel's name is *Fu Yuan Yu Leng*."

"Any numbers?"

Colt paused. "Five hundred or six hundred. I'm not entirely sure."

In a matter of seconds, Colt had piloted their Super Hornet up to five thousand feet above the water and entered a shallow orbit over the blue-and-white ship. It wasn't the only one in those waters either, and they had spent the last thirty minutes circling a turbulent patch just north of the Senkaku Islands—swooping low and zooming past one fishing trawler after another.

"Copy," the Hawkeye controller replied. "Intel can review your tapes when you get back."

"What's so important about these ships?" Doc asked. Unlike the weapon systems officers who were accustomed to riding in the back seat while manipulating the myriad of sensors the Super Hornet had at its disposal, she was an air wing flight surgeon who had only wanted to go for a ride.

"Maybe nothing," Colt replied. "But China has invested heavily in a fleet of fishing boats that some think is part of a maritime militia."

"A maritime militia?"

She saw Colt's helmet bob. "They have a history of using these boats to stake a territorial claim in contested waters—like around the Spratly Islands in the South China Sea."

"Or the Senkaku Islands in the East China Sea."

They made eye contact in the mirror again. "I thought they paid you to be a doctor."

"And I thought they paid *you* to fly planes," Doc jibed.

Colt laughed. "Now you sound like a real *wizzo*," he said, referring to the WSO who normally occupied Doc's seat. "I'm just a stick monkey to you, aren't I?"

Doc leaned back in her seat and reached up to unclip the oxygen mask from her helmet, letting it dangle to one side. She propped her elbows up onto the canopy rails and relaxed as if she were nobility and the seventy-million-dollar fighter jet her royal carriage.

"Diamond one hundred, Tiger," the Hawkeye controller said.

Doc saw Colt bring his oxygen mask to his face before answering. "Go ahead."

"Got another one for you, bearing three five zero degrees for ten miles."

Doc watched Colt manipulate the cursor on their displays, directing the AN/APG-79 AESA—active electronically scanned array—radar into surface search mode. He found the contact and designated it as a target, then turned to point the Super Hornet north.

"Five bucks says it's another fishing trawler," Doc said.

So far, their SSC—surface surveillance and control—mission had been utterly boring. During the Cold War, carrier air wings employed the S-3B Viking with radar, sonar, and magnetic anomaly detection equipment to find and track surface and subsurface vessels. But after the Viking's retirement in 2009, the surface search mission fell to the air wing's Hornets and Super Hornets.

"No way I'm taking that bet," Colt replied. Obviously, he agreed that their mission amounted to little more than a joy ride without much tactical or strategic value. "Starting down."

Doc reached up and clicked her oxygen mask into place, then craned to look around Colt's ejection seat as he nosed the Super Hornet over and made his approach toward the vessel from the stern. Doc could just make out the white froth of the vessel's wake, but the ship was still obscured from view.

"One mile," Colt said.

Again, Doc reached across the cockpit and braced herself. As Colt increased his pull, puffs of vapor formed along the Super Hornet's LEX, or leading edge extension—the wide, flat surface along either side of the canopy that stretched back to the wings. Again, the jet hummed through the air, and Doc couldn't help but smile at her good fortune.

If only my dad could see me now!

As the vessel came into view, she chuckled. "That's five bucks."

"I didn't take..."

Colt fell silent, and Doc looked forward to see what had distracted the pilot. Suddenly, the jet banked hard to the right, and she caught sight of a dark object floating from right to left across the canopy. It disappeared

under the LEX and was followed a moment later by a sudden jolt and a
sickening screech of metal.

"What the hell was that?"

But Colt didn't answer.

"ENGINE LEFT...ENGINE LEFT."

Doc tensed with the first of several audible bangs that sounded like
somebody was taking a ball peen hammer to the side of their jet, and her
eyes were drawn to the left display when the first caution appeared.

"What's going on, Colt?"

"Fuck," the normally calm pilot replied.

In a matter of seconds, Colt had processed the flood of information
assaulting him from every direction—the dark speck that caught his attention as they reached the stern of the fishing trawler, followed closely by the
engine surging, rising exhaust gas temperature, and loud banging and
violent shaking consistent with a compressor stall. He didn't even need the
cautions to help him diagnose the problem, because the remedy was the
same.

Throttle affected engine – Idle.

He pulled the left throttle back while beginning a climbing turn away
from the trawler to put altitude between them and the water.

Speed is life. Altitude is life insurance.

"What the hell was that, Colt?" Doc asked.

"Looked like a drone," he said, but his focus was on his engine indications that showed a steady increase in temperature and decrease in RPM.
Without thinking about it, he raised the left finger lift and pulled the
throttle to OFF, cutting fuel to the engine.

"A drone?"

Colt understood Doc's confusion, but he had more important things to
worry about. Foremost was the presence of a miniature drone flying in the
middle of the East China Sea that brought back memories of a swarm of
mysterious lights swirling around a Navy cruiser off the coast of Southern
California. He had never learned what the lights actually were, but the

memory of losing control of his F-35C Lightning II Joint Strike Fighter immediately after seeing the orbs was more than enough to give him a healthy dose of skepticism about unidentified aerial phenomena.

"Diamond one hundred, Tiger, status?"

Colt shook his head to clear away the memories. "Tiger, I'm declaring an emergency," he said, keeping his tone calm and measured. "We hit something and took damage to our left motor. I've shut it down."

"Copy," the Hawkeye controller replied.

As Colt continued climbing away from the water, he noticed long lines of contrails made by commercial jets arcing across the sky from the east, destined for China's most populous cities, like Shanghai, Beijing, or Guangzhou. Shaking away the thought that the airlines' passengers were oblivious to the dangers lurking beneath them, he glanced back over his shoulder at the blue-and-white fishing trawler and noted that it looked almost identical to the others they had rigged during their SSC mission. Maybe it was coincidence, but it sure looked like there was truth to the claims that China was flooding disputed waters with a fleet of fishing vessels.

"What did you hit?" the controller asked.

Colt didn't answer right away. "Doc, what did you see?"

"Not much. Just a speck, really."

"Was it a bird?"

"I don't think so," the flight surgeon replied.

Colt keyed the microphone switch on his right throttle. "Tiger, we think it was a small commercial drone."

"Copy," the controller replied again.

"Why do you think there was a drone flying way out here?" Doc asked.

But Colt didn't have a definitive answer for her. On the one hand, it was entirely possible that fishermen were now using drones to help guide them onto a school. But, on the other, if the fishing trawlers were employed in a military or intelligence-gathering capacity, the drones could be used in a more nefarious manner.

Like the ones around the Mobile Bay?

"I don't know," Colt replied. "I'll let intel figure that one out. How about we focus on getting ourselves back to the ship in one piece?"

"You don't think they'll divert us?" Doc asked with a slight tremor in her voice.

Honestly, Colt thought it was fifty-fifty and depended on who was in the tower and had the Air Boss's ear. Ultimately, it would be the captain's decision to either recover them aboard the carrier or send them to the divert at Kadena Air Base in Okinawa.

But before he could answer, the Hawkeye controller spoke again. "Diamond one hundred, push button twenty for your rep."

"One hundred," Colt replied, then reached up to select the right channel on his secondary radio.

"Colt, it's Rucas. You up?"

"Yeah, go ahead," he replied.

"What's going on?"

Colt ran him through what had happened, including each of the cautions that had appeared on his display.

"Has the compressor stall cleared?" Rucas asked.

"Affirm," Colt replied. After shutting down the left engine, the RPMs had dropped and the banging and accompanying vibration stopped.

"Copy that. Do you feel comfortable bringing her back single engine?"

"No problem," he said, adding a touch of bravado for Doc's sake.

"Okay, I'll let the Air Boss know. He wants to bring you back, but he's talking it over with CAG and the captain now."

Colt understood that the decision was out of his hands. If either the commander of the air wing or the carrier's commanding officer felt it was safer to divert him, they wouldn't hesitate to send him to Kadena. It was almost a certainty that if he had been a first-tour nugget, that decision would have already been made.

But Colt was a senior lieutenant with several hundred traps under his belt. Aside from the deployments he had made during his first sea tour, he had volunteered to support air wing training while instructing at TOPGUN —the US Navy's Fighter Weapons School—and had flown from aircraft carriers in both the legacy and Super Hornet as well as the new Joint Strike Fighter.

"Standing by," Colt said.

"Diamond one hundred, Tiger. Switch strike."

"Diamond." Colt switched from the Hawkeye's control frequency to check in with the ship. "Strike, one zero zero, Mother's two eight zero for fifty-five, angels twelve, state nine point oh. Emergency aircraft, single engine."

On board the carrier, a sailor took note of his side number and annotated his fuel state as nine thousand pounds while another sailor interrogated his transponder code. Only after ensuring he was squawking a friendly Mode IV code and that his side number matched the transponder's Mode II would they permit him to enter the fifty-nautical-mile Carrier Control Area.

"One zero zero, sweet, sweet. Mother is VFR, case one. Contact Marshal."

"One zero zero," Colt replied, then switched to the Marshal frequency.

He reached up with his right fist and slapped down on the handle near his right knee to extend his tailhook as he repeated his check-in with the Marshal controller.

The controller's reply sounded rote. "One zero zero, case one. BRC is zero one five, expect to Charlie on arrival. Report see me."

He reached down to the Course Select switch and held it to the right, watching a needle swing through the symbol for the ship's TACAN—or tactical air navigation station—on the display between his legs and steady up on the ship's heading, or Base Recovery Course, pointed north-north-east. Then, he pointed directly at the ship and scanned the ocean's choppy surface for the speck of gray they expected him to land his seventy-million-dollar fighter jet on.

He leveled off at two thousand feet and angled his jet to the right to enter the holding stack above the carrier on the downwind leg. Crossing inside ten miles, he spotted the aircraft carrier and reported it to Marshal. "One zero zero, see you at ten."

"One zero zero, switch Tower."

Colt switched to the tower frequency.

The voice of the USS *Ronald Reagan*'s Air Boss boomed over the radio. "One zero zero, Tower."

"Go ahead, sir."

"Charlie."

2

Shanghai Pudong International Airport
Shanghai, China

Lisa's ears popped as she chewed a stick of spearmint gum.

She sat buckled into the R4 jump seat on the starboard side of the aft galley as she tugged at the hem of her dress and inched it toward her knees. The last time she had worn the uniform, they were referred to as *stewardesses*, but she doubted the dresses had gotten shorter over the years. Or even that she had become more modest. More than likely, it was just the sheathed ceramic blade strapped to her inner thigh that made her self-conscious.

She glanced over her shoulder at the other flight attendant. The perky twenty-something-year-old brunette had her phone pressed to the door's tiny window and snapped pictures of Shanghai, oblivious that she was sharing her galley with a spook.

Instagram or TikTok? Lisa wondered, then turned back to her own window to look down on the largest city in the People's Republic of China. As usual, smog blanketed the city, but even through the haze at five thousand feet, she could tell Shanghai had changed over the last quarter century since she'd first visited. China had been a sleeping dragon then.

And now, the dragon was stirring.

The Airbus A330-900neo continued its descent into Shanghai Pudong International Airport, located on the coast, nineteen miles east of the city's center. She leaned back from the window and mentally ran through her emergency procedures, doing her best to fulfill her flight attendant duties, even if it was only just a cover.

She continued chewing her gum, and her ears popped one last time as the Airbus's main landing gear touched down on the asphalt runway. She felt the auto brakes engage and the thrust reversers spool, pressing her back into her seat. Within seconds, the jet slowed and exited on the high-speed turnoff to taxi between the parallel runways on the east side of the airport.

"I've always wanted to visit China," the brunette across from her said. "This is so exciting!" Her name tag said *Jenn*, but they had done little more than exchange pleasantries before taking off from Los Angeles.

Lisa nodded, then looked out her window again as the jet turned onto the ramp and approached their gate.

"First time?" Jenn asked.

"No," she replied, casually reaching between her legs to adjust the knife.

The purser's announcement over the public address system halted further conversation. "Flight attendants, disarm doors, cross-check, and stand by for all call."

She unstrapped from her seat and reached down to disarm the emergency slide and prevent it from automatically deploying when the door opened. She glanced across the galley at Jenn's door to verify she had done the same to hers, then picked up the inter-service phone.

Her crew began chiming in as each of the working flight attendants checked in with the purser, or lead flight attendant, and verified they had disarmed their doors. As two of the more junior flight attendants on the crew, she and Jenn were last, at their stations in the aft galley.

"Jenn, L4, disarmed, all clear."

"Lisa, R4, disarmed, all clear."

"Thank you," the purser replied. When she clicked off, the flight attendants hung up their phones and began preparations to disembark the passengers.

Several minutes later, as the last of the almost two hundred and seventy economy passengers exited through L2, Lisa placed her smaller carry-on atop her roller bag and waited for Jenn to finish gathering her things.

"Sorry," Jenn said, aware she was holding up the crew from beginning their thirty-hour layover.

"Take your time," she replied, though she didn't mean it. She glanced at the small Breitling Chronomat with diamond-set bezel on her wrist and mentally calculated how long she had to make her meeting. "I'm in no hurry."

As far as the others knew, she was one of three flight attendants who didn't speak Mandarin. That she had undergone months of rigorous language training was something she kept to herself, and she spent the forty-five-minute ride from the airport to the hotel pretending not to understand those who spoke the native language.

Jenn and the other excluded flight attendant spent most of the van ride taking pictures of the scenery outside their windows. But Lisa feigned disinterest while intermittently eavesdropping and looking at the minute hand on her watch ticking gradually closer to when she was supposed to meet her contact at the Lujiazui Central Green.

"Well? Do you, Lisa?"

It took her a second to realize Jenn had asked her something. "I'm sorry," she replied. "What did you say?"

Jenn laughed at her startled expression. "Girl, your head is still in the clouds! I said, Betty and I are going to walk the Bund. Do you want to join us?"

It had been several months since she last visited Shanghai, but she remembered walking along the promenade on the west bank of the Huangpu River quite well. It had been spring then, and she remembered enjoying the leisurely stroll to Huangpu Park, the country's oldest public park, at the north end where she first met with Shen Yu.

But today she was to meet him at Lujiazui.

"No, I'm sorry, but I'm beat," she said. "Maybe we can meet up tomorrow? I've always wanted to see the Jade Buddha Temple."

Jenn's disappointed look quickly disappeared, and she sat up tall and clapped her hands with a broad smile on her face. "This is going to be *so* much fun!"

An hour later, Lisa exited the Jinmao Tower through the eastern entrance. The hotel occupying the top thirty-five floors inside the eighty-eight-story building was in the heart of the Lujiazui financial and business district, and most flight attendants appreciated the easy access to restaurants and shopping. But Lisa only cared for its proximity to the park.

She turned north on Dongtai Road, walked underneath the large pedestrian walkway, and crossed Lujiazui Road to enter the green space. She was running a few minutes late, but she knew Shen Yu would wait for her. He had made it clear he would speak only with her, and he needed to do it immediately.

Must be important for the Agency to pull strings and get me on that flight, she thought.

She turned onto the red brick walkway circling the park and looked toward the pond in the middle. Shen Yu had indicated he would wait for her near a sculpture of what looked like two tree trunks stretching into the sky to become winged angels. The sculpture was easy to spot. Shen Yu was not.

"You're late," he said, suddenly appearing alongside her.

She startled but recovered quickly. "Shen Yu. You have us all very worried."

"With good reason." He looked at his watch before scanning the busy street behind him. "I need to catch a flight back to Hunan."

"So soon?" She followed his gaze. The sun was still high in the sky, and the smog gave it a milky glow that was oddly beautiful. But the park was empty, and they were alone. "Shen Yu, what is so important that I had to fly halfway around the world?"

"I'm sorry," the scientist replied. His face was downturned, and his eyes pleaded with her in a way even her childhood golden retriever couldn't have competed with. "I uncovered something I shouldn't have."

She felt her heart quicken. "What?"

He stared into her eyes, and she could tell it was a struggle for him. She knew the respected biochemist had shown a certain hesitancy to trust the Americans, but the consensus at Langley was that her feminine touch was exactly what he needed to overcome his reluctance in helping them.

"Shen Yu. Talk to me."

He took a deep breath and exhaled slowly with his chin tilted skyward. "I'm afraid they will execute me when I return," he finally said.

Instinctively, she reached to her right hip, where she would have carried her gun were she back in the United States. The hair on the back of her neck stood on end, and she felt cold as she contemplated the potential extraction scenarios they had considered for this exact situation. At the time, she had shot down every single one, believing they were too dangerous and that she still had more time.

"Then don't go," she said. She wasn't about to let him return to face a sentence she had committed him to. "We can get you out. *I* will get you out."

Shen Yu shook his head. "It's too late for that."

She reached out and took his hands in hers. They made eye contact, and his lip quivered with a fleeting look of shame that vanished as he steeled himself to do what he believed was right.

"Please," she said. "What did you find?"

His eyes darted around the park as if searching for hidden assassins. "A splinter element within the Ministry of State Security has developed a synthetic bioweapon designed to start a war."

"What element? Where?"

He ignored her questions. "I uncovered the plot months ago and thought I had more time to stop them, but I'm too late."

"Too late?" She struggled to wrap her brain around what Shen Yu was telling her. "It's never too late..."

He shook his head. "I'm sorry, but it is. They are going to use it against an American aircraft carrier."

She swallowed hard. "But Shen Yu..."

"*Listen to me*," he hissed. "I couldn't stop them, but maybe you can."

She stared at him in disbelief. Shen Yu knew his death warrant had already been signed, and still he had requested this meeting. He had her fly halfway around the world so he could look her in the eye and give her the chance to do what he could not—stop a war.

"How?"

"Did you bring what I asked?"

She nodded and blinked away her tears, then reached into her purse to pull out the envelope. She handed it to him, and he took it carefully in both hands.

Opening it, he removed a small stack of photos and smiled.

"There is still time, Shen Yu," she said again. "You can be with them again. It's not too late."

He looked at the pictures of his wife and daughter living comfortably in the San Diego suburbs. "One day, three autumns," he said, then muttered what sounded like *yaoshi*—*if* in Mandarin—and kissed his fingers and pressed them to his wife's face.

Then he slipped a flash drive into Lisa's hand and walked away.

3

USS *Ronald Reagan* (CVN-76)
Carrier Intelligence Center
East China Sea

Colt stood over the enlisted intel specialist as he reviewed the video taken from his AN/ASQ-228 ATFLIR—Advanced Targeting Forward-Looking Infrared—sensor pod. Under normal circumstances, they would have only reviewed footage of the vessels he had rigged as part of the SSC mission. But the foreign object he had ingested in his left motor changed things.

"Nice recovery, Colt."

He turned and saw Commander Rob "Flap" Roy, the Diamondbacks commanding officer, with a concerned look on his face. "Thanks, sir. Added a little too much power in close," he replied honestly.

But Flap waved him off. "No such thing as too much power when you're single engine."

Colt didn't necessarily agree with him. Before even flying out to the carrier, they had spent weeks flying FCLPs—field carrier landing practices —and had simulated a multitude of emergencies, including being single engine. He knew Flap was only trying to make him feel better about his

"Fair" pass, but it was a hallmark of carrier aviation that pilots were critical of their landings.

"Sorry for breaking your jet," Colt said.

Again, the Diamondbacks skipper dismissed the idea. "Don't worry about it. Just glad you made it back in one piece."

"Thanks for letting me take Doc flying." Colt was the training officer for the Diamondbacks' sister squadron, the Maces of Strike Fighter Squadron Twenty-Seven, but he was allowed to fly with the other air wing's squadrons by letter of agreement. The arrangement was put in place to facilitate training, but Colt hadn't hesitated using it to take one of his friends flying.

Flap chuckled. "Bet she got more than she bargained for."

Before he could respond, the petty officer called out to him. "Sir, I think I might have something here."

Colt turned back to the computer monitor and leaned in close. Even though the ATFLIR was a significant improvement over the older AN/AAS-38 Nite Hawk pod, it was a far cry from what he had grown accustomed to while flying the F-35C Joint Strike Fighter.

"What am I looking at here?" Colt asked.

The petty officer tapped on a few keys, then spun a jog wheel to rewind the video several frames. In the middle of the screen, the targeting pod's crosshairs were centered on the stern of a fishing trawler. In the upper right corner of the screen, Colt noticed a black speck appear from out of frame. "Now, watch this spot here as I advance the video."

The sailor gripped the jog wheel and rotated it clockwise. A counter in the lower right corner of the screen displayed the number of frames, but Colt's eyes were glued to the dark speck that grew larger and floated from right to left. The sailor continued to spin the wheel and advance the video at an agonizingly slow pace. At almost thirty frames per second, it took several complete rotations before he reached the last frame with the object visible.

"What does that look like to you?" Flap asked.

Colt cocked his head to the side as if trying to decipher a pictogram. He placed his finger against the screen and traced what looked like a lopsided X. "Could be a quadcopter," he said.

"That's what I thought too," the sailor replied. He opened a control window and adjusted the brightness and contrast, then ran it through several filters to crisp up the image. But no matter what he did, it was still too grainy to make out any significant features.

"At least we can be certain it's not a UAP," Flap said.

Colt turned and looked at the commander. He could tell by the look on his face he wasn't making a dig at the rumors that had circulated following Colt's encounter with the swirling orbs over the USS *Mobile Bay*, but it still made him uneasy.

Why do these things always happen to me?

Colt shook his head. "I still don't know why they would be flying drones out in the middle of the ocean."

"Maybe to spot fish," Flap suggested.

Colt had considered the same thing, but something about it didn't ring true to him. His eyes shifted from the blurred image of the drone to the fishing trawler in the background. "I don't think so, sir."

"Why not?"

Colt pointed at the ship on the screen. "Because they're not trawling."

"How can you tell?"

"See this here?" He traced his finger along the tall steel structure at the stern of the ship. "This is the gallows and is used for operating the trawl, but you can see that they don't have any rigging out."

"It's still the most logical answer," the commander said. "What else could it be?"

That was a question Colt didn't have an answer to. It was the most logical answer *if* the ship was really a fishing trawler. But if it was part of China's maritime militia or a collection vessel for the Ministry of State Security, there was no telling what they were using the drone for.

The sailor saved Colt from having to answer. "I'm going to send this video to Pacific Fleet. Maybe they can figure it out."

Flap didn't seem interested, and he slapped Colt on the back. "Glad you made it back."

Colt nodded, but he was lost in thought.

He left CVIC a few minutes later and headed for the cross-passageway where most of the CAG staff had their offices. Though Doc spent most of her time bouncing from squadron to squadron—usually to cajole the scheduling officers into adding her onto the flight schedule—she spent the remainder in CAG's spaces when the senior medical officer didn't force her to run sick call.

Colt rounded the corner and walked through the open door where several officers were gathered around her as if she were a celebrity.

"...and *WHAM!* Out of nowhere, this thing slams into us." Doc punched her open palm for dramatic effect.

"Telling sea stories, Doc?"

The flight surgeon turned and gave Colt a sheepish grin. "I was just telling them how you handled that *like a boss.*"

Colt shook his head. "Like a boss?"

"Yeah, like losing an engine was no big deal."

A few of the others saw the amused look on Colt's face and dispersed to return to their routine tasks that kept the air wing operational while on deployment. He suspected the CAGMO—the air wing's maintenance officer—would be especially busy ensuring the Diamondbacks had everything they needed to replace the damaged engine and get *100* back into the air.

"I just wanted to check in on you," Colt said. "But it looks like you're doing just fine."

She nodded, then reached back and brought her hair into a ponytail.

"Colt Bancroft," a gravelly voice said from behind him. "Just the man I wanted to see."

He turned and saw the imposing figure of Captain Noah "Cutty" Sark, the Deputy Air Wing Commander, standing in the doorway. "Am I in trouble, sir?"

"Not unless you've been avoiding me."

Colt studied the older fighter pilot's face but saw nothing to indicate Cutty was in a playful mood. "Not at all, sir. What can I do for you?"

Cutty gestured for Colt to join him in the passageway. "Let's go to my office."

Colt slapped Doc on the shoulder, then turned to follow DCAG from the room, quickening his pace to keep up with the former Division I line-backer. Whether it was his broad shoulders or the silver eagles sewn onto his flight suit, sailors simultaneously stepped aside for Cutty and flashed Colt uneasy smiles.

When they reached DCAG's office, Cutty opened the door and propped it open before gesturing for Colt to take a seat in one of the two chairs in front of his desk. Colt sat and waited for Cutty to do the same before the two locked eyes in silence.

"Well?" the old man asked.

Colt narrowed his eyes, unsure how to respond. "I'm not sure I follow, sir."

"You know you're going to have to tell me something."

"About..."

"The *Lincoln*?"

As if someone had flipped a switch and turned a lightbulb on over his head, Colt understood immediately what Cutty was alluding to. "Oh."

"Well?" he asked again.

Colt dropped his eyes to the floor for a moment, then looked back up to the senior pilot who had been the TOPGUN commanding officer when Colt had gone through as a student. He remembered Cutty demanding nothing short of excellence from his staff, and he knew a half-assed answer wouldn't cut it.

"You know I'm not supposed to talk about this."

Cutty nodded.

"And you've heard the rumors?"

Again, Cutty nodded.

Colt hesitated for a second, then got up and closed the door to give them some semblance of privacy. "What do you think, sir? Do you think I was flat-hatting?"

Cutty narrowed his eyes. "No. I don't."

"Good. Because the truth is, the Chinese developed a weapon to hack into the JSF and control it remotely." He paused to assess Cutty's reaction. "They hacked into mine that night off the *Lincoln* and attempted to crash it into the *Mobile Bay*."

Cutty bit his lip and narrowed his gaze on Colt as if evaluating whether the younger pilot was telling the truth or bullshitting him. After a few seconds, he asked, "Why would they do that?"

Colt felt an easing of the knotted tension in his shoulders. "The popular opinion was that they were hoping to eliminate the *Lincoln*'s air defenses before they commenced the attack on their real target."

"Which was?"

Colt hesitated.

"The *Lincoln*?" Cutty asked, having already drawn his own conclusion.

He nodded. "But the hack failed, I regained control, and the *Mobile Bay* survived."

Cutty leaned back in his chair. "How do you know their real target was the *Lincoln*?"

Colt's vision clouded as he remembered piloting a VX-31 F-35C over the darkened Pacific Ocean to chase down his friend. Then he shook himself back to the present. "Because they continued with their plan and launched an attack the next night."

The captain narrowed his gaze on Colt. "What happened?"

"The Dust Devils were in Point Mugu for a test of the Joint Strike Missile. Their test plan called for them to launch two anti-ship missiles against the former *Bonhomme Richard* in the Pacific Missile Test Complex."

"I remember the test," Cutty said, reminding Colt that the captain's last assignment had been at the Pentagon under the vice admiral for warfighting development.

"At least two Chinese operatives set up the experimental weapon on Santa Cruz Island and waited for the test platform to launch from Mugu. When it did, they took control of his jet and turned it on the *Lincoln*."

"Are you kidding me?"

Colt shook his head. "Wish I was."

"So, what happened? How do you know all this?"

Colt swallowed. He wasn't sure how much he should tell Cutty, but after several uncomfortable minutes, he said, "I went to Mugu with an NCIS special agent and tried convincing Jug to delay the test."

"McFarland?"

"Yes, sir."

"I know him. Smart kid. He didn't listen?"

Colt shook his head, ignoring that Cutty obviously also considered him just a kid. "He understood the risks but was under a lot of pressure from leadership to keep the test on timeline."

"So, what happened?" Cutty asked again.

"The special agent flew to Santa Cruz Island to find the operatives and shut them down before they could launch the missiles at the *Lincoln*."

"You didn't go with him?"

"Her," Colt said. "And no."

"You went after Jug, didn't you?"

He nodded.

"In what?"

"The spare test aircraft."

Cutty furrowed his brow and looked as if he was about to read Colt the riot act for going after the hijacked fighter on his own. But then he burst into laughter and slammed his palm flat on the table. "Holy *fucking* shit, Colt! You *stole* an F-35?"

"I *borrowed* it," he said, though he knew it was a matter of semantics.

"No wonder Big Navy wants to keep this quiet! Not only is there a weakness in the F-35's system architecture, but one of their most accomplished aviators stole one!"

"*Borrowed*," Colt repeated, still feeling as if the senior pilot was scolding him.

But Cutty didn't seem angry. "Well, I know the *Lincoln* is still floating, so you might as well tell me how you stopped the Chinese from sinking her."

When Colt looked up, he saw an amused expression on the captain's face and realized he'd misread the older man's reaction. "I wish I could say it was something heroic—"

The older pilot cut him off. "Stealing a Joint Strike Fighter is pretty fucking heroic, Colt."

He ignored the praise. "By the time I reached Jug, the Chinese had already taken control of his jet and were preparing to launch the missiles. But they spotted me first and pitched in."

"What did you do?"

"I had no choice but to dogfight." He replayed the fight in his mind.

"Did you shoot him?"

He nodded, and Cutty gasped. "But I didn't hit him."

"Holy shit. You *actually* fired on him?"

"I didn't *want* to, but I couldn't let them sink the carrier. As it turns out, it didn't even matter." When Cutty remained silent, Colt continued. "They ended up launching both missiles against the carrier. The *Mobile Bay* shot one down, and the *Lincoln*'s CIWS took out the other. When it was all said and done, Jug and I diverted into San Clemente on fumes."

Cutty reached under his desk and removed two tumblers and a small bottle of whiskey. He uncorked the bottle and filled each glass with one finger of the bronze medicinal liquid, then pushed one across the desk to Colt. As Colt stared at the contraband liquor, Cutty lifted his glass into the air. "Here's to you, Colt, for having the balls to do what needed to be done."

Colt picked up his glass and clinked it against the captain's, then brought it to his lips.

4

Jinmao Tower
Shanghai, China

After her meeting, Lisa went straight to her room and ran a hot shower, where she sat on the tiled floor and sobbed. She knew when Shen Yu returned to Hunan, he would be arrested for spying and executed without due process. His death wouldn't be reported, and the world would continue to spin believing China was a modern nation far removed from its violent past of Communist oppression.

After almost twenty minutes on the floor of her shower, she stopped feeling sorry for herself and resolved to honor his last wishes. She picked herself up, turned off the water, and climbed out to dry off. Sitting in her robe at the foot of the bed, she ran a brush through her damp, dark hair and contemplated how to get the flash drive and its contents back to Langley before Shen Yu's ominous warning came to fruition.

If what he had said was true, they were already watching her. She couldn't assume the flash drive would be safe concealed in her luggage or transmitted electronically back to Langley. She put the brush down and stared out the window at the remarkable Shanghai skyline while contemplating her options.

The phone on her nightstand rang and broke her from her trance.

"Hello?"

"Lisa!" Jenn's perky voice broke through her fatigue. "What are you doing?"

"I was just getting ready for bed," she replied, hoping the younger flight attendant caught the hint.

"Want to have a nightcap and watch the sunset?"

"I don't know..." She was about to decline, but a glance at the flash drive resting on the nightstand gave her an idea. "Maybe. Do you have a computer I can use?"

"Yes! Come on over!"

"I'll be right there," Lisa said.

After hanging up, she got dressed in a pair of jeans and a faded, loose-fitting concert T-shirt, then tucked the flash drive into her front pocket, armed herself with the nonmetallic G10 blade concealed in a sheath along her waistline, and snatched her room key off the dresser. She surveyed her room once more, then tucked the Do Not Disturb sign between the jamb and the door as she closed it and stepped out into the brightly lit hall.

Before Lisa could knock, Jenn opened the door and pulled her inside. "There's my computer," she said, pointing to a worn MacBook sitting on the desk across from her bed. "I'll pour you a glass."

Lisa thanked her, then sat down at the desk and inserted the flash drive into the computer, thankful it was an older model with USB-A ports. She had more experience working with the Windows operating system but knew enough about the Mac OS to create a hidden folder and transfer the contents of the flash drive for safekeeping. She would still hide the flash drive in her roller bag's secret compartment, but she felt more comfortable knowing she had duplicated the information onto Jenn's computer. Just in case.

Once complete, she ejected the flash drive, tucked it back into her pocket, and opened Safari to navigate to her web mail. She thought back on what Shen Yu had told her, before crafting a carefully coded email to her boss.

> *Monty,*
> *Wish you were here. Jenn and I have been touring the city. The cherry*

blossoms are so beautiful, and I can't wait to show you my pictures when I return.
Miss you.

    Lisa

"Are you done yet?"

"Almost." She sent the email and logged off, then closed the MacBook. Turning to Jenn with the biggest smile she could muster after one of the longest and most emotionally draining days of her life, she graciously accepted the offered wineglass.

"Here's to a wonderful layover," Lisa said.

"I wish Andy were here to see this," Jenn replied.

"Who's Andy?"

Jenn wiped at the corners of her eyes before replying. "My boyfriend."

"Is he back home in..." She couldn't remember where Jenn had said she was from.

"San Diego? No, he's in Japan."

"Japan?"

"He's in the Navy."

Lisa understood all too well the challenges of being with someone in the military, so she remained silent and watched the sun setting behind the neighboring buildings from the twin chairs Jenn had arranged to face the floor-to-ceiling windows. As much as she couldn't stand the perkiness of the younger woman, Lisa had to admit it was a rare and beautiful moment. Especially in her line of work. She finished her glass with a silent toast to Shen Yu and, without having to fake it, yawned and made her excuse to leave. Reluctantly, Jenn relented and gave her one last hug.

"Breakfast?"

She nodded. "But not too early." She hesitated for a moment before saying what had been on her mind. "Can I give you some advice?"

Jenn gave her a confused look. "Sure."

"Take some time off and go see your boyfriend." Jenn looked as if she was about to protest, but Lisa cut her off. "Trust me. You won't regret it."

Jenn's eyes glossed over as if imagining their reunion. "Thank you."

With a knowing smile, Lisa left the other flight attendant's room and scanned the empty hall before turning toward hers, trying to fend off her own memories and the mental fog that came with hours spent trapped in a steel tube miles above the earth. Between her long duty day and the glass of wine, it would have been too easy to forget she was isolated and become complacent. But she understood the risks.

All her senses were keenly attuned to her surroundings. Behind her, a door opened and closed, followed by the soft plodding of feet on carpet moving closer.

Two...no, three people.

Because the elevator was in the opposite direction, the hair on the back of her neck stood on end, and she was immediately alert. She pictured the approaching threat in her mind, a picture that became clearer as she inhaled the faint scent of body odor, poorly masked by cheap cologne. Her eyes twitched at their shadows cast onto the walls on either side of her, and she braced herself for what she suspected was coming.

But above it all, she choked back the sour taste of fear and prepared for a fight.

She slowed her pace while pretending to reach into her back pocket for her room key, but instead slid her hand to her waistline where she had concealed the nonmetallic G10 knife. She felt more than heard the first one reaching for her, and she quickly drew the blade and spun to face him.

His eyes locked onto hers with a startled look, but she quickly registered that he wore the uniform of the People's Armed Police. Without hesitation, she plunged all three inches into his chest and saw his grip relax on the syringe he had been about to stick into her neck.

She withdrew the blade as the syringe fell silently to the floor. In that instant, adrenaline flooded her body and her training kicked in. She shoved the uniformed man into the closest of the remaining two, then subtly shifted her weight onto her back leg and prepared for the coming attack.

Her mind swam with questions that were better left for later. *Who are they? What do they want?*

The second man darted forward, but she had prepared for his attack and snapped her leg upward in a sharp front kick, connecting the ball of her foot with his nose. He staggered backward a step, but his experience in the martial arts was evident as he shook it off and quickly resumed his advance. She pivoted on her back foot and caught the side of his head with her outstretched heel in a hook kick.

But it had little effect on him. Before she could retract her leg, he snatched it from the air and pulled her off-balance. She fell to the ground on top of the man she had stabbed, but quickly rolled away from her attacker and scrambled to her feet to resume the fight.

They had her hemmed in on all sides. The walls limited her lateral movement, and a man blocked her path in either direction. There was nowhere to go, and she was left with only one option.

Fight.

She lunged at the third man, slashing the blade at the air in front of his face. He deftly dodged the knife, then disarmed her in a flurry of strikes she never saw coming. Stunned, she countered with a quick jab and cross combination, but the blows to her ulnar nerves had left her arms feeling numb and heavy. Her target easily parried the punches, and she felt the jab of a needle in her neck before she could defend against it.

Lisa cried out just as a gloved hand clamped down over her mouth, but it was too late. The fast-acting drug had already taken hold, and there was nothing she could do but stare defiantly into the humorless eyes of the man standing in front of her.

Then, her world went dark.

5

Wizard 323
Navy P-8A Poseidon
East China Sea

Lieutenant Commander Ashley Mitchell glanced up from the paperback she was reading to look at the magenta line on the navigation display in front of her. The heavily modified Boeing 737-800 banked left as it reached the north end of the racetrack and began its turn back to the south. She rotated the lever to unlock the sun visor from the track over her left shoulder, then leaned over to stow it in the pocket next to her seat.

She looked through her side window onto the water beneath them. "There are a lot of boats down there," she said, more to herself than anything.

"Ma'am?"

Ashley turned and looked at Logan, the young lieutenant junior grade who had just joined Special Projects Patrol Squadron Two as a replacement pilot. "Oh, nothing you don't already know. Just looks like the Chinese are putting more and more boats in the water."

Logan nodded, then returned to studying the material he had been given to prepare for the lengthy process of becoming an aircraft commander. Though she had come up through the normal patrol squadron community, she knew Logan's experience wouldn't be much different. Sure, the plane they were flying had "borrowed" its bureau number from an unfinished P-8A fuselage that had fallen off a train and into the Clark Fork River in Montana almost a decade earlier, but to the pilots, it flew just the same.

"Is that normal this time of year?"

Ashley shrugged and slipped her bookmark into the novel she had been reading. "Normally, they hold their large naval exercises in the spring. But occasionally, Russia will send destroyers, corvettes, and submarines from their Pacific Fleet to participate in a joint exercise."

As the P-8A Poseidon rolled out on a southerly heading, Logan turned and looked through his side window at the crowded seascape beneath them. "Think any of those are Russian?"

"We can only hope."

She knew Logan understood. Their squadron's entire reason for existing was to serve as a communications intelligence platform and eavesdrop on the enemy to pinpoint their forces. In this part of the world, that included China and, if they were lucky, Russia. That hadn't changed since the late 1960s when the Navy sent four-engine EC-121M Warning Star surveillance aircraft out over the Sea of Japan to monitor Soviet communications.

The voice of her tactical coordinator broke in over the intercom. "Ma'am, we're starting to pick up some interesting signals patterns between smaller vessels."

"Military?"

"I don't think so," Ed replied. "Seems like most are fishing trawlers, but they have military-grade equipment on board and are communicating with fleet headquarters."

She knew the East China Sea was the responsibility of the East Sea Fleet of the People's Liberation Army Navy based in Ningbo, Zhejiang Province. It wouldn't be unusual for smaller vessels that had been conscripted as part of a maritime militia to maintain constant contact with fleet headquarters.

"Maybe they are just routine position reports," Ashley suggested.

"Tony doesn't think so, ma'am."

First Class Petty Officer Tony Delgado was one of their squadron's most gifted cryptologists who also happened to speak seven foreign languages fluently—including both Russian and Mandarin. "What does he think?"

"He thinks they're receiving deployment orders to…" Ed's voice trailed off, and Ashley could hear Tony's voice in the background over the ever-present hum of electronics. "Sorry, ma'am. He thinks they are being ordered south to support the South Sea Fleet."

"And he's sure these are fishing vessels?" Ashley looked over and made eye contact with Logan, who had been listening to the entire conversation through his David Clark headset.

"They are definitely trawlers. But your guess is as good as mine whether they are civilian, military, or MSS."

Logan mouthed, *What's MSS?*

Ashley held up a finger to let him know she would answer his question, then said, "Copy that. Have Tony draft his report, and let's get it sent back to Pacific Fleet for analysis. The last thing I want to do is sit on something that could be a cover for a full-scale invasion."

"Aye, ma'am."

When Ed's voice fell silent, she turned to Logan. "MSS is the Ministry of State Security—China's intelligence and security agency."

"They have boats?"

She nodded. "There's been some evidence that they're using fishing vessels as cover for surveillance gathering." When she saw his dubious expression, she added, "Yeah, I know. Sounds funny when we're the ones out here drilling holes in the sky doing exactly what we're accusing them of doing."

"It really is spy versus spy," Logan said.

Ashley caught the reference to the comic strip published in *Mad* magazine depicting stereotypical and comical espionage activities. In her mind, it wasn't far from the truth. Each side seemed to be caught in a never-ending struggle to gain an advantage over the other. But whereas the cartoon was always humorous and showed spies often trading victories, the real-world consequences of global espionage were far more serious.

"Let's hope not," she said.

6

San Diego, California

Special Agent Emmy "Punky" King crested the rise on the Coronado Bridge, and her gaze fell on the city's skyline, stretching north away from Logan Barrio. Its modern skyscrapers contrasted the ornate spired roofline of the Hotel del Coronado in her rearview mirror, and she felt like she was slipping through a wrinkle in time to transition from one world into another.

Her phone vibrated, and a notification popped up on the touchscreen display in the center of her dash. She tapped on it to read the message.

CALL ME.

Punky clicked the left paddle and downshifted the reinforced ZF eight-speed transmission as she swerved into the left lane and stomped on the gas pedal. The supercharged 6.2-liter V8 roared as she powered her Hellcat Redeye through eighty miles per hour onto the downward slope. The Hellcat didn't have the panache of her dad's old Corvette Stingray, but she had to admit it had a lot more power and a bit more in the way of gadgets.

Using the steering wheel's controls, she selected the number for her boss and placed the call over Bluetooth while moving back into the right lane and outpacing the slower-moving traffic.

He answered the call after only two rings with a curt, "Camron Knowles."

"Camron, it's Punky." Her nickname sounded strange, even as she said it. She had embraced the epithet from the moment her father's best friend had bestowed it on her, but it had special meaning now.

"You're coming into the office, right?"

She glanced in her mirrors, easing off the 797-horsepower engine as she touched ninety miles per hour. "Not this morning."

There was a pause on the other end. He was new to the Supervisory Special Agent role, and Punky knew he had his hands full with her. "Where are you going?"

"I'm following up on a lead."

He knew exactly what she meant. "Punky, *KMART* isn't a threat."

But, of course, he was. The traitorous sailor aboard the USS *Abraham Lincoln* had conspired in a plot to sink the aircraft carrier, and she was no closer to discovering his identity than she had been before coming face-to-face with an operative from China's foreign intelligence service. Before she killed the woman known to her as *TANDY* and severed her only link to the traitor.

She clenched her jaw. "Yeah, he is."

"Listen, Punky—"

"I don't want to hear it, Camron," she said. "The Ministry's West Coast network is more active than ever."

"And still we've heard nothing from *KMART*."

"Yeah, because I killed his handler! You don't think they've assigned someone new by now?"

Camron sighed. "Fine. Where are you going?"

Punky slammed on the brakes to avoid ramming her Challenger into a slower-moving Kia sedan, then jerked the wheel left and stomped on the gas. "La Jolla."

"La Jolla?"

She bit the inside of her cheek and debated filling him in on her plans. As a special agent assigned to the counterintelligence task force, Punky was authorized to conduct investigations to protect against espionage. But Camron was the head of that task force and had a right to know.

"Punky, *why* are you going to La Jolla?"

She decided to open her kimono just enough to satisfy him. "I've been monitoring the communications from a new individual operating in the San Diego area who the Ministry refers to as *SUBLIME*."

"Named for his outstanding spiritual, intellectual, or moral worth?"

"No, for the band," she said sarcastically. "I have no idea, Camron."

"Go on."

"Over the last several days, his frequency of communications has increased, and they all mention UC San Diego."

"And?"

Punky rounded the bend to merge onto Interstate 5 and downshifted again, surging past another Challenger—a yellow 305-horsepower SXT model—that attempted to accelerate and keep pace before quickly giving up. She flipped him off and continued racing north toward the city.

"I'm on my way to meet with a professor who is giving a lecture this morning."

"Okay?"

Punky couldn't tell if he was just humoring her or if he thought she was on to something. Either way, she could tell he was losing his patience. "The professor is from China."

"And what? You think *SUBLIME* is targeting this person?"

She glanced in each of her mirrors before answering. "You would too if you knew her field."

"Enlighten me."

"She is a professor with the Global Health Institute and serves on the university's Global Infectious Diseases working group." Punky paused before dropping the hammer. "She is regarded as an expert on next-genera-tion biowarfare and has written several articles about synthetic bioweapons."

Camron was quiet for a moment, and she found his silence more disconcerting than anything. "What are you thinking, Cam?"

"Honestly, I don't know," he said. "You might be on to something, but I think you're pushing the boundaries of your mandate. Did you forget that you're supposed to be investigating threats as they pertain to the Navy?

Maybe we should hand this off to the FBI and let them look into *SUBLIME*."

The last thing she wanted to do was hand over months of her hard work so somebody else could take the credit. But she had one more card to play. "The last message *SUBLIME* received mentioned the *Reagan*," she said.

"Reagan? Or the *Reagan*?"

She thought Camron was splitting hairs. "Does it matter?"

"Yeah, Punky. It does. There are at least a half dozen schools named after him in California, not to mention the presidential library and headquarters of the California State Republican Party. There are a lot more plausible explanations than to assume the message was referring to a nuclear-powered aircraft carrier."

But she disagreed. Maybe it was because she had found herself in the middle of a Chinese plot to sink an aircraft carrier off the coast of California. And maybe because the traitor who had made that even possible was still walking around and enjoying his freedom.

"Okay," Camron said. "You can look into it. What's the professor's name?"

"Tan Lily."

"I'll dig around and see what I can find out."

"Thanks, Cam."

"But, Punky..."

"Yes?"

"Don't make me regret this."

Guo Kang sat on his balcony overlooking San Diego Bay's placid waters while sipping his morning tea. He had grown accustomed to the leisurely pace of being a problem solver—only called on when his unique skills were required—and he took full advantage of the perks that came with his position. A luxury condo on the water. Boats in the marina. High-end European cars and motorcycles.

He set his cup down and leaned back in his chair with a contented smile on his face. It was shaping up to be a beautiful Southern California fall day. Sunny. Seventy degrees. Cool ocean breeze. Maybe he would go for a ride into the hills east of the city. Or take the ferry across to Coronado. His options were limitless.

His tea finished, he stood and stretched his athletic frame. Though the sun had barely crested the horizon, the city was already buzzing thirty stories beneath him. Leaving his teacup on the balcony table, Guo Kang headed inside and crossed the cool hardwood floors to his bedroom, where he undressed before walking into his spacious shower.

It was a luxurious setup with three powerful jets on either side of him and a large rainfall showerhead. The digital readout on the wall in front of him displayed the temperature at a steady ninety-nine degrees—warm enough that it eased the aches and pains he had sustained from a hard life. After washing himself, he reached up and rotated the knob counterclock-wise until the temperature dropped below sixty degrees.

The initial shock of the cold water took his breath away, but he calmed his breathing and found the Zen he sought each morning. By the end of the three minutes, he felt completely at ease.

After his shower, Guo Kang toweled off and walked back into the bedroom, where he saw his phone light up with a missed call. He scooped it up from the nightstand next to his king-size bed—already made with taut, military precision—and saw a message waiting for him in Signal.

His day of leisure momentarily forgotten, he opened the app and read the message, then tapped on the phone icon to place an encrypted call over his wireless network.

The General answered after only one ring. "Where are you?"

"At home," he said, already feeling a burgeoning arousal.

"I have another task for you."

Though he had been looking forward to the day, a task from the General portended even greater pleasure. His heart thundered with eager anticipation. "Go on."

"One of our scientists was discovered revealing details about our opera-tion to an American in Shanghai."

"What do you need me to do?" Guo Kang was a weapon to be aimed and didn't need to know why—his trust in the General was absolute.

"Free your schedule and stand by for your instructions."

After the call ended, Guo Kang received an encrypted file containing a complete target package. It was obvious the General had been keeping his eye on the doctor for some time, and he scrolled through the photos with increasing excitement and memorized the information. He knew where the doctor lived and worked. He knew where her daughter went to school and at what times the school bus picked her up and dropped her off.

After committing the target package to memory, Guo Kang dressed in a pair of black jeans and dark gray sweater and slipped on a pair of all-white Nike Air Force 1 shoes. Satisfied with his appearance, he exited his condo and took the elevator to the parking garage, where he approached the Nardo Gray Audi RS6 Avant parked in one of his two spaces. He slipped into the Valcona leather seat while reaching down to press the button that started the twin-turbocharged V8, smiling at the low harmonic of almost six hundred horses at his disposal.

Guo Kang took his time to adjust the climate control settings and turned on his heated seat, then put the high-performance wagon into gear and pulled out of the garage. The San Diego scenery blurred as he drove north from downtown to La Jolla.

7

University of California–San Diego
La Jolla, California

Tan Lily pulled into her reserved parking space in the lot off Gilman Drive, just a short, shaded walk down a flight of stairs from her office in the Medical Teaching Facility at the University of California San Diego. She wore a long gray pencil skirt and matching wool sweater over a loose white blouse, enjoying the mild temperatures before autumn gave its last gasp and surrendered to winter. She locked the Volvo V60 and walked up the concrete steps to the entrance on the northwest corner of the building.

Smiling at the students and researchers she passed, she realized her mind was already focused on the lecture she was to give that morning. That always seemed to be the case, and she acknowledged that her work consumed her. It wasn't something she was overly proud of, especially because it interfered with her ability to pay attention to her daughter.

With a sigh, she pushed her increasing guilt aside. Maybe after her lecture she could quiet her mind, if only for the weekend. She grinned at the thought of taking her daughter to the San Diego Zoo and strode across campus, ignoring the simplistic beauty in the medical school's industrial-looking buildings on either side of her.

Tan Lily walked inside and took the stairs to her office in the Global Health Institute, nodding at her colleagues on the Global Infectious Diseases working group as she made her way to where she had hung her white lab coat from a hook behind the door. She paused to slip the coat on over her sweater, then took a seat behind her desk, where the notes for her lecture sat unfinished in front of her computer.

She was only in her second year with the Institute and had already made a positive impact in their work, helping to identify three strains of carbapenem-resistant enterobacterales—a class of bacteria that caused common diseases, such as *E. coli*. The Centers for Disease Control had identified CRE as one of the nation's top five most urgent antibiotic resistance threats, and discovering the strains was the first step in learning how to defeat them. She was proud that their work would have a meaningful global impact.

But she was passionate about the topic of that morning's lecture.

"Are you ready?" The voice startled her, and she looked up to see the smiling face of Wang Li, a postdoctoral research associate.

"Almost," she replied, scooping up her notes to review the handwritten comments she had added to the margins.

"Well, I'm eager to hear your lecture, Tan Laoshi."

With a smile, the girl walked out of her office. Tan Lily appreciated her use of the traditional Chinese form of address—referring to her as *Teacher Tan*—but it reminded her of what was at stake. She looked at the framed picture of her husband and daughter and felt a tightness in her chest at seeing her once happy family.

With a deep breath, she forced aside her feelings and went back to preparing for her lecture.

An hour later, Tan Lily stood behind the podium and adjusted the microphone as her colleagues and students filled the auditorium. She squinted through the bright spotlights shining down on her, looking for a friendly face she could focus on to help her get through the lecture. Her heart raced with anxiety, but she tamped back her fear. This was an important topic, and she needed to get people to listen.

The crowd quieted into a soft murmur of hushed voices as the last of her audience settled into place. She turned away briefly to clear her throat, then spoke confidently into the microphone.

"Show of hands," she said. "How many of you tested positive for COVID-19?"

She saw more than two-thirds of the audience proudly raise their hands, almost as if they were displaying a survivor's badge of honor.

"You're not alone. There were over seven hundred and fifty million confirmed cases over the course of the pandemic. Six million deaths. But our global response to the coronavirus was slow, lethargic, and ineffective. Worse, it gave a road map to terrorists and hostile states intent on harnessing the power of fear."

She saw their hands drop, and she pressed a button on the remote to bring up a slideshow of photographs on the screen behind her, showing people dining in plastic bubbles on the sidewalk, wearing face masks in public parks, and being arrested on the beach. "Lockdown measures were put in place to temporarily protect the vulnerable from an unknown danger, giving the scientific community an opportunity to find a solution. But over the course of the next two years, the draconian measures put in place to protect...began to harm. Their long-term effects on the mental health of the population—especially vulnerable groups, such as those in poor socioeconomic conditions, the homeless, or immigrants—resulted in a one thousand percent increase of calls to the national suicide hotline."

She clicked the button again, and the picture changed to show a group of Islamic terrorists wielding AK-47 automatic rifles. *Click.* The picture showed a gathering of armed white men wearing camouflage fatigues and displaying a furled Gadsden flag with its motto "Don't Tread On Me." *Click.* The picture showed a mob of masked black-clad individuals carrying cudgels and hurling Molotov cocktails.

"Regardless of political bent or affiliation, our response to the coronavirus only demonstrated that one need not wait for a pandemic to cripple a nation." *Click.* The picture changed and showed a nuclear-powered aircraft carrier at sea. "In January 2020, the first two cases of COVID-19 were reported aboard the aircraft carrier USS *Theodore Roosevelt*. A week later, ship's leadership began taking precautions against transmission. One month after that, the ship placed thirty-nine individuals in quarantine due to the potential of having come into contact with two British citizens at a hotel in Da Nang, Vietnam. Two days after that, the World Health Organization declared a worldwide pandemic."

Click. The screen went dark.

"Now imagine what life was like in those early days. It's March 2020, and the news is continuing to report the worst potential outcomes. Cholera, bubonic plague, smallpox, Spanish flu...zombie apocalypse."

The audience laughed.

"We are told that this will change our lives forever." *Click.* The screen showed an aircraft carrier in port. "Aboard the *Roosevelt*, four sailors are identified with COVID and taken off the carrier. The next day, the number jumps to thirty-three. Two days later, forty-six. The next day, fifty-three. The numbers are spiraling out of control, and the media uses the Navy ship as an example of how deadly the virus is."

Click. The number one appeared on the screen, and she held up one finger as she surveyed the audience.

"In the end, an American nuclear-powered aircraft carrier was side-lined in a part of the world where its presence represented peace and stability. The commanding officer was relieved of command while trying to keep his crew safe from a virus we knew little about. And only *one* sailor lost his life after contracting the virus. Sad. Tragic. But hardly the end of times that was being reported."

Click. The screen went dark again.

"But the real tragedy is that the world now knows how little it takes to cripple the most powerful nation on Earth."

Tan Lily set the remote down and picked up a bottle of water to take a sip. The last several minutes had only been intended to grab the attention of her audience. She had wanted to show them how woefully unprepared the world was to combat a virus most scientists generally agreed had been a natural mutation.

"What if I were to tell you that genetic engineering is no longer a skill set relegated to an army of PhDs? Would that worry you?" She saw a few heads nod, but she zeroed in on the ones who still seemed skeptical. "Would you agree that in our lives, the greatest fear has been from a nuclear threat?" A few more heads nodded. "But we know that nobody can make nuclear material without first having access to specialized centrifuges, so we target those and restrict who has access. We sanction nations who try. We sign treaties." More heads nod.

"There is nothing like that for biology."

The heads stopped moving.

"In the early 2000s, graduate students were lauded for having completed an initial characterization of a single gene. In less than three years, graduate students were doing experiments on twenty to thirty *thousand* genes. All at once."

She stepped away from the podium and reached behind her to turn on the microphone clipped to her blouse. "I can already hear many of you saying, 'So what? What's the big deal? Isn't this the whole purpose of science? To understand pathogen genomes? Bacterial? Viral? Isn't that a good thing?'

"In 2004, a group of mathematicians and engineers from MIT created a competition called iGEM—International Genetically Engineered Machine. The worldwide synthetic biology competition was initially aimed at undergraduate students but has since expanded to include high school students." She paused to let that sink in. "What was initially five teams of thirty-one participants has grown to over three hundred and fifty teams and almost eight thousand participants." Another pause. "Here are some of the top entrants from last year."

Tan Lily walked back to the podium and picked up her notes. "Graduate students from the University of Copenhagen in Denmark created biodegradable fishing nets by combining spider silk—that has a comparable strength and flexibility to nylon—with mussel foot protein." She flipped the page. "Undergraduate students from the University of Technology Eindhoven in the Netherlands tackled the challenges faced by over one million people affected by the inflammatory disorder ANCA-associated vasculitis. They created a Modular and Personalized Autoimmune Cell Therapy by engineering mammalian cells that detect the autoantibodies and subsequently produce the anti-inflammatory cytokine interleukin-ten, which results in suppression of the autoimmune response."

She looked up and studied the crowd. "This is good, right? This is why we chose to go into science and medicine. This is why we are here right now."

The lights dimmed and the screen lit up behind her, divided into quadrants with pictures of scientists in each. "Who can tell me what these scientists are working on?"

Not a single hand rose from the crowd.

"The exact same approach iGEM uses to encourage students to engineer genes for the benefit of our environment or to improve the human experience through therapeutics is being used...*right now*...to create devastating bioweapons. Everything we love about biology can be flipped."

The lights came on again, and Tan Lily stood at the center of the stage, surveying the audience. The hushed murmur that had been present at the beginning of her lecture was gone. The crowd of doctors, researchers, faculty, and students was silent.

"My name is Dr. Tan Lily, and today I am going to talk to you about genetically engineered pathogens and how they pose the greatest risk to global security." She paused. "Most importantly, I am going to talk to you about what we—the scientific community—can do to protect against it."

8

Punky sat in her car in a parking lot off Gilman Drive, across the street from the Leichtag Biomedical Research facility. Her eyes were glued to the door as she waited for a sea of people to leave the auditorium following Dr. Tan Lily's lecture. Punky still wasn't sure what to make of the doctor, but there was no way she could ignore *SUBLIME*'s messages.

He was her best chance at finally uncovering *KMART*'s identity.

She leaned back in her Alcantara and Laguna leather seat and stared across the satin black–painted hood, wondering if she was going to be forced to return to the Southwest Field Office with her tail tucked between her legs. She had already pissed off Camron enough with her routine absences and going off on her own for what he thought amounted to a wild goose chase.

But, then again, she was the only special agent on his team who had prevented an operative from China's Ministry of State Security from sinking an aircraft carrier. If she wanted to focus her energy on preventing something like that from happening again, she figured she had earned that right.

Her cell phone vibrated in her pocket, and she looked away from the door to see Camron's name pop up on the caller ID. She took a deep breath, already fearing that he might clip her wings and recall her back to the office.

"Hey, Camron."

"Did you find her?"

Punky paused before answering. "She's giving her lecture right now, and I'm waiting for it to end. Unless you want me to barge into a lecture hall full of doctors and med students and wave my gun and badge around."

"You don't have to be such a smartass," Camron said.

Of course, she knew he was right. Ever since she had taken down *TANDY* and prevented the attack on the USS *Abraham Lincoln*, she had become almost obsessed with dissecting the Ministry's West Coast network. She hadn't done it alone, but she had led the charge and identified at least three operatives in California.

Still, he didn't deserve her attitude. "Sorry."

Her view was momentarily blocked by an Audi that parked in front of a bus stop with its windows rolled down. She briefly considered moving to a different parking space to preserve her vantage point on the building's entrance, but then thought better of it. The lecture would be ending soon, and she didn't want to miss her opportunity to speak with the doctor because she was monkeying around for a better spot when the one she had was good enough.

Despite her contrition, Camron had clearly had enough. "Satisfy your curiosity, but I want you back in the office this afternoon."

She opened her mouth to say something sarcastic but snapped it shut when movement in the Audi caught her attention. She narrowed her gaze on the driver to make out features beyond his jet-black hair but could only discern that he clearly had no intention of moving from that spot.

Great.

"Is that clear?"

The Audi's driver lifted a cell phone to his ear but never took his eyes off the building's entrance.

Now what's he doing?

"Punky?"

For a moment, she had been so engrossed in the dark-haired stranger that she forgot Camron had just proclaimed an end to her investigation. "Yeah?"

"Did I make myself clear?"

Before she could answer, the doors to the biomedical research building opened and a crowd of people spilled out into the Southern California sunlight. She scanned the crowd for a face that resembled the photo she had seen of Dr. Tan Lily on the UCSD website, but with the Audi in her way, she wasn't sure she would be able to make a positive ID from where she sat.

Then, she saw a woman, slight in stature, who could have been a match.

But it wasn't the sudden appearance of a woman at the center of the crowd's attention that made her stomach drop. It was the driver of the Audi who also seemed to notice her.

"I need to call you back," she said.

"Punky..."

She ended the call and climbed out of the Challenger's bolstered seat, her gaze alternating between the woman—*that has to be Tan Lily*—and the Audi's driver, who had also exited his vehicle.

Shit!

As the dark-haired stranger crossed Gilman Drive and made a beeline for the doctor, Punky swept back the hem of her blazer and rested her hand on the butt of her service pistol. The last thing she wanted to do was draw her sidearm in the middle of a college campus, but she suddenly wondered if *SUBLIME*'s intercepted messages were in reference to an assassination attempt.

Her cell phone started ringing again, but she ignored it. Punky poured all her focus into the man walking several paces in front of her, searching for some sign that he was carrying a weapon and was a threat that needed to be put down.

She rested her thumb on the holster's lever and was prepared to release the automatic locking system that held her pistol firmly in place.

Please be wrong.

As the man reached the outer ring of people leaving the auditorium, she saw him weave through the crowd as he attempted to cut off the doctor. Punky picked up her pace almost to a jog, bumping into several students and faculty who would be caught in the crossfire if her intuition proved right.

When the man stepped in front of the doctor and reached into his coat, she drew the pistol and brought the tritium front sight post up to center mass and shouted, "Federal agent! Freeze!"

The man's head whipped around, and a look of shock registered on his face, but he didn't appear caught off guard—almost as if he had expected somebody to be there, protecting the doctor. He locked eyes with Punky, then his gaze dropped to the pistol she had pointed at his torso.

"Show me your hands," she yelled. "Slowly."

His eyes twitched toward the doctor, almost as if checking to see if she had taken the momentary distraction to make her escape, then he looked back to Punky once more. "Okay," he said. "I'm pulling my hand out of my pocket."

Punky recognized her body's response to the stress of the moment. The auditory exclusion. The tunnel vision. Her heart hammering in her chest. But she slowly inhaled through her nose for a count of four and held it for another count of four. Slowly, she let out her breath in a thin stream through pursed lips as she fought to regain control of her senses.

As the world around her came into focus again, she noticed the crowd had scattered, and she was left standing with her pistol aimed at an Asian man who stood less than ten feet from the woman Punky had come to see. Dr. Tan Lily and a male colleague remained frozen in place as if any attempt to move on their part would result in certain violence. But from who, they weren't certain, as both looked back and forth between Punky and the man standing in her crosshairs.

"Do it slowly," she said. Her voice had developed a slight tremor.

His movement was so slow, she almost missed him removing his hand from his breast pocket. His fingers were wrapped around a black billfold that he allowed to fall open, exposing a set of credentials that were too far away for Punky to make out.

What the...

She looked from the billfold up to his face and saw a sardonic smirk crack his otherwise stoic expression, but she wasn't quite ready to back down. "Don't move."

"I'm not."

She took several steps closer, rolling her Under Armour Strikefast boots silently across the ground, but kept her pistol and gaze leveled on the stranger. He appeared at ease—despite the gaping maw of a .40 S&W pointed at his chest—and she struggled to make sense of him. He had not exhibited any of the classic predictors of violence, like facial grooming, hard looks, or a definitive weight shift, but he was still an unknown variable.

When she was within arm's reach, she turned her body slightly and shielded her pistol as she reached out with her other hand to snatch the billfold from his grasp. He raised his eyebrows with amusement but waited for her to satisfy her curiosity before saying anything further.

With the billfold in her hand, Punky shuffled back a step before risking a glance.

Shit.

Her shoulders drooped as she read the words "Central Intelligence Agency" above a declaration that the bearer was an accredited representative of the United States government engaged in official business. His photograph, signature, and the crest of the Central Intelligence Agency spanned the bottom. Punky reluctantly lowered her pistol.

"I'm a good guy too," he said, his smirk widening into a mirthful grin.

Punky holstered her pistol, then pulled back the left side of her blazer to reveal the gold Naval Criminal Investigative Service special agent badge clipped to her belt. "Special Agent King," she said. "NCIS."

"Jax Woods," the man said. "You already know who I'm with."

"What are you doing here?" Punky asked.

Jax turned to look at Tan Lily and her colleague. Both appeared completely stunned that a federal agent and Agency officer had descended onto their quiet campus. He turned back to Punky. "I came to see her," he said. "Why are *you* here?"

For the first time since seeing Jax step out of the Audi sedan, Punky looked away from him and studied Dr. Tan Lily. She was a petite woman with a naturally athletic figure and looked to be in her late twenties or early thirties with intensely focused eyes. "Maybe we should go somewhere with a bit more privacy," Punky suggested.

Jax nodded. "I agree."

"Excuse me," Tan Lily said. "Can one of you please tell me what is going on?"

Her male colleague stepped forward and partially blocked Tan Lily as if trying to protect her from them. "I think you owe us some answers," he said, suddenly more confident with taking charge of the situation.

Punky glanced at the Medical Teaching Facility. "Do you have an office where we can speak in private?"

Her colleague answered for her. "We're not going anywhere with you until we have some answers."

"We're not asking *you* to go anywhere with us," Jax said, then nodded at Tan Lily. "We came to speak with her."

But she folded her arms across her chest. "He's right. I need to know what's going on. Right here. Right now. Or I'm not going anywhere with you."

Jax and Punky traded glances, and she gestured for him to take the lead.

"Ma'am, I work for the Central Intelligence Agency," he said. Punky thought she saw a nervous look shimmer across the doctor's face, then disappear as quickly as it had come. "One of our officers has gone missing, and we believe your husband is somehow connected."

Her husband?

9

Punky closed the door and sat in one of the two chairs across from Dr. Tan Lily. The CIA officer sat with his legs crossed in the other, and he watched her with veiled amusement. His eyes sparkled as she took her seat, then turned to face the doctor, who leaned forward and rested her forearms on the desk between them.

"I know why he's here," she said with a nod at Jax. "Now, why are you here?"

Jax turned and studied Punky, and she couldn't help but notice how handsome he was. His Asian features made him seem somewhat exotic, but she focused on the doctor instead. She was more certain than ever that the doctor was whom *SUBLIME* had referred to in the intercepted messages. But she wasn't sure how Jax Woods or the CIA factored in.

"I'm curious about that too," Jax said.

Punky ignored him and struggled with how to explain her presence, knowing full well she still didn't understand how the doctor was connected to *SUBLIME*. There was a small chance that Tan Lily was somehow complicit in a Chinese conspiracy and that anything she said might unintentionally give the enemy an advantage. And she wasn't okay with that.

She turned to Jax. "You said you believe her husband is somehow connected to the disappearance of one of your operations officers?"

He nodded but remained silent.

She understood his reluctance to read her in on more details, but it still aggravated her. "My name is Special Agent Emmy King, but everybody calls me Punky. I work counterintelligence for NCIS and have been investigating a network of individuals from China's Ministry of State Security operating on the West Coast."

She gave them just enough information so they would know that Tan Lily was somehow connected to her investigation, but not enough to give away her means or methods. Still, Jax remained silent.

"Before I can comment on an active investigation, I need to know how you think her husband is connected."

Jax looked away and made eye contact with the doctor, but Punky saw hesitation cross his face. She understood why he was unwilling to share more details, but without them, she was afraid they were at an impasse. At last, he nodded. "You understand that I can't tell you everything, but I want us to trust one another."

She wondered if it was even possible to trust someone who worked for an organization built on a foundation of lies. Trickery and deception were the bread and butter of the nation's civilian foreign intelligence service. But she had to try.

"Okay."

Jax leaned back in his chair. "Yesterday, at approximately zero nine hundred hours Zulu time, we received a coded message from our operative stating that they were bringing back intelligence of the highest priority."

"Back from where?" Punky asked.

"Shanghai, China."

Punky saw Tan Lily frown, but neither woman interrupted.

"Our operative was working an asset who was a respected biochemist at the Hunan Institute of Science and Technology."

"My husband," Tan Lily said, her tone confirming that she either already knew or had suspected as much.

Jax nodded. "But our officer did not make the return flight, and all attempts to make contact have been unsuccessful."

"You're saying you think your officer was abducted," Punky said.

He nodded.

"Do you believe her husband is a suspect?" She was unable to keep the law enforcement side of her brain from approaching the case of the missing operations officer like any other investigation. If Tan Lily's husband was the last person known to have associated with the CIA officer, then he was the most likely suspect.

Jax glanced at Tan Lily, then dropped his eyes and shook his head.

Punky was afraid she knew what that meant, so she tried redirecting the conversation back to something she could hopefully tie back to her investigation into *SUBLIME*. "What kind of information was her husband providing?"

Jax kept his eyes averted. "I'm afraid I'm not at liberty to say."

"I am," Tan Lily said. "Like me, my husband is an expert in genetic engineering. We were asked to develop synthetic bioweapons for the People's Liberation Army. I declined and fled with our daughter here to the United States. He stayed behind."

"Why?" Punky asked.

"He knew he couldn't stop them from the outside."

Punky turned to Jax. "What was your officer's objective in going to Shanghai?"

"I don't know," he said, then held up his hands to forestall her objections. "I really don't. All I know is that her husband reached out through emergency channels and requested the meeting. We believed it warranted the face-to-face meeting, given the veracity of the intelligence he had previously provided."

"What happened to my husband, Mr. Woods?" Tan Lily asked, her voice surprisingly calm given the circumstances.

"I'm sorry," he said. "I don't know. We have been unable to reach your husband through our normal protocols."

Punky studied Tan Lily's reaction, but it seemed the doctor had already come to terms with the idea she might never see her husband again. For all Punky knew, she had come to terms with that before even fleeing Communist China.

"Recovering the information our officer collected from her husband is the National Command Authority's top priority," Jax said, making it clear that the president of the United States himself wanted whatever it was the officer had intended to bring back.

"But not your officer?"

Jax stared directly at her, not shying away from her accusation that the president cared more for the intelligence than the person who had sacrificed everything to collect it. "We are making every effort to locate our missing officer and bring them home safely. But the classification that was used to describe the information is only used for an imminent threat of weapons of mass destruction."

"What was the message?"

Jax stared over Punky's head as he recalled the message from memory. "It said, 'Wish you were here. Jenn and I have been touring the city. The cherry blossoms are so beautiful, and I can't wait to show you my pictures when I return. Miss you.' End quote."

Punky shook her head. "Yeah, sounds real ominous."

"The code word 'cherry blossoms' indicates information pertaining to an imminent threat."

"Aren't there cherry blossoms in Shanghai?"

"Not in October."

She bit the inside of her lip. "Who's Jenn?"

"I'm afraid I can't say."

Punky's analytical brain was shuffling the tiny morsels of information around, trying to connect them with other clues and piece together a rational explanation for the operative's disappearance. But beyond that, she was still stumped as to why the university had come up in *SUBLIME*'s communication. She knew they were somehow connected, but she still couldn't see the whole picture.

"Your turn," Jax said.

Punky had been thinking how best to explain what had led her to the University of California San Diego, and she concluded that there would be no way of sugarcoating it. If *SUBLIME* had pointed her to Dr. Tan Lily, it could only mean one of two things—either she was a willing participant in a larger conspiracy, or she was a target.

Based on what Jax had told her, she feared it was the latter.

"As I said, I've been investigating a network of individuals from China's Ministry of State Security. Last year, I came upon an operative who had recruited a sailor aboard the USS *Abraham Lincoln* and convinced him to turn over classified material pertaining to the F-35C Joint Strike Fighter."

Tan Lily furrowed her brow, likely wondering what any of this had to do with her.

"We were successful in stopping the operative, but we lost our only lead on the sailor known as *KMART*."

"So, *KMART* is still out there," Jax said.

Punky nodded. "I've spent the last year trying to track him down but have only managed to uncover more Chinese operatives on American soil. The latest—and most promising—is one in the San Diego area known as *SUBLIME*. The frequency of his communications has increased lately and mention what I believe to be the aircraft carrier USS *Ronald Reagan*."

Tan Lily lifted her hand off the desk. "What does any of this have to do with me?"

Punky glanced over at Jax before answering. "The last several messages have mentioned the university."

Jax closed his eyes in a sign of exaggerated frustration. "As a target?"

"The messages are encrypted, and the NSA has only been able to provide partial transcripts, so we can't see it in context," Punky said to the CIA officer, almost ignoring the doctor. "But given the doctor's specialty and what you just told us, I think it's safe to say that the Ministry has targeted her."

"For what?" Tan Lily asked.

Punky turned back to her. "I don't know. Maybe to finish something your husband started? A synthetic bioweapon, maybe?"

Tan Lily shook her head. "The whole reason Shen Yu remained behind in China was to *stop* them from developing a viable weapon. He wouldn't have helped them achieve success in such an endeavor. He just wouldn't."

But Punky could see the wheels spinning behind Jax's brown eyes.

"What if he *did* help them? What if he got them close and now they need someone with his same skill set to complete the weapon?"

The doctor straightened her back and sat tall. "I wouldn't do it," she said, matter-of-factly.

But Jax was on a roll. "What if they found some leverage to use? Like your husband?"

She shook her head, but Punky saw her eyes glisten with the advent of tears. "When my daughter and I fled China for the United States, I knew there was a good chance I would never see him again. We both understood the risks involved."

Punky could tell Tan Lily loved her husband, but she agreed he probably wasn't sufficient leverage to convince her to complete the engineering process on a synthetic bioweapon. There had to be something or somebody else that meant enough to convince Tan Lily to betray the very reason she had fled China with her...

"Did you say you had a daughter?"

Tan Lily nodded almost as if Punky had asked her about something more pedestrian, then her eyes grew wide as it dawned on her. She looked at Jax and saw the same worried look on his face.

"Where is she?" Jax asked.

"At school."

He jumped up. "We need to go."

Punky broke out in gooseflesh when she realized that Tan Lily's little girl was defenseless at school while she and Jax bickered over whose mission took priority. They would have time to figure out what the Ministry of State Security wanted with Tan Lily later. What mattered right now was that they moved the doctor and her daughter somewhere safe.

"Do you have somewhere you can take her?" she asked Jax, then stood and fished for her car keys.

"Where are you going?"

"I'm going to get her daughter."

"Not without me," Tan Lily said, already out of her seat and moving toward the door.

"I'll take her," Jax said, moving to escort the doctor.

Punky relented. "Fine. Call ahead to the school and have them pull her out of class to wait for you in the principal's office."

"I know what I'm doing."

Tan Lily yanked open her door and raced through the hall toward the elevator with Jax hot on her heels. Punky hesitated for only a moment as her mind scrambled to make sense of things. If the doctor really was at risk, then maybe her investigation into *SUBLIME* was more important than merely using it as a lead into discovering *KMART*'s identity. Maybe there was another attack afoot, and the doctor was the key to preventing it.

Jax and Tan Lily disappeared into the elevator, and she waved them on when Jax made a move to hold the door. "Get to her daughter," Punky shouted. "Then call the Southwest Field Office, and they'll patch you..."

The door closed.

Punky stabbed at the call button and anxiously waited for the elevator to return and carry her to the ground floor. When it did, she found herself bouncing with nervous energy, as if she were in a race against an invisible opponent. And that opponent had a head start.

"Come on, come on," she muttered, watching the floors tick down at an agonizingly slow pace.

When she reached the lobby, the doors opened, and she ran outside and turned toward Gilman Drive and her frostbite-blue Dodge Challenger in the parking lot across the street. She saw Jax's Audi S3 sport sedan pull a U-turn away from the curb and head east.

Then she saw a matte gray Audi sport wagon pull out behind them.

10

Guo Kang cursed when he saw the doctor exit the Medical Teaching Facility with a tall man he had never seen before at her side. He hadn't expected getting to Tan Lily would be easy, but he never thought she would have a personal protection detail either. And there was no question about it —the man next to her knew his business.

He watched the man tuck her into the passenger seat of an Audi S3 sport sedan, then get behind the wheel. He made a phone call and checked his surroundings before pulling away from the curb and making a U-turn to head east on Gilman Drive. Guo Kang hesitated for only a second—*Who is this guy?*—before putting his sport wagon into gear and pulling out behind them. If the General's target package was accurate, the doctor and her protector would most likely be headed to retrieve her little girl from Torrey Pines Elementary School.

Guo Kang felt the engine's restrained power purring like a snow leopard as he turned the corner and passed an idling campus bus. He was in no hurry and knew it was best to hang back to avoid detection, but he was comforted by the knowledge he had the horsepower available if he needed to hasten the hunt. So what if they reached the little girl? It would only make his job that much easier if both were in the same place.

He followed his quarry south toward La Jolla Village Drive, observing the way the S3 maneuvered in and out of traffic with practiced precision. The man had obviously been trained in evasive driving, and Guo Kang couldn't help but wonder who was behind the wheel. FBI? Local law enforcement? He was certain he and the General had done nothing to alert authorities to their activities, but the imposing man driving the sedan was evidence to the contrary.

The Audi S3 turned left onto La Jolla Scenic Drive just as the light turned red. Guo Kang coasted to a stop. He knew that Torrey Pines Elementary School was only a short drive through a residential area filled with mid-century modern homes adorned with red tile roofs. But the best part was that there was only one way in and one way out. The doctor would not escape him.

Guo Kang pulled out his cell phone and opened the Signal app to send a simple six-character alphanumeric message to the General: *60%fe3*. The code didn't quite portend disaster, but it indicated the need to speak with the General immediately.

His phone rang ten seconds later, and he answered the encrypted call with a tone of reverence. "General."

"What is it?"

"The doctor has left her office for the girl's school."

The older man grunted in acknowledgment. "That doesn't fit her normal pattern of behavior but is not in itself troubling. Maybe the little girl has a doctor's appointment. Or..."

Guo Kang didn't want to interrupt the General, but he needed to amend his instructions and the clock was ticking. "A man is with her."

"A colleague?"

The light turned green, and he smoothly accelerated into the intersection, turning left into the La Jolla neighborhood. He thought about the General's question for a moment but quickly dismissed it. "I don't think so. He moves like a professional. The way he carries himself. The way he drives."

"Law enforcement?"

"I don't know," Guo Kang said, but he dismissed that possibility as well. If the doctor had somehow fallen under the scrutiny of law enforcement, he doubted they would have escorted her off campus in an unmarked vehicle—a European sport sedan at that—and taken her to her daughter's school.

"Okay. What is your assessment?"

This time, there was no hesitation as he voiced his concerns. "I believe she is now under the guardianship of a personal protection detail. Who or why, I am not sure." He paused. "It is just one man, and I am certain I can complete my tasking. Do you want me to continue?"

The General sighed. "No. Continue to observe, but do not approach. I don't want to give whoever has her in their custody an excuse to increase their presence. But be on the lookout for additional security. Where there is one, there will probably be more."

"Yes, General." Of course, Guo Kang knew this. But his eyes flicked to each of his mirrors as if the General's words had suddenly reminded him of the gravity of their operation. He couldn't afford to be careless.

Only one car had turned to follow him through the intersection—a brilliant blue Dodge Challenger.

"Find out who is guarding the doctor," the General said.

"Yes, General."

"Keep me updated." The call ended.

Halfway to the school, the four-lane road narrowed into two, divided by a wide median filled with trees. His eyes darted left and right, but they kept returning to the modern muscle car shadowing him. It neither closed the distance nor fell back, and by the time they reached the intersection leading to the elementary school, he had convinced himself it was part of the doctor's detail.

Only one way of finding out.

He made the turn toward the school, knowing it was the only way in and out. Up ahead, he saw the Audi S3 parked in front of a gray wrought iron fence surrounding the elementary school. The passenger door opened, and Tan Lily jumped from the car and sprinted for the gate leading to the administration building. His eyes fell to the car's license plate, and he memorized it.

Passing the sedan, he circled the cul-de-sac and retreated toward La Jolla Scenic Drive. His eyes fell to the Challenger's front license plate, then up to the dark-haired woman behind the wheel. She stared back at him as he coasted past.

The doctor has more than one person protecting her.

Guo Kang pressed on the accelerator and made his escape back to his condo in San Diego.

The General will not be pleased.

11

Villagehouse Hirata
Iwakuni-shi, Yamaguchi-ken, Japan

Navy Lieutenant Andy Yandell parked his Jeep in his assigned parking space in front of the off-base apartment complex. The Marine Corps Air Station in Iwakuni sat on the southwestern tip of Honshu and was only twenty-five miles southwest of Hiroshima, but he wouldn't have known it by the surrounding landscape of rugged hillsides covered in pine, bamboo, and hardwood trees.

Climbing out of his Jeep, he glanced up at the spartan exterior of the four-story apartment complex, then walked up the narrow sidewalk at one end of the building to the exposed staircase. Looking forward to one last evening on shore before flying out to the ship, he let his mind wander and scrambled up the steps to his apartment on the third floor. After unlocking his door, he pushed it open, but the sounds from inside caused him to pause at the threshold.

Somebody's inside.

Instinctively, he reached for the pistol he would have carried concealed on his right hip if he had been back in the United States. But his temporary assignment to Det 5 in Japan had stripped him of that right.

"Hello?"

He pushed the door open further and glanced once more over his shoulder before taking a hesitant step inside. It was the absolute wrong thing to do if he suspected an intruder, but he couldn't help himself. If somebody was inside his apartment, he didn't want to wait for the police to arrive. He wanted them gone.

"Hello?" he yelled again, peering around the corner into the cramped living room on his right. Directly in front of him, a shoji—a sliding door made of latticework and translucent white paper—closed off his bedroom from the rest of the space. And he thought he saw a shadow move on the other side.

He froze.

Suddenly, the shoji slid open and revealed a shadowed figure standing in the doorway.

He stumbled back a step and clutched at his chest. "What the..."

Jenn sauntered across the floor, her heels clicking on the laminate wood floor. "I'm sorry. I didn't mean to scare you."

As she stepped into the light, he took in her beauty. She wore her signature purple Delta flight attendant uniform and had her short, dark hair pulled back into a tidy bun, each strand meticulously placed. He was so transfixed by her green eyes as they bored into him that he barely noticed the freshly applied bright red lipstick on her heart-shaped mouth.

Jenn Evers was a beautiful woman, and he was lucky to call her his girlfriend.

"What are you doing here?"

"I needed to see you," she said, falling into his arms and pressing her body against his. She inhaled deeply, then let out a quiet sob.

The fear had vanished, and all Andy felt was an overwhelming need to comfort her. "What's wrong?"

She looked up at him and shook her head. "I don't..."

Andy quieted her with a kiss and led her to the sofa. "How did you get here?"

"When we got back to Los Angeles, I jumped on a flight to Tokyo-Haneda, then took the train here."

Andy looked into her tear-rimmed eyes, trying to understand what could have possessed her to spend twelve hours on a plane and four hours on a train after an already long day. "Why?"

"Because Lisa..." The last shred of restraint she had been clinging to seemed to dissolve, and she broke down. He pulled her into his arms again and held her head to his chest while she cried in a much-needed emotional release. At last, the sobbing stopped, and she pulled away to wipe at the tears streaking her cheeks.

"Tell me what happened," Andy said.

So, she did. She told him about her flight from Los Angeles to Shanghai and the older flight attendant she had watched the sunset with. She told him how Lisa hadn't shown at their appointed lobby time the following day and couldn't be reached by phone. She told Andy that when hotel staff went to her room, they found it completely empty, as if it hadn't even been occupied. It was almost as if the woman had disappeared into thin air.

"What is the airline doing about it?" he asked.

She shrugged. "Nothing. They got us another flight attendant, and we flew back to Los Angeles like nothing even happened."

He tipped his head forward and kissed her, not caring if he smeared her perfect lipstick. It had been weeks since they last saw each other. "Well, you're here now," he said.

She pulled back from the kiss and licked her lips, but he felt her body deflate with relief. "Yes. I'm here."

Jenn stood and turned so that her back was to him. She looked over her shoulder and waited for him to do what she knew he would. Andy was more than happy to oblige. He rose from the sofa and reached for the small zipper at the top of her dress and pulled it down slowly, bringing his lips to her back and kissing his way down.

He kissed every inch of her spine, brushing his lips past her bra and down to her lower back. He lowered himself to his knees as her body wiggled gently under his lips, sighing as his kisses sent waves of delight through her body. As his lips reached the top of her panties, she shrugged off the top of the dress and let it fall to the floor.

She stepped away and turned to face him. He looked up at her as she reached back to unhook the clasp of her bra and saw the sparkle in her eyes. He knew what she wanted, but he couldn't stop himself from taking his time to admire her form—from her high heels and stockinged legs to her smooth and flat tummy and perfectly round breasts. She was the sexiest creature he had ever seen.

Jenn placed her hands on her hips and smiled at him, enjoying that he wanted her as much as she did him. She reached out for his hand, and he took it without thinking. The missing flight attendant momentarily forgotten, he stood and let her lead him into the bedroom on the other side of the shoji.

He was spellbound and would follow her anywhere. From the moment he first met her, and she'd coyly asked, "Coffee, tea, or me?" he knew what his answer would always be.

12

Lisa hurt.

From head to toe, her body was bruised with open wounds from the endless hours of abuse. She was naked, and had been since she regained consciousness, except for a suffocating hood they kept over her head. They had bound her wrists behind her back, and the plastic restraints cut into her skin. Her hair was wet and hung haphazardly as she tilted her chin to her chest and fought for a few moments of painless sleep.

She didn't know where she was. She had been in at least four trucks, two trains, and one airplane. She may have even been in a boat at one point, but she was in and out of consciousness for most of her journey and had a hard time keeping her thoughts straight. She sat on a short block of four-by-four wood bolted to the floor in a damp, concrete cell.

She thought she heard scurrying across the floor, but so far, the rats and other critters had left her alone. Suddenly, the door opened, and she jerked her head up, though she could only see shadows and faint outlines through the thick burlap.

"No sleeping!"

She cowered under the guard's heavily accented English, then tensed when he dumped a bucket of ice-cold water on top of her, dousing her already soaked skin.

The door slammed shut, and she cried.

It was agony, and she fought through the endless torture and mind-numbing emptiness by thinking only of her reason for being in China. Shen Yu had given her critical information he hoped she could use to prevent a war and stop thousands of innocents from dying.

That was her purpose. Her reason. Her why.

She just hoped her message had given Langley the clues they needed to access the information before it was too late.

Her teeth started chattering, and her body convulsed from the cold and the awkward position they forced her to suffer. She didn't know how long she had been there or how long they intended to keep her there, but she clung to the hope that Shen Yu's defiance would not be in vain.

The door flew open a second time, and a shadow rushed toward her. She flinched at the noise but couldn't see the punch that hit her square in the face. Her head snapped back, and she lost her precarious balance on the edge of the wooden block, falling backward onto her bound hands. Unable to break her fall, her head struck the concrete and opened yet another wound in her frail skin.

"You sit!" the guard yelled.

He bent over and grabbed her breasts, violently dragging her back into a seated position on the wooden block. "No move!"

Even after the guard released her, she felt his clammy hands squeezing her, and her stomach turned at the inability to prevent him from doing whatever he wanted with her. Even through the throbbing at the base of her skull, she felt a surge of adrenaline and clarity.

Then he hit her again.

Her head rocked back once more, and her nose broke with a flash of pain, but she kept her balance and remained stationary on the block. She glared up at him through the hood and dared him to hit her again.

He did.

Blow after blow, she felt new variations of pain she had never experienced before. He hit her broken nose several more times, and she felt a tooth losing its struggle to remain in her mouth. When the guard stopped, he ripped the hood off her head.

Without warning, he dumped another bucket of ice-cold water onto her battered body, and she inhaled sharply through her teeth and clenched her jaw. The guard behind her replaced the hood and kicked her between the shoulder blades, sending her flying off the wooden block. Her face hit the concrete floor and threatened the loose grip she had on her sanity.

She struggled to breathe through the rough fabric pressed tightly against her bloody nose and mouth and could sense she was losing her battle to stay conscious. She fought against it, struggling to focus on her firm belief that she had not been forgotten. Langley and the might of the entire US military would pour all their energy into locating her and bringing her home. All she needed to do was hold out.

But do they know I'm even missing?

She clenched her jaw at the thought. Of course they knew. She hadn't shown for her return flight to Los Angeles. Monty had received her coded email. They knew she was in danger. They would come for her. That knowledge comforted her, but she also sensed the warm and welcoming promise of blacking out blanket her body.

So, Lisa gave in.

13

USS *Ronald Reagan* (CVN-76)
East China Sea

Colt sat strapped into the armed ejection seat with his oxygen mask covering his face. He was parked in the area just forward of the carrier's superstructure with his Super Hornet's tail hanging out over the deep blue water and his main landing gear tires pressed up against a raised piece of metal ringing the edge of the flight deck, known as a scupper.

His jet was chained to the flight deck, and a yellow shirt walked up and patted his chest to show he was taking control. The aviation boatswain's mate instructed the brown shirt sailors to break down his aircraft and remove the chains, securing him to the deck of the ship. He looked around in awe at the organized chaos of cyclic operations, then up into the sky at the jets circling the *Ronald Reagan* like frigates waiting to roost.

Unlike in early carrier aviation, where the ship's straight deck required planes to take off to make room for landing aircraft, the angled deck of a modern aircraft carrier allowed both to occur at the same time. So long as the landing area was clear and launches were only conducted on one of the two bow catapults, jets from the previous event could begin the process of returning home to mother.

The jet to his left moved forward and inched along at a crawl toward the landing area where it would line up behind the number four catapult on the port side of the ship. Colt watched it for a moment, then craned his neck upward at a pair of Super Hornets orbiting overhead. When he looked back down, the yellow shirt indicated that his chains had been removed and began moving his hands in slow arcs to control the pace at which he taxied. Colt's control of the jet was intricately linked to a man he had never met.

After moving only a few feet, the yellow shirt tapped his cranial—a protective head covering that resembled an armored radio headset more than an actual helmet—and pointed at another yellow shirt in the landing area. The new taxi director raised his arms above his head and waited for Colt to turn and look at him.

When he did, the new yellow shirt gave a command for a slight left turn.

Colt added pressure to the left rudder pedal, then released it, demonstrating to the yellow shirt that he was looking at and following the commands of the right person.

All around him, jets moved, propellers turned, and sailors scampered about near one another in what appeared to be nothing more than a tangled mess of metal and flesh. But all of Colt's focus was on the yellow shirt who continued guiding his jet into position on the second catapult in the landing area. Slowly, the yellow shirt closed his hands into fists, and Colt pressed on his brake pedals to stop his forward movement. He reached down and set the parking brake and took a moment to relax before the launch started, looking to his right at two Super Hornets lined up on the bow catapults, just forward of where his jet had been parked.

Being on the flight deck with an entire air wing embarked was exhilarating, but preparing to launch for an air-to-ground training sortie with live one-thousand-pound bombs loaded on each of his pylons was icing on the cake. The yellow shirt spoke into the boom microphone attached to his cranial, then raised his hand again to get Colt's attention. He gave him the signal to release brakes and taxied him forward before passing him off to another yellow shirt who straddled the catapult track in front of him. As his jet moved across the lowered jet blast deflector, the new yellow shirt gave him the signal to spread his wings.

Colt reached down and rotated the handle near his right knee and stole a quick glance over each shoulder to ensure his wings moved into position. In his mirror, he saw the jet blast deflector raise behind him, protecting others on the flight deck from being knocked over by his exhaust when he went to full power during the cat shot.

Colt looked left at the weight board and moved his hand in an upward motion to let the sailor know his jet was heavier than expected. The sailor pulled the box down, rotated a knob, then showed it to him again. Colt gave him a thumbs-up and returned his attention to the yellow shirt who guided his launch bar into the shuttle.

Thunk.

Colt took a few more deep breaths to prepare himself for the launch. When it began, one of the two Super Hornets on the bow catapults would launch before him and the other after. The bow and waist catapults would continue to alternate until every jet in the cycle was airborne. After each launch, the catapult shuttle would retract into position as the JBD lowered and permitted the next aircraft in line to taxi into position. The process would continue, flinging fourth- and fifth-generation fighters into the air every thirty seconds, until the cycle was complete.

Colt knew once the jets staged behind the waist catapults were airborne, the flight deck crew would scramble into action to prepare the landing area for recovery. Even while they continued launching aircraft from the two bow catapults, the jets holding overhead would descend and break into the landing pattern. It was chaotic, and it was dangerous.

And it was the most beautiful thing Colt had ever seen.

The roar of a jet at full power drew his attention to a five wet Super Hornet on the bow preparing to launch into the sky. It was from the Dambusters of VFA-195—a squadron that traced its lineage to the TBM-1 Avenger and Bull Halsey's Naval Task Force in World War II—and the five external fuel tanks were a dead giveaway it was launching to fill the airborne tanker role.

The boat shuddered when the catapult fired, and the jet raced down the short track until it reached the end, where it dipped below the flight deck before beginning a slow climb away from the water. The pilot immediately banked right while raising the landing gear and flaps and accelerating away from the ship.

The yellow shirt interrupted Colt's focus on the tanker and taxied him forward until he felt tension from the holdback fitting. Another signal to hold brakes, then he put Colt in tension and gave him the signal to run up to full power.

Colt pushed his throttles forward to the stops and spooled up his engines to military thrust—the highest thrust setting before afterburner. He immediately wiped out the controls, moving his stick in a boxlike pattern, and pressed on both rudder pedals to ensure his flight controls moved without binding. He scanned his engine instruments for anything amiss, then saluted the Shooter.

The Shooter, or catapult officer, was a pilot assigned to the ship who was responsible for the final safety check before firing the catapult. He returned Colt's salute and lowered his hand to the flight deck before raising and pointing it at the bow of the ship as the signal for the catapult to fire.

With his left hand on the throttles and right hand gripping a handle on the canopy bow, the holdback broke, and his jet hopped before racing for the edge of the flight deck. It happened so fast, Colt barely had time to acknowledge he was flying before instinct and training kicked in. His right hand reached for the stick to bank left while his left hand reached for the landing gear handle and flap switch, cleaning up as he screamed through two hundred and fifty knots a scant two hundred feet over the water.

Doc Crowe watched Colt's jet take flight from the black-and-white closed-circuit video that played on the *Ronald Reagan*'s internal cable network, known as "Ship's TV." Taken from the PLAT—or Pilot Landing Aid Television—video from the flight deck was broadcast to every space aboard the ship, and it was almost guaranteed to be on in each ready room during launches and recoveries.

"Not going flying today, Doc?" Lieutenant Luke "Rucas" Mixon asked.

Doc brought her reclined ready room chair back to an upright position, then stood. "Unfortunately, I have to go down to sick call."

"Think you can get ahold of some of them no-go pills?"

It was no mystery that most air wing pilots ascribed to the belief that improved quality of life through pharmaceuticals was an appropriate mechanism for dealing with life on the ship. In the early years of the Global War on Terror, flight surgeons often prescribed amphetamine—known as "go pills"—for fatigue management during lengthy combat sorties. But the flip side of that coin were hypnotic medications—known as "no-go pills"—designed to ensure adequate rest. Temazepam, zaleplon, and zolpidem were all approved for use by aviators.

Of course, many weren't keen on the idea of spending eight months at sea, and they looked for ways to shorten their sentence. Sleep was the obvious choice. "Having trouble sleeping, Rucas?"

"No, but if I sleep twelve hours a day, then cruise is only half as long."

Doc shook her head. "Sorry, but that's a no go."

Rucas groaned at the obvious pun, but Doc knew he hadn't really expected her to pony up medication he didn't really need. At least, not while they were only floating in the middle of the East China Sea as a deterrent against China invading Taiwan. Maybe if a shooting war kicked off, CAG would authorize it. But until then, they would just have to fall asleep the old-fashioned way—consuming a greasy slider at mid rats followed by hours on the Xbox.

"Yeah, well, if you change your mind, you know where I live."

Doc hung her squadron coffee mug up on the peg over the coffee station, then exited the ready room into the passageway on the starboard side of the ship. Turning right, she walked aft toward one of the ladders she knew would take her to the main medical department just below the hangar deck between frames 90 and 120. As one of the Carrier Air Wing's flight surgeons, she remained under CAG's administrative control while embarked but under the cognizance of the Senior Medical Officer as a fully integrated member of the ship's medical department.

That meant, as much as she wanted to, she couldn't sit around in the ready room all day, drinking coffee and fending off pilots who wanted to sleep their lives away.

She found the ladder she was looking for and descended from the gallery deck, also known as the "oh three" level, to the second deck. Located just beneath the hangar, it was the first level above the ship's waterline and home to most of the amenities—few as they were—that made shipboard life bearable. The ship's store, post office, laundromat, and enlisted mess halls were all on that level. Wedged between them was the main medical department, known as "Sickbay."

"What's the latest, HM1?" Doc asked when she walked in and saw First Class Hospital Corpsman Diona Browne making notes in a medical chart.

"Just the usual, ma'am. Fever, cough, nasal congestion, and sore throat," she replied.

"Anything we need to be concerned about?"

Diona shook her head. "Nobody has been too bad. I gave them decongestants and ibuprofen and sent them on their way."

Doc nodded and took a seat on a stool located in the Sickbay's ward where sailors came to be treated. Not unexpectedly, more than a few came with the hopes of receiving an "SIQ" chit—or Sick in Quarters—that permitted them to remain in their racks instead of toiling in the machine shops or on the flight deck. But for those who were genuinely ill, it was an opportunity for them to receive medical treatment and return to duty as quickly as possible. Fortunately, both types were relatively rare, despite the closeness of almost six thousand people.

"Just wait until after our next port call," Doc said.

Diona laughed. "I've already put in the requisition for more penicillin."

Doc furrowed her brow as she tried remembering where their next port call was. "We're not going to Thailand next, are we?"

The first class petty officer deposited the completed chart in the filing cabinet, then picked out another. "Busan, I think."

"South Korea," Doc mused. "Could be just as bad."

"That's why I requested it."

14

Lisa floated in a lake. No, it was an ocean. The water was clear, and she saw a sandy bottom and bright, colorful fish swimming under her. The water was warm. No, it was cold. Her body tensed as the gentle swells carried her up and down, and she struggled to find comfort. Then, suddenly she realized she wasn't wearing a swimsuit. Not a one-piece. Not a two-piece. She was naked and exposed to the world, and she tried lifting her head from the water to see if anybody was watching from shore.

But she couldn't lift her head. It felt like a hand pressed down on her, holding her face in the water and forcing her to look at the sandy bottom. No, it was rocky. The water wasn't clear. It was dark and murky, and creatures slithered in and out of view as she fought against the hand on the back of her head. For a moment, she forgot she was naked or worried who might see. Her lungs burned for oxygen, and she needed to breathe.

I'm drowning.

She opened her mouth and felt a shock of cold water rushing in, threatening to invade her lungs. She wanted to scream but kept the air sealed tight in her chest, concerned what might happen if she gave in to panic.

Suddenly, it stopped. She felt the hand release her head, and she tried lifting it but discovered she wasn't floating facedown in the water at all. She was lying flat on her back on a concrete floor with unseen hands pinning her arms to either side, the surrounding darkness caused by a burlap sack still over her head. She opened her mouth to breathe and inhaled icy water that she quickly expelled with a violent coughing fit.

"Again," the emotionless voice said.

The burlap sack pressed tighter against her face before a deluge of water poured over her nose and mouth. Her lungs screamed for air, and her mind swirled in a panic as the biting water filled her nasal cavities and mouth. She coughed and choked and struggled to keep from being pulled under into the turbid abyss.

I'm drowning!

Then the water stopped. Again, she used every ounce of breath in her chest to clear her mouth, then quickly gasped. Before she could fill her lungs, the onslaught resumed. She tried closing her throat off before inhaling any but was too late. Her vocal cords spasmed and seized up, and she once again teetered on the precipice of passing out. Her body relaxed as she succumbed to the inevitable, incorrectly believing that blacking out would save her from the torture.

Again, the water stopped.

They ripped the hood from her head, and she coughed, fighting to breathe. The room's brightness stunned her, but through her good eye she could make out three uniformed guards and a man in a suit she had never seen before. She locked her eyes on him, silently pleading for him to make it stop.

"Lisa Mitchell," he said, using the fake last name from her airline crew identification badge. "We know you have stolen from us, *shagua*."

She recognized the term of endearment that literally meant "silly melon" but shook her head vigorously to deny the accusation. "No…I'm just a flight attendant."

He knelt over her naked body and held a flash drive in front of her face. Seeing it reminded her why she was there and shored up her weakened resolve.

"We know Shen Yu gave this to you," he said. "There is no sense in denying it."

She rocked her head from side to side. Her throat was still constricted, and she was only able to draw in brief wisps of air. As much as she wanted to speak and deny the accusation, she focused all her energy on breathing. On staying conscious. On staying alive.

But he was unfazed by her silence. "Who do you work for?"

She worked her mouth to answer, but no sound escaped.

He leaned closer and brought his ear near her lips. "Who?"

"Delta," she whispered in a raspy voice.

He made a soft clucking sound, then stood and placed the flash drive back into his pocket as he looked down on her with sadness in his eyes. "I don't want to hurt you, *shagua*."

When the hood snapped down over her head again, she reflexively gasped and took a deep breath before the water came. But it never did. The hands pinning her down lifted her to her feet. The sudden motion left her disoriented and woozy, as if the room had started spinning around her.

The voice whispered in her ear. "One more chance. Who do you work for?"

She wanted more than anything for the torture to end and to go home. She wanted to be warm. She wanted to be clothed. She wanted to feel something other than pain radiating from every part of her body. Lisa broke down and cried.

Without warning, a fist slammed into her stomach and knocked the wind out of her. The invisible hands holding her up prevented her from doubling over from the blow, then dragged her limp body across the floor. Before she could recover from the punch, they picked her up and set her down in what felt like a box.

They crossed her ankles and drove her down onto her knees. Even through the pain, it felt different than the concrete floor she had been sequestered to. They pulled her body back so her buttocks rested on her heels and pushed until the pressure against her ankles became unbearable.

Before she could shift her weight to find a modicum of comfort, they bent her body over at the waist and brought her hooded face within inches of her knees, her thighs pressing against her bruised breasts. The hands twisted her arms and pulled them behind her back before abruptly letting go. She tried sitting up but met solid wood pushing down on her from above.

She fought against it, but the wood continued driving her down until her battered face pressed against her knees. Then, she heard the latches fall into place as her captors locked her inside the cramped box.

Lisa waited until the room outside was silent before probing her surroundings. She tried moving her hands to her sides, but they were pinned above her lower back. Her ankles screamed in pain, but no matter how she tried shifting her weight, she couldn't relieve the pressure. With every attempt to gain an ounce of succor thwarted by the wooden boundaries, Lisa's heart raced, and she struggled to avoid panicking.

At last, she gulped a painful and ragged breath.

And she screamed.

15

Mace 210
Navy FA-18E Super Hornet
East China Sea

Colt felt his jet lurch as the last of his Mk-83 general-purpose one-thousand-pound bombs fell away. He snatched back on the stick, straining under the G-forces to raise his nose above the horizon, then banked left and looked over his shoulder at the smoke marker bobbing in the water. A second later, his bomb detonated on top of the smoke with a disappointingly small splash.

"Two one zero, off safe," Colt said, before glancing at his fuel and turning his focus ahead of him to spot the other air wing jets circling the target. "I'm Winchester and on ladder."

"Nice hit," Cutty said.

"Thanks, sir." He climbed to twenty thousand feet to orbit overhead and wait for the others to finish dropping their bombs. Without bombs or extra gas, Colt had little else to do but watch the sun set over the horizon and find the ship. Unlike Air Force pilots, who could count on the airport being in the same place as when they left, Navy pilots could only fly to where they thought the ship would be and hope it was there.

When deployed in international waters, the aircraft carrier steamed in a self-declared operating area to give pilots a general idea where she could be found following their missions. Where exactly she was within that area changed based on the weather and winds. But for each launch and recovery, pilots were given a PIM, or Position of Intended Movement, that was a best guess.

"One zero five, in hot."

Colt watched Cutty roll in on the smoke marker and release his final bomb. From his position overhead, he could just make out the dark speck racing toward the water and impact just shy of the bright red smoke.

"One zero five, off safe," Cutty said with an obvious tone of disappointment, then quickly added, "Don't say a word, Colt."

"I would never, sir." He grinned behind his oxygen mask and rolled out to point his nose at the PIM.

"Uh-huh."

Colt reached up to select the "air-to-ground" master mode and put his radar in surface search. If they weren't operating under an emissions control restriction, the carrier's TACAN would be on, and he could pinpoint its location with ease. But he knew better than to rely on somebody else to get him back home.

Colt looked down at the color moving map between his legs and saw nothing but blue with a few specks of green uninhabited islands dotting the vast ocean around him. The spot in the upper left corner of the display that normally showed his bearing and range from the carrier was still blank. He groaned.

"Anybody picking up the TACAN?"

"Nope," one of the others replied.

Colt tuned his radio to the frequency monitored by the air wing E-2D Hawkeye. "Tiger, two one zero."

"Go ahead."

"Any idea where the aircraft carrier is?"

"Say status of timber."

"Green," Colt replied, letting the controller know his datalink was functioning normally.

"Stand by."

He brought up his Situational Awareness display and watched as the Hawkeye populated it with air and surface contacts, including the aircraft carrier ten miles from the PIM he had scribbled on his kneeboard. He selected the track file and calculated his bearing and range from the ship.

"*Gracias,*" Colt said.

"*De nada.*"

He rotated the knob on his radio to turn it to the strike group's air defense controller. "Red Crown, two one zero, mother's two eight zero for seventy-four, angels twenty."

"Two one zero, sweet, sweet, contact Strike."

After repeating his check-in with Strike—who cleared Colt into the Carrier Control Area—he was instructed to contact Marshal for his Case III instructions. During the day and with good weather, aircraft proceeded directly overhead to hold in a stack above the carrier for a Case I recovery. But at night or in inclement weather, aircraft held on a radial away from the ship and flew an instrument approach.

"Marshal, two one zero, two zero eight for fifty, angels twenty, state eight point oh." Colt reached up and slapped down on the handle near his right knee to extend his tailhook.

"Two one zero, mother is VFR, altimeter two niner niner four. Case three recovery, CV-1 approach. Marshal on the two four five radial at twenty-five, angels ten. Expected final bearing three four five, expected approach time three one. Approach button seventeen."

Colt read back the instructions, then turned his jet to the piece of sky twenty-five miles southwest of the ship where he would hold at ten thousand feet. He still had close to twenty minutes before commencing the approach, and he compared the fuel he had left with the ladder he had built to make sure he had enough. It was a rough estimate, but he figured he'd have to dump no more than five hundred pounds.

Nearing his holding point, he descended from twenty thousand feet and leveled off at ten. The first aircraft to commence its approach held twenty-one miles from the carrier at six thousand feet—the lowest altitude Marshal assigned. The next held at twenty-two miles and seven thousand feet, and each subsequent aircraft held one thousand feet higher and one mile further away. That meant Colt was fifth in line to begin his approach.

Reaching the holding point, Colt slowed to two hundred and fifty knots and engaged the auto throttles, letting the jet maintain the correct speed while he adjusted his angle of bank to enter the holding pattern. "Two one zero, established angels ten, state seven point five."

After announcing his presence in holding—as much for the Marshal controller as for the surrounding aircraft—Colt dropped his mask and reached into his helmet bag for a bottle of water. There was nothing left to do but watch the fading orange glow on the western horizon and wait another twelve minutes until it was time to commence his approach. Because he had taken off during the day and flown his mission in daylight, he hadn't brought night vision goggles he could use to find the other aircraft in holding. But the weather was perfect, and he spotted their blinking strobe lights and fading silhouettes with ease.

"Ninety-nine, altimeter two niner niner four, final bearing three five zero."

With four minutes to go, Colt recognized he was slightly out of position and needed to turn a little earlier on the downwind leg to reach the holding fix at the appointed time. He adjusted his angle of bank and continued making mental calculations every fifteen seconds until his Super Hornet crossed the twenty-five-mile fix exactly on time.

"Two one zero, commencing, state seven point oh."

He pulled his throttles to idle, extended the speed brakes, and nosed the Super Hornet over to establish a four-thousand-feet-per-minute rate of descent at two hundred and fifty knots.

"Two one zero, switch approach, button seventeen."

Colt rotated the knob on his primary radio to the approach frequency. "Two one zero, checking in, state six point eight."

"Two one zero, final bearing three five zero."

Colt banked his Super Hornet to the right as he crossed inside twenty miles and adjusted his heading by thirty degrees to correct to the landing area's extended centerline. Just over a minute later, his radar altimeter warning let him know he had descended below five thousand feet.

Whoop! Whoop!

"Two one zero, platform."

He retracted his speed brakes to slow his rate of descent to two thousand feet per minute and maintained it until leveling off at twelve hundred feet over the water. At fifteen miles, he turned to place the carrier on his left wingtip and arced at twelve miles from the boat until he reached the extended centerline.

"Two one zero, fly bullseye."

Colt guided his Super Hornet onto the vertical line in his Heads Up Display, representing the lateral portion of the Instrument Landing System. At ten miles, he lowered his landing gear and flaps, then slowed until the angle-of-attack indexers lit up amber next to his HUD. But his focus was on the speck of light straight ahead—the faint, tiny speck of light they expected him to land on.

Colt had over one hundred night landings, but it still got his blood pumping.

He took a deep breath and exhaled slowly when the symbology in his HUD blinked to indicate the carrier had locked up his jet with the Automatic Carrier Landing System.

"Two one zero, say needles."

The ACLS guidance cue, a small circle with a tick mark at the twelve o'clock position, blinked steady three degrees above the horizon but centered up on his heading. "Fly up and on," he replied.

"Fly your needles," the approach controller said.

Colt watched the ACLS cue move downward until the circle fit perfectly inside his velocity vector. As it dropped below the horizon, he decreased power and allowed the velocity vector to lower until his rate of descent equated to a three-and-a-half degree glide path.

He took another deep breath and exhaled slowly. Passing through eight hundred feet, he glanced at the number representing his distance to the ship and saw that he was two miles away. Exactly where he was supposed to be. It wouldn't have been the first time the ship locked up the wrong aircraft and sent erroneous commands.

"Two one zero, three-quarters of a mile, call the ball."

Colt had already transitioned his scan to the IFLOLS. "Two one zero, Rhino ball, six point oh."

Ducky's voice came over the radio. "Raaaaah-ger, ball!"

Meatball. Lineup. Angle of attack.

His eyes danced between the meatball on the left side of the ship, the row of lights extending through the middle of the landing area, and the dim amber circle just left of his HUD.

Meatball. Lineup. Angle of attack.

Colt added a touch of power just as the ball dipped low in relation to the datums. His power addition worked, and the ball crested back to where it had been. But before he could congratulate himself, the red wave-off lights strobed, and his left hand instinctively pushed both throttles forward. He kept his angle of attack constant and allowed the added power to change his trajectory upward and away from the looming flight deck.

"Wave off, wave off, foul deck," Ducky's disgusted voice said.

Colt gave a little shake of his head as he flew up the landing area and climbed to twelve hundred feet to join the bolter/wave-off pattern. But he had enough gas for at least two more looks before he had to hit the tanker, so he took a deep breath and fell back on his training.

"Two one zero, say state."

Colt glanced down at his fuel display. "State five point seven."

There was a delay, and Colt continued driving upwind while waiting for the approach controller to call his turn to downwind. "Two one zero, your signal is Texaco and divert."

Divert?

Colt reached down and selected the waypoint for Marine Corps Air Station Iwakuni, stunned to see they had opted to send him to the tanker and then to a field over two hundred miles away when he had more than enough gas to try again. He was about to key the microphone to question the decision when he heard the LSO's familiar voice break the silence.

"Two one zero, paddles."

"Go ahead."

"A Rhino's landing gear collapsed in the LA. It's going to be a while before they can clear it, so we're sending you to the beach for the night."

"Two one zero."

There wasn't much left to say. Colt was already thinking about the cold beers waiting for him.

16

Officer's Club – Club Iwakuni
Marine Corps Air Station Iwakuni
Iwakuni-shi, Yamaguchi-ken, Japan

Four hours later, Colt had completely forgotten his frustration at being sent back to Iwakuni instead of loitering overhead the carrier while he waited for them to clear the fouled landing area. It was amazing what some hot food and a few cold beers did to his outlook on the night. And it didn't hurt that the Greyhound crews who hadn't yet flown out to the ship were there to welcome him with open arms and a blank check to pick up the tab.

"Another round?" Andy Yandell asked, tilting his bottle back to drain the rest of the Sapporo American-style lager.

Colt stared across the bar at the handful of Marine F-35B Lightning II pilots from the Green Knights and the Bats. He knew the Marine variant of the Joint Strike Fighter featured a vertical lift fan and pivoting engine nozzle for vertical landing and short takeoff capability and differed from the carrier variant he had flown. But he couldn't help but wonder if it also suffered from a weakness that allowed a hostile threat to hack into it.

"Colt?"

He looked over to the COD pilot sitting next to him. "Sorry?"

"Another round?"

Colt knew he had to lead a flight back to the carrier in the morning. But morning seemed so far away. "You bet," he said, though he knew he would probably regret the decision.

Andy pushed his empty bottle across the bar's surface and gestured for the bartender to bring them two fresh beers. The bartender returned a moment later and set them down in front of the two drunk pilots.

"Long way from the I-Bar," Andy said, referring to the iconic bar located on North Island Naval Air Station in San Diego.

"You got that right." Colt picked up the fresh beer and clinked the long neck against Andy's. "Thanks for the beer."

"It's the least I can do."

Colt took a sip and looked over his shoulder. Part of him was envious that the COD crews were able to spend much of their deployment living at home in Iwakuni or in five-star accommodations in various locations around the Pacific while washing down resort food with cold beer. But the fighter pilot in him still longed for his flat-top home in the middle of the ocean.

"They do a good imitation of a One-Eyed Jack," Colt said, tossing his napkin onto the empty plate.

"What's that?"

Colt turned and studied the younger pilot with something close to incredulity. "What's a One-Eyed Jack?"

Andy nodded.

"A Barney Clark?"

He shrugged.

"How much time would you say you've spent on a carrier?"

Andy took another sip of beer to delay answering. "A few nights here and there."

Colt pointed to the crumbs on his plate and said, "That was a One-Eyed Jack." When it was apparent Andy still didn't quite grasp his meaning, he added, "It's a slider topped with a fried egg."

"What's a Barney Clark?"

Colt laughed. "Also a slider topped with a fried egg."

"Why's it called a Barney Clark?"

"Because it has so much cholesterol, you'll probably need an artificial heart like the one ol' Barney Clark received."

Andy thought about it for a moment, then shrugged, apparently uninterested in a history lesson on the Jarvik 7 or the slang unique to carrier aviators. Like Colt, he had eaten the burger made from eight ounces of spicy seasoned beef, topped with bacon, fried garlic, cheese, and egg.

Colt's eyes sagged, and he glanced at his watch. "I should probably try and get some sleep. I haven't seen the air plan yet, but I'm assuming it's going to be a god-awful early recovery."

"Hold on a second," Andy said, fishing his cell phone from his pocket. "I think I have it in my email."

Colt tipped back his beer and took another pull while he waited for the Greyhound pilot to tell him just how little sleep he was going to get before strapping back into his jet and flying out to the ship. He already knew he was well within the twelve-hour limit of "bottle to throttle," but he wasn't about to pass up the opportunity for free beer—his shipmates still on the boat would have demanded nothing less.

"Yeah, here you go," he said, handing Colt the phone. "Looks like you've got a zero seven hundred Charlie time."

Colt groaned. That was a little less than six hours away and didn't account for the transit or time needed to brief. Even clouded by fatigue and several bottles of beer, Colt knew he could count the hours of sleep he would get on one hand and still have a few fingers left over. "I need to get some shut-eye."

"Yeah, me too," Andy said. "My girlfriend just left, and a few of us are going to head up to Hiroshima in the morning."

Colt slid off the stool and gave the COD pilot a sideways glance. "You do know this is a deployment, right?"

Almost as if he didn't get the gibe, Andy brushed him off. "Yeah. I'll be back out in two days."

"To bring me my mail."

"And food and other supplies," he added.

Colt took a hesitant step away from the bar, somewhat surprised to find he could still maintain his balance. The Marine pilots shot him a questioning look, and Colt couldn't help but wonder if they were talking about what had happened to him on the *Abraham Lincoln*. He shook it off and followed Andy on the short walk from the Officer's Club to the Kintai Inn. Though there had been some truth to his barbs, Colt knew the Greyhound crews provided a vital link to the carrier and were an asset to the team.

Even if they treated deployment like a vacation.

At the air station's main gate, a panel van passed between a pair of flags and an FA-18C Hornet on display and came to a stop underneath the guard shack's arched white awning. The Japanese driver reached for the clipboard resting on the center console and lowered the window to wait for the Marine sentry to approach.

"*Konbanwa*," Hiro Yamada said, beaming his trademark smile.

"Back again?"

He switched to heavily accented English. "Apparently somebody really likes seafood."

The guard smiled back and leaned against the door. "Gotta see your paperwork."

"Yeah, I know." Hiro lifted the clipboard and handed it to the guard.

"I'll be right back."

"Take your time with that," Hiro hollered after him. "I could use the break."

"You and me both," the lance corporal yelled back, then disappeared inside the building.

Hiro shifted the lever into park and leaned back into the worn vinyl seat. Normally, vehicle traffic entering and exiting the base would have necessitated he pull off onto the wide shoulder while security personnel verified he had the required documentation to enter the base. But in the middle of the night, there was nobody waiting behind him in queue, so he was content sitting in the idling van and listening to the wind furling and snapping the American and Japanese flags over his shoulder.

His cell phone lit up. He glanced at it resting in the cupholder and contemplated letting the call go to voicemail. But he knew what would happen if he did that. With a groan, he scooped the phone up and answered the call.

"Yeah?"

"Where are you?" the gruff voice asked. Hiro recognized it immediately.

"Making my delivery to the base."

"You're late."

Hiro rolled his eyes and glanced through the open window at the guard shack, hoping to see the Marine returning to wave him through. The sooner he finished his delivery, the sooner he could get this guy off his back. He opened his mouth to reply when the door opened and the guard stepped out, adjusting the patrol cap perched atop his head.

"Did you hear me?" the man asked, clearly frustrated with Hiro.

"I'll call you back," he replied, then tapped on the button to end the call, before tossing the phone back into the cupholder.

"Checks out," the Marine said, handing the clipboard back.

"As usual."

"I assume you know which way you're going?"

He nodded and rested the clipboard on the center console. "Just another day," he said.

"Those squids sure do eat well," the Marine added, nodding at the crates filling the rear of the van.

Hiro grinned. He had been making deliveries for the fishermen's cooperative going on five years. Whether he was delivering fresh parrot fish and tilapia to Club Iwakuni or frozen stock to be flown out to Navy ships, he hadn't spent much time thinking about what he was delivering. Seafood in Japan was a staple.

But his delivery tonight was different.

The Marine sentry rapped his knuckles against the side of the van. "See you next time?"

"*Mate ne,*" Hiro replied, then shifted the van into gear.

As the lance corporal stepped back and Hiro eased off the brake, he couldn't help but glance in the rearview mirror at the crates stacked neatly behind him. Each one was packed with frozen seafood, but one crate was special. He stuck his hand out the window and waved at the guard as he accelerated through the gate, already pushing thoughts of that special crate from his mind.

17

Valley Center, California

Punky slowed in the middle of the road when the Audi S3 turned left and stopped in front of a closed gate. She knew Jax was leading them to a safe house run by the CIA, but it seemed a little too conspicuous for her liking. She didn't think a multimillion-dollar property bordering a private runway in a gated fly-in community had the low profile she was looking for.

But, then again, Jax was the declared expert on the subject.

She watched the CIA officer enter a passcode into the control panel, then waited for the large metal gate to swing open and permit them access. Once the Audi sedan began rolling, Punky steered the Challenger off the main road and followed. She stopped just inside the gate to block the private road until it had closed, scanning her mirrors for any sign of the dark gray Audi sport wagon she had seen outside the school.

There had been no sign of it since leaving La Jolla, but something about it had set off her internal alarms.

She took her foot off the brake and let the muscle car idle down the paved road that appeared to double as a taxiway for private airplanes. Looking left, she saw several large homes in varying architectural styles ranging from Mediterranean and Tuscan to modern and contemporary, each with its own private hangar set apart from the house.

Punky was halfway down the private airstrip when she saw the Audi turn left onto a driveway that angled toward a Tuscan-style monstrosity set back from the road and surrounded by trees and shrubs. From a distance, the landscaping appeared to have been planted for aesthetic purposes. But upon closer inspection, she recognized the obvious seclusion it gave the house within the fenced-in and gated community, while still preserving angles from which to defend the property.

She followed the Audi up the drive, and they came to a stop in front of a woman in her late forties, standing outside with a Black Mouth Cur heeling next to her. Punky instinctively elbowed her service pistol on her right side while studying the woman and her dog. But when Jax stepped out of the car and walked up to the woman to give her a hug, she relaxed.

Punky killed the ignition and climbed out from behind the wheel, taking a moment to study their surroundings. She spotted several security cameras and motion sensors around the property, but she knew those were only the ones she was supposed to see. If the safe house was as secure as she suspected, there would be several hidden deterrents and countermeasures even a trained expert would have difficulty exposing.

"Punky, this is Margaret," Jax said, gesturing to the woman, who eyed her suspiciously.

"Pleased to meet you," Punky said, walking forward to shake the woman's hand.

"You as well." Margaret whispered something, and her athletic and muscular dog leaned into her as if protecting her from Punky. "This is my trusty sidekick, Cher."

At hearing her name, one of the cur's ears popped upright, but she never let her gaze stray far from the strangers who had parked their cars in the middle of her driveway. She tracked Jax's movement as he returned to the Audi and opened the rear door to help Tan Lily climb out.

Margaret looked past the doctor at the little girl who remained hidden behind her mom. "And who might this be?"

Jax placed his hand on Tan Lily's shoulder. "This is Doctor..."

"Not *her*," Margaret said, then gestured to the little girl. "*Her*."

If Tan Lily took offense to the woman's brusque nature, she didn't let it show. "This is my daughter, Shen Li."

Margaret whispered something to Cher, and she scampered forward to sniff at the little girl, who giggled and tried retreating from the dog's lapping tongue. Satisfied that Shen Li would be an acceptable houseguest, Cher nudged her with her nose, then turned and bolted into the yard in a rotary canter. She skidded to a stop after a few beats and spun to see if Shen Li was following.

"I think she wants to play," Margaret said.

Shen Li looked up at her mother. "Can I?"

Punky could tell by the worried look on the doctor's face that she didn't like the idea of her daughter playing outside with only a dog watching over her—even one as large as Cher. "I can stay here with her."

But Margaret wasn't having it. "She is perfectly fine."

Tan Lily gave the older woman a skeptical look. "Maybe she should stay with me. At least for today."

"Nonsense. My house. My rules. Let the girls play."

Punky saw the doctor bristle at the notion that a perfect stranger could dictate how she was going to parent her daughter—especially when they had been escorted to a CIA safe house by an operations officer and a special agent from the Naval Criminal Investigative Service. But when Cher barked in encouragement, she relented.

"Stay where I can see..."

But Shen Li had bounded off after Cher, who gleefully fled from the girl's pursuit.

"Great. Now, let's get you settled," Margaret said, turning toward the house.

Punky watched Margaret climb the steps to the front door, apparently oblivious to the barking and giggling that seemed oddly out of place for the seriousness of the moment. She traded glances with Jax, then gestured for Tan Lily to follow the older woman inside.

"Are you coming?" Margaret asked over her shoulder.

Guo Kang leaned back into the Audi's bolstered seats and slapped the steering wheel's paddle shifter to drop the sport wagon into a lower gear. The tuned German engine surged instantaneously, and he weaved into the left lane and passed several motorists who drove like they were on perpetual vacation. The deepening blue skies hid behind a thin layer of clouds he might have found beautiful if he took the time to appreciate it.

But the General hadn't sent him to Valley Center to enjoy the scenery.

He had sent him to find Tan Lily. And her daughter.

Finding the safe house had been easier than he expected. After providing Ministry technicians with the two license plates he had memorized, they went to work scouring government databases to discover whom the vehicles belonged to. Names, residences, liens. The driver of the Audi S3 had done a good job of hiding that information, and the technicians found nothing but a black hole. But the woman in the Dodge Challenger, not so much.

Fucking amateur.

The ninety-thousand-dollar car was purchased with cash and registered to a woman named Emmy King who lived on the island enclave of Coronado. A very rudimentary follow-on search by the technicians uncovered all manner of information about the woman who had followed him to Torrey Pines Elementary School. She was a San Diego native and had gone to college at the University of Southern California—which explained the "FIGHTON" license plate—where she played water polo, before graduating and joining the Naval Criminal Investigative Service as a special agent. She didn't have much of a social life, but her favorite beer was an Aloha Sculpin IPA from Ballast Point Brewing, and she frequently paired it with Pla Choo Che to-go from Swaddee Thai Restaurant on C Avenue.

But the best discovery made by the Ministry technicians was complete access to Mopar's Electronic Vehicle Tracking System. Without any effort at all, he had been able to follow the Dodge Challenger north from La Jolla without putting himself at risk of being spotted.

Guo Kang wrapped the Audi around tight bends into the rocky hills east of the interstate, making his approach to the intersection where his quarry had exited the road. As he neared, he slowed and drove past the gated entrance to an upscale fly-in community, studying the security measures put in place to deter only the most casual of criminals—an automatic gate that could be accessed through a control panel or RF transmitter, a white estate fence bordering the property, and a handful of security cameras that were easily defeated.

This will be child's play.

Guo Kang continued around the bend at a leisurely pace, looking through the trees at the private airstrip and million-dollar homes on the other side. Despite the presence of the NCIS special agent and a man whose identity he still didn't know, Guo Kang knew the doctor and her daughter were inside one of those homes. With a grin, he continued past the gated entrance to another estate community and turned south, down a road lined with white ranch rail fences on both sides. He drove away from the airport and pulled off onto the dirt shoulder before turning the ignition off.

18

Punky stared through the front window at Shen Li and Cher chasing each other. The little girl's laughter was infectious, and she couldn't help but smile at such a heartwarming scene. It was a shame it had to happen under such ominous circumstances.

As if sensing the need to bring her back to reality, Margaret walked up to her and said, "Do we know who is after her? Or why?"

Punky turned and looked at the older woman and saw genuine concern on her face. Jax had introduced her as a Security Protective Officer—an accredited law enforcement officer charged with the protection of Agency facilities. Of course she wanted to know more about the threat. Punky shook her head, then glanced over her shoulder at Tan Lily, who sat on the edge of the sofa with an anxious and forlorn look on her face. "Maybe we should find out."

Punky turned away from the window and sat in a chair across from Tan Lily. Margaret followed and hovered at her side, but Jax remained standing at the floor-to-ceiling windows overlooking the runway. She chewed on her lip, hesitating to broach the subject of trying to figure out who was after the doctor. Punky wasn't a mother, but she had a good sense of the myriad of emotions Tan Lily would be feeling.

But the doctor was the one to break the silence. "Why are they after me?"

Jax turned and looked at Tan Lily, then made eye contact with Punky.

"Why do you think?" Punky asked.

Tan Lily focused on her. "It must have something to do with my husband working for the CIA."

"Did you know he was working with us?" Jax asked.

She nodded. "Before I took Shen Li and fled, we talked about how to stop the regime from moving forward with their plan to develop synthetic bioweapons. The last time I spoke with him, he had said he believed they were going to scrap the program and focus their efforts in other areas."

"So, why would they still need him?" Punky asked.

"And why are they after me?" Tan Lily said, repeating her initial question.

Jax joined them in the living room and sat down in a chair next to Punky. "Why don't you tell us more about these synthetic bioweapons, and maybe we can figure that out."

Punky saw the doctor relax, as if the topic was something she was comfortable discussing. "You have to understand that when we're talking about synthetic bioweapons, we're not talking about something that is extremely difficult to do. This isn't science fiction. It's science fact. Twenty or thirty years ago, it might have been difficult. But not today."

"What would it look like?" Jax asked.

Tan Lily nodded as if formulating her thoughts to put them in a way they could understand. "There's two parts to it. First, there's the construction of the weapon. Then, there's what we will call switches, that will turn the weapon on."

"Like a trigger," Punky said.

Tan Lily nodded. "In the early days of biological warfare, scientists would take a naturally occurring virus and weaponize it. Today, I don't need to go to Africa and find a sample of Marburg. I can buy a DNA synthesizer that is completely untracked and construct the virus at home. The recipe is out there. How do I create Marburg? The genome is there, and all I have to do is take bits and pieces and ligate them together."

"Ligate?" Punky asked.

Tan Lily gave a little shake of her head. "It means to join molecules or molecular fragments together through a new chemical bond. It's something even high school students are capable of."

"How long would it take a group of teenagers to do this?"

Tan Lily shrugged. "If they wanted to, they could create—from scratch —one of the world's most deadly pathogens in only a few weeks."

"A few weeks? Wouldn't that be cost-prohibitive?" Jax asked.

"Oh no. It would cost maybe only thousands."

"So, constructing the virus isn't difficult," Punky concluded. "Why would they need someone with your husband's expertise? Or yours?"

"Because developing the trigger is a bit more challenging."

"And what does that look like?" Jax wasn't taking notes, but Punky could tell he was hanging on the doctor's words.

"When constructing the pathogen, you can create a switch so that exposure to a drug or a molecule will trigger what is known as promotion, or the expression of these genes." Tan Lily paused before locking eyes with Punky. "Did you have chicken pox as a kid?"

Punky nodded, though she had been so young she couldn't remember it. "When I was four or five."

"Chicken pox is caused by the varicella-zoster virus, also known as human herpesvirus three, and it has been embedded in your central nervous system since you were four or five. When you turn fifty, you will be exposed to something that will trigger the virus and cause shingles."

"What triggers it?"

Tan Lily shook her head. "We don't know. We don't understand that yet, but we *do know* how to engineer switches so that a molecule—like caffeine, for example—could be used as a ligand to activate a gene. You could do this at the DNA level or the RNA level and promote the production of those genes—either through more RNA, which leads to more protein, or more protein right off the bat."

Punky shook her head, still trying to gain an understanding of the biology and chemistry involved in making something like this work.

"These *switches*, called riboswitches, are nature's way of turning a gene on or off. Technically, it's a regulatory segment of a messenger RNA molecule that binds a small molecule and results in a change of production of the proteins encoded by the mRNA. But, because we are so smart and like to play God, we have figured out how to take these switches and insert them into a constructed pathogen."

"Why?"

"Because exposure to an innocuous or ubiquitous chemical would promote the pathogen's efficacy."

Punky held up her hand. "Wait a second. Are you saying that you could infect a large group of people with a pathogen that might go undetected until exposed to a second chemical?"

Tan Lily nodded. "I just told you that you have the varicella-zoster virus in your system now, but you haven't had any symptoms or adverse effects since the chicken pox and won't until that switch is triggered when you get older. Yes, you could infect a population with a pathogen that remains dormant until you trigger it."

"Why would you do that?" Jax asked.

"I can tell you why we were asked to look into it."

Punky's skin broke out in gooseflesh. "Why?"

USS *Ronald Reagan* (CVN-76)
East China Sea

Andy Yandell felt the C-2 Greyhound cargo plane shudder underneath him as the eight-bladed propellers spun to a stop. With practiced motions, he completed the engine shutdown procedure from memory while his copilot read the checklist out loud and verified each step had been done properly. After the final one, Andy took a deep breath and readied himself for spending a night at sea.

As if reading his mind, his copilot said, "Thank goodness we're only here for one night."

Even if he shared the sentiment, his conversation with the Navy fighter pilot over beers at Club Iwakuni still resonated with him. "You know you're in the Navy, right, Greg?"

"Hey, man, there's a reason I became a COD pilot. Let the fighter guys get all the glory. I'll just keep their girlfriends company and rack up my Bonvoy points and per diem."

Andy shook his head, then unstrapped from his seat and stepped over the center console to make his way aft from the cockpit and down the steps into the cargo hold. Sailors from the *Reagan's* supply department were already swarming up the ramp to retrieve their requisitioned cargo while his crew chief worked to unstrap pallets from the steel decking.

Andy stepped around a stack of crates marked with "Fishermen's Cooperative" but paused when he caught a whiff of a pungent aroma wafting up from one of them. He wrinkled his nose and squatted down for a closer look at the suspected culprit.

"What's that smell?" Greg asked, descending from the cockpit. "Please tell me it's not dinner."

"It's not dinner."

Andy reached out to touch the liquid seeping through a crack in the wooden crate and rubbed his gloved finger and thumb together. The liquid had an oily texture that turned his stomach, and he thought better of bringing it closer to his nose for a second whiff. Instead, he wiped it on his flight suit pant leg and stood.

"But, just to be safe, I'd stay away from the fish sticks."

Greg groaned. "Next you're going to say I can't have hot dogs either."

Andy chuckled and watched the other pilot duck through the hatch on the port side and descend the ladder to the flight deck for a breath of fresh air. He didn't think that was such a bad idea, and he had more important things to worry about than seafood that had already spoiled.

"Hey, Mike," he yelled to his crew chief. "Make sure you get this one off here quick. It's gonna stink the bird to high heavens!"

19

When Lisa regained consciousness, she struggled to orient herself. Her legs and arms were numb, but every joint in her body ached with tension. She was trapped in the box again and strained each second to keep control over the panic threatening to overwhelm her. She wanted to thrash about and flail against the wood keeping her constricted but knew it was futile.

She was on the edge of losing her mind inside the small space when she heard the latches release and felt the pressure on her back abate. She wanted to cry with relief when two pairs of rough hands grabbed her shoulders and lifted her from the box.

They carried her across the floor and set her on a steel chair. As the blood began flowing once more to her limbs, millions of pins pricked every inch of her body, but she welcomed the pain. It was a feeling of confirmation that she was finally free from the container's claustrophobic confines.

She squirmed on the cold chair before a pair of hands grabbed her arms and pulled them roughly behind her back and tied them to the chair, straining her already tender shoulders. She breathed stale air through the burlap hood and flinched at each soundless shadow.

When they finished tying her arms behind her, more hands grabbed her thighs and spread them apart. She sobbed, utterly helpless and unable to stop them from doing whatever they wanted. She rolled her head from side to side and silently begged for the torture to end.

After each of her legs was tied to the chair, the hands vanished. She fought to stifle her cries and took sharp and erratic breaths as she waited for them to soak her. She tightened her core and braced herself for another punch or a kick. With each passing second, she felt closer to insanity.

Then, the hood was ripped off.

The man in the suit stood in front of her with his arms folded across his chest. "Who do you work for?"

Her eyes rolled with confusion, and her lips trembled as she answered him, "I...I don't know."

What do I say?

The part of her brain that wanted the pain to stop pleaded with her. *The truth*, it urged.

She shook her head, and he stepped closer to her. "Who do you work for?"

The other part of her brain silenced her weakness. *Anything but the truth.*

She looked at him with genuine fear in her eyes. "Please," she said. "I don't know what you want from me."

She broke down again and dropped her chin to her chest with a faint whimper. But he tilted it upward with delicate fingers and stared into her eyes, and she gasped at the kindness he exuded. Lisa blinked away her tears, and he nodded.

"I'm sorry," he whispered, then let go of her chin.

He walked to the heavy steel door and rapped on it with his fist. The door opened, and he stepped aside as a guard dragged another prisoner into the room. The man's head hung low, and he held a bandaged hand close to his chest. Her breath caught when he lifted his head.

Shen Yu.

The man in the suit addressed the scientist. "Who did you give state secrets to?"

Shen Yu looked up and stared at Lisa, saying more with his eyes than he could with words. He apologized for what had been done to her. He apologized for failing her and for asking her to come to Shanghai. And he apologized for doing what they were forcing him to.

"To her," he said, nervously working his bandaged hand.

The man in the suit continued. "And who does she work for?"

Shen Yu's eyes filled with tears, not wanting to forsake the woman he considered a friend. Lisa cried at seeing his turmoil and nodded to him, letting him know it was okay to betray her. She wanted to survive and return home, but she would never forgive herself if she did so at the expense of somebody who had trusted her. She would accept the blame if it meant Shen Yu could live to see his wife and daughter once more.

He shook his head, refusing to accept the gift she had offered him. His honor would not allow him to sacrifice her, even if it meant he would never see his family again.

"Shen Yu," Lisa said, pleading with him to answer the question.

"*Who* does she work for?" the man in the suit repeated.

Shen Yu shook his head and hardened his jaw, and she saw that he had made up his mind and that nothing she could say or do would make him renounce her. With tears streaming down her cheeks, Lisa looked away.

"I work for the CIA!" she screamed.

The man in the suit looked at her and smiled. "Thank you, *shagua*," he said. "I have found you guilty of espionage and hereby sentence you to death." He reached inside his coat, pulled out a pistol, and shot Shen Yu in the head.

The guard released his grip on Shen Yu's body, and it collapsed in a heap on the ground in front of her. Without another word, the man in the suit left the room, followed by the guards, who stepped around the growing pool of blood under Shen Yu's body.

The door closed, and she was plunged once more into darkness, accompanied only by the scent of gunpowder and death hanging in the air amid the scurrying of rats.

20

Honolulu, Hawaii

Jenn's eyes shot open, and she focused on the beam of light stretching across the ceiling, then turned her head slowly to see where the offending light was coming from. She had used a hanger to clip the drapes together, but the pesky light found its way into her room anyway. It was just one of the many hazards of being a flight attendant.

Groaning, she rolled onto her right side and tried closing her eyes to block out the light that prevented her from getting a full eight hours of sleep. Not that she needed a full eight hours, but her stomach had been bothering her and she was hoping to sleep it off.

Three minutes into staring at the insides of her eyelids, she finally gave up and opened her eyes again. If she couldn't sleep, she might as well enjoy a cup of coffee on the balcony and take in the beauty of Waikiki Beach that her friends assumed she enjoyed on every overnight thanks to her Instagram feed.

She tossed back the covers and stretched her lithe frame, enjoying the way her naked body felt on the cool sheets. The air conditioner sensed her movement and kicked on, and she shivered and rolled away to look at her phone plugged into the nightstand.

There was no little red bubble over the Messages app on her phone showing that she had a waiting text message, so she opened her email application, hoping to find an email waiting from Andy. If there wasn't, she could always go back and read an older one, finding comfort in the loving words he never failed to use.

Not yet, at least.

Her inbox was devoid of new messages, so she scrolled to the last one he had sent and started reading while imagining him sitting at his apartment in Iwakuni or in front of a computer on the aircraft carrier. His words never failed to make her smile or feel loved, and she was lucky she had thrown all propriety out the window and flirted with him almost a year earlier.

While she was on duty, no less.

With a mischievous grin at the memory, Jenn set her phone down and sat up, swinging her legs off the bed to feel the soft carpet under her sore feet. The heels she wore walking up and down the aisle on the plane were designed for fashion and not comfort. And though a few of the seasoned flight attendants wore more sensible shoes, or at least had the good sense to change into ones that were little more than slippers once airborne, she wore her tall heels with pride. And she paid for it.

Jenn stretched and reached with both hands for the ceiling, lengthening her spine and inhaling deeply. She rose from the bed and continued stretching from side to side, taking inventory of the minor aches and pains she would need to care for during the day.

Giving up on the notion of going back to sleep, she strode across the carpet, unclipped the hanger from the drapes, and threw them open. The sun had just risen and wasn't shining directly onto her room, but the brightness of the cloudless morning still invaded her sanctuary. Pressing her nose to the sliding glass door, she looked down on the empty beach and counted a handful of surfers already paddling out into the water.

I want to bring Andy here, she thought.

She looked across the water and knew he was out there somewhere, floating on an aircraft carrier hundreds of miles from shore.

Turning away from her southeast-facing view of Diamond Head, she walked to the bathroom to start the shower. But before reaching it, she stopped and clutched her stomach as it knotted up with a sudden and inexplicable wave of nausea. In a panic, she raced the rest of the way and instead of reaching for the knob to run the water in the shower, she dropped to her knees in front of the toilet and lifted the seat to empty the contents of her stomach into the porcelain bowl.

What the hell?

Her stomach had bothered her the last couple of days, but she just assumed it had been something she ate. Food poisoning wasn't that uncommon in her line of work. But this wasn't food poisoning.

The wave of nausea subsided, and Jenn wiped her mouth with toilet paper before flushing it. She stood and looked at her reflection in the mirror, pleased that her hard work in the gym and disciplined diet had paid off. She refused to be one of those flight attendants who let themselves go and spent more time at the seamstress getting their uniforms altered than in the hotel gym.

But the mirror was playing tricks on her. Her muscular and toned body somehow looked softer.

Shrugging it off, she brushed her teeth to rid the taste of vomit, then turned on the shower and let the steam fill the cramped bathroom. Her stomach felt better, but she knew she still had a long way to go before she could safely assume she was out of the woods.

Climbing into the shower, Jenn pulled the curtain closed and stood underneath the hot water, letting it soak her aching muscles and wash away the fatigue that never seemed to go away. The nomadic lifestyle of a flight attendant wasn't nearly as glamorous as she had imagined as a young girl— or as she portrayed on her social media. Gone were the romantic days of air travel.

She ran her hands down her body and felt the bruises that seemed to appear out of nowhere. She could place the origin of maybe one or two as an errant bump into a beverage cart or misplaced armrest, but most remained a mystery. Her hands stopped as they crossed her abdomen, and she looked down. It definitely looked bloated, which was odd considering she had just thrown up and hadn't eaten much in the past day or two thanks to the nausea.

Nausea...

Nope.

She shook away the thought, refusing to let her mind go there. To further distract her inquisitive subconscious, she reached for the bottle of shampoo and squeezed half its contents into her open hand, then ran her fingers through her hair and scrubbed her scalp until she had a thick, fragrant lather. She stepped forward under the stream of water and felt the shampoo rinse from her head and run down her face, between her breasts, and down to her round stomach.

No way.

She turned to rinse the shampoo from the back of her head and felt the water caressing her shoulders and continued running her fingers through her hair while ignoring the voice in her head. It was doing a damn good job of convincing her of what she knew was a definite possibility.

What if I'm pregnant?

Jenn groaned and turned around to shut off the water. She stood in the shower and let the water drip from her body. Until she knew for certain, she would continue to worry. And what worried her most was how Andy would react. She knew he loved her and knew they would be together forever, but she didn't know how he felt about children.

Throwing open the shower curtain, she grabbed a towel hanging from the rack over the toilet and dried herself off. She left the bathroom and reached into her open suitcase to pull out a pair of Athleta yoga pants and a loose sleeveless workout top, then slipped on her running shoes and hurried back to the bathroom to brush the tangles from her wet hair. Satisfied she was somewhat presentable, she grabbed her wallet and room key and left for the drugstore on Kalakaua.

That one question consumed her every thought as she made her way to the drugstore and back to her room, where she slipped into the bathroom with another bout of nausea. With her stomach somewhat settled but her nerves shot, she ripped open the package and hovered over the toilet to take the first test she hoped she failed.

She pulled the stick out from under her and replaced the cap before setting it on the counter, where she tried her best to ignore it. Picking up the box, she read the instructions again, then started a timer on her watch for three minutes.

The longest three minutes of her life.

She stood and pulled her yoga pants up, then walked out of the bathroom to avoid looking at the pregnancy test on the counter, taunting her with a visible control line. She went to the nightstand and picked up her phone, hoping to see an email from Andy.

When she saw that her inbox was still empty, she cursed him, then quickly chided herself for her lack of patience. He would write when he was awake. He always had. He was dependable and would be there for her when she needed him.

And she needed him now more than ever.

Has it been three minutes yet?

She set her phone down and walked to the window overlooking Waikiki Beach and saw that more surfers had joined the early morning wave riders, braving the dawn to harness mother nature. She wondered how many of them were pregnant or had children of their own.

Is this what my life has become?

Would she forever live her life through the lens of somebody who has seen two pink lines side by side in a small window on a cheap piece of plastic? How long would she be able to keep flying before she had to give up working for the person growing inside of her? Would Andy accept that he was the father and welcome her and their baby into his home? Would they build a family together?

Inhale.

She took a deep breath and closed her eyes to the beauty outside her window and the turmoil inside her racing mind.

Exhale.

She breathed out the stress that overpowered every other emotion. She trusted Andy, and she trusted what they had together. He was a man of honor and would be an amazing father to their child.

Jenn turned away from the window and walked back into the bathroom, staring at her reflection in the mirror. No matter how hard she tried, she couldn't see herself as a mother. She was little more than a child herself. How could she be a mother?

She shook her head and looked down at the test on the counter.

And cried.

21

USS *Ronald Reagan* (CVN-76)
East China Sea

Andy rolled over in his rack and clutched his stomach as a sharp and sudden pain woke him from his restless sleep. He opened his eyes and stared at the beige underside of the bunk above him. With a trembling hand, he swiped at a heavy coat of perspiration on his face and felt heat radiating from his skin.

What the hell?

He rolled onto his side and ripped open the blue curtains, exposing him to the darkened stateroom. He slid his legs out from under the thin sheet and contorted his body to lower himself to the ground. On unsteady feet, Andy braced himself against another stab of pain deep in his stomach. He wasn't sure which end it was going to come out of, but he didn't want to wait around to find out.

"You okay, bro?" Greg asked, looking down at him from the top rack.

Andy opened his mouth to answer but quickly snapped it shut. Instead, he shook his head and took a hesitant step toward the door. He knew it would take all his strength just to make it to the head, several frames down the passageway.

"Andy?"

He stopped walking and doubled over as another wave of nausea slammed into him. "I don't feel so good."

As the feeling ebbed, he stood and again set his sights on the stateroom door. But his vision narrowed until all he could see was the handle. He took another step closer and swallowed back his fear. His heart raced faster as his body burned to fight off whatever held him in its grip. He was so focused on reaching the door that he didn't hear his copilot climb down from his bunk and approach him, resting a hand gently on his back for support.

"What can I do?"

"I...I don't know," Andy said. He stopped, closed his eyes, and took a long, slow breath. When he opened them, the room started spinning, and he felt his body listing to counter the roll. "Get Doc."

"Whoa," Greg said, gripping his arm to keep him upright. "Easy now. Let's get you back to bed."

The nausea had subsided, but he wasn't convinced returning to his rack was the best idea. Still, he was too weak to argue, and he allowed himself to be steered back to the bunk. Halfway through the turn, his vision again narrowed, and he knew instinctively he wouldn't be able to stop it. His knees buckled, and he sagged to the floor. But before his copilot could help him back to his feet, his vision went black, and he passed out.

Doc Crowe sat in the Mace's ready room, reclined in a chair reserved for guests with her feet propped up on the one in front of her. A projector bolted to the overhead streamed a movie onto a pull-down screen at the front of the room, and she tossed buttered popcorn into her mouth while trying to enjoy a few minutes of normalcy before heading to her rack. The time-honored tradition of watching a "roll 'em" at the end of flight operations was just one way for Doc to forget she was trapped on the aircraft carrier for weeks at a time.

The duty desk phone rang, but Doc was engrossed in watching Ryan Gosling charging up the steps and dancing around trained assassins while dispatching them with ease. She heard the duty officer answer the phone in a hushed tone so as not to interrupt the movie, just as the actor's advance was cut short by a man in white pants and a trash 'stache.

"Doc," the duty officer said in a stage whisper. "It's for you."

She popped another handful of popcorn into her mouth, then groaned as she climbed out of the ready room chair. She had already spent a full day managing sick call and visiting each of the ready rooms on the ship but still managed a flight in a Growler. All she wanted to do was enjoy the movie without interruption and check off another day on her deployment calendar.

She reached the desk and snatched the cordless phone out of the duty officer's hand. "Doc Crowe," she said.

"Doc, it's Goldy."

She turned back to the screen just as Ryan Gosling hurled himself through a window, moments before the room exploded. "Hey, Goldy, what's up?"

"It's my roommate, Andy. He's really sick."

"Have him sleep it off and go to sick call..."

But the Minnesota native wasn't having it. "I'm worried about him. He's *really* sick."

With a grimace, Doc passed the half-eaten bag of popcorn across the top of the desk to the duty officer. "Where is he?"

"In our room." Goldy gave her the bullseye—the unique identifier that included numbers and letters and told Doc the C-2 pilots resided in one of the staterooms one deck below in what was known as "Sleepy Hollow." Doc wrote the information down.

"Let me get my stethoscope, and I'll be right there."

"Thanks, Doc."

She hung up the phone, tossed one more look at the movie on the screen, then headed for the door. Stepping out into the passageway, she was struck by the darkness of the ship and the red glow of lights that gave everything an eerie appearance. The last thing she wanted to do was collect her stethoscope from her office and check in on a sick pilot, but that just came with the job.

I swear by Apollo Healer, by Asclepius, by Hygieia, by Panacea, and by all the gods and goddesses, making them my witnesses, that I will carry out, according to my ability and judgment, this oath and this indenture.

Doc chuckled. *Indenture.*

Sometimes being a flight surgeon was a rewarding profession that gave her opportunities to care for some of the finest aviators on the planet. But, most times, it was akin to being tasked with keeping a group of drunken toddlers alive. Fortunately, they hadn't had their first port call yet, so she still had a relatively high opinion of most of them. But she didn't know Andy all that well at all.

Doc turned down the darkened cross-passageway and ducked into the CAG staff's spaces where she kept her stethoscope. She snatched it off her desk and turned for the door but not before the Safety Officer spotted her.

"Everything okay?"

Doc shrugged. "You know pilots."

The lieutenant commander didn't reply and went back to one of the many reports he was required to prepare for CAG, and Doc stepped back out into the darkened passageway and made for the ladder that led down to Sleepy Hollow. After passing through several knee-knockers, she reached the ladder and climbed down into an even darker and quieter part of the ship where several of the air wing's pilots were berthed.

She squinted at the bullseyes above each door, comparing them with the one she had written down. When she found the right one, she knocked, and Goldy opened the door.

"Where is he?"

Greg pointed at the rack against the far wall, and Doc walked over to where the COD pilot writhed in agony atop his sheets.

Bit melodramatic, she thought.

"Hey, Andy," Doc said. "How you feeling?"

Andy rolled over and looked up at Doc with a pained look on his face. "Not good."

Even through the stateroom's dim red lighting, Doc could tell the pilot was pale and sweating. "Where does it hurt?"

Andy pinched his eyes shut and clutched at his stomach, though he was mostly in a supine position. Doc slipped the earpieces of her stethoscope into her ears, then pressed the diaphragm—the larger flat side of the drum

—over Andy's right lower quadrant and immediately heard an abnormal increase in gurgling and rumbling sounds made by the movement of fluid and gas in the intestines.

"Hmmm," Doc said, removing the earpieces and letting the stethoscope dangle around her neck. "What are you experiencing? Diarrhea?"

Andy nodded.

"Vomiting and nausea?"

Again, he nodded.

"Obviously stomach pain."

Andy winced.

"What have you eaten?"

"Nothing yet," Andy said. "We just flew on tonight."

Doc gave a little shake of her head. "From Iwakuni?"

"Yeah." Andy pinched his eyes shut. "We're supposed to fly back tomorrow."

"Any drinking?"

"Not last night."

Doc turned and walked over to the sink next to the door and washed her hands, pulling up her sleeves to scrub her forearms. "You should probably be okay. Could be food poisoning, or maybe even norovirus. But both will resolve themselves within one to three days. My guess is you'll feel a lot better tomorrow. Just make sure you stay hydrated."

Greg seemed skeptical. "He was fine when we flew on just a couple hours ago."

"It can take anywhere from twelve to ninety-six hours for symptoms to present themselves. He's going to be just fine. But if it gets any worse, he can go to sick call in the morning."

Greg nodded. "Thanks for coming, Doc. Sorry to waste your time."

"Not a waste," she replied, glancing at her watch to decide whether it was worth heading back to the ready room and catching the end of the roll 'em.

Maybe it was a waste after all.

22

The door flew open and caused a few of the more timid rodents to scatter. The daring ones continued their pursuit of finding morsels littering the filthy concrete floor where she huddled. Lisa's stomach knotted in pain, and she squinted, unable to focus against the brilliance of light streaming in.

"Get up," the guard commanded.

She closed her eyes and ignored the rat crawling across her legs in a hasty retreat from the advancing brute. But she didn't move. She found the soft pattering of rodent feet on her skin far preferable to the way her captors touched her.

"Get up!" the guard shouted, his voice cracking into a high-pitched shriek that made her question his age. But her idle curiosity vanished when he kicked her in the stomach.

She grunted but didn't move. She had eaten nothing in days and allowed the rats to have their fill of the putrid food served to her on plastic trays. The last time she had braved eating, the food quickly ran its course through her system, and she ended up soiling the floor with explosive diarrhea.

But by that point, she was beyond caring. They had forgotten her and left her to rot in a cage. It was her fate. She had accepted it.

They're not coming for me.

Her eyes still closed, she ignored the guard's kicks and knew he would eventually tire of tormenting her and leave her alone with her nightmares and rats. But instead, he grabbed a fistful of her hair and jerked, lifting her limp body into a seated position.

"Go away," she muttered in Mandarin.

Her scalp screamed in agony and was almost a welcome distraction from the empty hell of her pitch-black cell. The guard punched her in the face and split open several wounds that had nearly healed since her last beating.

"Stand," the guard said. When she didn't move fast enough, he punched her again.

She opened her eyes and glowered at him as he continued to pummel her broken nose while holding her upright by her knotted hair. She wanted to cry but couldn't summon the strength to feel sorry for her condition. She wanted to scream but couldn't find the breath.

All she could do was watch in hopeless fascination as the guard's gloved fist punched her face until it was so swollen, she could see nothing but her own bruised and bloody flesh. The hand holding her hair let go, and her weakened body collapsed to the concrete floor with a hollow *thud*.

She felt hands grab for her ankles, pulling and twisting upward until she rolled onto her back. It took several seconds of her shoulders and head skipping across every imperfection in the concrete before she realized she was being dragged from the room by her feet.

The reddish-hued light she could make out through the swollen flesh around her eyes grew brighter, and the surrounding noises echoed less. Part of her knew they were only moving her to a new location, but a larger part of her was beyond caring.

"Put her in the truck," a voice commanded.

"It's a long ride to the dock," another replied. "Want to take turns with her?"

Lisa's stomach lurched at the thought of their disgusting hands on her. They hadn't raped her yet but had violated every inch of her body, and just the thought of their clammy hands on her made her want to vomit.

So, she did.

She didn't move her head, and what was mostly bile spilled from her lips in a weak cough that covered her face and neck. She coughed again as her stomach continued heaving against the gripping nausea, and the hands holding her ankles quickly let go, letting her bruised feet slam to the ground.

"Hose her off," the first voice said. "You can have your turn with her. But she smells terrible to me."

Another voice chuckled, but Lisa couldn't make out who it belonged to before ice-cold water showered her naked body and took her breath away. She made no move to avoid it and savored one of the few things that didn't bring pain. The cold water washed away the blood, dirt, grime, and vomit she had accepted as her only clothing.

She didn't move when they groped her again, looking for a hold on her wet body to lift her and dump her into the back of a truck. She collapsed in a heap on the rough wooden bed and choked on diesel exhaust as the engine sputtered to life. Within seconds, the truck lurched and began bouncing down the road. To where, she had no idea.

Apparently throwing up on herself had been enough to keep the guards at bay. Other than a sharp jab of a boot in her ribs or an open-handed strike to her bare skin, they didn't touch her. For over an hour, she rode in the back of the truck and winced with each pothole or speed bump. When their drive ended, she heard the ocean and knew they were moving her someplace new.

But why?

It doesn't matter.

She had long since given up hope of being rescued. For all she knew, she was already a star carved into the Alabama marble wall and a blank space in the Moroccan goatskin–bound Book of Honor.

The diesel engine turned off, and she heard the tailgate being lowered. Unseen hands grabbed her ankles and pulled her toward the edge, breaking off splinters from the rough wood into her skin. She prepared herself for the drop as best she could, knowing her captors enjoyed watching her naked body fall to the ground in what had become almost a sport to them. They laughed every single time.

But there was no drop. Instead, another pair of hands grabbed her under her arms and carried her a short distance before lowering her onto what felt like a cot. Her body tensed, and her eyes darted back and forth, trying to see beyond her swollen flesh while she waited for the rain of fists she had grown accustomed to. Instead, someone draped a blanket over her.

The cot lifted into the air, and she grasped its edges, afraid of falling as her head spun with a severe case of vertigo. She couldn't tell if they were moving her forward or back, left or right, and she felt like she was tumbling end over end. But the stretcher was stable, and the itchy wool blanket felt warm on her exposed skin.

They carried her a short distance, then set her down on the ground long enough for the fluid in her ears to stabilize. The swelling in her left eye had eased up, and she saw a small sliver of her surroundings through the slit in her eye. She was on a dock next to a fishing trawler.

"Where are you taking me?" she asked in Mandarin.

A guard grunted in reply, apparently not wanting to divulge anything with even a vague answer. Instead, they lifted the stretcher and carried her across a short gangway and lowered her onto the boat's exposed deck. She contemplated rolling off the stretcher into the water but knew that entertaining such a fantasy would be foolish. She had zero strength and would only sink to the bottom of whatever body of water they were on.

But before she could consider attempting her suicide further, the deck vibrated, and the boat's engine sparked to life. It sounded like a large diesel motor and, based on the stable platform of the deck, she assumed the trawler was destined for open seas.

The wind across the deck picked up as the boat gained speed away from the pier, catching the wool blanket and peeling it away from her battered feet to expose her naked body from the waist down. But she ignored her nakedness and focused on the warmth draped over the upper half of her body. It was a foreign but welcome sensation. And she savored it.

But the boat ride was short-lived. In what seemed like only a few short minutes, the boat slowed and made its approach to a pier with a flurry of activity as sailors scurried around to tie off the boat to their new home.

Her captors lifted the stretcher off the deck and carried it to the gangway to transfer her to shore. They placed her in the back of a gas-powered cart that immediately began driving. She bounced in the stretcher as the cart motored away from the pier and began a quick climb into the hills rising away from the coast.

She had no idea where she was but knew her torture was far from over.

23

Wizard 323
Navy P-8A Poseidon
South China Sea

With a yawn, Lieutenant Commander Ashley Mitchell reached up and pressed the button to engage the autopilot. She was fighting fatigue and needed to stretch her legs. She unbuckled from her sheepskin seat and turned to her copilot. "You've got the aircraft. I'm going into the back to stretch for a few minutes."

Logan nodded as she took her headset off and set it on the glare shield. Ashley contorted her body and lifted a leg over the center pedestal, then left the flight deck and made her way to the back.

She stopped to pour herself a cup of coffee before moving to where her sensor operators were busy scanning the electronic emissions from Hainan Island and cataloguing them. Her tactical coordinator, Lieutenant Edward Turner, saw her approaching and removed his headset. "What's going on?"

"Just stretching my legs." She took a sip of the hot coffee. "Get anything yet?"

He shook his head. "Nothing out of the ordinary. But we still have time."

She had commanded missions in the South China Sea countless times, but there was an urgency with this one she hadn't felt before. Partly, it was because the fleet of fishing vessels they had observed in the East China Sea had moved south, as they suspected. But mostly, it was because a missing American intelligence officer drove the stakes even higher.

"Keep me posted," she said.

Ed nodded and placed his headset back on his shaved head. She moved down the aisle to watch her sensor operators manipulating the plane's surveillance equipment. Each had an insulated coffee mug in a cupholder at their console to stave off the fatigue she knew was taking a toll on each of them.

As she reached Petty Officer Delgado's station, she leaned over and saw him position the electro-optical sensor's crosshairs on a small boat. He scrunched up his face and made notes in his logbook, cross-referencing the sensor's position with a digital map of the waters around Hainan Island.

"Where is that?" she asked quietly.

Tony continued scribbling notes into his logbook, then reached up to shift the sensor through its various modes, switching between electro-optical and infrared as he took temperature readings to compare with their catalog of Chinese naval ships. She tapped him on the shoulder, and he jumped as he ripped his headset from his head.

"Sorry, Commander," he said.

Ashley smiled at him and patted him on the back. "I didn't mean to startle you." She nodded to the screen. "Where is that?"

Tony sat back down and zoomed in on the digital map he had been referencing. "Fenjiezhou Island. It's about fifty miles north of Sanya, a mile off the east coast of Hainan Island."

"Military base?" she asked.

Tony shook his head. "Actually, it's a tourist destination. Mostly uninhabited except for tourists vacationing there and the resort staff. Which is interesting..." He trailed off in thought.

Ashley squatted down next to him and looked at the notes he had been making. She was unable to decipher his chicken scratch but knew it probably had significant meaning to him. "What's interesting?"

He shifted in his seat to look at her. "Okay, I look for patterns. If there is normally a lot of traffic on the road, I take note when the traffic is light. If there are no boats running between Hainan Island and Fenjiezhou Island, I take note when there are."

"But if it's a tourist destination, then doesn't it make sense to have boat traffic there?"

He nodded. "Normally, yes. But this time of year, tourism is at an all-time low, and this boat traffic doesn't fit any existing patterns." He turned to look at the boat moving steadily across the water toward the uninhabited island.

"It doesn't look like a military boat to me," Ashley said.

"It's not. It's a fishing trawler."

Ashley wrinkled her nose. "Help me out here, Tony. I'm not seeing what's so interesting about this."

He turned back to her. "Why is a fishing trawler carrying passengers to a tourist destination?"

She felt goose bumps on her arms and stood, her eyes fixed on the screen as the boat slowed to make its approach to the pier. Tony turned back to his console and manipulated the controls to zoom in on the deck of the boat.

Could it be?

"Does that look like..." she started.

"A stretcher?" He nodded. "Yes. Yes, it does."

She stood motionless as deck hands secured the boat to the pier and lifted the stretcher to carry it from the deck across a gangway. The men loaded it into the back of a utility cart, then drove off the pier into the thick canopy of trees covering most of the island.

Holy shit.

"Commander!" Ed yelled, waving her forward to his station near the front.

"Good work, Tony," she said, and gave his shoulder a squeeze before turning to walk up the aisle toward her tactical coordinator.

"We just intercepted a phone call that mentions our missing officer," Ed said with increasing excitement.

"Read the transcript," she said.

He picked up his logbook and read from it. "The Ministry assesses that the potential...indecipherable...American spy. Movement to..."

She interrupted him. "Fenjiezhou Island?"

He nodded with wide eyes.

"Transmit everything back to base immediately." She lifted the Styrofoam cup to her lips and drained the remaining coffee, feeling fully awake.

Ed put his headset back on to pass instructions to the rest of the crew while Ashley strode forward to the flight deck. She ducked as she stepped into her seat and reached up to place her headset back on her head. "I've got the aircraft," she said. She reached up to spin a heading into the window on the Mode Control Panel and turned them away from Hainan Island.

"What's up?" Logan asked.

"I think we found her," she said with a wide grin.

24

Valley Center, California

Punky blew through the front door and stepped out into the crisp evening air. She was having a hard time believing that what the doctor had just told them was a coincidence. Jax followed her out onto the front porch, and they stood in silence for several minutes before Punky spoke.

"It has to be the USS *Ronald Reagan*."

Jax shook his head. "Just because they looked into it over a year ago doesn't mean they succeeded. You heard the doctor; they hadn't yet perfected the switch they needed to make something like this work."

But she didn't see it the same way. She wheeled away from Jax and walked away from the house while puzzling over the messages the NSA had intercepted from *SUBLIME*. It seemed pretty clear to her that whatever the Ministry of State Security wanted with Tan Lily, it had to do with the aircraft carrier *Ronald Reagan*. That it was at sea—at that very moment—defending the Strait of Taiwan against the threat of an invasion only made it more likely.

Jax followed her off the steps, then stopped when his phone rang. Punky was deep in thought but still heard his half of the conversation.

"What? When?"

She turned to him and grew concerned when she saw the look on his face.

"What are we doing about it?"

Jax looked at his watch, then furrowed his brow.

"We have her here, but we think there's something going on."

Even though Jax had played devil's advocate and forced Punky to consider alternate explanations for the Ministry's interest in Tan Lily, his comment to whoever was on the other end of the phone clearly showed he was worried. Like it or not, they had stumbled into the middle of something bigger than benign espionage activities on the West Coast.

Jax looked up and made eye contact with her. "The sooner, the better. Keep me posted."

He ended the call and joined Punky at the edge of the lawn.

"What was that about?"

"That was my partner, Connor Sullivan," Jax said. "We found her."

"Her?"

"Our missing operations officer," he said. "A Navy P-8A Poseidon surveillance aircraft was re-tasked from monitoring Chinese naval activity in the East China Sea after a fleet of fishing vessels received instructions to transit south. It appears they stumbled upon one of the trawlers transporting our officer from Hainan Island to a smaller island off the coast."

Punky shook her head. "That's a long way from Shanghai. Are we sure it's her?"

He nodded. "The P-8A also intercepted transmissions that mentioned moving an American to Fenjiezhou Island."

She pinched the bridge of her nose as if to stave off a headache brought on by trying to solve the puzzle. Even if the Navy had discovered the missing CIA officer's location, she didn't see how that fit with what Tan Lily had just told them. "It doesn't make any sense."

Jax clenched his jaw. "This is why I came here—to find our missing operations officer."

"Hear me out..." She trailed off as she looked into his determined eyes and tried stitching together the random and seemingly unrelated pieces of information they had collected. "I've been investigating the Ministry of State Security here in California for years. I've come face-to-face with their operatives and know what they are willing to do to accomplish their objectives."

"Punky..."

She held up a hand. "I understand we need to get your officer back. I'm not advocating that we don't. What I'm saying is that somehow this is part of their plan."

Jax rolled his eyes. "Rescuing an intelligence officer they kidnapped is part of their plan? Come on."

"You don't understand. While you and I play checkers, they are busy playing chess. They have thought two, three, four moves ahead, and the best we can hope for is a draw. What I'm saying is that we need to be even more cautious, especially if what Tan Lily told us is true."

Jax opened his mouth to reply, then quickly closed it.

She saw the look on his face and knew he was holding something back. "What?"

"We're launching a rescue operation to bring her home. Connor is on his way to Clark Air Base in the Philippines to debrief her as soon as she is rescued, and the Navy is sending the USS *Ronald Reagan* south to support."

She felt her heart sink. This was exactly what she had feared. "We're playing right into their hands and practically giving them the perfect target."

"This is what the Navy does—go into harm's way."

"But..."

Jax placed a hand on her shoulder. "It's done, Punky. We're going to get our officer back. My job was to find out if the doctor had any information that could help us do that."

Maybe it was the way he had said it, but it almost sounded to her like he was willing to toss Tan Lily and her daughter aside now that they had found their missing operations officer.

"And now?"

He narrowed his eyes. "And now I am going to keep her safe until you find out who is after her and why."

Her mind flashed to the dark gray Audi sport wagon she had seen out front of Torrey Pines Elementary School. She didn't have any evidence to support her suspicion, but she believed the driver of that car was the person she was looking for.

And now she knew he wanted the doctor to activate the weapon's switch.

Punky and Jax returned to the safe house to plan their next moves. She knew a Chinese operative was pursuing the doctor, and with the USS *Ronald Reagan* moving into the South China Sea, she couldn't help but fear that an attack was already underway. She sat in the chair across from Tan Lily.

"Why use an engineered biological weapon?" Punky asked.

The doctor looked relaxed as she sat on the sofa and answered the question without emotion. "To take out a targeted ship at a specific time without firing a single shot."

"But *why*?"

"To remove the only thing standing in the way of reunification."

"You mean an invasion of Taiwan," Jax said.

Tan Lily nodded. "It was believed that an engineered biological weapon gave them the greatest chance of success to accomplish that task. However, the fear was that whatever they infected the crew of the targeted ship with would also infect their own forces."

"So, they wanted you to engineer a switch," Punky said, tying it all together.

Tan Lily nodded. "It's called a binary weapon. It could be through an engineered switch at the DNA or RNA level, or it could be through paired infections that can later combine for a desired effect."

"But I thought you said this was child's play. Why would they need you?"

She chewed on the inside of her lip, hesitating to answer the question. "Maybe..." She shook her head.

"What?" Punky asked, urging her to finish her thought.

Tan Lily closed her eyes and took a deep breath before answering. "My husband and I discussed the possibility of creating what we called a tripartite weapon. To our superiors who had instructed us to create the synthetic bioweapon, it would look just like an engineered pathogen with a switch constructed into it—just like they wanted."

"Tripartite...you mean three parts," Jax said.

She nodded. "It was our fail-safe. If we couldn't sabotage the program and needed to move forward with synthesizing the pathogen, we would add a second switch to render it harmless. The thought was that if they ever managed to employ the weapon and activate the first switch, we could neutralize it by leaking the formula for something readily accessible or easily synthesized."

"Like what?"

Tan Lily shook her head. "It was just an idea, and I fled with our daughter before we could begin testing it. I don't even know if it was something Shen Yu investigated further."

But Punky had latched onto the theory. "So, it's possible that Shen Yu developed a synthetic biological weapon with an on switch *and* an off switch?"

"It's possible," the doctor admitted.

"Could you figure out what that switch was?"

"If I had a blood sample of someone infected with the pathogen that had already been activated," she said. "But even then, there are over one hundred million potential compounds, and it would take a long time to find the right one."

Punky groaned, then turned to Jax. "Could this be what Shen Yu gave your officer?"

He shrugged. "Could be, but that's an awfully big assumption."

She looked back at the doctor. "So, what you're saying is that unless you knew where to look, you would have to wait for someone to get infected with the weapon before even having a chance to discover the off switch?"

Tan Lily nodded.

That wasn't an acceptable answer. There were lives at stake, and Punky knew she needed to stop playing defense if they were going to have any chance of preventing another attack. She needed to get out there and uncover why *SUBLIME* was after the doctor. And she needed to stop him.

Punky stood, and she looked at Jax. "I'm going to put an end to this."

"What are you going to do?"

"I'm going to find *SUBLIME.*"

A short while later, she had her foot to the floor as she pressed her Dodge Challenger Hellcat Redeye to its limits and screamed west down from the hills toward Interstate 15. She feared the Navy was playing right into the Ministry's hands by moving the *Reagan* into the South China Sea, but unless she found out who was after the doctor, there was nothing she could do to stop it.

She didn't think anybody had followed them to the safe house, but she also hadn't thought anybody would be so brazen as to ambush her in broad daylight while driving her dad's 'Vette either. That event had permanently changed her outlook on the world. For better or worse, it had gifted her with a keen sense of paranoia that refused to permit her a moment without constantly evaluating and assessing those around her as either threats, friendlies, or allies.

As she merged onto the interstate, a faded yellow Chevrolet sedan inched closer on her left side, and she turned to study its driver. *Friendly.*

A lifted two-door Jeep Wrangler moved into the lane behind her, and she ducked her head to look at it through her side-view mirror. *Friendly.*

A black-and-white California Highway Patrol cruiser raced by in the left lane, its lights off but obviously in a hurry. *Ally.*

In her rearview mirror, several cars back, she spotted the single headlight of a motorcycle one lane over. There was nothing particularly troubling about it, but she loosened her seat belt anyway and drew the hem of her blazer back around the butt of her pistol. *Threat?*

The motorcycle quickly accelerated and left Punky's Dodge Challenger behind.

She breathed a sigh of relief and continued south while scanning for threats, but her mind was focused on the task ahead of her. She just hoped she could convince Camron of the danger.

25

USS *Ronald Reagan* (CVN-76)
200 nautical miles east of Taiwan

Colt sat with his ready room chair reclined as far back as it could go and had his feet up on the armrests of the chair in front of him, chasing away the remnants of his hangover from the late-night beers in Iwakuni. At the front of the room, a television hung from the ceiling in the corner and streamed various closed-circuit camera angles of the flight deck. For most pilots, watching flight operations was a favorite pastime when not actually flying, and Colt was no exception.

"Attention on deck!"

He popped to his feet before he heard Cutty's voice say, "Carry on."

Recognizing the Deputy Air Wing Commander, he relaxed and turned to the rear of the ready room where Cutty breezed past the duty desk with a stern look on his face, focused on Colt. He braced himself for bad news. "What's up, sir?"

"I've asked your skipper to put you on for an Alert Five tomorrow."

"Alert Five?" The vertigo subsided and his hangover seemed to dull. "What's going on?"

"I can't say yet," Cutty replied. "Just that we're stopping flight operations early and clearing the deck for a priority mission."

"So, this is real world?"

Sitting the Alert wasn't new to Colt, and he understood what DCAG was asking. An Alert 30 meant that aircrew could be anywhere on the ship if they could dress in their flight gear, man up their aircraft, and launch within thirty minutes. An Alert 15 required them to be in the ready room, already dressed in their flight gear, and launch in half that time. But the Alert 5 was the highest level of readiness and the most cumbersome for the pilots tasked with it.

"If it wasn't, I wouldn't have asked for my best."

On an Alert 5, Colt would strap into the aircraft with all his systems up and running except for the engines. There was nothing fun about sitting in a jet that wasn't flying for hours on end, and Colt wasn't looking forward to it. But the prospect of launching to support a real-world operation intrigued him.

"What *can* you tell me?"

"You'll get the full briefing tomorrow." He looked around, then lowered his voice conspiratorially. "But just between you and me, you might be interested in seeing what flies out here in a few hours."

"What?"

Cutty just winked. "You'll see. In the meantime, do yourself a favor and go talk to Bubba in CVIC."

If anybody could clue Colt in on what was going on, Ensign Dan "Bubba" Gump could. He was the Mace's intelligence officer and practically lived in the Sensitive Compartmented Information Facility known as the Carrier Intelligence Center, or CVIC.

"Aye aye, sir."

"Good man," Cutty said, before turning to leave through the door at the rear of the ready room.

After he had gone, Colt watched the first Super Hornet go into tension on the television, then decided his time was better spent preparing for whatever was coming. A few other squadron pilots sat in their respective chairs reading paperback novels or studying tactics and ignored him as he walked past the duty desk for the passageway on the starboard side of the ship. The door closed behind him, and he turned left toward the blue tile of Officers' Country.

Approaching midships, Colt ducked into the alcove for CVIC and entered his code to unlock the door with an audible *click*. He walked through the large open room into the back where the squadron intelligence officers worked.

During combat operations, the rooms were full of charts depicting strategic and tactical targets, but where they were operating near Taiwan, identifying surface contacts seemed to be the most important task. He spotted Bubba bent over a table, poring over photos of what looked like a naval base. Colt stood behind him and peered over his shoulder, wondering what the spy found so interesting in the art of studying satellite imagery.

"What's that, Bubba?"

"Huh?" The intelligence officer startled but relaxed when he saw Colt. "Oh, I didn't see you there."

"Yeah, you were pretty focused. Where is that?"

"Yulin Naval Base on Hainan Island. Fleet intelligence thinks the Chinese are growing their submarine presence here, but I think there's something else going on. If you look right here..."

Colt cut him off, uninterested in the People's Liberation Army Navy order of battle. "Yeah, so anyway, what's up with CAG assigning us Alert Fives?"

Bubba grunted. "That's a good question."

"You mean you don't know?"

Bubba looked around to see if anybody else was within earshot before leaning in close. Like many intelligence officers, Bubba was a prior-enlisted sailor and understood the importance of scuttlebutt better than most. Like the water cooler in a modern-day office, the scuttlebutt—a cask used to serve water aboard sailing ships of old—was a common gathering place for sailors and a hub for gossip. Over time, the two became synonymous.

"We're seeing a tremendous increase in signal and electronic intelligence coming in from various sources all centered on Hainan Island. That's why I'm looking at these photos. I'm trying to figure out what's got everybody so worked up."

"But we're not planning some big operation?" Colt asked, looking for confirmation.

"Not that I know of," Bubba replied. "But look, there is definitely something brewing. We've been operating with the *America* for several weeks, and they just departed station for the Philippines. Big Navy ships don't do that without reason."

"Port call?"

Bubba shook his head.

Colt looked at the imagery Bubba was studying and figured if he had to stand an Alert 5, he might as well prepare himself with as much intel as he could get. "Listen, can you get me a breakdown of any surface-to-air threats and an air order of battle for this area?"

Bubba nodded. "Sure thing. Give me about ten or fifteen minutes. Want me to bring it to the ready room?"

Colt had a bad feeling about this. "I'll wait."

A few hours later, Colt stepped onto the flight deck forward of the island and turned to look west at the sun setting over the bow. It was oddly quiet without the air wing's jets and airplanes preparing for a launch or finishing a recovery. He spotted a few yellow shirts milling about in the landing area, but otherwise the flat top was devoid of human life with most air wing personnel having been ordered below.

He turned his collar up at the wind howling across the deck, then turned and looked aft at a handful of LSOs in white float coats standing on the platform on the port side of the ship. He frowned and wondered who they were there to recover when the 5MC loudspeaker above his head erupted with the Air Boss's voice.

"*Greyhound at five miles, clear the landing area.*"

Colt walked toward the landing area and ducked underneath an E-2D Hawkeye chained to the deck when his ears picked up the faint sound of an approaching turboprop. He craned his neck and spotted a dark speck just above the horizon in the distance.

Remaining well clear of the painted line that would foul the deck and prevent the COD from landing if he crossed it, Colt watched the turboprop cargo plane lumbering closer on a long, straight-in approach. No matter how long he had been in the business or how many times he had seen carrier operations up close, he still found beauty in the insanity of landing an airplane on a boat in the middle of the ocean. He, and those like him, were a rare breed.

Rare and crazy, he thought.

After the C-2 Greyhound landed and caught the third wire with its stubby tailhook, Colt wondered why Cutty had sent him to the flight deck to watch what he had seen countless times before. He watched the cargo plane fold its wings and turn right to clear the landing area, and he was about to turn back for the catwalk when the 5MC squawked to life again.

"On the flight deck, clear the landing area for helicopter recovery, spot six."

Colt stopped walking and looked up at Primary Flight Control, known as Pri-Fly, where the Air Boss sat in his perch overlooking the flight deck. Through the thick glass, he saw the commander with a set of binoculars pressed to his face, looking at a spot behind the ship.

Slowly, Colt turned and moved out from underneath the Hawkeye, careful to remain well clear of the landing area and avoid drawing attention to himself. Over the turbine whine of the COD's engines, he heard the rhythmic thumping of a helicopter's rotors growing louder. He squinted at a speck on the horizon and watched it materialize into a shape he recognized as a helicopter. But not an American one.

What the heck is this?

As it drew closer, Colt stood in rapt fascination as he noticed the large helicopter was painted in a unique camouflage pattern and devoid of markings. It was clearly not a US military helicopter. The yellow shirt LSE, or Landing Signal Enlisted, stood in the landing area just forward of the island with two wands held overhead, giving the pilot the signal to "prepare for guidance."

As the helicopter descended over the flight deck, the LSE gestured for it to move forward, then held the wands out to his side as it hovered over the desired landing spot. Within seconds, the pilot had deftly maneuvered the helicopter to the non-skid surface, and flight deck personnel swarmed it with chocks and chains to tie it down to the ship. A door just aft of the cockpit on the starboard side slid open, and several gruff-looking men dressed in nondescript black fatigues hopped out and made their way toward the island.

Colt stood dumbfounded as the men approached and wondered who they were and what they were doing on his ship.

26

United Airlines Flight 65
36,000 feet over IKELA Fix

The pilot dressed as a United Airlines first officer picked up his handheld microphone on the starboard bulkhead and selected the cabin public address system. "Ladies and gentlemen, we are over the South China Sea and two hours from Bangkok." He reached up to the overhead panel and flipped a switch to turn the seat belt sign off. "Right now, the computer is showing us right on schedule, and we should have you at the gate three minutes after eleven o'clock. Please sit back, relax, and enjoy the rest of your flight."

The captain looked at his watch and grinned, proud of himself for putting them over the exact fix right on schedule. For a flight that was almost seven hours long, nailing the timing was a monumental feat—especially with the headwinds they had encountered near Taiwan.

With his PA announcement complete, the first officer returned the microphone to its cradle and turned to look at the captain. "Should be anytime now."

Almost on cue, the annunciator panel lit up, and both pilots instinctively glanced at the cabin pressurization system.

"Looks stable," the captain said.

The first officer extinguished the light and nodded, then he reached down for the Flight Management Computer near his left knee and began tapping on the miniature keyboard. They were too far away for a safe insertion, so he entered a lateral offset from their planned route on the airway, executed the change, and leaned back in the faux sheepskin–covered seat as the autopilot adjusted course to the west and brought them closer to Hainan Island.

The captain locked eyes with the first officer, hesitant to voice his apprehension. Both knew there were over three hundred passengers blissfully unaware of the clandestine ballet that was about to take place beneath their feet.

Godspeed, gents.

In the Boeing 777's bulk hold, four men bent at the waist and stepped from the heated pod, before shuffling to the now open cargo door at the aft end of the massive jet's lower deck. They moved carefully, burdened by heavy layers of dark clothing to combat the extreme cold they were just beginning to feel.

Each man wore a rig with both a main and reserve chute on his back and a navigation system strapped to his chest. Clipped to their harnesses, just below their waists and hanging almost to the floor, were kits containing everything they might need to complete their tasks once on the ground.

"Jesus, it's cold!"

They had trained for exactly this scenario and had experienced the extreme cold temperatures before, but they never got used to it. Their memories of the frigid Coronado surf were distant, but the lessons had been ingrained in them, and they huddled closer together as they waited.

"Thirty seconds," the jumpmaster said.

Their communication system was state-of-the-art and allowed them to speak to each other through line of sight. But once they exited the airplane, they would be connected to the entire team—including the QRF aboard the USS *America*—via satellite.

Each man took his place in line. The fourth and final jumper closed the hatch on the pod they had just exited and sealed it for the return trip to Hickam. The pod itself was necessary for a mission like this. It contained four jump seats bolted to opposite bulkheads and four spartan bunk beds that had been lifesavers during the long flight. The four jumpers had boarded the pod at a warehouse in Honolulu, carrying with them their free-fall rigs and kit for the mission. Though each man carried supplemental oxygen, the pod contained its own life support system and was both heated and pressurized.

After the airline loaded the pod onto the plane, the men struggled to make themselves comfortable while they waited for the Boeing to take off and fly almost five hours before reaching the drop zone. Four hours into the flight, an alarm sounded, and the men began preparing for their jump. They added extra layers of clothing, checked and rechecked their rigs, then strapped into their parachutes and adjusted their kit bags.

Fifteen minutes after the first alarm, a second alarm sounded, and the lights in the pod extinguished and were replaced with a night vision–compatible faint, green glow. Each man grabbed a mask from the bulkhead next to his jump seat, placed it on his face, and inhaled pure oxygen.

Jumping from high altitude posed several challenges to a human body not designed to live at 36,000 feet, and each jumper spent forty-five minutes breathing one hundred percent oxygen to flush any residual nitrogen from his system. At sea level, nitrogen was harmless, but during rapid changes in pressure—such as when they depressurized their pod in preparation for the jump—any nitrogen in their system could cause decompression sickness and incapacitate the jumper.

But these men were experts. Each had hundreds of high-altitude jumps, and the routine of pre-breathing was second nature. Another positive result of breathing one hundred percent oxygen was that it increased their visual acuity, and as their eyes adjusted to the low light environment of the pod, they made out the shapes of the other jumpers around them. Their eyes were adjusted fully to the darkness by the time their pre-breathing cycle had ended and the pod depressurized.

"Thirty seconds," the jumpmaster said. He didn't shout. He didn't have to. Each man wore a mask pressed to his face with a small microphone seated inside just below his nose.

With the pre-breathing cycle complete, each man removed the masks affixed to the bulkhead and replaced them with the supplemental oxygen masks they carried on their rigs. Each wore a heavy balaclava over his face, pulled down just below the chin to allow the oxygen mask a tight seal. Over that, they wore Peltor headsets and lightweight bump helmets with night optical devices clipped to a bracket on the front and flipped up to allow an unobstructed view through their thick goggles.

Graham reached up and tapped the helmet of the man in front of him. "Four ready."

Ron repeated the gesture. "Three ready."

"Two ready," Todd said.

"Go," the jumpmaster said.

"On me!"

Without hesitation, Senior Chief Dave White leaped through the cargo door. The wake of the massive Boeing 777 slammed into him, but he tucked into a streamlined shape and dove for the earth, seeking clean air below the jet.

As the air smoothed, he looked over each shoulder and grinned inside his mask. The entire team descended in a beautiful formation and tracked away from the jet directly behind them.

"Now," he said over the radio.

As one, the four men steered ninety degrees to the left and flew west toward Hainan Island.

The phone at the first officer's right knee rang and startled him. Although he and the captain were two of only six pilots in the Air Force qualified to fly these missions, it was only his second such operation. But it was the first real-world mission either could remember.

"Hello?"

"Jumpers away," the jumpmaster said. "Cargo door sealed."

"Fantastic!"

The line went dead, and the first officer unplugged the phone and secured it in his flight bag as the captain removed the offset and adjusted course back to the east and their assigned airway. He glanced at his watch and noted the time. The door light had been illuminated for two minutes.

27

USS *Ronald Reagan* (CVN-76)
South China Sea

The Air Boss's voice boomed over the carrier's 5MC flight deck public address system. *"On the flight deck, aircrews are manning up for the twenty-two hundred launch. The temperature is eighty-four degrees, the altimeter is three zero one nine. It's now time for all unnecessary personnel to clear the catwalks and the flight deck. All flight deck personnel are in a complete and proper flight deck uniform: helmets on and buckled, sleeves rolled down, goggles down. Check chocks, tie-downs, and all loose gear about the deck. Check your pockets for FOD. Check all rotor clearances for the go aircraft for the twenty-two hundred launch. Start 'em up."*

At the conclusion of the announcement over the loudspeaker, the calm on the flight deck became a flurry of activity. Charlie Mauzé and his copilot, Roger Rholdon, strapped into their seats aboard the Russian helicopter sitting on spot six, just forward of the two waist catapults on the port side of the ship. Two Super Hornets sat on the bow catapults in an Alert 5 posture, with two additional fighters chained to the flight deck aft of the jet blast deflectors.

Charlie selected the secure satellite channel for the Tactical Operations

Center at Clark Air Base and keyed the microphone. "Scar Nine Nine, Dusty One, radio check, over."

After a slight delay, he heard a calm voice reply, "Five by five."

"Say status of QRF."

Charlie knew Dave's four-man fire team had already exited the jumbo jet and were on their way to the target, and he was committed to launching. Regardless of the Quick Reaction Force status, he would launch to reach the release point on timeline.

"Green, green."

As the Mi-17's twin turbine engines began turning, he shared a glance and exchanged fist bumps with Roger. On the deck of the *America*, two Marine Corps MV-22 Ospreys were prepared to deliver a TRAP team or second squad of SEALs if they ran into trouble. Between them and the four Super Hornets, he felt confident they would reach the objective and make it back to the ship.

The two air branch pilots returned their focus to their systems and resumed functional checks to verify the former Soviet helicopter was ready to fly across open water to their release point off the coast of Fenjiezhou Island. Once there, they would loiter and wait for the signal to exfil.

They were at a critical moment in the timeline, and failure was not an option.

With the engines stabilized, Charlie signaled to the yellow shirt that they were ready to engage. The LSE relayed the signal to the tower as the ship started a turn to starboard.

"Dusty One, mother's steadying up heading three five zero. Winds are straight down the deck at fifteen knots. Happy hunting."

Roger gave Charlie a thumbs-up that he was ready to go, and Charlie keyed the microphone to reply. "Dusty One."

Unlike the standard Soviet version, the Agency bird had been retrofitted to allow them the ability to start their motors while keeping the rotor brake engaged. An amber light illuminated, and the LSE gave the arm signal to engage rotors. The five-bladed single rotor started spinning, and Charlie again checked their engine parameters before turning on their infrared lighting. The LSE waved both wands in an upward motion, and Charlie pulled up on the collective and danced on the pedals, making slight corrections with the cyclic to establish a stable hover over the flight deck.

With the LSE's right wand pointed at the port side of the ship, his left wand motioned for the Hip to sidestep out over the water. Charlie complied but kept his focus on the LSE until he pointed both wands to the west, then he shifted his attention from the yellow shirt's guidance to the empty blackness in front of them.

Remaining low over the water, he lowered the nose and accelerated toward the release point. Outside ten miles, Roger changed the radio from the *Reagan*'s tower frequency to the pre-briefed alert frequency, then selected the encrypted satellite channel.

"Scar Nine Nine, Dusty One is airborne. Proceeding to holding point Alpha."

After clearing the flight deck, the *Reagan* immediately began a turn to the south to steam away from Chinese territorial waters. Although national waters only extended out twelve miles according to the 1982 United Nations Convention on the Law of the Sea, China had notoriously—and illegally—claimed waters well beyond that. The United States Navy routinely challenged their claims and sailed in the disputed waters, but the *Reagan* wanted to draw as little attention as possible to the helicopter flying ever closer to Chinese airspace.

"Dusty One, Scar Nine Nine, green north. Continue."

The operations personnel in the TOC monitored continuous satellite and drone feeds as well as real-time electronic surveillance emissions for indications the Chinese had been alerted. Labeling their direction of travel as green indicated it was safe to continue without expecting resistance.

But Charlie would have continued anyway. He knew there were Americans relying on him to get them home.

USS *America* (LHA-6)
South China Sea

The amphibious assault ship bobbed in the dark waters with two Marine Corps MV-22 Osprey tilt-rotor aircraft from VMM-265 (Reinforced) chained to spots four and five in an Alert 5 posture. In the back of the first Osprey was a squad of SEALs, relaxed and calm while their brothers hurtled themselves through the night sky at a darkened island. In the back of the second were Marines and sailors assigned to Fox Company, 2nd Battalion, 4th Marines. Specially trained, the Magnificent Bastards' Fox Company served as the Expeditionary Strike Group's TRAP team.

Normally, the team responded to requests from the Joint Personnel Recovery Center after a pilot had already gone down, but they were given a list of eleven personnel and their attached ISOPREPs to review before boarding the tilt-rotor aircraft. It was unusual, but given the short notice nature of the operation, most of the Marines didn't give it a second thought.

The ISOPREP, or Isolated Personnel Report, was a classified document that personnel at medium to high risk of isolation were required to fill out. The information contained in the report included basic identifying information such as height, weight, hair and eye color, and descriptions of scars or tattoos with accompanying photos. In addition, each person required to complete one filled out four personal statements from which four separate questions could be asked to prove their identity to rescuing forces.

The Marines adjusted their body armor, wiped sweat from their camouflaged faces, and studied the reports while wondering who these people were. Most agreed that eight of the eleven were Navy SEALs—an assumption made because the second Osprey was filled with squids—but it was the other three that had them baffled. Two men—both of whom looked like civilians—and a beautiful older woman.

"She must be a hostage," one of the Marines commented.

"Or a diplomat's wife," another suggested.

"Who ran off with some Chinese businessman," a third grunt added.

The idle and irreverent chatter continued unabated as they waited for the call to spring into action. Most believed nothing would come of it, and they would get the order to stand down after being forced to sit in the back

of the Osprey for several hours. But a few of the less jaded still believed this
was their chance, and it didn't really matter who they would be called on to
rescue.

USS Ronald Reagan (CVN-76)
South China Sea

Colt craned his neck and looked over his shoulder as the Russian-made
helicopter lifted off the flight deck and turned out to sea.

"Where do you think they're going?" Lieutenant Anthony "Ducky"
Golemi asked.

"No idea," Colt replied, turning to look at his wingman on the other
catapult. "But by the looks of it, they're expecting some heavy resistance."

"What makes you say that?"

A third pilot in the division spoke up. "Because they put four of us on an
Alert Five to be ready for trouble?"

"But in the brief, they said they were just going to recover an isolated
person and bring them back and that we were on call just in case."

Colt shook his head. Ducky was one of the nicest and most competent
pilots he had ever met, but it seemed he was having a hard time accepting
the gravity of the situation. "Ducky, when was the last time you saw a helicopter like that taking off from the carrier without lights in the middle of
the night?"

"With a bunch of frogmen on board," the fourth pilot added.

To his credit, Ducky remained silent. Colt turned back to try and spot
the Hip, but it had disappeared into the inky night. All that was left for him
to do was sit and wait for a call he hoped never came, but one he was
prepared to answer.

28

Fenjiezhou Island

Dave looked down on the island through his night optical devices and tried ignoring the enormity of the challenge facing them. The uninhabited speck of land sat a little more than a mile off the coast of Hainan Island and comprised some of the most inhospitable terrain imaginable—something the overhead imagery and surveillance photos they had studied during the mission briefing failed to prepare them for.

But that was exactly why men like them existed.

Dense vegetation covered two hills at each end of the island. A narrow draw divided them and connected the rocky and cliff-like eastern side with a narrow, sandy beach on the leeward side. Scaling the cliffs to reach the objective would have provided them the greatest chance of avoiding detection, but it would have been treacherous under the best of conditions. Following a night HAHO insertion, it would have been foolish.

Dave continued descending around the southern tip of the island to approach the beach from the south. Without looking, he knew the others were stacked up behind him in perfect formation to land on the vacant beach. The island was blanketed in darkness, but a handful of lights glowed from the hotel villas dotting the southern hill.

She's in there, he thought.

The sound of waves crashing beneath him grew louder as he descended below the crest of the hill and made his approach for landing. He made a brief turn away from the island, then reversed course and approached the beach from the west. He flared his canopy at the edge of the beach and slowed his descent while allowing his forward momentum to carry him into a slow walk.

Easy day.

He gave himself half a beat to feel pride in jumping into hostile territory from a Boeing 777 almost seven miles in the air and fifty miles away, then quickly collapsed and gathered his chute and moved inland to the edge of the jungle. He dropped to his knees and began burying the chute in the deep sand at the base of the sharply rising hill to the east. By the time the last SEAL touched down, he held his rifle at the ready and scanned the dark jungle for threats.

"Scar Nine Nine, Mariner One Zero," Dave whispered, without removing his cheek from the M4's polymer stock. "In position and moving to the objective."

"Mariner One Zero, Dusty is green. Continue."

Dave looked over his shoulder for confirmation that the others were good to go. The clock was ticking, and they needed to find the captured Agency officer and exfil before the Hip ran out of gas. Any undue delay put them at risk of being stranded on the island.

"Mariner One Zero, out." Dave rose and slipped into the foliage. Although the island was devoid of tourists, multiple P-8A Poseidon and MQ-4C Triton surveillance missions pinpointed the captured officer's location to within four villas halfway up the hill on the southwest corner of the island. Their task force's intelligence specialists assessed they would encounter little armed resistance, but he knew better than to take that at face value.

As far as Dave was concerned, half the Chinese army waited for them under the jungle canopy, and he took in his surroundings through the white phosphor night optics that bathed everything around him in an almost natural soft white hue. Compared to older generation night vision goggles that changed everything to a green color, the newer devices put less strain on the eyes and made it easier to spot threats.

Behind him, Todd, Ron, and Graham brought up the rear. All three carried suppressed SOPMOD M4 rifles, but Graham also carried his breaching tool of choice—the Benelli M1014 shotgun loaded with fourteen Aguila Minishells—slung across his back.

The four-man fire team moved with well-rehearsed precision and spread out as they disappeared into the thick foliage and ascended the steep hill. They struggled for several feet of near-vertical elevation gain, then stopped and listened to the wind and insects surrounding them over the noise of their pounding hearts. Despite the intel assessment, they expected to encounter resistance and were on alert for signs of human life, knowing it was early enough to assume guards were still awake. An insertion later in the evening would have been ideal, but they were constricted by the airline's flight schedule from Honolulu to Bangkok.

Following their brief rest, Dave again led them up the hill. They clawed and scraped for each foot, testing the limits of their ability to remain silent. The terrain was brutal, but they pressed on to the objective, alternating between short bursts of movement and even shorter periods of rest. After their fifth such pause up the hillside, Dave signaled for them to stop and hold their position, then lowered his body into the dense ferns.

The four SEALs rested on the edge of a clearing and peered up at a villa through their NODs. Dave felt the incessant ticking of an internal timer, reminding him that time was one thing they didn't have in their favor. But he pushed it aside and refused to rush.

Slow is smooth, smooth is fast.

He had complete faith in his team's ability to clear the villas until they found the captured Agency officer. But whether they were able to do so without encountering armed resistance was beyond his control. No amount of planning or preparation could guarantee that because the enemy always got a vote.

He took a deep breath and gritted his teeth.

It's go time.

Lisa woke with a start and flailed her limbs in fright. Her right eye had swollen shut, but her left opened just enough to see she was still in the bathtub with her wrists chained to the heavy chrome faucet. The room was dark, but she had grown used to the familiar shadows, and they no longer terrified her. It was the silence that held her frozen, waiting to be shattered by the crash of a door, the stomp of a boot, or an angry voice descending on her.

The brief reprieve from her captors' torment came to an end not long after they chained her to the tub. She glanced down at the four inches of cold water and noticed it had turned a dark pink, shaded by blood that seeped from multiple open wounds across her body. She shivered, and gooseflesh broke out down her arms and legs, but she was too weak to move. Her body ached from the constant abuse, and her mind swam with horrific memories of unspeakable trauma that gripped her stomach with a sudden bout of nausea.

She took several breaths to regain control over her emotions and looked down at her throbbing feet. A faint sob escaped her lips when she saw the battered flesh, remembering with sudden clarity how her captors had smashed them with a hammer. Each of her ten toes were flattened and bent at unnatural angles, and chunks of skin had been flayed away where fragments of bone protruded. Even if she had the strength to attempt escaping, the blood oozing into the frigid water reminded her she wouldn't get far.

I can't make it another day, she thought.

Her eyes slipped closed again, and she tried to imagine a host of rough men descending in the night to free her from her torment and return her to safety. But it was futile. It was a hope she had once longed to manifest into reality, and the one she had given up on days ago.

Just let me die.

29

Dave remained crouched in the vegetation for several minutes before deciding it was safe to advance into the clearing and on to the first villa. In the distance, he heard waves breaking against the rocky southern shore and hoped it was loud enough to drown out their movement. At last, he motioned to the others that he was moving into position.

Taking point, he rose out of the trees and crossed the narrow cement walking path that circled most of the island and approached the first villa. It was identical to each of the other two-story target buildings with a large, curved deck at the rear, suspended eight feet in the air and facing the ocean. Dave made his way under the deck to inspect the posts anchored into concrete footings and dismissed it as a viable option for gaining entry.

He continued around the side of the villa and sighted over his SOPMOD M4 as he made his way up the hill to the front. He knew the main entrance was more exposed, but the need to find the hostage in time outweighed the potential risk of being spotted. He crested the hill and paused for only a second before stepping from the vegetation into the level clearing. A cursory scan of the open space through his NODs confirmed they were alone, and he hurried to the front door with his rifle at the ready.

Dave felt the others stack up behind him as he neared the front door. In his mind, he saw images of the resort's accommodations from photos they had studied before the mission. He knew they lacked actual floor plans, but most agreed that the first floor was likely a living area furnished with couches and chairs, and a staircase leading to the sleeping area on the second floor. He had trained in kill houses with far less information than that, and he felt a familiar sense of calmness that only comes after hundreds of hours of training in a skill.

He was ready.

Dave reached for the handle and applied gentle pressure to test for resistance. It turned easily, so he paused, reached behind his back, and signaled to prepare for entry in...

Three...two...one...

He turned the handle and pushed the heavy door inward, quickly stepping inside and pivoting to the right to move toward what he saw was a wet bar in the room's corner. Todd followed on his heels, turned left, and advanced along the wall toward the sliding glass door leading out onto the deck. Their infrared lasers swept the room in overlapping arcs as they scanned for threats.

"Clear right," Dave said.

"Clear left," Todd replied.

Ron and Graham stepped into the villa and took up positions on opposite sides of the front door. Graham nudged it closed behind him, then moved to the staircase on the far side of the room. With his rifle pointed up, he leaned his upper body out over the steps, craned his neck to look into the room above, and motioned for the others to advance.

Dave moved first and carefully placed his foot on the bottom step, hoping the humidity had caused the wood to swell and eliminated the potential for unwanted creaking. He held his breath and eased his body weight onto the solid wood tread. When no sound followed, he exhaled.

Step by step, he crept up the stairs and twisted his body to keep his rifle pointed at the empty space above. If he hadn't been wholly focused on looking for threats, the villa's ornate teak woodwork might have impressed him. But he only had time to focus on the beam of infrared light through the white hue of his NODs as he scanned the stairwell.

Dave felt Todd press a hand against his lower back to let him feel the slightest pressure of his presence. He trusted from experience that the other SEAL had his rifle aimed in the opposite direction to ensure they covered every angle, and he moved with confidence.

Reaching the second floor, Dave paused a moment before exposing himself to the room above. When Todd gave him an encouraging tap on his lower back, he lifted his head to scan the darkened space, then bolted up the remaining steps and crossed quickly to the canopy bed draped in mosquito netting. Todd followed on his heels and turned in the opposite direction to clear the cramped bathroom.

"Clear right," Todd said.

"Clear left," Dave replied.

Dammit!

Despite knowing the odds were slim they would find the captive Agency officer in the first villa they cleared, he was disappointed. The longer it took to find her, the greater the risk of being discovered. He wheeled for the stairs and descended to the first floor, where Ron and Graham waited anxiously. He gave them a quick shake of his head, then moved to the front door and prepared to lead them to the next villa.

Dave keyed the push-to-talk on his plate carrier to provide the TOC a situation report. "Scar Nine Nine, Mariner One Zero, villa one cleared. Negative Tangos. Negative Eagles. Moving to villa two."

"Mariner One Zero, Scar Nine Nine, Dusty green, continue."

From over his shoulder, Dave heard Graham whispering into Todd's ear. "If the door's locked, we'll have to go loud. It's reinforced, and a kick won't do it."

Todd tapped him on the shoulder to spur him into action, and Dave took a quick breath before stepping out into the night. The soft rustling of wind through the brush and faint crashing of waves below them were the only sounds. Nothing had changed since they entered the first villa less than five minutes earlier, and he moved swiftly across the crushed shell clearing to the second villa, further up the hill.

They had planned to clear the two villas at higher elevation next before moving back down to the fourth and final one. If they struck out and came up empty on all four, they would continue moving up and down the hill and follow the terrain to the northeast until they found her, or until the Mi-17 reached bingo fuel. At that point, they would have no choice but to beat feet down the hill and catch their ride back to the *Reagan* with their tails tucked between their legs.

That's not gonna happen, he thought.

Dave reached the edge of the level clearing and plunged into the vegetation on the other side, beginning his ascent with smooth and deliberate movements. His pace was quicker than it had been climbing from the beach to the first villa, but the timer in his head seemed louder and more urgent, propelling him upward with fervor. The rest of the team followed as before and paused when he reached the second clearing fronting the higher two villas. After a few seconds of respite, he swept around the corner to the front door and waited for the others to stack up behind him.

Again, Todd squeezed his shoulder, and he reached up to test the knob. He shook his head and motioned for Graham to breach.

"We've gotta go loud," Dave whispered.

This is gonna get messy.

The reinforced door, hinges, and deadbolt were too strong for their preferred method of entry, but they didn't have much choice. If they wanted to rescue her and get her to safety, they needed to clear each villa as quickly as possible.

Graham moved forward, raised the shotgun to the hinges, and quickly fired two shots into each. The deafening blasts shattered the night's stillness, and Dave sensed that the night had changed. The insects and animals that had provided the soundtrack for their movement fell silent, and the wind and waves seemed like little more than a hint of a whisper.

Graham kicked the door off its hinges, and Dave threw caution to the wind and blew into the room, aiming his rifle left toward the sliding glass door.

Before he had taken two steps, he saw a figure reaching for an AK-47 rifle propped against the far wall. He shifted his aim, squeezed the trigger, and sent two suppressed rounds into the man's back before his third step.

Todd entered a split second later and turned right, gliding across the wood floors to the wet bar in the far corner. Ron raced for the stairs and ascended two steps at a time with Graham hot on his heels.

The element of surprise was gone—speed and violence of action were all that mattered now.

30

Lisa jerked her head upright at two loud blasts and the sound of the door downstairs being kicked off its hinges. It was immediately followed by a flash of light and what sounded like a suppressed gunshot, but through the ringing in her ruptured eardrum, she couldn't be sure. Nothing seemed real anymore.

Through the bathroom's open door, she watched the shadowed figure of her guard rising from the bed. But before he could finish sitting upright, a spitting sound followed another flash of light and sent him reeling back onto the mattress. She whimpered and closed her eyes like a child, blocking out the evil that had descended into her own personal hell.

Heavy footsteps ascended the stairs as a menacing presence filled the bathroom and hovered over her. She tensed and prepared for another cruel swing of the hammer or steel pipe and inhaled sharply, wincing at the stabs of pain radiating from her broken ribs.

"Clear right," a voice said from across the room.

"Clear left," another replied.

English?

Her mind was playing tricks on her. That's all it was. Mandarin filled her head, and the unfamiliar voices confused and disoriented her. But she had been so certain. She opened an eye and saw a large man crouching over her and reaching out with a hesitant hand for the chains binding her wrists.

She flinched and kicked her battered feet against the tub, trying in vain to move away from him while pleading in Mandarin.

"Whoa," he breathed and pulled his hand back to give her some distance. "Easy now. We're here to bring you home."

Lisa thrashed in the cold water, but the word resonated with her.

Home?

At last, she relaxed and hung limp from the chains restraining her to the faucet, but her one open eye bore into the man who maintained eye contact while continuing to reassure her that she was going to be safe—that she was going home.

A second man entered the room, and her eye flashed to the new shadowy figure.

"Easy now," the first man said again. "Can you tell me your name?"

Lisa, she thought.

But her mouth opened, and a string of Mandarin phrases spilled out.

"You're safe now," he replied. "I need to know your name so we can take you home."

Home.

She worked her tongue across the inside of her mouth and tried to form the word she knew he needed to hear. But her mind was terrified of hope. Hope was the one thing that would totally break her and send her into an endless abyss of torment and agony.

Lisa, she thought again.

"Li... Li...," she stammered, trying to speak the name that brought with it parole.

But he was patient, and he spoke softly to encourage her. "It's okay. Just tell me your name."

"Lisa," she finally said. "Mourning." As the name escaped her lips, an invisible wall in her mind crashed down around her, and the truth of her situation became real.

"We're here to bring you home, Lisa," he said.

Dave helped Todd lift her from the bathtub and carefully lower her to the floor, then moved out of the way so Ron could examine her injuries. He stood in the doorway, watching the battered officer writhe in agony, and felt his anger boil over into blood lust for what the Chinese had done to her.

He reached up for the push-to-talk on his chest. "Scar Nine Nine, Mariner One Zero, jackpot. I say again, jackpot. Package secured and moving to extract."

"Mariner One Zero, Dusty One copies. Seven minutes out."

"How bad is she?" Dave asked.

Ron stood and led him into the bedroom and out of earshot. "She's in rough shape."

"How bad?"

"Probably moderate to severe pain with mostly superficial wounds. We don't know the extent of her internal injuries, but she likely has some that could result in pulmonary or hemodynamic compromise."

"English, Doc."

"It means she's lost a lot of blood and I don't know how stable she is. Giving her the wrong medication could be dangerous, but she's not ambulatory and we'll have to carry her out. We can't safely do that with the pain she's in."

"What do you suggest?"

"I can give her fifty milligrams of Ketamine intramuscularly. It'll take close to five minutes before providing any relief."

Dusty will be here in six.

Dave nodded. "Okay, do it. We need to get moving."

Ron returned to the bathroom and knelt next to her. "Lisa," he said quietly. "I'm going to give you something for the pain. Do you understand?"

She nodded. Dave watched him insert the needle into her thigh and slowly depress the plunger. He knew the dosage would likely break the dissociative threshold and put her into a trancelike state while still preserving her airway reflexes and spontaneous respiration. Aside from relieving her from the pain she'd endured, it would temporarily help her forget what was about to happen.

Five minutes.

"Mariner One Zero, Scar Nine Nine, we're picking up chatter indicating hostiles are inbound to your position. Recommend you beat feet."

"Roger," Dave said, then turned to Ron. "We need to move. Now."

Ron placed a comforting hand on Lisa's shoulder and rolled her onto her side. She groaned, but it was obvious the Ketamine was already having an effect. Dave helped Ron roll her back onto a soft litter that was little more than a hammock with handles on either end, then he covered her with a poncho liner and stood.

Four minutes.

"Ready?" Dave asked.

Ron nodded.

Dave turned for the stairs, followed by Ron and Graham carrying Lisa between them, and Todd bringing up the rear as they descended to the first floor. They stacked up on either side of the open door and paused for a moment, then surged out into the darkness.

Three minutes.

After the cacophony of gunfire disturbed the peaceful evening, the night sounds were slowly beginning to return to normal. But he could still sense a difference.

There's movement in the jungle.

"We've got company," he whispered, motioning for Ron and Graham to move deeper into the foliage.

He and Todd fanned out and scanned the surrounding darkness while bounding from tree to tree in a well-rehearsed cadence to cover for each other. Just before reaching the level clearing in front of the lower villas, he froze and signaled for Todd to halt.

Hostiles.

He didn't know if the Chinese knew where they were, but it was the only way to the beach. With their escape route blocked, they would have to shoot their way to safety.

"Dusty One, status," Dave whispered.

The reply was instantaneous. "Two minutes."

"Roger, this will be a hot extract." Dave looked at Todd.

He nodded, and together they stepped out into the clearing. Dave swept his rifle to the left while Todd aimed straight ahead and to the right. Before taking two steps into the gravel opening, Dave placed his IR laser onto the figure of an armed soldier and squeezed the trigger. His SOPMOD M4 coughed, and two rounds caught the man in the chest.

To his right, he heard Todd engaging targets. Two shots. Then four. The SEALs never stopped moving across the clearing, continuing around the lower villa with Dave on the left and Todd on the right. Behind them, Ron and Graham muscled the litter and hurried to follow in their wake.

Before Dave descended into the tree line, a machine gun opened up on his left and sprayed bullets into the air over his head. He dropped to the uneven ground and rolled to his right to look for cover, then sighted over his rifle and returned fire, walking rounds closer to the muzzle flashes coming from the jungle.

"Contact left!"

But Todd had already heard the machine gun and reversed course up the hill to flank the threat from higher elevation. "Keep moving," he growled.

Dave knew it was meant for the litter bearers, but he took it as a reminder that they couldn't afford to get bogged down in a firefight with the helicopter less than a minute from the LZ. It would be a sitting duck on the beach, waiting for the SEALs to climb aboard.

They needed to keep pressing to the extraction site.

The ineffective machine gun fire stopped, and Dave took advantage of the lull to rise to a knee and empty his magazine into the trees. When his bolt locked to the rear, he dropped the empty magazine and indexed a fresh one just as he heard the distinctive chopping sound of an AK-47 on full automatic in the jungle opposite the villa. The staccato of the Chinese rifle was followed quickly by the booming report of Graham's shotgun.

Todd had heard the same thing. "Mariner One Two, status."

When the query was met with silence, Dave felt a chill down his spine. But before he could worry about the others, he had to deal with the threat directly in front of him. He slapped the bolt catch along the side of his rifle to chamber a round and rose from his knee to charge the reloading machine gunner.

31

Lisa felt good. Whatever the man injected into her hadn't eliminated the pain but masked it to where she no longer winced every time she moved. And she was moving a lot in the litter they had made for her, wrapped in a soft and warm cocoon that made her feel as if she were floating through the air and swaying gently from side to side.

She kept her one good eye open, although it focused on nothing and seemed to take in everything without recognition. She saw a thick canopy overhead and twinkling stars in the gaps, but she couldn't remember where she was or how she had gotten there. Had she just woken up? Had she always felt so warm? Had she ever been in pain? She couldn't remember, but she thought so.

She heard the heavy breathing and occasional grunt of the two men who labored to carry her cocoon through the jungle, but she didn't know who they were. She only had the vaguest sense that they were there for a good reason and that she was happy they came. But to where? Where was she?

A thundering crack like splintered wood shattered the silence of her cocoon and sparked a dim feel of worry deep in her mind. But she didn't flinch. She blinked her one good eye slowly in the only reaction she could make and explored that worry.

What was she worried about? Yes, there had been a loud noise, but the world was full of loud noises. Why had that one been any different? Because she knew it, and she felt...annoyed? Frustrated? She recognized the sound and couldn't connect it to where her brain retained the memory of it. But the men carrying her reacted with urgency and dropped her cocoon to the ground.

One of them climbed on top of her, and she felt even more comforted. She closed her good eye and enjoyed the feeling of being wrapped inside a protective ball where nothing could hurt her. She could no longer feel her body, just a suggestion of pressure weighing down on her and making it difficult to breathe. But even that didn't bother her or pin down her fleeting mind, despite the man's musky smell giving her a singular thing to focus her attention on.

She heard a loud boom and saw a flash through her closed eyelids that triggered an emotion she recognized as fear. Only, she wasn't afraid. She knew she should be, but she wasn't. Whatever drug they had given her had removed that part of her brain. Or hidden it.

"Tango down," another voice said. She'd heard the voice before but again had a hard time following her thoughts to resemble anything close to a name or a face. It was a feeling more than anything else.

"Watch our flank," musky man said.

"Drag her down the hill. I'm hit."

"You okay?" He shifted his weight and pushed her deeper into the protective ball.

"Took out my radio, but the plate stopped it." He sounded different.

They were speaking quietly, little more than whispers, and she could sense the fear in their voices. But she didn't feel afraid at all. The only thing she felt was the protective warmth of her cocoon and the reassuring pressure of a man who had come to take her...

Home.

Suddenly the pressure abated, and she opened her eye when she felt herself floating again. The stars above her winked out, and the trees shifted. Another loud boom and a flash lit up the canopy overhead for a moment, showering her with an assault of color that was muted, as if she was seeing the world through a dirty window.

Somebody should clean that.

She closed her eye. Her cocoon bumped against something hard, and the musky man who had injected her with confusion suddenly let go. Her eye opened and twitched in his direction, then quickly closed as a series of flashes turned darkness into light. Again, something told her to flinch at the din of metallic scraping noises and loud coughing that accompanied each flash of light. But she remained still.

"Contact front!" musky man shouted.

What was his name?

Seven...eight...nine.

A tinny voice in her head counted the number of flashes, but she didn't understand why. She heard the other man yelling in response but couldn't make out his words over the coughing.

Fourteen...fifteen...sixteen.

Had she skipped any numbers?

Another sound joined the racket, a bark more than a cough. It mattered to some part of her, but she didn't understand why the stars no longer twinkled through the gaps in the canopy or why a new smell permeated the air. Bits and pieces of paper-thin flecks fell onto her like snow, and her cocoon jostled as another man—a different man—collapsed on top of her. His breathing was heavy, and he smelled of tobacco and coffee. But neither was quite right.

Another lucent boom and deafening flash rived the night directly over her. This time, she did flinch, but tobacco and coffee pressed down on her to keep her encased in her cocoon.

Pain.

It was the first time she remembered feeling that, and she didn't like it. She groaned, willing it to go away.

"Shit," tobacco and coffee said. "She needs another dose."

Another dose of what?

Thirty.

There was a pause in the scraping and coughing sounds followed by the twang of a spring and a plastic clicking sound. She knew she should recognize the sounds that pierced the fogginess of her brain, but it didn't make any sense to her. She could only feel the warmth of her cocoon and the pressure of tobacco and coffee on top of her and...

Pain!

It was more pronounced now, and she gasped. The pressure on top of her no longer comforted her, and she moaned and panted as if she had just sprinted a mile. With sudden clarity, she recognized the surrounding sounds as a chorus of gunshots. Some were suppressed, but the loudest sounded like AK-47s.

How do I know that?

"Ron, give it to her!"

The weight on top of her lifted, and the shadowed figure of tobacco and coffee moved from her vision and dissolved into the darkness. Another boom of the shotgun was answered by several loud cracks and a staccato of flashes from an AK-47. A second figure scurried into view, and she looked up into musky man's kind eyes for reassurance.

"Hang in there, Lisa," he said.

Who's Lisa? Wait... Am I...?

PAIN!

She pinched her eyes shut against the sensation that suddenly overwhelmed everything else. The sounds of gunfire lessened as if somebody had turned the volume down, and her vision blurred into a reddish hue of trees and sky and shadows. The beating of her heart throbbed throughout her body and drowned out every other sound, even the suppressed gunshots and louder cracks of Chinese automatic rifles. It was loud, and it hurt. And she felt nauseous.

A prick in her thigh broke through the crippling pain. It hurt but was so insignificant compared to her agony, she almost didn't notice. But she noticed a sensation spreading from her thigh and inching its way across her body, like liquefied warmth filling her from her toes to her chin. It pushed out the pain and reddish hue and dimmed the flashing lights and scraping, coughing sounds that echoed all around her.

"Get her to the beach! Now!" It was another voice, but one she knew she had heard before.

Her cocoon lifted into the air and moved again. She floated through the darkness, only casually aware of the brief interludes of light flashing around her. She knew she should flinch, but she didn't. She knew she should be scared, but she wasn't. The pain was gone again, and she couldn't even remember why she had been worried.

32

Dusty One
Air Branch Mi-17 Hip

Charlie stared at the dark island through his night vision goggles with detached calmness. He saw flashes of light break through the dense jungle near the landing zone and knew the SEALs were engaged in a firefight, giving the enemy hell as they retreated down the hillside toward the beach. But his observation was merely another data point and didn't change his focus from the looming approach.

Coming in from the sea meant he wouldn't have to account for rising terrain or other obstacles impeding his flight path, but it also meant his approach would be over a mostly flat surface, and he wouldn't have an opportunity to calibrate his depth perception. That was a challenge anytime flying on goggles, but tonight he needed to be extra cautious to avoid overshooting the LZ.

"You're point two from the zone," Roger said.

While Charlie focused on the green-hued scene through the forward windscreen, his second pilot sat in the seat to his left and called out the estimated range to touchdown, giving him another tool he could use to ensure he flared to stop his forward travel over the correct spot. Charlie was thankful their model of Mi-17 had large windows in front of each pilot's pedals and one in the centerline that allowed excellent forward visibility when landing.

Roger reached up and flipped the switch to activate hydraulics and lower the cargo ramp at the rear of the helicopter—a much appreciated improvement over the typical clamshell-style doors. Both side doors were open, but they weren't sure which direction the SEALs would come from, and every second counted. The quicker they were aboard, the quicker they could lift off and return to the safety of the sea.

"Point one," Roger said.

Charlie glanced to his right and saw an increase in the gunfire breaking through the jungle. It was going to get really interesting really quick.

Charlie keyed the switch to speak over the intercom. "We need someone on the guns."

"On it," came a SEAL's reply.

Without taking his eyes off the approaching landing zone, Charlie knew what was happening behind him in the main cabin. Each of the four SEALs had been trained in operating the miniguns before taking off from the *Reagan*, and two were taking up positions at the side doors and preparing to rain hate down on the enemy. After clipping the safety tethers' carabiners to their rigger's belts, the SEALs would remove a cotter pin to unlock the pivoting system and swing the guns out over the water.

The electrically driven six-barrel rotary machine guns were capable of firing 7.62 x 51mm rounds at a rate of over three thousand rounds per minute. Though there were no optics or lasers on the guns, they were loaded with a three-to-one tracer mix that would allow the operators to walk their fire onto the targets. Both SEALs flipped their switches to turn on the guns' power supplies, then free-spun the barrels.

"Dusty One..." There was heavy breathing on the radio. "We're thirty seconds out."

"Mark yourselves with IR strobes," Charlie replied. "We're in the flare."

Within seconds, flashes of light from separate IR strobes began blinking through the dense foliage. Two were directly in front of the helicopter, and two were to Roger's left, further up the beach. He craned his neck to keep sight as the Mi-17 crossed the beach line and flared to stop its forward movement with the nose pointed at the first two strobes in the jungle. Charlie gave it left pedal and pivoted the helicopter to give the SEAL on the starboard GAU-17/A the widest field of fire.

"They're on our heels," a voice said over the radio, just as two blinking IR strobes broke through the tree line. Within seconds, Charlie was able to make out two men leapfrogging toward the waiting helicopter, taking turns to stop, pivot to the jungle, and fire several rounds into the trees while the other bounded ahead. He heard the minigun spool up behind him.

As the first two SEALs reached the open door of the Mi-17, two additional strobes broke through onto the beach to their left. Charlie could tell they were carrying a heavy load between them and was about to key the intercom switch when he heard Dave shouting.

"I'm going to help!"

Charlie looked over his shoulder in time to see the senior chief—who had just climbed aboard—leap from the port door and sprint up the beach toward the second pair of blinking strobes.

Ting!

He snapped his head right as a round plinked into the Mi-17's armor plating aft of the side door. Fortunately, the SEAL manning the starboard minigun needed no other encouragement to respond, and Charlie heard the satisfying zipper of hot rounds flying through the night air. The SEAL pivoted the gun slowly from right to left and walked the rounds across the trees where only moments before two of his brothers had exited the jungle. Charlie looked away and focused on the two remaining SEALs struggling to drag the rescued spy across the sand forward of the helicopter.

Come on! What's taking so long?

"One minute," Roger said, letting him know they had already been on the ground longer than either wanted.

Charlie wanted to fire back an acerbic reply but knew it was pointless. All he could do was listen to the minigun laying down covering fire and wait for the last of the frogmen to carry the rescued Agency officer onto the helicopter.

Dave sprinted toward the others while firing his rifle into the jungle behind them, doing his best to keep their pursuers at bay. He saw Ron turn and stumble in the deep sand, almost dropping his single-handed grip on the litter, but he regained his footing and continued shuffling toward the waiting helicopter.

"Come on!" Dave yelled.

Over his shoulder, he heard a second minigun open up on the jungle to give them a heavy blanket of covering fire. He reached Ron and Graham and took one of the handles at the front of the litter, turning to help them drag the battered operations officer. With the added muscle, they moved quicker through the sand and reached the Hip within seconds. Dave leaped aboard and pulled the litter up onto the helicopter's sloping ramp. Graham followed half a beat behind and helped him tow her deeper into the helicopter and hopefully better protected by the sparse armor plating.

Ron stepped up onto the ramp and shouted, "Last man!"

Dave watched him collapse in a heap next to the Agency officer, then moved quickly through the cabin to complete a head count. The last thing he wanted to do was leave anybody behind.

"All aboard," Dave shouted, tapping Charlie on the shoulder. The pilot nodded and raised the collective, lifting the Russian-made helicopter from the sand. Less than ten seconds after the last SEAL stepped onto the ramp, the air branch pilot had the helicopter nosed over and accelerating away from the island. Exhausted, Dave slid to the floor and watched the SEALs on the door guns continue to spew thin tails of fire into the darkened jungle behind them.

Slowly, the gunfire ebbed, and the SEALs flipped off the miniguns' electric motors and locked their mounts in place. As the sound of the beating rotor blades and wind whipping in through the open doors replaced the sound of gunfire, Dave plugged his Peltor headset into an intercom jack on the bulkhead. He surveyed his surroundings and saw bullet holes pocking the fuselage and brass casings and steel links littering the aluminum floor.

"Scar Nine Nine, Dusty One, the package is secure, proceeding to mom," Charlie said.

Dave breathed a sigh of relief, thankful to be out over the water and heading home. But his relief was short-lived.

"Copy all, Dusty One." The voice paused. "Chatter indicates the Chinese have launched fighters to intercept."

"How long—"

Roger's voice chimed in. "Looks like we're leaking fuel."

Well, shit.

33

USS *Ronald Reagan* (CVN-76)
South China Sea

Colt groaned and shifted his weight to try to find a modicum of relief from the discomfort caused by his parachute harness digging into his thighs after four hours strapped to the ejection seat. He brought his Garmin Fenix in front of his face and pressed the button to light it up so he could read the time.

Only ten more minutes, he thought.

He had come to regret his decision to volunteer for a second back-to-back shift and gave up on his Kindle in favor of staring out into the pitch-black nothingness to pass the time. He looked over at the jet on the catapult next to him and saw what looked like the flicker of a screen lighting up his wingman's face.

"Hey, Ducky, how's your night vision?"

Ducky looked up and glanced in Colt's direction. "Great. You still over there?"

He shook his head and reached down to further dim his cockpit lighting, but no matter how dark he made it, he still couldn't make out a defined horizon. It was just one of those nights.

A loud banging on the side of his jet drew his attention down to the bottom of the ladder, where he saw his plane captain, a third class petty officer whose name he couldn't quite remember.

Ramirez or Rodriguez? Something like that.

"Sir, I think your relief is coming," he yelled up to him.

Colt nodded and felt a glimmer of hope that he would finally be released from his prison. His stomach growled at the thought of descending from the flight deck for the dirty shirt and a slider at mid rats, but he had to take his PC's word for it. Sitting on the bow catapult, he had an unobstructed view of the ocean but couldn't see anything other than Ducky's Super Hornet on the adjacent catapult.

What's his name? Rosales?

Colt put the thought from his mind and started cleaning up the nest he had made for himself. He stuffed the trash in his helmet bag's side pocket next to two emptied and crushed water bottles, then turned up the cockpit flood lights to make sure he hadn't missed any Clif Bar wrappers. Satisfied he wasn't leaving a mess for his relief, he uncapped his last water bottle and drained it in one long pull.

It's Martinez.

As the blood began flowing again to his limbs, Colt reached down and started unstrapping his leg restraints so he could finally climb out of the seat. He froze with his hands on the buckles when the 5MC's loudspeaker boomed across the flight deck.

"*Launch the Alert Five aircraft!*"

What did he just say?

He sat up and turned to Martinez with a shocked look on his face. "What did he just say?"

But before Martinez could reply, the 5MC flight deck address system blared again. "*All crew on the flight deck, start up the Alert Five aircraft. Launch the Alert Five aircraft, initial bearing heading two seven zero.*"

Out of the corner of his eye, Colt saw his plane captain stow his ladder and give him the waggling three-fingered signal to start his Auxiliary Power Unit. Without thinking, he reached for the APU switch and flipped it on while simultaneously lowering the canopy in place to shut out the soft whine of four jets starting up.

One minute.

After the APU came online, he flipped the engine crank switch over to the right side and began spooling the right motor. It helped that he was already pointed into the wind and the engine's core was rotating with the airflow through his intakes. Seconds later, he advanced the throttle and introduced fuel and ignition to the combustion sequence. The engine lit off with a low growl, and he watched the RPM rise and stabilize at idle.

His hands flew across the cockpit in well-rehearsed motions that were second nature. Because his inertial navigation system already had a stable alignment, and he had already powered on his radar and weapons systems, his sole focus became starting his engines. He cranked the left motor.

Two minutes.

"Tower, three zero seven for a rep," Ducky said.

Colt advanced the left throttle and waited for his left engine to light off before glancing at the Super Hornet next to him. A squadron white jersey troubleshooter had plugged into the communications panel on the starboard side of his nose and was talking to the pilot to address whatever issue he was having.

"Three oh seven, are you having problems?" the Air Boss asked.

"Yes, sir," came the dejected voice. "I need to be spun off the cat."

Colt's second engine stabilized, and he shut down the APU and gave Martinez the signal to disconnect external power from his jet. The plane captain removed ground power, then turned and shouted something to the yellow shirt, who immediately gave the signal to break him down. As sailors scrambled underneath Colt's jet to remove the chocks and chains keeping him bound to the flight deck, the yellow shirt gave him the signal to lower his launch bar. Colt felt it drop into place.

"Hey, Colt, I'll try to catch up with you," Ducky said over their tactical frequency. "Try to save some for me."

Colt double-clicked the radio transmit switch on his throttle in reply but kept his focus on the yellow shirt straddling the catapult track. He was focused on one thing and one thing only.

Three minutes.

Colt took a deep breath, exhaled slowly, and bent at the waist to double-check his upper and lower leg restraints were still buckled and connected to his seat. Sitting up, he swept his hands across his lower Koch fittings that kept his butt attached to his seat, then the upper that anchored him to the parachute in the head box. He knew the clock was ticking, but he was never so rushed that he skipped steps in the checklist.

Mask on. Seat armed.

I'm ready.

Four minutes.

He looked at the sailor holding the weight board and made a circular gesture with the green finger light strapped on his left hand to indicate they had his correct weight. After another deep breath, the yellow shirt gave him the signal to take tension and advance power. He felt his nose squat under the strain, and he pushed his throttles smoothly to military-rated thrust while watching his engine instruments. Satisfied the engines were stable, he wiped out his flight controls as the final step required for launch, then reached his pinky for the light switch on his throttle and turned on his external lights.

The shooter saluted him and lowered the lighted wand to the flight deck and pointed it at the dark nothingness beyond the bow. Colt braced his head against the headrest when the holdback fitting broke, and the steam shuttle hurtled his seventy-million-dollar jet down the catapult track. The dim flight deck edge lighting raced underneath him, and he felt the jerky transition from being pulled off the boat to being pushed by twenty-six thousand pounds of thrust.

Five minutes.

Clark Air Base, Philippines

"Scar Nine Nine, Dusty One, the package is secure, proceeding to mom."

Connor felt like a fish out of water and stood at the back of the ad hoc Tactical Operations Center they had set up in a hangar on the air base. Every other person in the room had a role to play in the ongoing rescue operation, but all he could do was run his fingers through his thick, luxurious hair and wait for information to filter down to him.

"Two Flankers launching from Lingshui," a sailor announced.

He knew enough to know that a Flanker was a fighter, but beyond that, his knowledge of the Chinese air order of battle was limited. In any event, it wasn't good news and meant the SEALs had kicked the hornet's nest.

"Copy all, Dusty One," the watch commander said. "Chatter indicates the Chinese have launched fighters to intercept."

He tried biting his tongue but couldn't help himself. "What about air cover?"

The watch commander turned and looked at him. "We have Super Hornets on alert aboard the *Reagan* and Joint Strike Fighters on the *America*."

He spun away and paced along the back wall, doing everything he could to avoid snapping at the men and women who were busy collating information with one solitary purpose—to get the Mi-17 back to the *Reagan* unharmed.

"First alert Super Hornet from the *Reagan* airborne," another sailor announced.

Go get 'em, boys!

He exhaled with relief as the watch commander relayed the information to the air branch pilots flying a blacked-out Russian-made helicopter over the pitch-black South China Sea. "Dusty One, Scar Nine Nine, a Super Hornet has launched from the *Reagan*."

"Copy," came Charlie's calm reply. "We have another problem."

Connor stopped pacing and faced the speaker.

"We took damage and are leaking fuel. Can't make it all the way back to mom."

The watch commander didn't hesitate. "Copy. Proceed to FARP Alpha."

"Dusty One."

Connor strode across the hangar's concrete floor and approached the watch commander. "What's FARP Alpha?"

He sighed with obvious frustration at Connor's continued interruptions, but he patiently pulled up a chart of their operating area and pointed to a speck of green hidden in the vastness of blue. "Passu Keah," he said.

"Is it a base?"

He shook his head. "It's a Forward Arming and Refueling Point on an uninhabited atoll in the southwestern part of the Paracels."

"So, there's gas there," Connor concluded.

The watch commander nodded. "A Marine Corps MV-22 Osprey from the USS *America* delivered a five-hundred-gallon fuel bladder there, but it's not the most ideal place to gas up."

Connor looked up at the screen showing two radar contacts flowing south away from Lingshui Air Base on Hainan Island and one flying north from the *Reagan*. "Can they make it?"

He shrugged. "Depends on how bad the leak is. If they drain the fuel bladder dry, they should have enough to reach the carrier, but there are just too many variables to be certain."

Connor watched the radar contacts slowly tick across the computer screen and felt a pang of guilt that he couldn't do more for the SEALs who had risked everything to rescue Lisa. He turned and strode back to the rear wall and resumed his pacing, wishing there was something he could do other than hope.

Hope was never a good strategy.

34

Escondido, California

Jenn walked into her apartment and kicked off her heels, watching them sail over the sofa in elegant arcs. She left her roller bag standing next to the front door and walked into the kitchen to reach for a wineglass before stopping herself. She needed to find a new way to unwind.

Shoulders slumped, she opened the empty refrigerator and pulled out a bottle of water. Maybe if she wasn't so thirsty, she wouldn't think about the unopened bottle of Malbec sitting on the counter. Taunting her.

"Oh, shut up," she spat.

Dropping the empty water bottle, she reached up and untied the neckerchief that had been slowly choking her all the way from Honolulu. It was fitting, she thought, as she felt the life growing inside her choking off the freedoms she had taken for granted as a sky goddess. It was amazing that a little pink line could have such an impact.

How could this happen?

She shook her head. She knew how it had happened. And, if she was being honest, she wasn't all that surprised. Andy's appetite for her was insatiable—a refreshing change from the empty and meaningless dalliances she thought she had been enjoying before he came into her life.

But it wasn't just his fault. She couldn't keep her hands off him either. Whether he was wearing his green romper—or jumpsuit, or whatever it was called—or in his trademark shorts, T-shirt, and flip-flops, she couldn't help herself. He was irresistible. Easily the most attractive man she had ever met.

And he loves me.

She swallowed hard. Jenn didn't want to admit it, but she was genuinely concerned that if she told him, he would disappear and leave her with a lifelong reminder of what could have been. It wouldn't be the first time a man had disappointed a woman.

Jenn glanced at the clock over the stove, mentally calculating what time it was wherever in the Pacific Ocean Andy was floating. Not that it really mattered. It wasn't like she could pick up the phone and call him. As much as she wanted to hear his voice reassuring her that everything would be okay, she knew it was just a dream.

Walking into the living room, Jenn reached back and unzipped the top of her dress, wriggling her arms free from the confining and itchy fabric. She let the top of her dress fall around her waist and flopped back onto the sofa, closing her eyes as she tried to ignore what surprises the next few months had in store for her.

She had three days off before her next trip—a two-day trip to Honolulu with a long layover—but she wished she could sleep for nine months and wake up when her nightmare was over. Better yet, maybe she could sleep for eighteen years.

She groaned.

No matter how hard she tried, she couldn't get her mind to switch off. The little voice in the back of her head wouldn't shut up.

He's going to say you trapped him.

He's going to deny it's his.

He won't even call you back.

And on and on.

She reached into the pocket of her dress and pulled out her phone, hoping a quick email to Andy would silence the voice long enough to let her sleep. She wasn't nauseous now and wanted to take advantage of it.

The message was short and sweet and straight to the point.

Let me know when we can talk.

USS *Ronald Reagan* (CVN-76)
South China Sea

Andy opened his eyes, somewhat surprised to discover that he was back in his rack. He couldn't remember if he had actually made it to the officer's head down the passageway. The gut-twisting cramps seemed to have receded, but the debilitating headache and fever had not. He lifted his head from his pillow, and the room immediately began spinning.

What the heck is wrong with me?

He dropped his head back to the pillow just as he heard the door open. A brilliant beam of light intruded on the pitch-black darkness of his stateroom, and he leaned his head to one side to see who had entered. But even that subtle movement was enough to bring his nausea back, and he groaned.

"Andy?" The voice of Lieutenant Commander Tom Wilson, his detachment officer-in-charge, startled him.

"Yeah?"

"You okay?"

He closed his eyes to quell the nausea and swallowed hard against the lump in his throat. From the moment he first raised his right hand and swore an oath to the Constitution, Andy had prided himself in putting the mission first. He had flown sick. He had flown tired. He had even flown injured. But this...

"Not really," he said, hating the words as they tumbled from his mouth.

Andy opened his eyes and noticed that the beam of light still shone into his room. Tom's voice hadn't come any closer and almost sounded as if he hadn't even crossed the threshold and was still in the passageway outside his stateroom.

"We need to get you down to Sickbay."

But Andy didn't want to go anywhere, and he shook his head. "Doc just said I need to sleep it off."

"You've been asleep almost a full day," Tom said. "And a lot more people are getting sick."

Andy swallowed again. "Food poisoning?"

Tom didn't answer right away. "We don't know. Doc wants to draw blood."

Frustrated, Andy swung his feet out of his rack and lowered himself to the floor. He braced himself against the metal bunk and waited for the vertigo to subside, then took a hesitant step toward the door. "What do you mean, *we don't know*?"

Tom retreated away from the door, as if the one step Andy had taken put him in mortal danger. "Hold it right there," he said.

Andy stopped. "What's going on, Tom?"

"Lots of people are getting sick."

"Yeah, you said that." A sudden stab of pain hit him square in the stomach, and he doubled over with a grunt. "What...the *fuck*...is going on?"

"Doc doesn't think it's food poisoning. But whatever it is, it's spreading quickly throughout the ship."

Andy took another step, but the spinning room's dizzying pace quickened, and he dropped to a knee in the middle of the floor. He had experienced food poisoning before, and he agreed that this didn't feel like that at all. This was worse.

"Are we in River City?" Andy asked.

"Probably."

Like most aviators, Andy never understood the games ship-drivers liked to play. They made a big deal about remaining under clouds during long transits to hide from foreign satellite surveillance and routinely shut off all outside communications during periods known as "River City." He assumed there was a strategic purpose, but it was mostly just a nuisance.

"I need to get a message to Jenn," he muttered.

"We'll get a message to her." Tom hesitated for a moment. "We need to get you down to Sickbay."

Andy closed his eyes and bit off a scathing reply. He knew it wasn't Tom's fault that he had eaten a bad Barney Clark or caught a virus. But the last thing he wanted to do was leave his stateroom and make his way down to the second deck and stand in line with a bunch of other sick people so Doc could jab him with a needle and suck blood from his veins.

"Do you need help?"

"No," Andy replied, just as another wave of nausea caused him to double over.

"Andy?"

"I'm fine," he groaned. "Let me get changed."

Tom quietly closed the door and plunged Andy into the comforting darkness once again. He took several calming breaths before pushing himself to his feet and staggered the short distance to his locker to retrieve his flight suit. It was the easiest uniform to put on over the boxers and T-shirt he had been sleeping in.

With the flight suit zipped up, he sat down in the chair and slipped his feet into his boots. Another bout of vertigo threatened to topple him over, but he gripped the arms and steadied himself as he waited for it to pass. When it did, he bent over and began tying his laces.

His vision narrowed, and he closed his eyes.

This isn't good.

With a grunt, he snapped his eyes open and focused on completing the simple task. It was one he had learned as a toddler, and he wasn't about to let food poisoning or a stupid virus stop him from completing it. But before he finished lacing up his first boot, his vision went black, and he fell forward from the chair and hit his head on the edge of the metal desk.

35

Dusty One
Air Branch Mi-17 Hip
Southeast of Fenjiezhou Island

Charlie's face was etched in emotionless determination. It was hot, and the turbulent air so close to the water was making him work harder than normal to keep the older helicopter flying toward their destination—almost another one hundred miles over the horizon. But despite this, his grip on the cyclic and collective remained loose and relaxed. Only his jaw clenched firmly.

"Dusty One, Scar Nine Nine, a Super Hornet has launched from the *Reagan*."

"Copy. We have another problem." He released the push-to-talk and spoke over the intercom to Roger in the left seat. "How we looking?"

"Definitely won't have enough to make it to the carrier," he replied.

"Shit!" Charlie took a calming breath, then pressed the button to transmit again. "We took damage and are leaking fuel. Can't make it all the way back to mom."

"Copy. Proceed to FARP Alpha."

Charlie gestured for Roger to load the waypoint into the navigation system and replied, "Dusty One."

With the new destination loaded, he banked the helicopter to put the isolated atoll on the nose. Passu Keah was significantly closer than the *Reagan* and made their fuel-time-distance calculations infinitely easier. Though there was still plenty to keep him tense, he relaxed his jaw slightly.

"Can we make it?" he asked Roger.

"Oh yeah. And then some."

He exhaled and turned his focus on the other bit of good news. The prospect of having Chinese fighters intercept them and blow them out of the sky before reaching safety didn't make the flight any easier on him. But with an American fighter racing to meet them, he knew he would at least have some top cover. He glanced over at Roger, who was looking at a computer showing their location in relation to the man-made islands the Chinese had constructed to claim territorial rights. "What's it look like out there?"

Overlaid on top of the situation display he was monitoring were several contacts that were broadcast over datalink from the various intelligence-gathering platforms supporting the operation. He already knew a Navy P-8A Poseidon was orbiting north of their position off the coast of Hainan Island and that an MQ-4C Triton drone was patrolling south of the Paracel Islands, and both were uplinking surface and air contacts to the network.

"No change to the surface-to-air picture. We are well outside their engagement zone and shouldn't be detected on this track." He tapped on a few icons with the stylus attached to the Toughbook computer.

"Surface traffic is normal, and there is no activity at any of the known naval bases between here and there." He selected another overlay on the laptop. "The only air threats are the fighters launching from Lingshui."

"How far?" Charlie asked.

"They just got airborne. One hundred miles."

But they'll eat that up quickly. Charlie grunted.

"Wait," Roger added. "I'm seeing the Super Hornet from the *Reagan* now."

Charlie wanted to glance across the cockpit at the dim screen but didn't dare take his eyes off the horizon through his NODs. He had several thousand hours flying at night, all below one thousand feet above the ground, but there was something unique about flying over the water at night.

In his previous life, he'd had the advantage of using terrain-following radar, but the former Soviet helicopter lacked that luxury. Nor did it have an LPIA—Low Probability of Intercept Altimeter—that would allow them to use the radar altimeter without fear of being detected by Chinese sensors. Instead, he was forced to rely on his barometric altimeter, and without any distinguishing ground features, it would be easy to dip the nose and fly right into the water. Especially on a night like this. He wasn't taking that chance.

"How far away are they?"

"Just one so far. One hundred twenty miles."

It was too close for his comfort, but hopefully the jet jockey knew what he was doing.

Mace 201
Navy FA-18E Super Hornet

All the hours of boredom strapped to the ejection seat dissolved from his memory the second his jet broke free from the flight deck. Colt was precisely where he belonged—at the controls of a Navy jet, taking the fight to the enemy. He retracted his landing gear and immediately turned to point his nose due west at Hainan Island.

Unlike normal cyclic operations, an alert aircraft wasn't restricted to flying straight ahead for ten miles before turning or climbing and descending within the CCA. He pushed his throttles into afterburner and pulled back on the stick to begin a climb for one of the most important things he would need in an engagement: altitude.

"Two zero one, take angels thirty, fly heading two five zero for cutoff."

Colt adjusted his heading another twenty degrees to the left and continued climbing through fifteen thousand feet. He was still in afterburner and accelerating away from the carrier, not wasting time worrying about whether the other two alert aircraft had launched. If they did, he would see them over the datalink soon enough.

"Two zero one," he replied.

"Two zero one, cleared to switch Tiger control."

Colt reached up and tuned his primary radio to the E-2D Hawkeye controller's frequency and leveled off at thirty thousand feet before keying the microphone. "Tiger, two zero one."

"Two zero one, Tiger, picture single group, BRAA, two six zero, one hundred and fifty, forty-two thousand, flank southeast, bogey, outlaw."

Outlaw?

Colt felt a flutter of excitement deep in his stomach, and he ran the cursors on his radar attack display along that line of bearing. The addition of the brevity code *outlaw* meant that the bogey aircraft had met point of origin criteria. They knew where the unidentified plane had launched from, but it hadn't yet satisfied criteria for declaring it hostile. He was surprised they had even called away the alert for that.

"Two zero one, commit," he replied, indicating he was taking ownership of the intercept.

"Tiger copies commit. Single group, BRAA, two five eight, one hundred and thirty-five, forty-two thousand, flank southeast, bogey, outlaw."

Colt pulled up the Situational Awareness display that showed both surface and air contacts the E-2D Hawkeye populated into the datalink network. Although still beyond his onboard radar range, the airborne threat's surveillance track moved rapidly away from Hainan Island at forty-two thousand feet toward another track flying well below one hundred. He placed his cursors over the low and slow-flying surveillance track.

"Tiger, declare contact, BRAA two zero zero, seventy-five."

The reply was immediate. "Contact BRAA two zero zero, seventy-five, friendly. I say again, friendly. Skip it, skip it."

What the fuck is going on?

He thought back to the Russian helicopter he had watched take off while sitting on the catapult and wondered if that was the low-flying contact. Colt swallowed, then moved his cursors back to the hostile group and designated it to pull up additional information in his Night Vision Cueing and Display, a hybrid between the Joint Helmet Mounted Cueing

System and the AN/AVS-9 dual tube night vision goggles. While not as powerful as the Helmet Mounted Display he had worn while flying the F-35C Joint Strike Fighter, the NVCD still provided him visual guidance to a computer-generated box in the sky where the invisible target was located. He selected his radar-guided AIM-120D AMRAAM, or Advanced Medium Range Air-to-Air Missile, and studied the depicted Launch Acceptability Region.

Still too far away.

The box centered around the lead J-11B Flanker in his NVCD abruptly rotated and became a diamond. Although he saw the correct symbology for a hostile contact on his Situational Awareness and radar attack displays, he still had a hard time accepting it and wanted the controller to declare it hostile and give him the authority to shoot. "Tiger, declare single group."

"Single group hostile."

Holy shit.

Dusty One
Air Branch Mi-17 Hip

Charlie dropped his eyes to look under his NODs at the red light flashing just under the glare shield on his forward instrument panel. It took him less than a second to recognize its position on the Hip's upgraded radar warning receiver.

Not good.

"Radar lock," Roger confirmed. "Six o'clock and correlated."

If there was a bright side to having a hostile enemy fighter locking you up on radar, it was that at least it wasn't a surface-to-air missile site that had gone undetected by their surveillance. The fighters rapidly closing in on them were still their biggest threat.

"How far?" Charlie asked, lifting his gaze to look at the augmented darkness through the forward windscreen.

"They're at sixty miles and closing."

"How far to Passu Keah?"

Roger zoomed out on his display that had become cluttered with additional icons as the *Reagan's* E-2D added additional surveillance tracks to the datalink network. "Also sixty miles. About thirty minutes of flying time."

Charlie keyed the transmit switch for the SATCOM radio. "Scar Nine Nine, Dusty One is thirty minutes from FARP Alpha." He omitted the fact that they were only thirty minutes from landing if the Chinese fighters didn't shoot them down first.

"Scar Nine Nine copies."

Charlie turned his attention back to the closest alligator to the canoe. "How far out is our savior?"

Roger didn't have to ask who he meant, since there was only one contact on his screen that had any chance of saving them from becoming a burning fireball in the night sky. "Seventy miles. One additional Super Hornet is ten miles in trail."

At least there are two now.

A second flashing red light drew Charlie's attention once more back to the instrument panel. But this one was accompanied by an annoyingly loud beeping sound.

"Fire control radar," Roger said.

The Chinese fighters who had their radars locked onto the helicopter were preparing to fire. In his previous life flying Blackhawks and Little Birds, he would have used the terrain to mask their position and avoid missiles fired at him. But over the open water, there was nowhere to hide. All he could do was run as far and as fast as possible.

He glanced down at the engine instruments and saw that he was already producing the maximum amount of torque and couldn't push the engines any further.

Come on, baby, you can do this.

"Fifty miles," Roger said.

Charlie clenched his jaw tighter and focused on inching even closer to the water, hoping the Chinese fighters' radars would struggle to hold a lock through the choppy surface clutter. His hands and feet remained relaxed on the controls, and they descended below ten feet, flying closer than he really wanted to in those circumstances.

"Hey, what's that alarm?" Dave asked, sticking his head into the cockpit.

Roger ignored the SEAL, who stared wide-eyed through the forward windscreen at the pitch-black nothingness in front of them. "Forty miles," he said.

The second red light began flashing, and the beeping sound changed to a klaxon siren.

"Fuck!" Charlie cursed. "Missile launch."

36

USS *Ronald Reagan* (CVN-76)
South China Sea

Doc Crowe stepped from the Sickbay and pulled the surgical mask down around her chin, leaning against the bulkhead to catch her breath. She had been going nonstop through the night. Ever since Goldy had called her to check on Andy, more and more people on the ship were coming down with the same symptoms.

What is going on?

The door opened over her shoulder, and Diona's head emerged. "Ma'am, you have a phone call."

Doc closed her eyes and willed herself to find the energy she needed to make it through the night. Then, she pushed off the bulkhead, lifted the mask to cover her mouth and nose once more, and spun back into the ship's medical department. "Thanks, HM1."

She walked across the ward and picked up the phone. "This is Doc Crowe."

"Doc! It's Goldy again."

She sighed and felt her exhaustion boil over into frustration. "I told you to get Andy here for—"

"He hit his head, and I can't wake him."

Her exhaustion disappeared as if someone had flipped a switch. "Is he bleeding?"

"It's bad."

"Keep pressure on it. I'll be right there."

Doc slammed the phone down and motioned to Diona. "Get your kit and come with me."

"What's going on?"

Doc spun back for the door and raced for the ladder. She didn't bother removing her mask and struggled to breathe through the polypropylene— a non-woven fabric designed to block dust and microbes. She didn't know what was spreading across the ship, but if there was one thing the pandemic had taught her, it was that it was better to be safe than sorry. Within minutes after seeing their first patient in sick call and recognizing the symptoms were like Andy's, she ordered the medical personnel under her charge to break out the masks.

"Ma'am!" Diona yelled.

But she ignored her. When she reached the ladder, she grabbed the handrail and launched herself upward, bellowing, "Make a hole!"

The sailors above moved aside and permitted her unfettered access to ascend to the "oh three" level while the corpsman raced to keep up with her bulky medical kit slung across her back. "Ma'am, what's going on?"

Stepping off the ladder, Doc paused and waited for the first class petty officer to catch up before answering. "One of the pilots hit his head. He is bleeding and unconscious."

"How bad?"

"I don't know," Doc said, turning for the passageway to make her way across the ship to the ladder that led to Sleepy Hollow. "He was the first one I saw with symptoms. Could be related, but we won't know that until we can draw blood."

Doc was on autopilot, moving through the ship's darkened corridors while thinking through the potential outcomes of an unconscious patient with a head injury. Normally, she would have to consider the potential for a concussion based on symptoms like nausea, headaches, and unsteadiness. But Andy had exhibited each of those even before hitting his head.

She reached the ladder and descended into Sleepy Hollow, listening to Diona's boots thumping softly behind her. But before she could knock on the door, it opened, and she saw Andy lying in a pool of blood.

"Shit."

"I don't know what to do," Goldy said, stepping aside to permit her entrance.

Though she rarely had to deal with anything worse than minor illnesses on the ship, she fell back on her training with ease. Doc swept into the room while pulling on a pair of latex gloves and fell to her knees next to Andy, squeezing his shoulders while calling out to him. "Andy, can you hear me?"

No response.

Though it was obvious what had happened, she followed the training she had received in tactical combat casualty care and swept his body, looking for other injuries while following the mnemonic MARCH.

Massive hemorrhage.

The wound on his head was the only source of bleeding, and she turned to Diona. "Place pressure on that."

The corpsman ripped open a package of gauze and placed it against the unconscious pilot's head while Doc continued her assessment.

Airway.

She leaned down and placed her ear close to Andy's mouth while looking down his chest to watch it rising and falling with his labored breathing. It didn't appear there were any obstructions to his airway, but she worried that with his nausea he was at risk of pulmonary aspiration.

"Let's move him into the recovery position," she said. "Control his head for me."

Though she didn't think there was a significant risk of a spinal injury based on where the wound was, she still wanted Diona to help stabilize the head while she rolled Andy onto his side. She lifted his right arm above his head and draped his left across his neck. Then, she bent his left leg upward at the knee and looked to Diona for confirmation she was ready.

"On three. One...two...three."

While the corpsman stabilized Andy's head, Doc rolled him onto his right side before continuing to evaluate him.

Respiration.

Andy's breathing was labored, but no more so than any of the patients she had already treated for the illness. And, aside from the head wound, she was certain he had no other injuries, so she skipped the next step of checking on circulation and moved directly to the last one.

"Grab me a blanket," she told Goldy.

The COD pilot spun away and ripped a wool blanket off the top rack and handed it to Doc. Even though Andy wasn't wet or cold, she knew he had lost blood—and therefore body heat—and was at risk of hypothermia. She wrapped his body in the blanket, then motioned for Diona to remove the gauze bandage to inspect the wound.

The laceration was above his left temple, and she softly manipulated the tissue around the wound until she was certain it hadn't fractured the skull. The cut was deep and would require stitches, but there was nothing life-threatening about it. She breathed a sigh of relief.

A blinding light consumed his consciousness, pushing aside every other sensation. The painful stomach cramps and worsening headache seemed to fade into the background as he registered only the brilliant white light.

"Andy, can you hear me?"

He noticed a feeling against the side of his forehead, and when the light moved on, he saw a hand moving something against his temple. He winced at the pressure and inhaled a whiff of a metallic smell that made his stomach churn, then knot up again.

"Andy, it's Doc Crowe."

He swallowed and tried working his tongue to form a response. "Doc?"

"You've had a rough day," she said.

His eyes took in his surroundings, surprised to find he was no longer in his stateroom. He felt something tug against his head, but it didn't hurt. It was just the vaguest notion of pushing and pulling. "What's going on?"

"There," Doc said, stepping back to look down on him. "How are you feeling?"

He lifted his hand to his head, but Doc stopped him.

"I just stitched you up."

"Stitched me..." Suddenly, the memory of tying his boots to make his way down to the Sickbay came back to him. "What happened?"

"Looks like you passed out and hit your head. Gave your roommate quite the scare, but it was nothing a few stitches couldn't fix." A corpsman handed Doc a sheet of paper, and Andy saw her face scrunch up with worry. "Are you sure this is right?" she asked the sailor.

"We ran it twice."

Doc looked back down at Andy and forced a smile. "Just rest here for now."

He swallowed again and nodded, then watched Doc walk to the phone a few feet away and dial a number. He still felt woozy—probably from hitting his head—and his stomach cramps hadn't seemed to let up at all, but he felt comforted knowing he was in medical and that Doc was taking care of him. All lingering feelings of guilt at not being able to fly were gone, and he resigned himself to resting in the bed until whatever bug he had caught worked its way out.

"Yes, sir, it's Lieutenant Crowe," he heard Doc saying into the phone. "The number of cases is increasing, and we just ran blood tests on the first patient we treated."

His ears perked up when he realized she was talking about him.

"It's something we haven't seen before. I recommend we initiate quarantine protocols and begin sanitizing the spaces. I'm going to send the results to BUMED."

The knot in Andy's stomach tightened as the fear he had kept at bay roared to the surface. If Doc thought whatever he was infected with warranted immediate notification to the Navy Bureau of Medicine and Surgery, then it was much worse than he thought.

37

Mace 201
Navy FA-18E Super Hornet

The bold word *SHOOT* stood out next to the symbology as a not-so-subtle reminder that Colt had satisfied the requirements of the Rules of Engagement. Even though the E-2D Hawkeye controller had already declared the Chinese fighters hostile, his onboard systems correlated the target and met the programmed criteria to engage.

He glanced at his radar attack display to ensure he had both Chinese fighters targeted, then reached up with his left hand to the master arm switch and moved it from SAFE to ARM.

He moved his trembling hand back to the throttle and said a small prayer.

Please, Lord, please don't let me fuck this up.

"Two zero one, Tiger, single group hostile."

It was yet another not-so-subtle reminder that he had a job to do and to stop hesitating when it mattered most. Without another thought, he squeezed the trigger and held it firmly until the first of his four AIM-120D AMRAAMs dropped away from his weapons rack. Its rocket motor ignited almost immediately and raced forward, leaving a mesmerizing, brilliant trail in its wake.

He tapped the button to switch targets to the second Flanker and repeated the process. He squeezed the trigger until his second missile dropped free and raced off into the night. "Two zero one, Fox Three, two ship, single group."

The missiles—as bright as they were initially—disappeared quickly as they accelerated to Mach 4 on their way to the Chinese fighters. Colt banked his jet and looked through the NVCD at the computer-generated diamond representing the Flankers' location. A dim blossom of light flared briefly inside the diamond, then faded to black. At first, Colt thought his first missile had impacted, but a quick glance to his radar display showed that he still had at least thirty seconds until it reached the target.

Then it dawned on him.

"Tiger, two zero one, single group just fired on the friendly."

The reply was a curt, "Tiger."

There was nothing left to do but continue tracking the fighters and hope his missiles reached their targets first. If the Chinese had fired a semi-active radar-guided missile, it would go stupid the minute the host aircraft blew up, courtesy of the AMRAAM's forty-pound high-explosive blast fragmentation warhead.

But an active missile would continue to guide on the friendly helicopter autonomously, no matter what happened to the Chinese Flanker.

Let's hope it's not active.

Dusty One
Air Branch Mi-17 Hip

Charlie clutched the helicopter's controls with a fear-induced, white-knuckled grip. He focused on what he could see of the horizon—which wasn't much—and aggressively banked the helicopter and climbed to the right, before reversing direction and descending back to the left.

For a helicopter not designed for high-performance maneuvers, his experience shone as they executed a modified weave designed to defeat the air intercept radars that remained stubbornly locked onto them.

"Still locked on," Roger shouted over the straining turbine engines.

Charlie ignored him and poured all his focus into maneuvering the lumbering helicopter as best as he could to defeat the missile without inadvertently flying them into the water. His focus was broken only momentarily by a blinking light appearing on the horizon.

"Passu Keah's in sight," Charlie muttered, before glancing down at his engine instruments to make sure he wasn't pushing the helicopter beyond its limits.

"Dusty One has FARP Alpha in sight," Roger said over the SATCOM channel.

"Scar Nine Nine."

Beads of sweat ran down Charlie's face and dropped from his eyebrows into his eyes, which he quickly blinked away. He couldn't take his hands off the controls to wipe at the sweat and hoped that the downward force of the Gs would draw it down his cheeks and keep his vision unobstructed. This was not the time to go blind.

"Fifty feet," Roger said, providing a quick warning that they were extremely low over the water.

Instead of replying, Charlie abruptly rolled the helicopter to the other side and brought their rotor blades perilously close to the water before beginning a climb.

Suddenly, the radar warning receiver went silent. Charlie continued his frantic maneuvers without acknowledging that the alarm had stopped blaring its tinny warning in the cramped cockpit.

"Charlie," Roger said calmly, his eyes still fixed on the rapidly changing needles on the vertical speed and altitude indicators.

Charlie ignored him.

"Charlie." Roger reached across the cockpit and placed a relaxed hand on his tense forearm. "We broke the lock."

He completed one more iteration of the weave maneuver before his muscles relaxed, and he allowed the helicopter's nose to track toward the flashing infrared beacon on the horizon. His chest rose and fell with rapid breaths, but as his heart dipped back to normal, his breathing slowed. "Thanks," he whispered.

If there had been any lighting in the cockpit, Charlie was certain Roger would have seen his pallid color and known how close they had come to flying into the drink. He had been in some harrowing situations before, but this was the first time he could recall when he thought they wouldn't survive. He glanced over at the screen in Roger's lap and saw the icon for their pursuer turned and pointed at the *Reagan's* Super Hornets.

Thank God those guys came along when they did.

Dave's shadowy figure appeared once more through the cockpit door. "What *the fuck* was that?"

Charlie glanced over at Roger, whose expression said everything. The two began laughing almost uncontrollably, earning a disgusted grunt from the bearded SEAL, who retreated once more to the interior of the helicopter. The two pilots continued laughing and released their pent-up tension as they prepared themselves for the rest of the mission.

"Scar Nine Nine, Dusty One is five miles out," Roger said over the SATCOM channel.

"Status?"

"We were fired on but avoided the missile. Thank the Navy for us." Roger ended the transmission and focused his attention through the windscreen as they neared the tiny atoll. The dim IR chem lights the Marines had placed to mark the landing zone were just becoming visible.

"LZ in sight," Roger said over the intercom.

"Copy," Charlie replied, and wiped the remnants of sweat away from his face to clear his vision for the landing. Even though he felt relief they had evaded the missile, he knew they could just as easily crash on the atoll if he misjudged the approach. There was no room for error when flying over the water in the middle of the night.

"Winds are calm. Recommend we approach from the west," Roger said.

"Concur."

As they approached the atoll, Charlie slowed their forward movement west of the landing zone and side-stepped to the small bluff, as if he was making a landing on a ship at night. However, unlike on a ship, he didn't have the lighted wands of an LSE guiding him, and he did his best to judge their movement through the side window. His thousands of hours were obvious as he expertly slid over the clearing and descended slowly to the earth.

"Ten feet," Roger said as they continued downward. "Five... four...three..."

Charlie lowered the collective and settled the Russian helicopter softly onto the ground and held it there while hacking an internal clock. Dave and his SEALs jumped from the side doors and scrambled to connect the fueling hose from the bladder to the Hip.

"Let's go, let's go," Charlie said to himself.

Mace 201
Navy FA-18E Super Hornet

Colt's fingers were sweating as he gripped the controls and continued flying straight at the Flankers. Part of him was tempted to fire another missile, but he knew it would be wasted if the first two reached their targets. Instead, he selected the AIM-9X Sidewinder heat-seeking missile and prepared himself to take follow-on shots if the Chinese fighters survived the initial salvo.

"Tiger, two zero four, angels twenty, picture."

Despite feeling as if he had a handle on the tactical situation, Colt was happy to hear another alert pilot's voice on the radio. He glanced at his Situational Awareness display and saw his position broadcast over datalink, ten miles in trail and closing rapidly.

"Two zero four, Tiger, single group, BRAA, one nine zero, sixty, thirty-eight thousand, flank southeast, hostile. Targeted by two zero one."

There was a slight pause on the radio, then Lieutenant Luke "Rucas" Mixon spoke again in a clipped, excited tone. "Tiger, declare contact one nine zero, ten, forty thousand."

Colt saw his radar warning receiver flicker with an indication that the other Super Hornet's radar had detected him. He didn't wait for the E-2D Hawkeye controller to reply and keyed the microphone switch. "Skip it! That's two zero one!"

"Two zero four," came the somber reply.

It was understandable that Rucas wanted to get in on the action, but he didn't want to end up getting shot down by an overly eager Naval Aviator. As it was, there would probably be some grumbling among the other squadrons in the air wing that Colt had taken all the glory for himself.

Assuming I don't fuck it up.

The thought brought him back to the fly-out cues on his radar attack display as they reached the targets. He looked through his NVCDs and saw a brief flash of light, followed by a dim glow as the first Flanker crashed into the water.

"Splash one!" he shouted.

Colt switched back to the second target and glanced at his radar attack display to see the second J-11B pitching in toward him. Obviously, his missile had caught them by surprise, but the surprise was gone.

"Tiger, two zero one, single group maneuver."

"Two zero one, Tiger, single group hot, hostile. One contact."

Almost immediately, his radar warning receiver lit up as the J-11B's radar locked onto his aircraft. It was obvious his second AMRAAM either didn't detonate or had gone astray somewhere en route to the Chinese fighter. Without giving it a second thought, he rolled his Super Hornet one hundred and twenty degrees to the left and executed a nose-low slicing turn away from the threat.

"Two zero one, out left."

Rucas's voice was giddy again. "Two zero four targeting single group."

Colt pushed his throttles forward into afterburner and felt the jet accelerating as his nose sliced through the horizon and he placed the threat at his six o'clock. Instinctively, he performed an anti-G straining maneuver, squeezing his thighs and glutes while taking short and punctuated breaths and flexing his core muscles. Combined with the inflating bladders of the anti-G suit, the straining maneuver helped keep his blood from pooling in his lower extremities and kept him awake.

"Two zero four, Tiger, single group hostile."

"Two zero four, Fox Three, single group."

As Colt rolled out with the J-11B at his six o'clock and his nose pointed forty-five degrees nose low, he glanced up and saw Rucas's missile racing toward the Chinese fighter over his head and breathed a sigh of relief.

38

Colt cracked the throttles back and eased the nose of his fighter up toward the horizon. A quick glance down at the datalink display showed the icon representing Rucas turning away from the advancing Chinese fighter.

"Two zero four, out right, cheap shot, single group."

Colt took the cue that Rucas was turning away after his missile went active, and he slapped his control stick into his left leg, then pulled it back into his lap and traded airspeed for angles as he pitched back into the engagement. "Two zero one, in left."

He had already designated the datalink track file representing the Chinese fighter, but with his nose pointed back to the northwest, his radar again swept the sky until it returned a hit. He selected his third and final AMRAAM and prepared to squeeze the trigger when the icon began flashing.

Colt relaxed his trigger finger and took a calming breath.

"Two zero one, Tiger, single group faded."

At last, the missile detonated and caused the icon to disappear from his screen. Colt was again left with nothing but darkness in front of him. For the first time since the alert had been called away, he had a moment of calm to process what had just happened.

"Did we just do what I think we just did?" Rucas asked over their tactical frequency.

Colt shook his head in disbelief. "Yeah, I think we did."

"Two zero one, Tiger, picture clean," the Hawkeye controller said. "Stand by for tasking."

Stand by for tasking?

"There's nobody left to shoot," Rucas said.

"There's always somebody left to shoot," Colt said, though he silently agreed with him. They were flying over the contested Paracel Islands and were certain to draw the attention of the People's Republic of China, but at that moment, they were alone. He switched back to the air intercept control frequency. "Tiger, say status of friendlies."

"Stand by."

Colt knew the Chinese fighters had launched to intercept a friendly helicopter and that he had been ordered to stop that from happening. But that didn't mean whomever the SEALs had with them on the helicopter was out of the woods yet. They still needed to get back to the ship.

"Two zero one, Tiger, stand by for coordinates."

Colt slipped the four-colored pen from the elastic loop on the side of his kneeboard and prepared to write down the latitude and longitude. But for what, he wasn't sure. "Ready to copy."

"Proceed directly to sixteen degrees, three minutes north, one eleven degrees, forty-six minutes east and establish CAP."

Colt scribbled the coordinates on his kneeboard card, then glanced down at his fuel quantity and furrowed his brow at the instructions. "Tiger, state intentions."

There was a pause before the controller's voice returned. "We're still trying to get all the details, but apparently a friendly helicopter is at that location. You are to escort them to Clark Air Base."

His confusion only intensified after he entered the coordinates into his flight computer and saw that the location was in the middle of the South China Sea. Manning a Combat Air Patrol for an indefinite period would strain his endurance with the fuel he had remaining, but then to follow that up with escorting them six hundred miles away? "I'm not going to have the gas to escort them there and make it back to the ship."

"You're to land there and await further instructions."

"Say again?"

"Colt, it's Cutty," the brusque voice of his DCAG said. "There's been an outbreak of some kind, and the skipper is putting the entire ship in quarantine."

Quarantine?

"Roger that, sir."

Clark Air Base, Philippines

The watch commander slammed the phone down in frustration, then brought his hands up to knead the tension from his temples. Connor leaned against the wall in the back of the room, watching the organized chaos of a dozen men and women working tirelessly to get the helicopter back to safety. He couldn't understand the stress they were under, and he admired them even more for it.

"Listen up!" the watch commander bellowed.

Heads whipped in his direction, and Connor shoved off the cold steel. He was on pins and needles waiting to learn the fate of the aging Russian helicopter. But something about the watch commander's demeanor told him it wasn't good news.

"The *Ronald Reagan* is no longer a suitable option for recovering Dusty One."

Connor took two quick steps forward as the room erupted in a chorus of nervous whispers.

"Quiet down!" the watch commander yelled, then paused and waited for the cavernous room to slip once more into silence. "We don't have time to lose our minds. We need to bring them back here."

"What's happened on the *Reagan*?" Connor asked.

The watch commander turned and appraised him, obviously frustrated by the interruption. But he answered the question anyway, likely to avoid distraction so his team could focus on the solution instead of the problem.

"There has been some kind of outbreak, and the commanding officer has declared the entire ship in quarantine."

Connor opened his mouth to press for more details, but the commander held up a hand and silenced him with a surprisingly patient gesture. "I know there are lots of questions, but we can address those after we get them back here." He turned and faced a Navy lieutenant commander with gold wings on his chest. "Air, does Dusty have the range to make it here?"

The baby-faced pilot plotted the straight-line distance between the FARP on Passu Keah and their location aboard Clark Air Base, then hastily scratched numbers down on a notepad. Connor watched him scribbling furiously while every head in the room was turned in his direction, waiting for his answer. At last, he looked up and said, "Maybe."

"Maybe? What does that mean?"

If the pilot was nervous, he didn't show it. He simply recited the facts as he saw them. "The standard range for the Mi-17 is three hundred and eight miles, but we'll call it an even three hundred to make the math easy. This particular bird has two two-hundred-and-thirty-gallon auxiliary fuel tanks installed. Each tank has approximately two hundred and twenty-seven gallons of usable fuel for an increased range of just under two hundred miles. Again—easy math—we'll call it two hundred and twenty-five gallons usable with a range increase of one hundred and ninety miles."

"Get to the point," the watch commander urged.

"It depends on how bad they're leaking and how much fuel they made it to the atoll with," he said. "With a full internal tank and two full auxiliary tanks, they should have a range of just under seven hundred miles."

"How far are we from Passu Keah?"

"Six hundred miles."

"So, what's the problem?" the watch commander asked.

"The fuel blivet at FARP Alpha is only five hundred gallons. If they were on fumes when they landed on Passu Keah, that's only enough gas to get them four hundred miles."

The watch commander snatched his phone off its cradle.

Dusty One
Air Branch Mi-17 Hip
Passu Keah Atoll

Charlie looked over his shoulder at the gaggle of men scrambling back aboard the helicopter. It was a slow process transferring fuel from the five-hundred-gallon fuel bladder on the atoll into the Russian-made helicopter, but he felt the tension in his upper back dissolve as he watched the needles creep upward on the fuel quantity gauges for his two auxiliary fuel tanks.

"We drained her dry," Dave said, poking his head into the cockpit.

"Is it enough?" Charlie asked.

Roger measured their distance on the atoll to the *Reagan's* Position of Intended Movement and nodded. "More than enough. Even with the leak, we should be able—"

The satellite radio squawked and interrupted his answer. "Dusty One, Scar Nine Nine."

Charlie pressed the transmit button. "Go ahead."

"What's your fuel state in gallons?"

Charlie shared a concerned look with Roger before answering. Normally, they spoke in units of time instead of quantity. "Just under six hundred gallons. More than enough to make it back to mom."

He released the push-to-talk switch and looked back at Roger. "What the hell is going on?"

The other pilot shook his head. "I have no idea, but I have a feeling we're not going to like it."

As if on cue, the radio squawked again. "Change in plans, Dusty. Mom is no longer a suitable destination. You are to proceed to Clark Air Base. How copy?"

"We can't make that," Roger said. "We've got maybe four hundred miles left."

Charlie took a deep breath before replying. "That's a negative. We don't have the range."

"Good copy, Dusty. Start heading that way while we work something out."

Charlie exhaled slowly and turned to Roger. "What do you think?"

"I think it's fucking stupid. They want us to fly east through known Chinese surface-to-air missile sites and over open ocean without being able to reach our destination?"

"Are there any other atolls between here and there that we can use as emergency diverts?"

Roger zoomed in on his tablet to look at satellite imagery of the ocean between their tiny speck of land and the Philippines. "Macclesfield Bank is about one hundred and ninety miles away, but the shoals are entirely submerged and won't do us any good."

"Dammit!" Charlie said. "Anything else?"

"Scarborough Shoal," Roger said. "It's just over four hundred miles away."

"Dry?"

"Maybe. The highest point should be six feet above sea level at high tide."

Charlie nodded and looked at Dave over his shoulder. "Everybody aboard?"

"Last man," he said.

"Pass out life vests and prepare the rafts for a potential ditching. We're going to another island."

Dave gave him a curious look but didn't argue and spun back into the cabin. Charlie increased torque, and he felt the Mi-17 get light as he lifted off the sandbar and hovered inches off the ground. After stabilizing in the hover for a second, he nosed over and quickly accelerated away from the atoll before keying the switch to transmit back to the TOC.

"Scar Nine Nine, Dusty One is airborne and proceeding to Scarborough Shoal. Request you launch Search and Rescue."

39

Mace 201
Navy FA-18E Super Hornet

Colt arrived at the coordinates the Hawkeye controller had passed to him
and oriented his CAP facing Hainan Island to the northwest. Even though
Vietnam also claimed rights to the Paracel Islands, if anybody were to
launch and challenge the two Super Hornets, it would be China.

"Tiger, two zero one established on CAP, angels thirty."

The controller replied with a clipped, "Tiger."

Colt looked over his right shoulder and saw the darkened outline of his
wingman's jet, a little less than a mile away. The anxiety he had felt after
launching from the *Reagan* was gone now that he was no longer alone in
the contested skies over the South China Sea. But the carrier in quarantine
brought with it an entirely new worry.

"In place right," Colt said.

He glanced over his shoulder again and saw the other jet come up on a
wing to begin his one-hundred-and-eighty-degree turn back to the southeast. They would flow cold—away from the threat sector—while relying on
Tiger's radar to alert them of potentially hostile aircraft launching from

Hainan Island. He started his turn, then looked down at the datalink display to verify Rucas had turned in the right direction, but his eyes focused on the icon for the slow-moving helicopter beneath them.

"Tiger, two zero one, picture."

"Tiger, picture clean," the controller said, then added, "Friendly helicopter, your position, cherubs five, flowing east."

"Two zero one."

Colt rolled out heading southeast, then banked ninety degrees and looked straight down at the pitch black beneath him. Through his NVCD, he saw a cluster of infrared lights glowing from an island he assumed the helicopter had landed on, but the helicopter itself was invisible. He rolled upright and settled in for a long night ahead of him.

"Two zero one, Tiger, friendly helicopter is proceeding to Scarborough Shoal."

Rucas spoke up first. "Where the hell's that?"

After relaying the coordinates for the emergency divert, the controller filled them in on what was happening almost thirty thousand feet beneath them. "Dusty One has a fuel leak and can't make it all the way to the Philippines. Two Ospreys from the *America* are en route to recover the passengers and take them the rest of the way."

Colt glanced down at his fuel gauge and knew that if they remained airborne much longer, the air branch helicopter wasn't going to be the only one experiencing a fuel emergency. "Tiger, any chance of getting a Texaco airborne?"

"Stand by."

He doubted there was an Air Force big-wing tanker—a KC-135 or KC-10 —they could join on to top off, and the situation aboard the *Reagan* probably meant they wouldn't be able to launch a five-wet Super Hornet to pass gas either. He was counting on only having what fuel remained in his internal tanks after his externals ran dry. But it never hurt to ask.

"Hey, Colt, how are you doing on gas?" Rucas asked.

He didn't want to give an honest answer, so he just said, "I'm good."

The double mic-click reply let him know Rucas understood his situation would turn dire if they loitered much longer. But with Dusty One proceeding east for the shoal, he should have just enough gas to make it to the Philippines. If China didn't send up any more fighters.

"Two zero one, Tiger, negative on the Texaco."

"Copy," he replied, biting off a string of curse words that would do little more than make him feel only marginally better.

"Two zero one, Tiger, chatter indicates fighters launching from Lingshui."

Well, shit.

With one more glance at the icon representing Dusty, he keyed the microphone and said, "In place right."

Clark Air Base, Philippines

Connor pulled out a chair to sit down at an empty computer station as he nervously chewed on his fingernails. He stared at the screen depicting their area of operations with the Philippines on the far right, Vietnam on the far left, and Hainan Island in the upper left corner. The icon representing Dusty One—the air branch helicopter carrying Lisa Mourning and her SEAL rescuers—was only a third of the way across the blue waters of the South China Sea.

How are they going to make it?

"Two J-15 Flankers airborne from Lingshui," somebody said to his right. "They're being vectored to Dusty One's location."

His eyes flicked across the screen as the datalink populated with two new icons representing the Chinese fighters. Two hundred miles of open ocean separated them from the slow-moving helicopter, but he knew the supersonic fighters would eat that distance up in no time.

They're not going to make it.

"What's the status of Search and Rescue?" the watch commander asked.

A young man on the opposite side of the room answered. "Both Ospreys are airborne and en route to Scarborough Shoal."

"ETA?"

Connor looked at the monitor and saw two additional icons flowing northeast away from the USS *America*. They weren't moving nearly as fast as the Chinese J-15 Flankers or FA-18 Super Hornets from the *Reagan*, but they seemed much quicker than the air branch helicopter.

"Sixty minutes," the sailor replied.

Connor didn't need to be a math whiz to see that the Marine MV-22 Ospreys would reach the shoal well before Dusty One. But if the Hip had enough gas to limp to the shoal, they could immediately transfer their passengers and crew over to the faster tilt-rotor aircraft and make a run for Clark Air Base. It all came down to time and fuel. They had too much time and not enough fuel.

Almost as if reading his thoughts, the watch commander queried the air branch helicopter. "Dusty One, Scar Nine Nine, say state?"

"Enough."

His eyes shifted from the slow-moving helicopter to the icons representing the Super Hornets as they closed the distance with the Chinese fighters.

Come on, boys, he thought.

Mace 201
Navy FA-18E Super Hornet

Colt pressed his throttles forward and spurred the Super Hornet closer to the speed of sound. But with two external fuel tanks, he knew he wouldn't break through the barrier without going into afterburner and harnessing every bit of thrust produced by his two General Electric turbofan engines. And dumping fuel directly into the hot exhaust section wasn't the smartest thing to do when he was already skosh on gas.

"Tiger, single group, one hundred miles, hot, bogey, outlaw."

The Chinese Flankers were still beyond radar range, but thanks to the Multifunctional Information Distribution System, known as MIDS, the Hawkeye controller transmitted their location to the Super Hornets via datalink. Even without his onboard sensors providing targeting information, Colt had everything he needed to run the intercept.

"Let's set up a grinder," he said to Rucas. "Two zero four, pump."

"Two zero four."

Colt watched his datalink display as his wingman turned to flow cold, increasing the separation between their two aircraft. He would let it grow to fifteen or twenty miles before he turned cold and directed Rucas to reverse direction and flow hot. The tactic, known as a grinder, ensured that at least one fighter was always pointed into the threat sector while keeping them stationary over a fixed spot on the ground. With the helicopter flowing east, they were all that stood between the Chinese fighters and the hapless Mi-17. This was the proverbial last stand.

An electric waterfall sound echoed through his helmet, and his stomach dropped.

"Two zero one, nails zero three zero."

"Two zero one, Tiger, clean zero three zero."

Colt stole a glance at his Situational Awareness display and saw the number 9 at the end of a dashed line. He cursed when he realized their luck had run out. "Looks like it's an HQ-9," he said, remembering that Bubba had highlighted the Chinese version of the Patriot Surface-to-Air Missile battery's location on Woody Island.

"Two zero four is naked," Rucas said, letting Colt know he hadn't been detected.

Colt looked at their separation.

Not enough, he thought. But he needed to do something before the missile battery locked onto his aircraft with a fire control radar. "Two zero one, out left."

On cue, his wingman replied, "Two zero four, in left."

Colt slapped at his stick and overbanked his jet before pulling it into his lap to begin a nose-low slicing turn away from the approaching Chinese fighters. He pushed his throttles into afterburner, then punched a red-painted button the size of a silver dollar on the canopy rail, ejecting bundles of chaff to disrupt the radar's attempt to lock onto him. He rolled out pointed southeast with his nose thirty degrees below the horizon, before pulling his throttles out of afterburner.

Not good, he thought. He was stuck between advancing fighters and a semi-active radar homing surface-to-air missile that had an employment range of close to two hundred miles. And he didn't have the gas to mess around with either.

"Two zero four, Tiger, single group, seventy miles, hot, bogey, outlaw."

"Two zero four, commit single group."

40

Dusty One
Air Branch Mi-17 Hip

Since launching from Passu Keah and turning east for Scarborough Shoal, Charlie had purposely ignored how dark and ominous it looked through his forward windscreen. He nervously scanned the horizon, looking for tracer fire or the tell-tale orange blossom of a missile launch from one of the Chinese outposts on the otherwise uninhabited Paracel Islands. But it was dark. Only a flashing red light on the forward instrument panel drew his attention down into the cockpit.

"What's that?" he asked.

"Surveillance search radar," Roger answered. But his voice was suspiciously calm.

"From what?"

When he didn't answer, Charlie stole another glance inside the cockpit and turned to look at the green glow on his copilot's face.

"Roger," he said. "From what?"

"An HQ-9," he replied, but quickly added, "But we're only picking up a side lobe. It appears to be targeting one of the Super Hornets."

Charlie returned his focus to the pitch black through the forward windscreen, blocking out the little voice in the back of his mind that told him they were easy pickings. It didn't matter that he'd felt that way his entire career as a special operations helicopter pilot or that the Mi-17 was equipped with state-of-the-art electronic countermeasures designed to defeat even the most robust air defense systems. He was still piloting a leaking four-decade-old helicopter at wave-top height with nothing but hundreds of miles of ocean in any direction.

"Should we start jamming?"

"Not yet," Roger replied. "If we do it before they know where we are, we could guide them right to us."

Reluctantly, he nodded. He felt naked without a protective curtain of electronic jamming between them and the searching radar, but Roger was right. Turning the jammer on too early was almost as bad as not having it at all. "How far out is Pedro?"

Two Marine MV-22 Ospreys had launched from the *America* with a company of Marines and were racing northeast from the amphibious assault ship to take them the rest of the way. Charlie thought the TRAP team was overkill on the uninhabited atoll, but it never hurt to have the most guns in a fight.

"Oh, shit."

Charlie's blood ran cold when he heard the tone in Roger's voice. "What?"

"There are a *ton* of surface ships out here, and the *Reagan*'s Hawkeye is picking up another airborne target between us and Scarborough Shoal."

He shook his head. "What? How? There's nobody else out here."

"Apparently there is," Roger said, before keying the microphone to transmit back to the TOC. "Scar Nine Nine, Dusty One, are you seeing the latest radar picture?"

There was a longer than normal delay in the response. "Affirm. It appears to be a helicopter, but there's some debate whether it belongs to the PLA Navy or not."

Charlie already knew. In this part of the world, even the fishing trawlers weren't out here to fish, and he wasn't willing to take that chance when they were already in danger of not making it. "Dave!" he shouted. "Get up here!"

For as loud as it was inside the helicopter, he was almost surprised to see the bearded frogman's head appear over his shoulder a moment later. "What's going on?" Dave asked.

"We're going to have company."

He was focused on the blank canvas of darkness ahead of them and couldn't see the look on the SEAL's face, but he knew Dave had to have been just as surprised. "What kind of company?"

"A helicopter."

"Hostile?"

"Unknown. But we're going to lower the ramp, and I'll need you and your guys to man the guns."

"The guns," Dave repeated, as if emphasizing that he understood their expected company was the type that might require such a response. "How long do we have?"

Charlie saw Roger manipulating the Toughbook from the corner of his eye and knew the other air branch pilot was measuring the distance between them and calculating their closure. It was a far cry from what the Super Hornets were likely experiencing with the Flankers from Lingshui, but at less than one hundred feet over the water, a closure rate of over one hundred knots seemed insane.

"He's at twenty miles," Roger said.

Charlie finished the thought for him. "Not long, mano."

Dave grunted something indecipherable and disappeared back inside the Hip's cramped cabin.

Dave turned and looked at the SEALs huddled together on the bench seats along the side of the fuselage. They seemed calm and relaxed, at home in their environment, and stared back at him with flat but determined eyes. He motioned for two to join him, and they quickly popped to their feet and scampered to where he stood just behind the cockpit.

"I need you two to man the door guns," he said. "I'll be on the ramp gun."

On cue, a hydraulic motor whirred to life, and the steel bulkhead at the rear of the helicopter slowly angled down from the ceiling and exposed a tapestry of pitch black behind them. All three SEALs turned to look over the heads of the other passengers.

"What's going on?" one of the SEALs shouted.

"A helicopter," Dave replied. "Not sure if it's hostile, but we have to assume it is."

"How long?"

Dave echoed Charlie's assessment. "Not long."

The SEALs turned for their respective doors and slid them open. With the two side doors and the ramp open, wind whipped through the cabin and jostled those still huddled protectively over the Agency officer. But they ignored the distraction and immediately went to work clipping into their safety tethers and swinging the miniguns out over the water to make them ready.

Dave looked down at Ron caring for his patient, then strode aft to clip into the safety line on the ramp. He removed the pin securing his minigun to its mount, then pivoted it left and right and prepared for a target to appear behind them. He hated that they wouldn't have advance notice of the enemy helicopter's approach, but he figured it would become apparent soon enough.

Charlie's muscles in his upper back tensed up as he continued flying the Hip on toward Scarborough Shoal. The red light on the radar warning receiver flickered occasionally to indicate they were still only detecting the side lobe of the HQ-9's surveillance radar, but that was no longer the immediate threat. Even the J-15 Flankers from Lingshui had taken a back seat to the rapidly closing helicopter.

Low on fuel, enemy fighters chasing us, a surface-to-air missile targeting us, and now an enemy helicopter? Charlie shook his head. He should have taken the Life Flight job in North Carolina instead of going to the dark side. *Closest alligator to the canoe, Charlie.*

"Five miles," Roger said.

"What the hell is it?"

Roger keyed the microphone again to call on their support network operating from the safety of Clark Air Base. "Scar Nine Nine, do you have any tipper on this helo yet?"

The pause was shorter this time. "We're not certain, but we think it's likely a Z-10."

"A what?" Charlie asked.

"It's an attack helicopter," Roger said.

"Armed with what?"

"It was designed for the ground forces as an anti-tank helicopter. Think of it like the Chinese version of the Apache. We can count on it having a chain gun, but it's also capable of carrying air-to-air missiles."

Super, Charlie thought.

Suddenly, the darkness just left of their nose tore open with the bright staccato of gunfire aimed in their general direction, and brilliant balls of fire streaked past them on their left side. Charlie flinched, but he gripped the controls firmly to avoid driving them into the water—the instinct to duck under the gunfire was almost overpowering.

"Get ready!" he yelled over his shoulder, though he knew the SEALs wouldn't be able to hear his warning over the wind noise in the cabin. He just hoped they had seen the incoming tracer fire and knew what was coming.

The gunfire stopped, and Charlie angled his nose toward the incoming helicopter in hopes of taking it close aboard to prevent it from articulating its nose-mounted chain gun after the merge. The one advantage they had over the Z-10 were the three Navy SEALs manning the miniguns.

Suddenly, the blinking red light on the dash flared brighter and was accompanied by an alarm that drowned out every other sound in the cockpit. Charlie saw the flickering light burn solid and didn't have to ask. He knew a fire control radar was now targeting them, and it didn't really matter whether it was from the helicopter or surface-to-air missile battery.

It's showtime.

A flurry of movement out of the corner of his eye drew Charlie's attention to an ominous shadow filling the left side of his windscreen. He abruptly shoved the collective toward the floor while yanking back on the cyclic, compensating for the reduced torque with left pedal before pivoting to fly underneath the merging attack chopper. It was a pure instinctive reaction, and he felt a bubble of fear catch in his throat.

He yanked up on the collective to arrest their descent toward the water, but before he could shout another warning over his shoulder to the gunners, the night split open with a buzz saw of fire from the left minigun.

Get 'em, squids!

41

Mace 201
Navy FA-18E Super Hornet

Colt watched his wingman prosecuting the intercept on his datalink display and tried ignoring the growing number of icons cluttering the already cramped battle space. Other than him and Rucas, the friendly air order of battle consisted of two MV-22 Osprey tilt-rotor aircraft from the USS *America* racing to meet up with the defenseless helicopter, a P-8A Poseidon surveillance aircraft and MQ-4C Triton drone from Guam, and an E-2D Hawkeye from the *Reagan*.

"Two zero one, Tiger, pop-up group, zero nine zero, one hundred miles, cherubs five, hostile."

Colt had been about to call in, but the pop-up group was dangerously close to the friendly helicopter they had been ordered to protect. He couldn't afford to ignore it. "Two zero one, target pop-up group," he said, then added, "Two zero four, press."

"Two zero four," Rucas replied, letting him know he understood that he owned the single group of J-15 Flankers from Hainan Island. He would be on his own, but it came with the job. "Fox Three, two-ship, single group."

Colt was tempted to look over his shoulder to try to spot the two AIM-

120D AMRAAM missiles racing from his wingman's Super Hornet toward the inbound fighters. But he knew it was pointless. His focus was on the pop-up group threatening the helicopter.

"Two zero one, Tiger," the Hawkeye controller said with a shade of panic in his voice. "Pop-up group is engaging the friendly helicopter! Recommend buster!"

Resisting the temptation to look at his fuel gauge and lament at the situation he found himself in, Colt pressed his left hand forward and pushed the throttles into afterburner. The intercept would likely take every drop of fuel he had on board, but there was nothing he could do about that. If he let the pop-up group take down the friendly helicopter, everything he had done that night would have been for nothing.

"Two zero one," he said through gritted teeth.

"Tiger," his wingman said. "Single group maneuver."

"Single group, beam west," the Hawkeye controller replied.

Even without moving his cursor over the icon representing his wingman's Super Hornet, Colt knew he had already fired his last two remaining radar-guided missiles and was left with only two AIM-9X Sidewinder heat-seeking missiles to finish off the Chinese fighters. He just hoped Rucas had waited to fire the AMRAAMs until he had closed the distance enough to prevent a simple ninety-degree beaming maneuver from defeating them.

"Shots trashed," his wingman said.

Colt cursed inside his mask but shook it off and focused on the pop-up group. Its icon appeared superimposed over the one representing the friendly helicopter, and he knew it would be more luck than skill if he managed to make it in time. And, even then, he would have to rely on the friendly helicopter pilot being skilled enough to separate and give him a clean shot on the hostile aircraft.

Using the pressure pad underneath his left index finger, Colt manipulated the cursor on his screen until it hovered over the pop-up group. He pressed down on the pad and designated the icon as the target, giving him range and bearing information and a dynamic Launch Acceptability Region for his last remaining radar-guided missile. Not that he would be able to employ it with as close as the target was to the friendly helicopter.

"Two zero one, say state," the controller said, probably prompted by some well-meaning senior officer aboard the carrier who knew Colt and the other alert pilot were dangerously low on fuel.

"Below bingo," Colt said, letting him know he was flying on fumes and had committed to burning it all to try to save the helicopter.

"Copy. Pedro is en route."

Colt glanced at the icons representing the Osprey Search and Rescue package and took note of their general location. Unlike the helicopter or tilt-rotor aircraft that could land on Scarborough Shoal, Colt knew there was no place for him to set down. Too far from the *Reagan*. Too far from Clark Air Base. Too far from any runway at all. He had resigned himself to the fact that he was going to have to punch out and ride the silk into the dark waters beneath him and wait for Pedro to come pluck him from the sea.

"Roger," he replied. "Declare pop-up group."

Dusty One
Air Branch Mi-17 Hip

Dave heard the left minigun open up and pivoted his gun to the right as he strained to peer into the darkness, looking for a target. Charlie's erratic flying had tossed him into the air, but his safety tether and firm grip on the GAU-17/A kept him from floating away.

There!

A dark shadow appeared above their tail, twisting and angling to follow the slower-moving transport helicopter as Charlie continued maneuvering aggressively to prevent the enemy from getting a clean shot. They suddenly banked right, and Dave was flung to the side before the safety line snapped taut. With a groan, he pulled himself back to the gun and angled it to follow the shadow that had rolled in behind them.

He depressed the trigger, and fire erupted from the six spinning barrels, but another hard jink to the left caused him to lose his grip on the gun's controls and fly in the opposite direction. Again, he grunted when the safety line snapped taut, then whipped him into the metal floor.

"Dammit! Keep us stable!"

Dave pushed himself up into a crouch and scampered back to the tail gun, clawing his way up the mount to regain his hold on the weapon. He knew Charlie was doing everything he could to keep from being eaten alive by the attack helicopter, but his abrupt maneuvers weren't making it easy on the SEALs to target the threat.

Focus on the solution. Not the problem.

With gritted teeth, Dave set his feet firmly on the floor and angled the minigun in preparation for their next turn. On cue, they banked hard to the right, and their pursuer's shadow appeared from behind their tail. He was ready and depressed the trigger again and spat fire into the dark shape.

Sparks flew as the 7.62 x 51mm rounds impacted the enemy helicopter and ricocheted into the night. He eased off the trigger and braced himself for Charlie to reverse course. When he did, Dave jerked the minigun around, using it to brace himself while aiming where he expected the attack chopper to appear.

But it didn't.

Instead of moving in a predictable flight path, the Chinese helicopter increased altitude and tucked itself high above their tail and beyond Dave's reach.

He turned and shouted over his shoulder, "He's above us!"

Even though he knew Charlie couldn't hear him, Dave felt himself floating off the metal floorboards as they dropped closer to the invisible water. He bent his knees and prepared for a jarring collision when the pilot stopped their descent, but he kept his eyes focused on the shadowed outline of the attack helicopter above them and willed it to reengage.

They leveled off, and Dave slammed back to the ground. But he had been ready that time, and he immediately angled the minigun upward and aimed to the side of the tail. If Charlie banked left, he might have another shot—albeit fleeting with little chance of success. But at the rate things were going, even a little chance was better than no chance.

Suddenly, the sky above them erupted in bright orange flame as the helicopter exploded in a flash. A split second later, Dave heard the high-pitched scream of a missile streaking through the sky and the thunderous detonation of it impacting with the Chinese attack chopper.

"What the…"

Charlie must have seen the flash too because he resumed his erratic flying. Unprepared, Dave whipped left and right, straining the carabiner he had used to clip into the safety tether.

"He's gone," he shouted. "Threat neutralized!"

But Charlie couldn't hear him, and the aging Russian chopper continued zigging and zagging through the night, whipping the SEAL and its other passengers around the cabin to avoid being taken down by the unseen threat. Dave slammed to the ground but quickly pushed himself up as if popping up on a surfboard, looking forward to the cockpit that seemed impossibly far away. He reached down to unclip from the safety tether just as the helicopter dropped out from beneath him.

Dave flew up toward the ceiling, then slammed back down, cracking his head into the metal floor. Stars ringed his vision, and he thought he heard what sounded like a fighter jet roaring overhead before he blacked out.

42

Mace 201
Navy FA-18E Super Hornet

Colt watched the AIM-9X Sidewinder missile guide into the Chinese helicopter and detonate just above its stubby wings on the starboard side. He had a split second of panic when he thought the helicopter might keep flying, but then it exploded in a brilliant flash that cast an ominous shadow onto the friendly Mi-17 Hip racing east.

"Splash one, pop-up group," Colt exclaimed with breathless relief.

"Two zero one, Tiger, green east."

Colt pulled back on the stick while dipping his right wing to watch the friendly helicopter again disappear into the pitch-black night. As the flaming wreckage of the Chinese Z-10 fell into the water, Colt kept his nose pointed skyward to gain as much altitude as possible.

Speed is life. Altitude is life insurance.

"*FUEL LOW...FUEL LOW...*"

He reached down and selected the waypoint he had created for Scarborough Shoal, knowing that if he had any chance of being rescued, he would need to eject in the vicinity of where the Hip and the two Ospreys were converging. He had long ago given up hope that he might make it all the way to Clark Air Base and was already mentally preparing himself for the ejection.

"Tiger, any luck with a Texaco?"

The response was quicker than he'd hoped and most definitely not what he wanted. "Negative. Two zero four is on a bingo profile to Clark Air Base at this time."

Passing through ten thousand feet, he pointed his nose at the distant shoal, then reached down and unclipped the kneeboard he had strapped to his right thigh. He tucked it into his helmet bag, then shoved the bag as far back on his right side as possible. Most pilots who ejected didn't have the luxury of preparing themselves for it, but with nothing left to do, Colt spent his last few hundred pounds of gas trying to get as close to the shoal as possible.

"Status of Pedro?"

The baritone voice of a Marine pilot answered. "Two zero one, Pedro One is twenty minutes from the shoal."

All that mattered was that he survived long enough for the tilt rotor to home in on his beacon and pluck him from the water. If he was lucky, he might even be able to make it close enough to the shoal that he could wade ashore and walk onto the Osprey. Even Navy pilots didn't like the idea of getting wet.

"Good to hear your voice, Pedro," Colt said. "Right now, I'm—"

"*ENGINE RIGHT...ENGINE RIGHT...*"

Shit.

Colt felt a sudden loss of thrust as the fuel-starved right engine spooled down from military thrust. With his throttles all the way up, he knew he'd burn through his fuel quicker, but he needed speed and altitude, and full power was the quickest way of getting it.

Of course, now that he had lost his first engine, he second-guessed his decision not to use a more fuel-conserving power setting.

"Pedro One, I just lost my right engine," Colt said, trying to sound as calm as possible.

"Pedro," the Marine pilot responded.

Though a safe ejection was possible at altitudes from the surface to fifty thousand feet, Colt had targeted somewhere in the upper teens to pull the handle. He couldn't remember the exact envelope for optimum ejection, other than that he wanted to have his wings level and be as slow as possible to reduce the risk of injury from the wind blast. Passing through fifteen thousand feet, he lowered the nose and used the remaining fuel in his feed tanks to propel him faster toward Scarborough Shoal.

"ENGINE LEFT...ENGINE LEFT..."

"There goes the left engine," Colt said. He knew that once the engine spooled down below sixty percent, his second generator would drop offline and plunge him into darkness. His standby instruments would continue working and the flight controls would revert to mechanical linkage, but his ability to navigate would be lost.

"Pedro."

With one more glance at the moving map display between his legs, Colt noted the distance and estimated his time remaining to the waypoint he had designated for Scarborough Shoal.

Fifteen miles. Less than three minutes.

The time would change once he lost thrust and began slowing and gliding toward the tiny speck of land in the middle of the ocean, but it gave him something to shoot for. If he kept his nose pointed in the same direction, allowed his jet to slow to less than two hundred knots, and glided back down to ten thousand feet, he could pull the yellow-and-black-striped handle in three minutes and feel confident he would come down somewhere near the shoal.

Suddenly, his cockpit was plunged into darkness. Each of the displays that had given him crucial information during the flight went blank, and he fought to quell the rising panic. He reached down to the battery switch and moved it from NORM to ORIDE, then felt along the outside of his left thigh for the green rubber ring to activate his emergency oxygen.

Two minutes.

Colt didn't count down the seconds, but he was keenly aware of his metronomic heartbeat that kept him focused. He dropped his eyes to the standby instruments and watched the airspeed needle drop below three hundred knots. When it reached two hundred and fifty knots, he lowered the nose and began a gentle descent.

One minute.

The large hundreds hand on his standby altimeter spun quickly downward as his seventy-million-dollar fourth-generation fighter became a lawn dart.

Fourteen thousand feet...thirteen thousand feet...

Despite his best efforts to remain calm, his heart rate increased the closer he got to ejection.

Twelve thousand feet...eleven thousand feet...

With one more deep breath, Colt keyed the microphone switch one last time. "Two zero one is punching out." Then, he released the stick and useless throttle and wrapped his fingers around the ejection handle between his legs.

Ten thousand feet... Here goes nothing.

He pulled the handle.

Like every Navy fighter pilot, Colt had been through aviation survival training more than once, and he knew what to expect during ejection. He knew to keep his heels on the floor, toes on the rudder pedals, and properly align his spine to prevent injury. He knew what the books and instructors at the aviation survival training centers had told him to expect.

But that didn't mean he was prepared.

Immediately after pulling the handle, he felt the inertial reels pull his shoulders back into the seat before his familiar and comforting surroundings erupted in chaos. The canopy over his head disappeared in a flash, and the wind slammed into him like a freight train. He half expected to black out from the G-forces as the catapult fired and propelled his seat up the rail, but he watched with detached wonder as the cockpit seemed to drop away beneath him. A split second later, his vision narrowed when the ejection seat's rockets fired and shot him clear of the stricken jet.

In rapid succession, a drogue chute deployed to stabilize and slow him, then the main parachute filled with air, and the opening shock yanked him clear of the seat. When his vision returned, he scrambled to recall his training and prepare himself for the landing using the oft-recited memory aid of *IROK*.

Inspect.

Colt looked up into the inky darkness above and saw the faint outline of his parachute canopy. It was a complete circle and not in an odd shape that might indicate a malfunction he would have to work his way through—like a partial line-over or streamer.

Inflate.

Colt felt down the front of his chest for the beaded handles attached to his life preserver unit and yanked on them to activate the CO_2 cartridges. The horse collar flotation device inflated with a violent *hiss*.

Raft.

He reached back for the seat pan still attached to his harness by the lower Koch fittings and felt around for the handle that would drop the raft beneath him. If he had estimated correctly, he might not even need it, but he couldn't count on Kentucky windage to keep him dry. He'd much rather wait for the Osprey inside a raft than bobbing like a cork in the water.

He found the handle and pulled it to the side, but he couldn't see if it did what it was supposed to do. A sudden *snap* a few seconds later let him know that the raft had fallen beneath him before the tether jerked it to a stop and activated the CO_2 cartridge to inflate it.

Options.

Colt had come to the step in the procedure he had the most control over. His options depended on numerous environmental considerations— whether it was day or night, over land or water, in friendly or hostile terri-tory—and it was the only step entirely up to him. He reached up to release both bayonet fittings on his oxygen mask and let it fall away. It dangled by the hose attached to the regulator on his survival vest. Then, he lifted his bulky visor and took in his surroundings.

Colt had no idea how high he was above the water. It was his first time under a parachute, but he knew his descent rate was faster than he expected. His instructors had cautioned him to keep his eyes on the horizon and to not look down at the ground racing up to meet him. But with as dark as it was, that wouldn't be an issue.

Koch fittings.

He reached up to the buckles that connected the parachute to his harness and prepared to release them once his feet entered the water. Too early and he would fall to his death. Too late and he risked getting tangled in the parachute lines and drowning.

Suddenly, the line connecting him to the raft and survival kit beneath him went slack, and he knew he was close.

Here we go.

43

NCIS Southwest Field Office
Naval Base San Diego, California

Punky bolted upright and gripped the edge of her desk to orient herself to the real world. She knew she had been burning the candle at both ends and that it had probably been a bad idea to stay late in the office to pore over the intercepted communications from *SUBLIME*. If she hadn't been sure, waking up at her desk was all the evidence she needed.

"I said I wanted you in the office. But that didn't mean I wanted you to sleep here."

Punky turned and saw Camron standing at the edge of her cubicle holding two steaming cups of coffee. He reached over and set one on the desk in front of her, then took a sip from the other.

"Camron, listen—"

Before she could launch into her explanation, he held up a hand. "Save your breath. I think you might be onto something."

The comment caught her off guard, and she spun in her chair to face him. "Why? What's happened?"

"I guess you haven't heard."

She bit off a snide remark. "Heard what?"

"The captain of the USS *Ronald Reagan* has put the entire ship in quarantine."

Punky jumped up from her chair. "What? Why?"

Camron seemed a little too calm for what she thought was a significant development. He took another sip of his coffee before answering. "There has been an outbreak of some kind, and people just have diarrhea or something. But that's pretty much my assumption for any cruise."

But Punky knew better. If what Tan Lily had told her was true, then what the crew of the *Reagan* was experiencing was part of a synthetic bioweapon attack. What she didn't know was whether the illness spreading across the ship was only half the weapon's potency. She felt dizzy as she tried puzzling through the myriad of scenarios.

"There's more to it than that," she said.

Camron gave her a queer look but waited for her to explain.

"There is no question Dr. Tan Lily is being targeted by the Chinese Ministry of State Security."

He rolled his eyes.

"I'm serious, Camron. Listen to me. She is at a CIA safe house *right now*."

His demeanor changed, and he lowered the coffee cup. "Why?"

"Because one of their officers went missing in Shanghai after meeting with her husband. Both are biochemists with the specific skill set needed to engineer a synthetic bioweapon." She paused for a breath to let that sink in. "Hell, she was giving a lecture on the topic when I met her."

Camron was silent for a moment. "What do you know about *SUBLIME*?"

Punky shook her head. "Not much. That's why I'm here. I believe the Ministry is targeting her either because she knows how to activate the bioweapon or nullify it."

"But if the ship is already infected..."

She waved him off. "It's over my head, but she said they likely engineered a pathogen with a switch." She didn't bother explaining the difference between a binary weapon and a tripartite weapon. "If we can get her a blood sample from someone infected on the ship, she can tell us how it was engineered and how to mitigate its impact."

He nodded. "We might be in luck. The flight surgeon who treated the first patient sent the results of the blood test to BUMED."

"Get me a copy of those results, Camron."

He hesitated. "I'll run the request up the flagpole. Your only task right now is to find *SUBLIME* and stop him."

As if she needed Camron to tell her that. "On it."

She yanked her jacket off the back of her chair and slipped it on as she made for the exit. If her hunch was correct, the Chinese operative would be under the gun to make a move on Tan Lily. If she wanted to stop him, she needed to convince the CIA to use the doctor as bait.

Guo Kang sat astride his Ducati motorcycle in a parking lot off East Harbor Drive across from the whitewashed walls surrounding the naval base. Through the wrought iron security fencing, he studied the stucco building with a red-tiled roof where Emmy King had spent the evening. It hadn't taken much sleuthing to discover that the building was home to the Southwest Field Office for the Naval Criminal Investigative Service.

Made sense for the special agent to be there.

But why is the Navy interested in the doctor?

The flow of traffic along the street increased as more and more cars made their way to the base's main entrance on 32nd Street, but he was content letting them pass. His thoughts were on the doctor and her daughter tucked away in a secure location forty miles north. For some reason, the American Navy had taken an interest in the biochemist, and he was hesitant to inform the General until he understood why.

A flash of blue shot through the intersection near the main gate, and Guo Kang recognized the Challenger immediately. He started the Ducati and darted out onto East Harbor Drive, racing toward 32nd Street to catch up with the NCIS special agent. He didn't need to know what the Navy wanted with the doctor to know she posed a threat to their operation and needed to be stopped.

The light turned red, but he goosed the throttle and darted between cars as he made the left underneath a pedestrian overpass. The flashing red lights and descending red-and-white-striped gates warned him of an approaching trolley, but he had already spotted the Dodge muscle car making its way north. He had sighted in on his target and would not be deterred.

The motorcycle shot across the tracks moments before a red streetcar rumbled north toward downtown. Weaving between slower-moving cars, he reached down to the phone mounted to his Hypermotard's triple clamp and tapped on a button to place a call. He heard the phone ringing through the Bluetooth connection in his helmet before a voice answered.

"Authenticate."

"Mandate of Heaven," Guo Kang said into the helmet's microphone.

"Go ahead."

"I need a mobile response team to set an ambush on Interstate 15 northbound near Lake Hodges."

"Capture or kill?"

"Capture," Guo Kang replied. *If I wanted to kill her, she'd already be dead,* he thought.

"Target?"

"Blue Dodge Challenger. California license plate Foxtrot India Golf Hotel Tango Oscar November."

"Armed?"

Guo Kang surged between two sedans and closed to within four car lengths of the blue muscle car. "Affirmative."

"Time?"

"Twenty minutes."

"Stand by for confirmation." The voice on the other end sounded frustrated, and Guo Kang understood the burden he had placed on the duty officer. It would be a challenge, but he knew it was possible. He had been a member of the team that was on call 24/7 to respond to urgent requests for support, and he knew they could reach Lake Hodges within fifteen minutes.

The Dodge drove underneath Interstate 5 and continued north on Escondido Freeway, but Guo Kang kept his distance while he waited for the operations center duty officer to return to the line with confirmation that the mobile team was en route. He could do it alone if he had to, but he knew that would likely result in the special agent's death, and that greatly increased the risk of not getting the information he needed.

Then again, maybe eliminating her wasn't such a bad thing.

"Confirmed," the voice in his helmet said. "The team leader will contact you when in position."

The line went dead before Guo Kang could say anything else. All that was left for him to do was sit back and avoid being spotted as he watched the Dodge Challenger drive north. Once the team was in place, he would cause a diversion that would harry the special agent and drive her right into his trap.

44

Twenty minutes after leaving the base, Punky felt the hairs on the back of her neck stand on end, and she glanced in each of her mirrors, searching for whatever had triggered her innate sixth sense. Seeing nothing, she turned to look up at the hills covered in scrub brush stretching away on either side of her but saw nothing suspicious.

Then, in her side-view mirror, she spotted a red-and-black motorcycle four lengths behind her.

She stared intently into the rider's dark-tinted visor and was unable to see his eyes, but she knew with certainty that he was staring back at her. She held his hidden gaze for a heartbeat before looking up to see that traffic ahead was slowing and being diverted to the exit on West Bernardo Drive. She shot a glance at the motorbike in her rearview mirror, then followed the cars up the off-ramp.

At the intersection, she saw a utility van blocking traffic trying to turn left across the overpass.

Where are the police?

Alarm bells started going off in her head, and she reached down to pull the hem of her jacket back around her holstered pistol. Something about this didn't smell right, and when she saw the technician directing traffic, she knew.

She pressed the button on the steering wheel to place a call, then drew the SIG from its holster and held it low across her lap while she waited for the call to connect.

"Punky?"

"Something's not right, Camron," she said, glancing up into the rearview mirror to see the biker take his hand off the throttle long enough to unzip his jacket and unveil a compact submachine gun slung across his chest. "I need backup."

"Keep the line open while I connect with the local sheriff..."

Before she could respond, movement through the windshield startled her, and she stomped on the gas pedal while cranking the wheel hard to the left. The Challenger's tires spun before gaining traction, and she ignored the long blast of a car's horn as she whipped out onto the overpass and narrowly missed the technician, who was sprinting for the van. Speeding west away from the interstate, she glanced into her rearview mirror and saw the motorcycle matching pace with her.

"Shit!"

If she'd had any lingering doubts about the biker, those vanished when he brought the submachine gun up and let loose a short burst that impacted the road to her left and kept her from entering the interstate in the opposite direction. She floored the accelerator and harnessed almost eight hundred ponies under the hood, launching the muscle car up the hill.

"What's going on?" Camron asked. "Was that gunfire?"

Punky's eyes never stopped moving, and she looked for an opportunity to disengage. But she was propelling a car that weighed over five thousand pounds compared to a motorcycle that weighed less than a tenth of that. Getting away from the biker was going to be a challenge.

"At least one armed individual on a motorcycle," she said, giving Camron whatever information he needed to mount a response.

At the top of the hill, she turned right into the Rancho Bernardo Community Park and felt the Challenger's rear let loose for the briefest of moments. It triggered a memory of fishtailing around corners in her father's Corvette Stingray the previous summer with Colt Bancroft sitting next to her. She couldn't believe it was happening again.

"Not this time," she said, reminding herself that she still got a vote in how this turned out.

Pressing harder on the gas pedal, she flew past basketball courts and a recreation center, scanning beyond her hood for something she could use to turn the tide in her favor.

"What's that?" Camron asked.

For a moment, she had almost forgotten her supervisor was still on the line. "Just send backup to the Rancho Bernardo Community Park!"

Punky looked in her mirror, surprised to see that the motorcycle hadn't closed the distance. The dual sport bike had more than enough power, but he hung back and seemed content with following her past the tennis courts to the rear of the park. She knew she was leading him deeper into a dead end, but his hesitation had bought her enough time to settle on a course of action.

"They're on their way, Punky."

"Fuck this," she muttered, then slammed on the brakes and jerked the wheel hard to the left, sliding the Challenger around an island at the end of the road. When her back end let loose, she gave it gas and turned the steering wheel to drift around the curve. Once her nose was pointing back at the biker, she eased off the gas to let her tires catch, then launched herself straight at the motorcycle.

As Guo Kang came around the corner, he spotted the Challenger drifting around an island at the end of the road. Other than a parking lot next to some baseball fields, there was nowhere for the NCIS special agent to go. He had her cornered.

The pavement was smooth, and the Ducati Hypermotard chewed up the ground, but he eased off the throttle when he saw the Challenger pointed back in his direction.

What's this?

But in the span of a second, it quickly became apparent what the female agent's plan was. He had less than that to develop his own and put it into action without hesitation.

He slipped the clutch and twisted the throttle again to hear the throaty growl of the twin-cylinder 937cc engine roar through the dual tailpipes tucked under his seat. At the same time, he swerved erratically to avoid the oncoming muscle car and engaged the clutch as he lurched toward the side of the road.

With feigned incompetence on the bike, he stomped on the foot pedal for the rear brake and felt the rear begin to skid before squeezing the brake lever to lock up the front. The result was a fishtail that twisted the bike sideways as his nose dipped and hit the curb. He used the momentum to fling his body clear of the bike, tucking to roll over his handlebars and into the weeds at the edge of the road.

His Ducati crashed hard to the ground and slid for several more yards before stopping less than twenty feet from the Challenger that had come to a screeching halt. He had timed his crash perfectly and came to rest in the weeds only a few feet from the road. He felt a few scrapes and bruises already beginning to form and had lost the subcompact machine gun in the process, but he knew his performance had been flawless. He remained still and waited.

Guo Kang listened to the soft purring of the idling Hellcat engine and the rhythmic pounding of feet as the special agent ran from her car to check on him. But he didn't move.

"Federal agent!" she yelled.

Through his darkened visor, he watched her scramble into view. Her pistol was held in both hands out in front of her and leveled on him.

"Don't move."

He didn't.

Guo Kang grinned inside his helmet and slowly twitched his limbs to let her know that he was alive but hurt. She hesitated for the briefest of seconds, then holstered her pistol and knelt over him to sweep his body for signs of trauma. She had done the hard work for him.

With surprising speed, Guo Kang reached his hand up and hooked it behind her neck, bringing her face crashing down against his dark visor. The special agent reached out to stop herself from collapsing onto the rider, but her shock was obvious. Guo Kang took full advantage of that and reached down to his right hip, drew his pistol, and aimed it up into her chest.

He squeezed the trigger three times and watched with fascination as the look on her face turned from shock to pure terror.

It was only when he heard the faint sound of approaching sirens that he realized he had ruined his only chance at finding out why the Navy was interested in the doctor. Like it or not, he was going to have to inform the General that their operation was in jeopardy.

The success of the coming invasion hung in the balance.

45

USS *Ronald Reagan* (CVN-76)
South China Sea

Doc Crowe groaned when she saw the line forming outside medical. Without even looking, she could tell they were all suffering from the same thing. And even though the captain had taken the senior medical officer's recommendation and put the ship under quarantine, that hadn't stopped the number of cases from rising. The line along the bulkhead only under-scored what she already knew.

We're in big trouble.

She reached up to check that her mask was in place over her nose and mouth, then cut through the line and into the medical spaces. She saw a few of the sickest heaving into trash cans they had brought with them, but that had become so commonplace that she barely even noticed. Of course, she had been up all night, treating the sick, so maybe it was just her exhaustion that prevented her from focusing on what she had come to accept.

We're in big, big trouble.

She stepped into the ward and saw Diona leaning over Andy with a worried look on her face. She waved off a few of the ship's company corpsmen and made a beeline for the sleeping COD pilot. "What's going on?"

"His blood pressure has been dropping," Diona said, reaching up to affix a 1000-milliliter bag of 0.9% sodium chloride solution to the tree above his bed. "And his heart rate has been increasing."

Doc knew what the petty officer was thinking, and she admitted that an intravenous injection of saline solution was exactly what she would have ordered. Andy needed extracellular fluid replacement and treatment for metabolic alkalosis in the presence of fluid loss and mild sodium depletion. In short, he was severely dehydrated, and Diona was doing precisely the right thing.

She glanced at the vital signs monitor and saw that the pilot's temperature was 104 degrees—well above what she would have expected for someone who was only dehydrated. Even for a person who was recovering from an infection that had triggered gastroenteritis, it was far higher than she was comfortable with.

"Anybody else with this high of a fever?"

Diona glanced at the monitor and shook her head. "It was less than one hundred just a minute ago."

Doc reached down and placed her hand on Andy's arm. It had been clammy when they brought him down from his stateroom, but now it was red and hot and dry to the touch. "Andy? Can you hear me?"

His eyes twitched behind closed lids, but he didn't respond.

She looked up at the monitor and saw his heart rate top 130 beats per minute. "Maybe the saline will help."

Diona opened the valve to allow the fluid into the IV port, then turned to Doc. "This is the third bag," she said, with just a hint of worry intruding on her normally calm demeanor.

"Has it helped?"

The corpsman shook her head.

Doc knew a good rule of thumb was 30 milliliters of fluid per 2.2 pounds of body weight, so it wouldn't be unexpected for it to take three bags of saline solution to counter the effects of extreme hydration. But she would have at least expected his pulse to stabilize closer to one hundred beats per minute and for his blood pressure to rise to within an acceptable range.

"I don't like this," Doc said.

"What should we do?" The corpsman was looking for reassurance, but Doc wasn't sure she had any to give. They were doing everything they could to keep him comfortable and replenish his fluid loss, but it didn't look like it was helping much.

"I don't..."

Andy's eyes opened. "Doc?"

"I'm here," she said, reaching down again to gently rest a hand on his chest.

"I don't feel so good," he said.

Suddenly, his body went rigid. Doc froze when she recognized the tonic phase of a seizure, but she kept her hand on the pilot's chest as she looked down into his pleading eyes. "You're okay, Andy."

She hadn't realized it, but she had been counting the duration while she waited for it to progress to the next stage of seizure, known as the clonic phase.

Six...seven...eight...

Andy's muscles relaxed, then he started twitching. Each jerking movement of his body seemed like an electric shock that underscored the dire situation the USS *Ronald Reagan* had found itself in. Doc kept her hand on his chest while he thrashed on the gurney, and she looked around the ward at the other sailors who had come in looking for medicine to make them well. Would they all burn hot with fever and become so severely dehydrated that they also seized?

"What do we do?" Diona asked.

At last, Andy's body fell still, and his heart rate slowed. It was only a few beats lower, but it was enough to give Doc hope.

Again, she surveyed the other patients. There were a handful who had come in not long after they brought Andy down, and she could already tell that they would follow a similar trend as the virus cooked them from the inside out. Even more were only showing the early signs of infection, but she knew that would soon change. If they didn't get help soon, the ship would be dead in the water without a crew to run it.

"Doc?"

Sierra looked up at the corpsman and shook off her paralysis. She saw that Andy had slipped back into unconsciousness and that his vitals appeared to have stabilized. "Electrolytes."

"What?"

She spun away from the COD pilot and looked for the pharmacy technician. The second class petty officer was the only one on the ship authorized to dispense medication, but it wasn't medication she was after.

"Salt tabs," she said. "Everyone on the ship needs to start taking salt tabs."

When Andy opened his eyes, he felt like he had been hit by a truck. His muscles ached with fatigue as if he had just completed a killer CrossFit workout, and he was racked with exhaustion.

"Doc?"

His voice was barely a whisper. He turned his head to the side and saw a machine displaying what he assumed were his vitals, and he studied the numbers with little more than idle curiosity. Like most pilots, he avoided the doctor at all costs and still didn't know the difference between systolic and diastolic. He understood heart rates, and his looked unusually high.

"Doc?" he asked again.

The room was abuzz with activity, and each of the other beds was occupied. He couldn't remember if that had been the case before, and he wondered just how many people had come down with the same illness. He vaguely remembered Tom telling him that lots of people were getting sick. Was this the result?

A corpsman appeared over his shoulder, and he focused his eyes on her, taking note of the mask and protective equipment she wore over her Navy Working Uniform.

"How are you feeling?"

"What's going on?" he asked.

"You and a lot of other people are getting sick. It's spreading quickly across the entire ship." She paused to look at his vitals, then checked the bag of saline solution hanging above his bed. "Are you feeling thirsty? Do you need to urinate?"

Andy shook his head. "I feel like I got hit by a truck."

The petty officer nodded. "Makes sense. You had a seizure, so your muscles—"

He cut her off. "A seizure?"

"We think it was caused by a combination of severe dehydration and high fever. We've given you several bags of intravenous saline solution to remedy the first, but your fever is still higher than we'd like. Even after giving you acetaminophen injections."

Andy looked at the patients in the other beds. "What about them?"

The corpsman winced and gripped her stomach before answering. "They're experiencing the same symptoms. We're doing what we can to keep them hydrated and cool them before it gets too bad."

As the reality of the situation hit him, Andy remembered that Doc Crowe had wanted to draw blood and test it for pathogens. He thought he remembered that she had just received the results before telling somebody over the phone that she recommended quarantine and cleaning protocols.

"What did the blood test show?"

The corpsman's eyes softened as she looked down at him, but she almost looked defeated. "I don't know. It's nothing we've ever seen before. But the Navy's best doctors are looking at it."

Andy closed his eyes and took a deep breath. He needed to make it home to Jenn. That was all that mattered.

46

Dusty One
Air Branch Mi-17 Hip

Charlie leaned forward and kept sight of the retreating Super Hornet for as long as he could. Its glowing exhaust was clearly visible through his night vision goggles, but one by one, even those turned dark and cold as the fighter jet ran out of precious fuel. Like most pilots, he watched with morbid fascination until the bitter end.

"Think he made it?" Charlie asked.

Before Roger could answer, they both saw a bright flash as the canopy jettisoned and the pilot ejected from the stricken jet. They were too far away to see the parachute deploy, and all they could do was hope he had survived.

"Can you see him?" Roger asked.

Instead of answering, Charlie keyed the microphone. "Pedro One, this is Dusty One. The Super Hornet pilot ejected, but we can't see a chute."

The Marine pilot replied immediately. "Roger. We have his beacon."

"What's our fuel?" Charlie asked.

As if his copilot understood what he was asking, Roger replied, "Not enough."

Charlie clenched his jaw in frustration. As a fellow pilot, he didn't like the idea of leaving the fighter pilot alone in the water. But he liked it even less since they would have been shot from the sky had he not shown up when he did. The fact that the fighter pilot had knowingly run himself out of gas to save them made it even more maddening that they had to continue to the shoal without looking for him.

But the Marine Osprey pilot set his mind at ease. "Dusty One, Pedro Two is en route to recover the pilot. Continue to Scarborough Shoal."

"Dusty One," Charlie replied.

The flickering red light on the radar warning receiver turned solid, and the relative silence was broken by an alarm neither wanted to hear. They were no longer detecting only the side lobes of the HQ-9's radar energy but were being targeted by the robust surface-to-air missile battery.

"Dusty One is spiked," Roger said, reaching down to activate their electronic warfare jammers.

"Dusty One, Scar Nine Nine, chatter indicates the HQ-9 battery is targeting you," the calm voice from the TOC said.

"No kidding!"

Another red light blinked on, and Charlie glanced down to see the low fuel warning he had hoped would remain extinguished for just a little while longer. They were already making best speed for the shoal, and there was nothing they could do to counter either problem—the enemy surface-to-air missile *or* the lack of fuel.

"How far?" he asked.

"Just five more minutes," Roger replied.

I don't think we can make it.

Wizard 323
Navy P-8A Poseidon
South China Sea

Lieutenant Commander Ashley Mitchell sat on the edge of her seat and pressed her face to the windscreen to look up at the brilliant stars twinkling overhead. It was hard to believe so much chaos could be happening around them. They had been on station for the duration of the operation to monitor Chinese naval activity—including the fishing vessels that had moved south in force—but things seemed to be spiraling out of control. It wouldn't be long before they needed to do more than just monitor.

"Ma'am, the HQ-9 is targeting Dusty One," Lieutenant Turner said over the intercom.

She reached for the rocker switch on the yoke, toggling it down to reply. "Fire control?"

"Not yet. But chatter indicates an imminent intercept."

She glanced down at the navigation display that showed their position relative to the Chinese surface-to-air missile battery located on Woody Island, then pressed the autopilot disengage button on the yoke to take command of the modified Boeing 737-800. She gripped the controls and banked the plane left to point their nose into the missile engagement zone.

"Scar Nine Nine, Wizard three two three," she said.

"Go ahead, Wizard."

"Electronic surveillance indicates missile battery designated one alpha targeting Dusty One. How copy?"

There was a pause as the task force personnel manning the TOC at Clark Air Base correlated their report with information received from other assets in the area. Ashley wasn't privy to what other ships and aircraft were participating in the operation, but she knew of at least one MQ-4C Triton drone flying high-altitude surveillance twenty thousand feet above them.

"Good copy, Wizard."

Her tactical coordinator spoke over the intercom again. "Ma'am, they're activating their fire control radar."

"Roger that," she replied, then turned to look at her copilot.

"What are you thinking?" Logan asked.

For as capable as the P-8A Poseidon was, they didn't have many options for targeting a surface-to-air missile system. Their internal bay included five hard points for carrying the Mark 54 torpedo and the HAAWC, or High-Altitude Anti-Submarine Warfare Weapon Capability, air launch accessory that allowed them to employ a torpedo from as high as thirty thousand feet.

But they did have one trick up their sleeve.

She pressed down on the rocker switch again. "Ed, load the HQ-9 coordinates into the SLAM-ER."

Logan's eyes widened in surprise. "Shouldn't we ask—"

"We don't have time," she snapped.

"The SLAM-ER, ma'am?" Lieutenant Turner asked, obviously sharing Logan's sentiment that employing the AGM-84K Standoff Land Attack Missile–Expanded Response without authorization would, at best, land them in hot water.

"You heard me," she said. "Let me know when it's ready. I'm maneuvering us into position." She reached over and pushed the thrust levers forward, increasing the output of the Poseidon's twin turbofans to their maximum.

Dusty One
Air Branch Mi-17 Hip

The tension in Charlie's shoulders turned into solid knots and ached, but he practiced his box-breathing technique to push through his anxiety and focus on the one thing he could control—flying the helicopter to the best of his ability.

"Scarborough Shoal in sight," Roger said.

"Pedro One is loitering north of South Rock," the Marine Osprey pilot responded.

In the distance, Charlie saw the triangular-shaped chain of reefs and rocks encircling a large central lagoon and angled their approach to the right, where he knew the highest elevation was located just short of a single inlet. The terrain of South Rock was supposed to be almost six feet above sea level at high tide, but he didn't know if it was flat or wide enough to allow a safe landing.

Not that it mattered. The chorus of flashing red lights from the Chinese surface-to-air missile and imminent fuel starvation meant he had no choice. They were going to put down as close to South Rock as possible, even if it meant they got wet in the process.

"Dusty One is making our approach to South Rock now," Charlie said.

"A quarter mile to feet dry," Roger said, letting him know the distance to their intended touchdown point.

"Let's hope it's dry," Charlie replied, the tension in his shoulders intruding on his voice.

Roger ignored the comment. "Fifty feet over the water, come forward four hundred."

With one more glance at the fuel gauges now reading empty, Charlie focused his attention on the looming landmass that appeared like little more than a slightly less dark patch of water. He slowed their approach and descended closer to the surface, paralleling the shallows at the south-western corner of the atoll.

"Forty feet over the water...thirty..."

Charlie heard Roger's calls but had tuned everything else out. He even ignored the klaxon sound of the radar warning receiver that indicated the HQ-9 had activated its fire control radar to guide the Mach 4 surface-to-air missile. None of it mattered now. Everything but the shoal on their left side and the water beneath them was a distraction from what he needed to do.

"Missile launch!" Roger shouted.

But Charlie ignored him.

Just one hundred feet more.

47

Wizard 323
Navy P-8A Poseidon
South China Sea

Ashley knew she was pushing the limits of their engines and endurance, but she wasn't about to sit idle while a Chinese surface-to-air missile shot down an American helicopter. "What's our status, Ed?"

"Just finished loading it," he replied.

"Fire," she commanded.

If her tactical coordinator had any reservations about launching the three-million-dollar weapon, he didn't show it. The fifteen-hundred-pound missile dropped free from its external hard point before the turbojet engine propelled it toward the target.

"Op away," Ed said.

Ashley immediately banked away from the target, turning to put the disputed Chinese territory at their six o'clock. When she had gone through one hundred and eighty degrees, she reached up and turned on the autopilot, letting the Boeing jet fly itself away from hostile waters.

"You have the aircraft," Ashley said to Logan, not waiting for the required response before unstrapping and climbing out of her seat to walk aft from the flight deck.

Lieutenant Ed Turner was standing behind Petty Officer Delgado at his console on the port side of the plane when Ashley walked up. Both men were focused intently on the screens that displayed telemetry data for the SLAM-ER missile as it made its way along a preprogrammed nap-of-the-earth profile bound for Woody Island.

"How much longer?" she asked.

"We should start receiving datalinked images in..."

A flicker on the screen cut off Tony's response, and three sets of eyes stared at what looked like a grainy black-and-white movie of the ocean surface taken from a shaking cameraman. Tony immediately grabbed the control stick next to his station and made a subtle adjustment to the crosshairs. After a slight delay, the camera shifted and centered on the new target.

"Good control," he said.

The AGM-84K SLAM-ER was known as the Frankenstein of weapons. Based on the Harpoon missile platform, the SLAM-ER added an infrared seeker from the AGM-65F Maverick and a modified Walleye datalink. Though it could fly autonomously using GPS and infrared terminal guidance, the datalink allowed for a "man in the loop" feature that gave the operator the ability to fine-tune its guidance.

In this case, Tony used the joystick at his console to adjust the crosshairs in the last few seconds of flight to ensure it hit the desired target.

"Is that it?" Ashley asked, pointing at a bright spot on the screen.

Ed leaned in close, but Tony answered, "Yes, ma'am. That looks like the HT-233."

"That's the radar?"

Tony ignored the question and continued adjusting the crosshairs to keep them centered on the large rectangular hot spot in the middle of the screen. She couldn't help herself and held her breath as the missile raced toward the target at over five hundred miles per hour. As the seconds ticked closer to impact, Tony refined the aim point several more times until the target filled the camera's entire field of view.

The screen went dark, and Ashley exhaled.

Dusty One
Air Branch Mi-17 Hip

Silence filled the cockpit, but Charlie had already committed himself to ignoring everything but the landing. As the Hip neared the dry land of South Rock, he slowed their forward movement and hovered over the shoal while peering down at the rocky and uneven terrain.

"Do you see a good spot?" he asked Roger.

He pivoted the helicopter to give his copilot a better view through the windows on their left side, keenly aware that every second he delayed setting the helicopter down brought them closer to running out of fuel. Then he'd have no say in the landing spot whatsoever.

"Nope," Roger replied. "It's all uneven."

With a silent curse, Charlie pivoted back to the left and slowly inched the helicopter forward over South Rock. He debated setting down on the highest point, but without a flat piece of ground to set down on, they ran the risk of the helicopter tipping over and falling into the water. Even though most of the people in the back had trained for an underwater helicopter egress, he wasn't eager to end the mission that way.

"I'm going to put us down in the shallows," he said.

They drifted north to the lagoon side of the reef, and he pivoted once more to align them with what looked like a large stretch of shore. Even though it would be a wet landing, he hoped it was shallow enough that they could at least have a stable and flat piece of earth to rest the twenty-thousand-pound helicopter.

Roger reached over and tapped on the fuel gauges. Both auxiliary fuel tanks had long been drained, and the needle indicating their internal fuel quantity had been pegged at zero for the last several minutes. Neither said anything, but both pilots knew the helicopter's engines were operating from only what was left in their fuel lines.

"Five feet," Roger said, looking down through the forward window at the approaching water.

Most pilots said that any landing you walk away from is a good landing, but that didn't mean Charlie was about to mail it in. He eased off on the torque and let the Hip gradually descend to what he hoped was less than a foot of water.

"Four...three...two..."

Their wheels touched down, and Charlie took a long, slow breath before lowering the collective and committing them to the landing. Just as the Russian helicopter came to rest, the twin turboshaft engines above their heads coughed and sputtered as the last of the fuel was atomized and burned out. As if the machine was a dying man giving its last gasp, the engines wound down and the helicopter went dark.

"Holy shit," Charlie said.

"That was close," Roger agreed.

North of Scarborough Shoal

Colt plunged into the water and waited a second too long before releasing himself from his parachute. He shot to the surface underneath a web of parachute lines and multicolored silk, but he quickly fell back on his training and reached over his head to pull fistfuls of parachute in front of him. He didn't kick his legs for fear they might become tangled in the lines and instead allowed his flotation device to keep his head above water.

Nice and steady, he thought.

After several minutes of patient and deliberate movement, he had successfully disentangled himself from the fabric and slowly sculled backward away from the floating mess. With that first order of business complete, he allowed himself a brief respite and leaned his helmet back against the flotation collar and looked up into the night sky. He knew Rucas was up there somewhere engaging Chinese fighters, a Marine Osprey was coming to look for him, and a host of surveillance aircraft were watching it all unfold.

"You're on camera, Colt. Let's go."

He lifted his head and looked around, trying to spot...anything. A raft, a boat, the reef, an airplane. Anything would have made him feel significantly better about his situation. The last thing he had expected when he woke up earlier that day was that he would find himself bobbing alone in the South China Sea.

"Can't change that," he said, verbalizing his ongoing battle to overcome his fears.

He swept his hands around his body, searching for the nylon tether that connected his raft to his seat pan. When he found it, he pulled the line in front of his face to locate the snap hook, then clipped it to his survival vest's D-ring. Then he reached underneath him to detach it from the seat pan.

It was another lesson they had ingrained in them from the very beginning of water survival training—never let go of a piece of equipment unless it's attached to you. Satisfied, he unbuckled his lower lap belts and felt the seat pan fall away beneath him. Without the extra weight pulling him down, Colt bobbed higher in the water.

Though it was relatively calm, the waves were significantly larger than what he had experienced in the indoor pools they used for survival training. It made it difficult to reel in his raft and pull himself inside. But by the time he had, he could hear the approaching Osprey and knew his time in the raft would be short-lived.

The loud thrumming of the Marine tilt rotor grew louder, and he looked up just as a spotlight turned on. Blinded by its brilliance, he followed the Osprey's approach until it hovered directly over him. Colt had never been plucked from the water by an MV-22 before—heck, he had never been plucked from the water by *anything* before—but they had taught him to let the hook drop all the way to the water to discharge the static electricity before trying to reach for it.

Squinting against the light and the spraying water, he spotted a steel cable with a rescue strop and heavy-duty hook attached at the end. He waited until both reached the water, then rolled out of the raft he had struggled to climb into and swam the short distance to where the strop floated on the surface. He unclipped the raft's tether from his survival vest, then rolled into the strop and clipped the end to the hook so that when they reeled him up, the padded sling would lift him by his armpits.

Again, acting on muscle memory from hours spent in the pool, Colt waved a hand over his helmet from back to front, making sure the cable wasn't looped around his neck, then held a thumb out to the side like he was hitching a ride, so the person operating the hoist could see he was ready. Within seconds, he felt the cable tug upward and pull him clear of the water.

48

Yulin Naval Base
Hainan Island, China

General He Gang sat at the borrowed desk in his makeshift office on the naval base. He raised the glass of Moutai and swallowed the contents in one gulp, feeling the immediate heat of the baijiu spread across his gut. He was a disciplined man, but his operation was at a critical phase, and he relied on the distilled liquor to calm his mind.

Unlike the pompous fools who declared themselves leaders of his country, He Gang didn't wear a customary uniform adorned with various medals awarded more for compulsory service to the state than any specific act of heroism. Instead, he wore a simple dark blue suit, plain white shirt, and Western-style tie. He had removed the tie hours ago but still sat erect in the high-backed leather executive chair with his suit jacket on.

The phone sitting on the desk blotter vibrated, and He Gang observed the number with curiosity for a moment before answering.

"Yes," he said.

"The Americans have rescued her." The voice was breathless with anxiety.

He took a deep breath and exhaled slowly, feeling the tension evaporate from his body. They had been careful to move the American spy to a secure location that was beyond the normal scope of US intelligence-gathering efforts to make it appear as if they were moving her someplace more secure.

"Good," the General replied.

"Sir?" The voice on the other end was understandably confused. There were only a handful of people within his ranks who knew the full breadth of their operation. And none of them were within the eighth bureau that was responsible for counterintelligence.

"I must meet with Admiral Qin Guoping immediately. Keep me advised."

The General ended the call and reached for his red silk tie resting on the blotter atop the simple wooden desk. With practiced hands, he flipped up the collar of his shirt, tied a flawless double Windsor knot, and smoothed out his collar before checking his appearance in the dirty mirror on the wall next to the door.

He had chosen not to divulge details of the operation with the military until this exact moment. And though it had come with risks, the result was more than ample to justify the means.

With one more glance in the mirror, He Gang stepped out of the office and walked briskly down the hall to the stairwell at the opposite end of the building. The Admiral's office was a short walk away, but there was no guarantee he would be there at this early hour. If he had to track the Admiral down at his quarters, it would add unnecessary risk to the timeline.

Let us hope he is there.

As he walked, he dialed a number and waited for the person on the other end to pick up. Regardless of the time of day, he always answered the phone.

This time was no exception as the hoarse voice answered after three rings, "Yes, General."

"The trap has been set."

The man on the other end grunted in acknowledgment. "And the doctor?"

He Gang pushed open the door at the end of the hall and stepped out into the clear and humid night. "Move in now."

"Yes, sir."

"Call me when it's done." He Gang ended the call and lengthened his stride as he hurried across the small courtyard to the building housing the South Sea Fleet's submarine headquarters on the installation. Based in Zhanjiang, the South Sea Fleet was one of the largest in the People's Liberation Army Navy due to the contested waters and islands off the coast of Vietnam. While the fleet's surface force was based in Zhanjiang, the submarine fleet was based in Yulin, and its commander was the ranking naval officer on the base.

He Gang walked through the front door and bypassed the helmeted guard at the quarterdeck who was largely ceremonial despite being armed with a polished QSZ-92 service pistol in a starched canvas holster. Whether the pistol was loaded with 5.8 x 21mm armor-piercing rounds was irrelevant to him. The sentry knew better than to stop the General.

He pushed through the double doors into an operations center abuzz with a flurry of activity as naval officers ran back and forth across the room. He Gang spotted the Admiral and hurried to close the distance between them.

The Admiral looked up to see the General approach and held up a hand. "It's not a good time. We are under attack, and I need to deploy our fleet to the safety of open water."

"We are not under attack, Admiral," He Gang replied calmly.

Admiral Qin Guoping set the phone he was holding back onto the cradle and considered him with curiosity. "Two of our frontline fighters and one helicopter have been shot down. What is that, if not a prelude to war?"

He Gang repeated himself. "We are not under attack, Admiral. May we speak in private?"

The Admiral gestured over his shoulder to the private conference room behind his desk on the floor of the operations center. He Gang led the way into the room and waited for the Admiral to enter before closing the door to seal them off from the commotion on the floor.

"Explain yourself," the Admiral said tersely.

"The Americans are responding to an operation that has been sanctioned at the highest levels. I can't go into the details. But if you'd like, I can get General Peng Biao on the phone for you to give you your orders directly."

The Admiral stiffened at hearing the Defense Minister's name. "What do you need?"

"I need you to direct your forces to Taipei, China," He Gang replied calmly.

The two men locked eyes and remained silent for several moments, each considering their options. Admiral Qin Guoping had to know his career hinged on the very next decision he made. He would either be favored by the Party and continue his meteoric rise within the PLAN, or he would be arrested as a traitor for allowing Western aggression to go unchecked.

He Gang knew the success of his operation was dependent on the Admiral allowing the Americans to abscond with their repatriated spy and focus his efforts on the reclamation of Taipei.

Their staring contest was broken by a soft knock at the door. Both men turned to look at a commander who opened the door and stepped inside and addressed the Admiral. "Sir, the Americans have destroyed a radar facility on Woody Island, and we are scrambling additional fighters to respond."

He Gang turned back to the Admiral. "Your decision?"

A few minutes later, Admiral Qin Guoping set the phone down and turned to He Gang with a somber look on his face. Not quite ashen, he was pale enough that several of his aides looked at him with concern and stepped closer to the older man. He waved them off.

"Is it done?"

The Admiral nodded. "Our remaining fighters are returning to base."

"Come with me," He Gang commanded.

They returned to the conference room, where He Gang dressed down the Admiral in a hushed tone that barely hid his boiling anger. "The next time I tell you to do something, you do it exactly as I say without hesitation. Is that clear?"

The Admiral nodded, then lowered his eyes to He Gang's feet.

"If you do not do as you are told, you will not only be removed from your position here, but you will disappear from the face of the earth. Along with your wife, your two sons, and their entire families. Your lineage will cease to exist."

The Admiral remained silent, but some coloring returned to his face at the mention of his wife and sons. Both his sons served in the People's Liberation Army Navy, and one was on the island as a junior officer assigned to a ballistic missile submarine. The Admiral knew that He Gang was not to be crossed.

"Our fighters that went missing were lost during a training accident," He Gang stated.

The Admiral looked up at him. "But the Americans shot them down."

He Gang shook his head firmly. "Listen to me very carefully because I will not repeat myself. The fighters that went missing were *lost during a training accident*. We are not at war with the United States."

Not yet.

"I must report this to the Fleet Commander," Qin Guoping persisted.

He Gang locked eyes with the Admiral as he reached into his pocket and pulled out his cell phone. Without looking at it, he dialed a number, put it on speaker, and handed it to Qin Guoping. The Admiral took the phone hesitantly.

When the call connected, a deep voice asked, "How can I help you, General?"

The Admiral's eyes flashed to He Gang with immediate recognition. "Admiral Fu Hai..."

Qin Guoping spoke with the South China Sea Fleet Commander almost daily and had known him for close to twenty years. He considered him a close friend and respected him as an officer.

"Qin Guoping, is the General with you?"

"He is," the Admiral replied.

"And are you accommodating his requests to support this operation?"

"I'm afraid I don't know anything about the operation," Qin Guoping replied.

"You are a good commander, Qin Guoping," Fu Hai said. "The General has committed his own vessels from the East Sea Fleet to this operation. Support them as they move on Taipei, and ensure that they succeed. Do as General He Gang asks, or you will be replaced."

It wasn't the same threat the General had made, but it was close enough.

"But the American aircraft carrier, USS *Ronald Reagan*..."

"Is out of commission thanks to the General. He has done his part. Do yours."

He Gang knew the Admiral was a good officer and would do as instructed so he could go home and crawl into bed with Wing Li and mourn the loss of their brave pilots in private.

"Yes, Admiral," he replied quietly.

The Fleet Commander was silent on the phone for a moment, as if contemplating whether his subordinate commander would do as instructed. "Please hand the General the phone."

Admiral Qin Guoping did as instructed and held the phone out to He Gang, who took it off speaker and lifted it to his ear. After several minutes, he ended the call with a simple, "Thank you for your time, Admiral. That will be all."

49

Clark Air Base, Philippines

Connor hadn't even had an active role in the rescue, but he was still exhausted from all the stress. He pushed through a heavy steel door and stepped out onto the tarmac, taking a deep breath as he stared across the airfield at the horizon's orange glow of the coming dawn. The air base was still closed, but he thought he could hear the faint bass drum of the Marine Ospreys making their way to shore from behind the hangar.

He tapped his foot, anxiously waiting to receive Lisa and begin the debriefing process. The stress of her rescue was one thing, but knowing she might be the only person who could prevent an attack ratcheted that up a notch. And he felt every ounce of the burden that had fallen on him to discover what knowledge she possessed and transmit it to Jax before it was too late.

The door behind him opened, and the watch commander stepped outside. He paused for a moment, then walked close and stood next to Connor in silence. Neither said a word for a few minutes as the thrumming sound of the tilt rotors grew louder and echoed off the surrounding buildings.

"You okay?" he asked.

Connor turned to him and nodded. He knew his fatigue was written all over his face.

"You probably don't see stuff like that very often, do you?"

He laughed. "You do?"

The watch commander reached inside his coat pocket and removed a cellophane-wrapped cigar. He studied it in the dim lighting for a moment, then offered it to the CIA officer. "Stogie?"

"Is this a tradition of some kind?" Connor asked, accepting the gift.

The watch commander removed a second cigar, slipped it from the packaging, and inhaled the fragrant maduro wrapper before snipping off the tip with a cutter. Connor followed his lead, then held a match to the end while puffing on it until it glowed red. They stood in silence on the tarmac, letting the smoke billow around them and waft into the air.

Less than one hundred yards away, flight crew scrambled to prepare the specially configured Gulfstream G550 they had flown in from the States to carry Lisa home. They hadn't planned to depart so soon and expected the *Reagan*'s medical staff to stabilize her aboard the aircraft carrier first. But with the ship under quarantine, their entire timeline had become compressed. Connor drew in another mouthful of the full-bodied cigar smoke, thankful it wasn't his problem to deal with.

The door behind them opened and a voice called out, "They're five minutes out."

The watch commander blew a thick stream of smoke into the air, then sighed. "We're on our way."

"Guess quiet time is over," Connor said. He dropped the cigar and ground the glowing embers with the heel of his boot as the watch commander disappeared inside the hangar.

He turned back to watch the pair of Ospreys materialize over the hills to the west and descend onto the runway. From a distance, they looked nearly identical to every other tilt rotor he had seen. But he knew these ones were different. Aside from the olive drab coloring, he knew they carried Marines, SEALs, an air branch helicopter crew, and a woman who had endured more than he could ever imagine.

And a fighter pilot who had single-handedly salvaged the entire operation.

The Ospreys taxied closer, and Connor squinted through the dawn haze as the sound reverberated through his chest. He brought his fingers up to plug his ears while they parked side by side, less than one hundred yards from the idling Gulfstream, then fell silent as the massive proprotors spun to a stop.

Suddenly, the parking apron sprang to life. From behind him, members of the task force raced out to greet the returning SEALs. Medical personnel descended from the Gulfstream and jogged to the closest Osprey, where Connor assumed they would stabilize Lisa before bringing her on board the business jet. From behind the second Osprey, he saw the shadowed outline of a gaggle of men he suspected were the clean-cut Marines who had plucked the Super Hornet pilot out of the ocean before rescuing the others from the shoal.

"All right," a booming voice called out. "Let's get her over to the Gulf-stream. I want to be wheels-up in ten minutes."

The other men nodded, then carefully hoisted a litter and shuffled toward the Gulfstream, where two orderlies waited to carry Lisa the rest of the way. The CIA G550 was configured as a medevac with a dedicated medical bay outfitted with hospital-grade equipment needed to stabilize patients for long flights. From advanced life support capabilities to X-ray viewing equipment, the doctors and nurses on board would be able to get an early look at the extent of Lisa's injuries during their flight home.

"You all set?" a bearded man asked.

Connor took a deep breath and exhaled slowly before answering. "That was a little more intense than I expected."

The SEAL furrowed his brow, as if reading into the statement. "I don't think anybody expected the Chinese to take it that far. But that's why they sent us to get her."

Connor looked over at the orderlies carrying an immobile Lisa into the Gulfstream. "If Langley is right, and she knows about an attack that is coming, we're running out of time."

"And that's why they sent you."

Connor nodded, then started walking across the tarmac toward Lisa. The sooner he found out what secrets she had brought back with her, the sooner they could stop whatever attack was coming. He paused as he crossed paths with a pilot in a soaking-wet flight suit making his way toward the hangar.

"Hey, good work out there," he said.

Colt eyed the stranger suspiciously but nodded in acknowledgment. "Just doing my job," he said.

The man continued toward the Gulfstream, and Colt hesitantly made his way across the tarmac, trying to figure out what to do next. He knew the carrier was under quarantine, but he felt uncomfortable being on solid ground when his shipmates were still on board the *Reagan*. Even more so, knowing that many of them were probably fighting off illness.

"Are you Lieutenant Bancroft?" a voice called out.

Colt stopped and turned toward a sailor dressed in the green Type III Navy Working Uniform. "Yeah, that's me."

The sailor handed him a satellite phone. "It's for you, sir."

Colt took the phone and brought it to his ear. "Lieutenant Bancroft."

"Colt, it's Cutty."

His heart raced with anxiety. Even though he knew he had done everything by the book, he still had a nagging doubt that second-guessed every decision he had made. From shooting down the Chinese fighter to running out of gas going after the attack helicopter, he knew he was about to be put under the magnifying glass again. "Sir, what's going on?"

"First thing's first," the old man said. "Are you okay?"

He felt himself relax. "Yes, sir. I'm fine."

"Fever? Headaches? Nausea?"

"No, sir. I'm fine."

"No symptoms?"

"Sir, what kind of illness is this?" he asked, worried that DCAG seemed more concerned with him being sick than what he had just gone through.

Cutty sighed heavily into the phone. "We don't really know, to be honest. Lots of people are in really bad shape."

Colt thought back to Sierra and wondered how she was handling things. "How's Doc doing?"

"She was the one who examined the first person to get sick."

Colt felt a knot in the pit of his stomach. Though he knew Doc often ran sick call with the other medical officers on the ship, it was more likely that the flight surgeon had been called to check on someone he knew. "Who was it?"

Cutty paused, and Colt knew it was a violation of patient privacy to reveal that information. But laws like that had a way of being overlooked when an aircraft carrier was being sidelined because of a strange illness. "Andy Yandell," Cutty said. "He's a..."

"COD guy," Colt finished for him. "Yeah, I had a few beers with him in Iwakuni the other night."

"I know. That's why I asked how you were feeling. We still don't know where he got it."

It could have been that he was being overly paranoid, but he started to feel his stomach churning. "I feel good, sir. What do you want me to do?"

"Normally, we'd want you back out to the ship to do a complete medical workup on you..."

Colt had expected as much. One didn't run a seventy-million-dollar fighter jet out of gas and crash it into the South China Sea without having some sort of investigation launched into the incident.

"...but with the ship in quarantine, we're going to keep you and Rucas there until things settle down."

"Rucas is here?" In the excitement of shooting down the Chinese helicopter and flaming out near Scarborough Shoal, Colt had forgotten all about his wingman. As if in answer to his question, Colt heard his name being shouted from across the tarmac. He turned and saw Rucas with a wide shit-eating grin on his face. "Never mind, sir. He just found me."

"Sit tight, Colt. I'll be in touch."

"Aye, sir."

He ended the call just as Rucas reached him and pulled him in for a hug. He was still soaking wet from his brief dip in the South China Sea, but the other fighter pilot didn't seem to mind. "You made it!"

"Did I?" Colt asked, still trying to process everything that had happened.

Rucas released him and stepped back. "Just what do you think you were doing out there?"

He scrunched up his face in confusion, but one of the SEALs walked up and answered for him. "His job, I reckon."

Colt glanced over at the SEAL and did a double take. "Senior Chief?"

"Hey, flyboy."

Rucas saw the bewildered look on Colt's face and the bemused expression on the SEAL's. "Do you two know each other?"

Colt opened his mouth to answer, but the SEAL was quicker. "Yeah, your flyboy here crashed his jet on my island last year."

"I didn't crash," Colt said. "This is Senior Chief Dave White."

"Seems like a dark cloud seems to follow you wherever you go," Dave said, though Colt could tell the SEAL was only poking fun at him. "First you crash on my island..."

"I didn't crash," he said again.

"...then you eject from a perfectly good airplane."

"First of all, I didn't *crash*, I *landed*. Second, it wasn't a perfectly good airplane, it was out of gas."

"I seem to remember that being your excuse last time too." Dave stuck out his bearlike paw to Colt. "Thanks for saving our bacon, flyboy."

"So that was you, huh?" Colt accepted the offered hand and squinted at a dark smudge on the SEAL's face. "What's that?"

Dave reached up and touched his forehead with a grimace. "Oh, just hit my head trying to fend off that helicopter while you took your sweet time getting to us."

Colt rolled his eyes. "Glad I didn't drag my feet any longer—it would have really messed up your devilish good looks."

Dave grinned. "We need to stop meeting like this."

"Yeah, I thought you said you'd be in touch. What gives?"

"I definitely will." He paused. "But I got a plane to catch right now."

Colt looked over Dave's shoulder and saw a patient being loaded onto the Gulfstream. "Where you headed?"

"Back to San Diego, my man." Dave nodded at Rucas, then turned and jogged to the business jet medevac.

Colt watched him leave before turning to his wingman, whose face registered nothing but confusion. "What the hell was that all about?"

Colt shook his head. "Long story."

50

The strange humming noise was becoming more prominent. It wasn't getting louder. It was just becoming more difficult to ignore. With the humming came a faint glow that was also becoming more difficult to ignore. Like a wedge, it was breaking apart the dark nothingness that had defined her for the last... How long had it been since she'd seen the light?

"She's coming around," the unfamiliar voice said.

Her eyelids flickered as if attempting to open but failing to do so. The humming was persistent, and the glow of light was filling her awareness to the point that she could no longer avoid it and retreat inside her comforting darkness. Lisa Mourning opened her eyes but quickly snapped them shut.

The split-second view she had managed to take in was terrifying. She was in a brightly lit tube with wires and hoses and vaguely familiar machines all around her. And then there were the people. They looked friendly enough, but she knew looks could be deceiving.

"Lisa," another voice said. "Can you hear me?"

It's a trap.

She knew her captors had used deceit to unbalance her and cause her unending pain. This had to be just another one of their ploys to catch her off guard, to humiliate and hurt her. She couldn't give in to the temptation, no matter how badly she wanted to go home.

Home.

A faint memory flickered.

We're here to bring you home, Lisa.

With tentative curiosity, she opened her eyes again and struggled to keep them open so she could examine her surroundings. She didn't recognize the two people hovering over her, but bits and pieces of information she knew came from her past began to fill in the void.

She was in a plane.

No, this is a jet.

The humming came from the jet engines.

She was strapped to a bed softer than anything she had ever felt before —especially not a concrete floor, wood box, or canvas stretcher. It was warm and soft and felt sinfully exotic.

"How are you feeling, Lisa?" the man standing over her asked.

She parted her lips to answer but felt a stiffness in her jaw she didn't recognize. She probed the inside of her mouth with her tongue and registered a few simultaneous realizations. She was missing a few teeth she used to have, and her mouth was bone dry.

"Thirsty," she croaked.

The doctor—*yes, that's what he is*—nodded to her and pushed an ice chip against her lips. She opened her mouth slightly and felt the coldness slip into her mouth and dissolve. The moisture felt heavenly, and she felt an immediate sense of relief flood her body.

"More," she whispered.

The doctor nodded again and pressed several more chips of ice into her mouth to gradually reintroduce water into her system. She was finding it easier to keep her eyes open and looked away from the doctor's face to examine the rest of the interior. A few words written on pieces of equipment provided more clues that she was no longer being held by the Chinese.

She startled when another man stepped into view. Thick, dark hair framed his tired eyes, but his face was calm and oddly familiar. He wasn't a doctor, but Lisa had the vague impression she had met him before.

"Hello, Lisa," the man said. "My name is Connor. Do you remember me?"

Connor.

The name sounded familiar, and she dug into the recesses of her mind to recall from where she had known the dark-haired man. Even his voice had a lyrical quality she knew she had heard before. But the man's appearance and voice filled her with a sense of dread, as if her body knew there was a reason to be afraid, but the memory remained hidden from her.

She shook her head.

"You are on an Agency plane," Connor said in a carefully measured cadence. "We are flying you back to California."

Lisa blinked and felt tears begin to roll away from the corners of her eyes. She didn't understand how she had come to be strapped to such a comfortable bed inside a jet flying to America, but she felt grateful. And relieved. And another feeling she couldn't quite place.

Connor shot a questioning look at the doctor, who had stopped feeding her ice chips. The doctor smiled down at Lisa and said, "The sedative is wearing off, but we've given her something for the pain. It may take a little while for her to remember what's happened."

"How long?" Connor asked.

Lisa looked up into Connor's brown eyes and felt the need to tell him... *What? What am I supposed to tell him?* It frustrated her that her addled mind wouldn't cooperate.

"An hour or two, at most," the doctor said.

Lisa cleared her throat and asked, "What day is it?"

She knew that wasn't quite right. *Day* seemed somehow too insignificant to warrant the effort from her curious mind. But it was close.

Connor shared a look with the doctor before answering, "It's Tuesday."

Tuesday.

No, that wasn't what she needed to know, but she was on the right track. She peeled back another cobweb from her mind and felt it become clearer with each passing second.

"What month is it?"

Yes, that's the question.

There was no shared look this time before Connor answered. "It's October, Lisa. You've been in captivity for a week."

The last of the cobwebs fell away, and every horrible memory of the past week suddenly flooded her mind. Nothing was spared as she recalled every brutal beating, every humiliating act. She felt phantom ropes digging into her chafed skin, and she struggled against the bed's restraints to free herself from bondage. Her body reacted on instinct alone, but her eyes filled with tears of relief.

"What happened?" Lisa asked, blinking them away.

Connor darted in close, and Lisa flinched. Even though she knew the man wasn't a threat to her, she suspected she would be skittish for some time. As if sensing her unease, Connor took a half step back but held her gaze.

"Do you remember me now?"

Lisa stared hard into his brown eyes but couldn't place where she had seen them before. She shook her head.

"Do you remember anything?"

She pinched her eyes shut against the torrent of memories flooding her mind. She shook her head to clear them away, then opened her eyes and looked up at Connor.

"Too much," she said.

Connor placed a gentle hand on her arm, and Lisa recoiled. Human touch had meant only pain and humiliation. But this touch was different. Slowly, she relaxed against Connor's hand and gave him a weak smile, hoping he wouldn't pull his hand away.

He didn't.

"Do you remember being captured?"

Lisa couldn't prevent the memory of being taken from overpowering every other thought, and she opened her eyes. Swallowing hard against the sour taste of fear, she nodded.

The hand on her arm squeezed softly. "You're safe now, Lisa."

"Thank you," she croaked. "Did you stop it?"

Connor looked over his shoulder at someone out of view. When he turned back, he asked, "Stop what?"

Maybe it's not too late!

"The attack. Did you stop the attack?"

Connor lowered himself to one knee. "There hasn't been an attack. What do you know about it? Do you know the target? Do you know when?"

Lisa's eyes fluttered as she tried processing the rapid-fire questions. "That doesn't make sense. It should have happened by now." Her conversation with Shen Yu flashed through her mind, followed immediately by the image of his head exploding in front of her. She choked back a sob.

"What should have happened by now?" Connor asked in a softer tone.

Lisa tried recalling specifics, but chunks of her memory were still missing. She shook her head slightly. "I don't know exactly. Only that they were targeting an aircraft carrier with a synthetic bioweapon."

"What do you know about this bioweapon?" Connor asked.

Lisa took a deep breath. "Shen Yu..."

Connor nodded. "You were meeting with him in Shanghai."

"Shen Yu said it was too late..." She trailed off.

"What did he tell you?"

The more questions Connor asked, the more Lisa remembered. She remembered the look of sadness on Shen Yu's face as he told her of what his country had done. And she remembered the strange proverb: *One day, three autumns.*

"Lisa?"

"*Yaoshi*," she muttered.

"What?"

"It was the last thing he said to me."

Connor cocked his head. "What does it mean?"

"If?" Lisa closed her eyes and shook her head. "I don't know."

"What did Shen Yu tell you before that?"

"He told me they had deployed a synthetic bioweapon against an aircraft carrier."

"Why?"

Lisa opened her eyes. "He didn't say. But I can only guess that eliminating a strategic asset like an aircraft carrier would make an invasion that much easier."

"Invasion?"

"Of Taiwan."

Connor gritted his teeth but remained silent.

"What is it?" Lisa asked, sensing his hesitation.

"The USS *Ronald Reagan* is in quarantine right now because of an outbreak on the ship."

"An outbreak of what?" Lisa asked, suddenly wishing she had pressed Shen Yu for more details.

"They don't know."

Lisa winced as a bolt of pain radiated through her body. Connor rose from his knee and said, "Doc."

The doctor walked over and leaned down to look at his patient. He looked at the readings on the monitor over the bed and nodded as if satisfied she was in stable condition. "How are you feeling, Lisa?"

"In pain," she replied. It had been hidden just below the threshold of the narcotics they had given her, but the opiates were wearing off.

"I'm going to give you—"

"No," she said. "No drugs." It wasn't unbearable yet, and the fog was just beginning to lift. She needed to honor Shen Yu's sacrifice and finish her mission. She fixed her gaze on Connor again. The pain was becoming more intense, and she needed to tell him what she knew before the doctor stepped in. "Shen Yu gave me something."

"What?"

"He didn't say. Just that I could use it to stop a war."

Connor removed his hand and stood. "Did he give you the antidote?"

Lisa's eyes filled with tears, as much from the pain as from the memory of what it had cost Shen Yu. "I don't know. I never saw what was on it."

"On what?"

Her thoughts were becoming more jumbled as another bout of pain swept through her. "A thumb drive."

"What happened to it?"

"When they arrested me, they took it." She swallowed against the bile creeping upward. "Then they executed Shen Yu in front of me."

Connor sagged in defeat as the doctor stepped forward and inserted a needle into her IV injection port. "She needs something for the pain."

This time, Lisa didn't argue and welcomed the warm sensation spreading up her arm. "But I copied its contents onto a laptop."

"Whose?" Connor asked.

Lisa's eyes sagged closed as the opioids the doctor had injected attached to receptors in her brain to block the pain. She tried visualizing the other flight attendant and could see her clearly, but her name remained just beyond reach. She replayed the events of the flight in her mind, fast-forwarding through the mind-numbing boredom of serving drinks and food over the Pacific Ocean. She recalled their conversation in the van on the way to the hotel and how she had brushed her off to make her scheduled meeting with Shen Yu.

"Lisa?" Connor asked, gently encouraging her to find the answer to his question.

Her eyes still closed, she recalled the girl calling to invite her to drink wine and watch the sunset. She thought about transferring the contents to her computer before sitting in the chairs overlooking the milky Shanghai skyline. The sunset had been truly magnificent, and she suddenly realized it had been the last sunset she had seen.

She had Jenn to thank for that.

Jenn.

Lisa opened her eyes and looked up at Connor with a triumphant look on her face. "Jenn," she said.

"Jenn Evers?"

Her eyes closed again, and she gave in to the drug's warm embrace.

Connor rubbed her arm. "You did good," he said.

51

Valley Center, California

Jax poured himself another cup of coffee, then rinsed the carafe and filled it with water to make a second pot. He let his cup cool on the kitchen counter as he went through the routine process of dumping the used grounds and preparing for another round. Though he and Margaret had been the only ones drinking coffee so far that morning, he suspected the others would appreciate a fresh pot when they surfaced.

The soft plodding of feet drew his attention to the hall, where Cher walked into the room ahead of Margaret. One of the cur's ears drooped low, but both eyes were fixed intently on Jax as he poured the water into the coffeemaker.

"How long do we expect the danger to last?" Margaret asked.

Jax stabbed at the button to begin the brewing process, then scooped up his mug and took a sip. "I don't know," he said. "Punky is looking into the Chinese operative who we believe is after her, but I think the threat will be gone once we've recovered our officer."

Margaret leaned against the counter, and Cher sat at her feet and looked up at them. "How much longer until that happens?"

He looked at his watch and tried doing the mental gymnastics to convert the time. He might have been off by an hour, but even so, he should have already heard from Connor. "Any time," he said.

Margaret nodded but remained silent, letting the sound of the percolating coffeemaker fill the kitchen. Jax looked down at Cher, who only stared back. It was going to be a long day if he had to wait much longer.

As if someone had heard his plea, his cell phone vibrated with an incoming call. He saw Connor's name on the caller ID and quickly answered. "What's the word?"

"We got her," he said. "We're on our way back to California now."

Jax exhaled, and he saw both Margaret and Cher relax at his change in posture. It was as if somebody had cut the tension in the room, and they could finally breathe. "Good. That's good. Have you debriefed her? Has she revealed anything about an attack?"

There was a long pause while Jax waited for his question to bounce across satellites to reach his partner somewhere over the Pacific Ocean. "She's banged up pretty bad, but I did get a chance to question her." There was another pause.

"What did—"

Connor continued, speaking over Jax. "She copied the contents of the thumb drive Shen Yu gave her onto a computer belonging to Jenn Evers."

"The other flight attendant?" Jax felt himself deflate. It had been too much to hope that Lisa would have been privy to the details of a looming attack, but that didn't mean Jax hadn't hoped anyway.

"How far are you from Escondido?"

"Escondido?" Jax furrowed his brow. "Maybe twenty minutes. Why?"

It was obvious Margaret was interested in the conversation, but she passed the time by pouring herself a cup of coffee and leaning over to scratch Cher on the head. The dog never took her eyes off Jax.

"That's where she lives."

He closed his eyes and groaned. Not that they wouldn't have sent a team in to rescue Lisa if they had known, but they could have long since had the intelligence with only a short drive down the interstate. "I'm going to retrieve it," he said. "How long until you land?"

"Not for another twelve hours," Connor replied. "But Jax?"

"Yeah?"

"Does the word *yaoshi* mean anything to you?"

"Not really. Why?"

There was a pause on the other end. "Lisa told me it was the last thing Shen Yu said to her."

Why would he say that?

"That doesn't make any sense, but I'll let you know what I find on the computer." He ended the call and turned to Margaret, who waited patiently for him to fill her in. "Lisa copied the intelligence onto another flight attendant's computer before she was kidnapped."

"And this other flight attendant lives in Escondido?"

Jax nodded, but he hesitated.

"Go," Margaret said. "Cher and I will take care of the doctor and her little girl."

He started to protest, but she stopped him.

"Just go. We know what we're doing."

"Thank you." Jax set his coffee cup down and turned for the door.

Only twenty minutes away.

Escondido, California

Jenn kicked off her tennis shoes and flopped down on the worn sofa, still wearing a pair of sweatpants and a loose-fitting tank top. She had left with the intention of going for a short morning run, but it had been more walking and less running. The pregnancy had sapped her of her strength far more than she expected, and she was looking forward to a relaxing day of watching a few episodes of her favorite show on Netflix.

She pressed play on the next episode of *Outlander*, hoping the supernatural love story of Jamie and Claire would help her forget her real-world problems. But before the opening sequence even began, her phone rang. With a groan, she pressed pause.

"This better be good," she muttered, then leaned over to pick up her phone from the coffee table. She didn't recognize the number, but it had a San Diego area code, and her heart jumped in her throat.

"Hello?"

"Jenn Evers?"

She leaned back into the plush cushions and closed her eyes, wondering what product or scheme the telemarketer was going to try selling her on. "I'm not interested."

"This is Commander Nicholas."

She suddenly leaned forward. "What is it? Is Andy okay?"

The naval officer on the other end sighed. "Andy is fine. But he wanted to get a message to you before you saw it on the news."

"Saw *what* on the news?" She grabbed her remote to exit Netflix and turned to one of the twenty-four-hour news channels. Her breath caught in her throat when she saw a video of an aircraft carrier with the words "Navy doctors scramble to discover cause of mysterious illness aboard USS *Ronald Reagan*" in a banner at the bottom of the screen.

"What's going on? Why are you calling me?"

"Andy is sick. We believe it's some sort of virus, but it's spreading quickly around the ship, and the captain has ordered a quarantine."

She heard his words, but they didn't make sense. She imagined lots of people got sick on deployment. But she didn't think squadron commanding officers ever called the families to let them know.

And I'm not even Andy's wife.

"So why are you calling me?"

There was a pause on the other end, long enough that she wondered if he was going to dodge answering the question. "This is a new virus of some kind. Andy was one of the first to get sick on the carrier, so I wanted to let you know that he's in good hands and..."

The knock at her door diverted her attention away from his vague answer.

Jax knocked a second time before stepping back from the door, wishing he'd been able to reach Punky to bring her along. He didn't know what it was like being a young and single flight attendant, but he imagined Jenn would be more than a little skeptical at seeing a man outside her door. He heard movement inside and knew Jenn was home but probably reluctant to answer.

Can't say I blame her, he thought.

"Can I help you?" she called from the other side of the closed door.

Jax held up his credentials. "Miss Evers, my name is Jax Woods from the Central Intelligence Agency. I'm sorry to trouble you, but may I have a few minutes of your time?"

There was a slight pause before the door opened. Jax saw a petite brunette in her early twenties wearing sweatpants and a tank top that she covered protectively with one of her toned arms. "Is this about Andy?"

Jax didn't recognize the name and pressed on with his rehearsed script. "May I come inside?"

Reluctantly, Jenn opened the door wider and permitted him access to her small apartment. "I'm sorry to bother you, but I'm hoping you can help me with something."

She led him into the living room, where she sat on the couch and tucked her legs up under her. The TV was on and tuned to a local station, and Jax noticed her phone sitting on the coffee table in front of her with the screen unlocked. He took it all in without consciously thinking about it and returned his focus to the beautiful flight attendant waiting patiently to understand why someone from the CIA wanted to speak with her.

"I just talked to Andy's commanding officer," she offered with a slight tremor in her voice.

"Who's Andy?" Jax asked.

"My boyfriend? He's a Navy pilot. I thought that's why you were here."

Jax squinted at the strange admission. "I'm actually here to talk about a flight attendant you recently worked with on a flight to Shanghai. Lisa Mitchell?"

Jenn opened her eyes wide. "Is she okay? Did you find her?"

"Lisa is fine," Jax said, recalling Connor's description of the operations officer's condition.

"What happened to her?"

He ignored the question and tried to regain control of the conversation. "Miss Evers, did Lisa use your laptop?"

Jenn leaned away from him and crossed her arms protectively again. "Do I need an attorney?"

"You're not in any trouble," he said, trying to reassure her and prevent her from stonewalling him.

"Then why are you asking about my laptop?"

"Did she use it?"

She nodded.

"Good. Can I see it?"

"Why do you need it?" she asked.

Jax sighed, then glanced up at the TV as a reporter began speaking about the quarantine aboard the USS *Ronald Reagan*. He looked back at Jenn and noticed her eyes filling with tears. "Where is your boyfriend, Miss Evers?"

She stared back at Jax with a blank expression.

"Is Andy in trouble?" he pressed.

"That's why his skipper called me." She swallowed as if choking back a sob. "He's really sick."

"What's on your laptop may help him. Will you get it for me?"

At last, she nodded.

52

Rancho Bernardo, California

Punky opened her eyes but could only see the dirt and gravel her face was buried in. She tried lifting her head off the ground, but a wave of nausea overpowered her, and her stomach clenched as she tried to vomit. That was when she knew she was in trouble.

She gently moved each of her limbs as she probed her body for injuries. Her chest was on fire, but the rest of her seemed okay. She tried rolling onto her back and struggled. Using her right arm, she pushed off the ground and onto her side. She looked down and could see a singed and torn shirt where the assassin's bullets had entered.

"Fuck me," she moaned as she flopped onto her back.

Looking up into the cloudless sky, she panted to keep the pain from overwhelming her again. She had been hurt before, but nothing quite like this. The memory came flooding back, and her body twitched with each of the three shots that replayed in her mind.

The biker.

Punky turned her head toward the sound of the approaching sirens, hoping Camron had been smart enough to send an ambulance as well. With her right hand clutching her stomach, she used her left to push into a semi-seated position. Supporting herself with a shaking arm, she shrugged out of her jacket and reached back to grasp the collar of her ruined shirt. Tugging on it, she pulled the shirt over her head and collapsed to the ground, exhausted and panting from the effort.

Lying flat on her back again, she pulled her arms free and let the shirt fall to the ground next to her. She took a few more shallow breaths, then reached down and ripped free the Velcro straps that held her body armor in place.

Punky moaned as she lifted her head from the ground and looked down to inspect the damage. Three bright red holes oozing blood were enough confirmation that the body armor hadn't absorbed all the bullets' energy. But she would have been dead without it, and she silently thanked Camron that he had insisted she wear it.

Picking up her shirt, she folded it in an eight-inch square with the cleanest fabric exposed on one side. She pressed the clean patch down against her midsection—covering all three holes—and held it there while she waited for another wave of nausea to pass.

Her vision narrowed, and she focused on taking slow and steady breaths while gritting her teeth through the pain. Her movements were short and choppy, aligning with the ebbs and flows of her energy. She knew she had lost blood and would be in real trouble if she didn't get the bleeding stopped.

But the sirens seemed closer.

She unbuckled her belt and pulled on it to remove it from the loops in her pants, letting her holster fall to the ground next to her.

"Motherfucker!" she moaned in pure agony.

With the belt clear, she placed the buckle on top of the folded shirt and pressed it tightly against her abdomen while she forced herself into a seated position with her other hand. Slumped over, she took two deep breaths in between sharp stabs of pain, then reached back to wrap the belt around her and loop it through the buckle.

Clenching her teeth, she cinched down on the belt hard, sending shards of pain through her entire body. She would've given anything for the Individual First Aid Kit she always carried in her car, but she knew her training was more than sufficient to make do without it. Her temporary bandage wouldn't last, but it was better than nothing.

She forced herself to focus on her training and immediately began assessing herself for the most dangerous life-threatening injuries.

Massive hemorrhage? *Well, the three new holes in my body probably count.* Airway? *I'm breathing. That's a start.*

Respirations? She took several breaths and listened for whistling or bubbling coming from her chest and abdomen that might indicate her lungs were compromised. Nada. *So far, so good. The bullets probably hadn't gone too deep.*

Circulation? Aside from the bouts of dizziness and nausea, her heart was still ticking, although it had probably been taxed far more than it ever had before.

Head injury? She reached up and remembered the headbutt to the helmet she had taken just before being shot. It was probably the cause of the wicked headache she had, but other than a small cut and a minor concussion, it wasn't anything to worry about.

Her self-assessment took less than ten seconds, and she was satisfied that she had treated herself as best as she could. All that was left was to wait for the ambulance to reach her.

Punky pushed herself over to one side and brought her knees up underneath her. She fought through the pain to bring one leg up. And then another. With an arm wrapped tightly around her abdomen—pressing hard against her makeshift dressing—she stood and waited for the dizziness to subside before taking a hesitant step toward the road.

She shuffled by the Ducati that looked mostly intact aside from the road rash it sustained during the crash, and she stopped when she realized that her Challenger was gone.

Bastard.

She bent over and lowered her head, hoping to tighten her grip on the consciousness that was slipping through her fingers.

I need to get to the ambulance.

She pulled out her cell phone and saw the words "No Service" in tiny letters at the top of the screen.

Fucking figures.

Punky shoved the phone back in her pocket and turned slowly back to the Ducati. She wasn't an experienced rider by any means and would probably only put the nail in her own coffin by getting on the thing, but she didn't have another choice.

She still needed to get to Jax and warn him about...

Tan Lily.

The thought struck her like a hammer. With her out of the picture, *SUBLIME* would most likely be on his way to the safe house in Valley Center. And nobody knew he was coming. The fear she felt caused adrenaline to surge into her body and gave her a boost of much needed energy. She was still in severe pain and struggled with every step, but a mask of determination fell over her face as she lifted the heavy bike from its side.

Standing next to it, her stomach twisted in knots. But she lifted a leg and swung it over the bike. She struggled to keep it upright as she lowered her chin to her chest and closed her eyes to fight off another wave of vertigo.

"Come on, Punky!" she yelled at herself.

She opened her eyes and checked to see that the key was turned on before pressing the red start button, listening to the Ducati's motor turn over before starting. She reached for the throttle and twisted it several times, hearing the throaty growl of the engine. She put the bike into gear and pulled away from the edge of the road, struggling to keep it upright as she turned back toward the park's entrance.

She worked the throttle in short bursts as vertigo fought to topple her. The bike surged and weaved as she crept closer to the help she desperately needed.

Hold on... Just hold on...

She felt herself slipping and silently chided herself for being weak. Her vision narrowed dangerously, and her hearing became muted. She was focused on the road in front of her, trying desperately to make it to the next reflective marker, the next crack in the road, the next anything that would get her closer to the ambulance.

Slowly, the road began to tilt. At first it was subtle, and she shifted her weight to counter it. She could hear her heart thumping in her ears and was distracted by the silence in between beats as they lengthened to the point where she thought her heart would simply stop. The road tilted again, and no matter how she shifted her weight, it became impossible to stop.

The soda straw of vision closed in around a road that was tilted almost ninety degrees, and she felt the impact on her hip and shoulder before blacking out.

53

Valley Center, California

Guo Kang leaned back into the bolstered seats, enjoying the Dodge Challenger far more than he thought he would. He had loved riding the Ducati but hadn't thought twice about laying it down to make his escape. That was what set him apart from his adversary. He was decisive in ruthless execution. The American had been weak.

He downshifted using the paddle on the steering wheel and felt himself sink deeper into the seats as the muscle car accelerated almost instantaneously.

Great taste in cars, though.

He accelerated up the switchbacks and, at the crest of the hill, steered the Challenger past the entrance to the fly-in community where the Americans had stashed the doctor and her daughter. To avoid drawing unnecessary attention to himself, he eased off the gas pedal and coasted through the residential area until the trees closed in around him.

He spotted them instantly. Parked along the opposite side of the road was a matte black Ford Raptor truck with two men sitting inside. Even through the tinted windows, he could tell they were parked there to observe traffic passing the gate. When he brought the Challenger to a stop, one of the men lifted a radio to his mouth to report his presence.

Perfect.

He didn't know what kind of protection surrounded Tan Lily, but if he wanted to maintain the element of surprise, he needed the men in the truck to report his arrival. He figured ten minutes was all it would take for word to make it back to the safe house that the NCIS special agent had returned.

Instead of following the road straight through the intersection and continuing east of the private airstrip, he turned right and drove into the hills south of the safe house. Looking at his watch, he started a mental clock.

Margaret stood in the living room and stared at the runway through the floor-to-ceiling window. She was on familiar ground and had Cher by her side, but she grew increasingly nervous as the hours ticked by without hearing from Punky. She had promised to return after neutralizing the threat, and her absence only underscored the danger to the woman under her protection.

"Base, this is Road One, over."

Margaret didn't flinch at the tinny voice coming through the speaker set into the portable radio on the kitchen counter. She turned for the kitchen with the cur at her heels and picked up the handset. "Go for Base."

"Yeah, Margaret, we just had an unidentified vehicle come through the intersection and turn south away from your location, over."

Margaret put her finger on a map stretched out on the counter and noted the location where she had placed her mobile team. "Copy that. License plate?"

"Blue Dodge Challenger..."

She felt herself relax.

"...California plates. Foxtrot India Golf Hotel Tango Oscar November, over."

"Good copy," Margaret said with relief, remembering the NCIS special agent's car. "That's a friendly. You can let her pass. Anything else?"

"Negative," the voice replied.

"Base out." Margaret put the handset down but scrunched up her face. She had been in this business long enough to know when to trust her gut. And right now, her gut was twisted into knots. She picked up her phone and called Jax.

"Everything okay?" he asked.

"Everything is fine," Margaret said, then paused just long enough to let him know something was bothering her. "Have you heard from Punky? Is she on her way back?"

"I haven't heard from her since she left," Jax said. "Why? What's going on?"

Cher inched closer to Margaret and pressed against her legs as if she too could sense looming danger. "Maybe you should call her," the senior agent suggested. "Something doesn't feel right."

"I'm on my way back with the laptop," Jax said.

"That's the key, Jax. Have you looked at it yet?"

"What did you say?"

"I asked if you looked at it yet."

"No, the other thing."

Margaret squinted. "That's the key?"

"*Yaoshi.*"

"Come again?"

"It's the last thing Shen Yu said to Lisa. In Mandarin, it can mean *if*, or it can mean..."

"*Key*," Margaret answered for him.

"We're missing something here. Let me give Punky a call, and I'll get back to you."

A low, ominous growl rumbled from deep within Cher. Margaret looked down at the normally calm cur and saw her hackles raised. "I'm going to harden our position here and fortify the entrance. Make sure you call before you reach the gate."

Jax paused before responding. "What's going on, Margaret?"

"I don't know," she said. "I just have a bad feeling."

"Hang on. I'm on my way."

"Hurry."

Tan Lily rolled to her other side and looked through the window at the hills in the distance. Under normal circumstances, it might have been a view she could have enjoyed while on vacation.

But these were anything but normal circumstances.

Even if she ignored for a moment that she was at a CIA safe house instead of in her lab at UCSD where she was supposed to be, she had too many thoughts running through her head to enjoy something as simple as the Southern California scenery. Chief among them was her husband's involvement with the CIA. Contrary to what she had told Jax and the female NCIS special agent, she had only suspected as much. Learning that he had been spying for the Americans erased any chance she would ever see him again.

What was he thinking?

The knock at her door jolted her from her anxiety-induced introspection, and she craned her neck to see it crack open. The woman who ran the safe house entered with her dog heeling beside her.

"We need to go," Margaret said.

She didn't seem nervous or excited, but Tan Lily could tell by the tone in her voice she was serious. She sat up and turned to the Security Protective Officer, letting her hair fall haphazardly across her shoulders.

"Where?"

Margaret walked across the room and closed the drapes to hide the view outside. "To a safe place," she replied. "We've been compromised."

Tan Lily kicked her feet off the bed and set them onto the scraped hardwood floors, but she felt dizzy as she considered what that meant. *Compromised?*

"I thought this *was* a safe place," she said with obvious frustration.

Margaret shot her a sideways glance, and Tan Lily could tell she wasn't thrilled with the situation either. Their reasons might have been different, but she knew that being openly obstinate wouldn't help her cause.

"I'm sorry," she whispered. Cher walked closer and sniffed her hand.

Margaret nodded in acceptance. "It's okay. You've been through a lot. Do you want to wake Shen Li, or should I?"

Hearing her daughter's name ignited a fire inside her. It was barely a flicker but enough to remind her that the situation was bigger than her and her own desires—there was a seven-year-old little girl sleeping in the bed next to her. She would do what needed to be done, but nothing absolved her from her duties as a mother.

"I'll do it."

Over her shoulder, she heard Margaret speaking into a radio. "Road One, we're preparing to move, over."

Tan Lily ignored the sound of static and gently brushed Shen Li's cheek to wake her. Her daughter's eyelids fluttered as she struggled to release the dreams holding her firmly in place, but Tan Lily persisted and gently whispered in her ear, "Wake up, Shen Li. Wake up, my precious."

Shen Li's eyes struggled to open, still in dreamland and not seeing her mother leaning over her. Tan Lily continued stroking her cheek and whispered softly to her daughter, persistent in pulling her back into the real world.

"Come now, little one," Tan Lily said. "We need to go."

She scooped her daughter off the bed and lifted her in her arms, turning her so that Shen Li's head rested on her shoulder, and her legs wrapped around her waist. She turned and made eye contact with Margaret, who nodded and gestured for her to leave the room.

Two of Margaret's men stood at either end of the hall, wearing body armor and carrying rifles at the low ready. Despite what she had been through and seen in the last day, seeing them armed for war sent a shiver down her spine and filled her with dread for what was to come.

The radio over her shoulder squawked again. "You're clear. Proceed as planned."

"Copy," Margaret replied.

She carried her daughter down the stairs, Shen Li's face nuzzled against her neck as she followed the Security Protective Officer across the living room's hardwood floors to the front door. Margaret paused to peer through the sidelight before opening the door and stepping through. Two pickup trucks idled in the circular drive with their rear doors open.

Tan Lily felt a strong hand rest on her upper back with its fingers wrapped loosely around her neck, applying gentle pressure to guide her to the truck. The grip wasn't oppressive or controlling. It comforted her as she carried her daughter to the Ford Raptor at the rear, placed her daughter on the seat, and climbed in after her. Cher bounded up into the cab and sat on the floorboard at her feet.

The moment she was inside, Shen Li climbed up into her lap and rested her head on her shoulder again. The door behind closed, and she looked up to see Margaret and one of her men climbing into the front seats. She looked through the windshield and saw two others climbing into the truck in front of them.

"Road One, we're on the move," Margaret said into the radio. She put the truck into gear and pulled slowly out of the driveway.

"Copy," came the reply.

The man in the front passenger seat turned to face her. "Ma'am, if things start to get scary, I want you and your daughter to get down onto the floorboard. Do not move until one of us tells you it's safe."

She nodded her assent.

He turned back around and held the short-barreled rifle in his hands as he scanned the landscaping on either side of them. The convoy reached the end of the driveway and turned south toward the air park's main gate. They drove slowly and listened to silence inside the truck and the low rumble of the tuned engine beyond its windows. By the time they reached the gate, she began to relax.

54

Jax ended the call after it went to voicemail for the fourth straight time. He thought it more than odd that Punky wouldn't answer her phone when she knew what was at stake. He downshifted the sport sedan and surged up the hill toward the fly-in community, wondering what was waiting for him when he got there. Margaret's call bothered him. Even more so after being unable to reach the NCIS special agent.

"Dammit!" He knew better than to let his frustration get the better of him, so he drew in one long, deep breath and held it while counting to four. By the time he exhaled, he had decided he wasn't willing to return to the safe house without knowing why she wasn't picking up.

He scooped up his phone and scrolled until he found the number for the NCIS Southwest Field Office. "Jax Woods for Camron Knowles," he said when a receptionist answered the call.

"One moment, please."

His call was placed on hold, and he seethed at the calming elevator music playing in the background as he waited to be connected with Punky's supervisor. The music ended.

"He's in the field," the woman on the other end said. Jax almost blew a gasket. "Transferring you to his cell phone now."

"Thank you," he muttered, then took another calming breath.

The phone rang a few more times before a gruff voice answered, "This is Camron."

"Camron, this is Jax Woods."

"Yeah?"

He could hear something in Camron's voice—*Fear? Anger?*—and he hesitated. "I've been working with Special Agent King on a case," he said.

"Oh..."

The tone in his voice changed again, but Jax couldn't quite pick up on it. "Yes, sir. I've been unable to reach her. And I was hoping—"

"She's been shot, Jax."

His heart rate spiked, and he felt his skin prickle with a dump of adrenaline. "Shot?"

"Her vest took most of the abuse, but there was some penetration. She's going to be fine, but she's banged up pretty bad."

Jax rounded the bend in the road and reached the last switchback before getting to the safe house. He remembered Margaret warning him to call ahead. "Can you pass along a message for me? I recovered Lisa's intelligence, but something is going on up here, and we're increasing the threat level. Have her call me before she drives up—"

"She might not be going anywhere for a while," Camron said. "Whoever shot her stole her car, but we've got an APB out on it and will track it down soon enough."

"Her car?" Jax didn't think an all-points bulletin was needed. He knew who had shot her and stolen her car, and he gasped when he crested the rise onto the straightaway in front of the fly-in community. "Shit!"

"Jax?"

"Send help," he said, then pressed his foot to the floor and launched the Audi S3 straight at the Mopar muscle car.

Guo Kang had a choice to make. Two identical matte black Ford trucks rolled toward the gate from the other side, carrying the doctor and her daughter. He didn't know where they were going and knew if he let them leave, he would no longer be able to control the situation. But if he forced the issue there at the gate, he would be outgunned and lose the engagement.

It's now or never.

He unrolled the driver's window, then quickly drew his pistol and leaned out to aim slightly above the lead truck's headlights, targeting where he expected the driver. The gun barked when he squeezed the trigger, then he shifted aim to the passenger side and fired twice more. The lead truck skidded to a halt, and he shifted his aim back toward the driver's side and emptied his magazine.

The truck's doors opened and emptied operators on either side before the air over his head crackled with returning gunfire. He dropped the empty magazine and reached for a fresh one when movement out of the corner of his eye drew his attention to the left and down the road toward the interstate. He almost choked when he recognized the nose of a car pointed directly at him and accelerating rapidly.

He stomped on the gas, trying to lurch clear of the kamikaze attack, but he was a beat too late. The Audi sport sedan slammed into his left quarter panel and spun the Challenger almost one hundred and eighty degrees. The air bags deployed, and his head rang with the impact and sound of shattered glass and splintered carbon fiber, but he quickly shook himself free from his paralysis.

He yanked on the door handle and threw his shoulder into it, spilling out of the driver's seat just as several rounds from the shooters in the pickup trucks plinked into the Challenger. He fell to the ground and rolled onto his back, spreading his legs wide and rising in a half crunch to aim his pistol toward the airfield where the rifle rounds were coming from. He sighted in on the passenger from the lead truck and squeezed the trigger.

Click.

In the chaos of the crash, he had forgotten to reload. He flopped back to the ground, found his spare magazine, then slipped it into the magazine well and released the slide to chamber a round. He craned his neck up and spotted a man racing toward the fence while firing his suppressed rifle at the Challenger.

The concrete on either side of Guo Kang splintered and flew into the air with the impact of dozens of high-velocity rounds. He squeezed off two more shots without taking aim, then rolled to his stomach and aimed at the Audi S3's crumpled nose where he expected the driver to emerge. But the driver's door was still closed.

He didn't waste time savoring his small victory of stopping Tan Lily from leaving the compound. He was pinned down by an adversary with superior firepower, and he ignored the rounds impacting around him to push himself upright and improve his fighting position.

Move!

Like a sprinter, he launched himself across the driveway to the low fence on the other side. He had taken fewer than ten steps when a red-hot hammer slammed into his upper back and pitched him forward. The impact jarred the pistol from his grip, and it skidded across the asphalt as he struggled to take a breath, wincing from the bullet lodged in his upper back to the right of his spine.

Get up, dammit!

Guo Kang pushed himself up, hobbled two steps to retrieve his fallen gun, then stumbled into the bushes on the other side. If he could get out of sight, he might have a chance of surviving the day.

And reaching Tan Lily.

Tan Lily's body shook as she stretched it to cover as much of Shen Li as possible. Her daughter trembled but remained quiet, crying silently as the truck reversed away from the gate. She had her arm around Shen Li's head and stroked her silky hair in between kisses and whispered words of comfort. But she knew it was her fault her daughter was in danger.

The truck's tires squealed, and her body flung sideways as Margaret quickly spun them around, then accelerated back toward the house. Tan Lily remained on the floorboard, her tensed body sheltering her shaking daughter while listening to the sound of gunfire retreating behind them.

"Mama?" Shen Li whispered in a muffled voice.

Tan Lily kissed her hair. "Yes, my precious?"

"Are we going to die?"

She opened her mouth to reply but couldn't find the words. When she had agreed to take Shen Li to the United States, she never expected she would have had to answer such a question. Yet here she was, lying on the floorboard of a pickup truck, preparing to sacrifice her body to keep her daughter safe from stray bullets.

She swallowed hard. "No, my precious. We're not going to die."

She sounded more confident than she felt, but she knew the time had come. She could no longer cower in the back of a pickup truck and wait for others to decide her fate. She needed to take matters into her own hands and get them out of this mess. There was no reason the sins of the mother needed to fall to the daughter.

She felt the truck fishtail as Margaret steered them off the street onto the long driveway and heard small rocks bouncing against the undercarriage. When they came to a skidding halt, Margaret put the truck in park and jumped out. Tan Lily kept her head down and kissed her daughter's hair, trying to comfort her even while her own heart and mind raced with fear. The back door opened, and she turned to see Margaret's outstretched hand.

"Come," she said. "We need to get you inside."

Tan Lily lifted herself off her daughter and pushed Shen Li to the open door. The little girl moved without hesitation and wrapped her arms around Margaret's neck and clung to her chest. Tan Lily followed Cher from the truck and hurried to keep up with the CIA Security Protective Officer carrying her daughter to the house.

They scampered inside and raced for the stairs. Margaret bounded up the steps with Shen Li in her arms, and Tan Lily followed barely two paces behind with the cur hot on her heels.

"What's going on?" Tan Lily asked.

When they reached the room at the end of the hall, Margaret lowered Shen Li onto the bed and pressed a soft hand onto her shoulder. "Do you mind if Cher stays with you?"

The fear etched on Shen Li's face eased, and she smiled at the dog who scampered close and kissed her cheek. She giggled softly and wrapped her arms around the dog's neck. "Can she, Mama?"

Tan Lily looked up at Margaret and saw the older woman nod, then forced a smile for her daughter. "Of course, my precious."

She leaned over and kissed her daughter gently on the forehead before turning for the door. She felt light-headed as she followed Margaret into the hall and closed the door behind them.

55

Rancho Bernardo, California

Punky winced when the medic removed the last piece of metal from her abdomen where the bullet had managed to penetrate her body armor. She knew she would have been dead without the vest, but it pained her to admit that Camron had been right in insisting she wear it. She looked up at her supervisor, who grimaced and put his cell phone away.

"Bad news?" she asked.

Camron pinched his eyes in thought, but he nodded. "That was Jax."

She shoved the medic away and sat up. "Jax? What's going on?"

"He said they're increasing the threat level and..."

Punky jumped up from the gurney and gritted her teeth against the pain and sudden bout of vertigo. Camron held up a hand to stop her, but she shoved him aside. "Let's go."

He shook his head. "You need to go to—"

But she wasn't listening to him. She jumped from the back of the ambulance, spotted his black government Chevrolet Tahoe with dark-tinted windows, and made a beeline for the driver's door. His heavy footfalls chasing after her were all the evidence she needed to know he wasn't about to let her run off on her own again.

"I'll drive," he said.

She opened the driver's door and climbed in behind the wheel. "The hell you will. I've seen you drive, and we don't have time for that."

Camron looked like he was going to argue with her, but he relented and jogged around the nose of the SUV and climbed inside next to her. Punky had the Tahoe in gear and her foot to the floor before he had even buckled himself in. "Whoa, Punky! We want to get there alive."

But she ignored him. She still felt light-headed and sluggish, but the idea of letting the Chinese assassin who had shot her get to Tan Lily and her daughter was all the motivation she needed. She had let her guard down once before and took three gunshots to the chest for it. It wouldn't happen again.

She raced the Tahoe through the community center, then skidded around the corner at the intersection onto West Bernardo Drive. She held the SUV's plastic steering wheel in a white-knuckled grip, longing for her Challenger's Alcantara-wrapped steering wheel—and its almost endless supply of horsepower.

"You need a new car," she muttered, guiding them across the overpass and onto the interstate headed north.

"I'd like to live long enough to drive one," he said, clutching the grab bar on the A-pillar while flinching as she weaved them through traffic at over one hundred miles per hour.

Punky's eyes darted across the freeway several car lengths ahead, projecting their path as they raced into danger. With one hand on the wheel, she fished her cell phone from her pocket to call Jax. She needed to find out what was waiting for them when they got there.

Valley Center, California

Jax opened his eyes and saw steam rising from his car's crushed nose, but the ringing in his ears was the only thing he could hear. He leaned back into the seat and winced at the throbbing in his skull, then tentatively brought a hand up to his forehead to feel a large knot growing where it had impacted the steering wheel. Even cushioned by the air bag, he felt far worse than he had expected.

That was stupid, he thought, remembering with sudden clarity how he had turned his compact German sedan into a missile and aimed it at the assassin in Punky's stolen car.

Assassin.

The thought was enough to erase the cobwebs that kept him fixed in place, and he scrambled to free himself from the seat belt keeping him immobile. He needed to get back to Tan Lily before it was too late.

It took some doing, but Jax managed to release the buckle and pry the door open. He pulled himself free from the wrecked car and stumbled out onto the driveway, scanning the carnage around him with an odd sense of detachment. The Dodge Challenger had damage to its driver's-side rear quarter panel and was spun around with its nose pointed away from the safe house. The driver's door was open, but the front seat was empty.

Filtered sunlight glinted off spent brass casings littering the ground, and he spun to look through the gate at where a Ford Raptor pickup truck sat idle with its doors open.

What the hell happened?

Jax reached back for the comforting feel of his Glock 9mm pistol but stopped when he felt his phone vibrating in his pocket. Still scanning the entrance and the surrounding grounds for any sign of the assassin, he pulled his phone from his pocket and answered without looking at it. "Yeah?"

"Jax!"

"Punky?"

"What the hell is going on?"

As if that simple question had suddenly brought everything into focus, he jumped into action. He ran past the bright blue muscle car and entered the gate code into the control panel and listened to the electric motor whine as the gate swung open. "The key," Jax said.

"What?"

Jax didn't wait for the gate to swing open fully and wedged through, then ran for the idling pickup truck. He didn't know where its occupants had run off to, but he only needed to get back to Margaret and the safe house before it was too late.

"He said she's the key. Hurry."

Tan Lily followed Margaret down the hall while contemplating her options. She knew Shen Li was tucked away in a bedroom with Cher and would be safe, but she wasn't willing to sit around and do nothing while things spiraled out of control.

"Base, Road One," a breathless voice said over the walkie-talkie in Margaret's hand.

The older woman brought it to her mouth and pressed the push-to-talk. "Go ahead."

"Target has moved into the woods west of the property. There's no sign of him, but we are pursuing on foot."

Margaret stopped in front of a door at the end of the hall and entered a code into the keypad set into the wall. The light turned green, and the door unlocked with an audible *click*. "Base copies," Margaret said, turning the knob to open the door into a darkened room. "Break. Road Two, come in."

Another voice answered. "Road Two."

"Move into the woods and set up a blocking position. Cher and I will protect the principal in the safe room."

Tan Lily felt her face flush at the comment. "Just you and Cher?"

Margaret reached inside and flipped a switch to turn on a set of overhead lights, illuminating what looked to be an armory with all manner of pistols, submachine guns, shotguns, knives, and cases of ammunition.

"Road Two," the voice replied.

Tan Lily heard the front door open and close beneath them as the only other person protecting the house left to pursue the unseen threat outside. Her heart raced when she realized that she and Shen Li were alone in the house with only Margaret and her dog.

But Margaret ignored her question and walked to the far wall to retrieve a short-barreled bullpup pump action shotgun from where it was mounted. Tan Lily followed closely behind, scanning the room for a weapon she might be able to arm herself with. Her eyes settled on a folding knife resting on the table in the center of the room, and she scooped it up without a second thought.

While Margaret opened the breech and began feeding 12-gauge shells into the shotgun, Tan Lily watched her closely while her thumb stroked the stud along the blade's handle. She had hoped it wouldn't have to come to this, but she knew she couldn't afford to squander the opportunity the Security Protective Officer had given her by sending the other man out into the woods.

Her thumb pressed on the stud, and the blade sprang open with a *click*.

Margaret slid another shell into the breech, then paused. She turned and locked eyes with Tan Lily, then glanced down at the knife in her hand. "What are you doing?"

Without a second thought, the operative known as *SUBLIME* shoved the knife up under Margaret's rib cage and pierced her liver before quickly pulling it out and stabbing straight into her neck to the side of the larynx. Margaret's eyes grew wide, and her fingers released the shotgun as Tan Lily yanked the blade sideways and severed the older woman's carotid artery and jugular vein.

Blood showered Tan Lily, but she only gave a subtle shake of her head as she watched the woman crumple to the ground at her feet. All she needed to do now was get Shen Li and escape before the Americans figured out that the man in the woods wasn't there to kill her.

He was there to rescue her.

56

Guo Kang stumbled and fell forward into a thicket of ferns, struggling to take a breath as he fought through the dense vegetation west of the safe house. He knew he wouldn't likely survive the ordeal. He could hear men behind him, pursuing him away from the front gate and deeper into the woods. They would harry him until he had no more energy left, and then they would kill him.

"This can't be happening," he muttered.

He was one of the Ministry's most skilled operatives, and the General had only tasked him with retrieving the doctor and bringing her in so she could activate the weapon aboard the USS *Ronald Reagan*. It should have been simple. But, for some reason, the Americans got to her first.

He pushed himself up and propelled himself onward. He had accepted his fate, but he wasn't about to quit without sacrificing himself for the operation. If he could get *SUBLIME* away from the Americans, then maybe she could still complete her mission. He wouldn't be around to receive accolades for his role in the reunification of Taipei, but his legacy would be cemented in the annals of history.

There, in the hills north of San Diego, he would sacrifice his life for the future of his people.

Guo Kang stumbled again and fell to his knees. He coughed and spat thick blood onto the dirt underneath him, fearing that he was in worse shape than he first suspected. He took a labored breath and heard a rattle from his chest, recognizing the symptoms of his lungs filling with blood. He tilted his head up and spied the safe house through the trees only two hundred yards away.

I won't make it.

He growled at the coward inside him and lunged upward once more. He refused to accept defeat and would use every last ounce of energy to reach *SUBLIME*. But to be safe, he needed to alert the General. If they stopped him before he could free her, he needed the General to know before he committed their forces to the invasion.

While struggling to put one foot in front of the other, he reached into his pocket and pulled out his cell phone. Forsaking standard protocols in favor of expediency, Guo Kang dialed the General's number through the Signal app and hoped their leader answered the call.

"What is it?" the General asked when the call connected.

"I am..." Guo Kang coughed, and his mouth filled with blood. He spat it onto the ground before continuing. "I am finished."

"Is she safe?"

The rattling in his chest was getting worse, and his odds of surviving were dropping with each step. But still he moved forward. *Never retreat. Only attack.*

"Not...yet," Guo Kang said.

"Are you hurt?"

He hated to admit it. In all his years as a commando in the People's Liberation Army and paramilitary operator for the Ministry of State Security, Guo Kang had never been wounded. He had never been bested on the field of battle, and he felt shame that it had happened in what was to have been his defining moment in service to the State.

"Yes," he said. "I've been shot."

He coughed again. More blood. His vision blurred, and he felt the world tilting around him as he struggled to remain conscious.

The General sighed on the other end. "Pull back," he said. "We will get to her another way."

"But..."

A searing pain erupted between his shoulder blades as a force slammed into him and toppled him forward. He barely had time to register the echoing sound of a gunshot behind him before he fell face first onto the ground. The impact knocked the wind out of him, and the rattling in his chest grew louder as blood poured from his mouth. He opened his mouth to warn the General, but nothing came out.

"Guo Kang," he heard the distant voice cry out. He spotted his cell phone on the ground three feet away, but he knew it was too far. He knew he wouldn't be able to sanitize it before his pursuers were on him, so he focused on staying awake long enough to make his last stand.

"Federal agent!" another voice called out.

Guo Kang lifted his pistol and pointed it behind him without looking. He squeezed the trigger and felt the gun recoil with each shot, but he didn't know if any had found their mark. He only knew that he would die as a warrior, with a gun in his hand.

Another round slammed into him, and his body twitched with the impact.

Guo Kang suddenly felt nothing at all.

Tan Lily opened the door and saw Shen Li clutching Cher tightly around her neck. The cur stood erect, blocking the little girl with her body as she watched the door open.

"Mama? What's happening?" Shen Li asked.

She crossed the room quickly, barely registering that the dog bristled as she neared and emitted a low rumble from deep within her chest. Then, she saw her daughter's eyes grow wide with shock, and she realized she was covered in Margaret's blood.

"We need to go," she whispered. Cher growled when she reached for her daughter's hand, and she stopped short.

"Mama, you're bleeding."

Tan Lily wiped a hand down her face, smearing the older woman's blood. As if the cur could smell her master in the metallic scent, Cher growled louder and barked at the doctor. But Tan Lily had heard the gunshots too. She knew that meant whoever the General had sent to rescue her had either been stopped or had bested the Americans. Either way, she was running out of time.

With a flick of her wrist, she drew the knife and slashed at the dog as the blade sprang open. She felt the sharp edge slice through the dog's skin, and Cher yelped in pain as she recoiled from the strike. Tan Lily took the opportunity and snatched Shen Li's wrist and yanked her off the bed.

"You hurt Cher!" the little girl shrieked.

But Tan Lily wasn't listening. For the moment, the loving mother and dedicated professor was gone. She was SUBLIME, the skilled intelligence operative and dedicated servant to the State. The only thing that mattered now was getting out from under the Americans' thumb and to a Ministry safe house, where she could activate the weapon.

Towing her daughter behind her, Tan Lily fled from the room as Cher alternated between whimpering and barking at the fleeing woman. Unfortunately, she hadn't hit any vital areas, and she needed to get out of the house before the dog finished licking her wounds and pursued her attacker.

"You're hurting me," Shen Li yelled, twisting and pulling to free her arm from her mother's grip.

"Stop it!" Tan Lily yelled. "We're leaving."

"No!"

She suddenly stopped and turned to strike her daughter across the mouth with the back of her free hand. She had never hit her daughter before, and she saw the immediate look of hurt and betrayal cross her little girl's face. Part of her regretted it, but the larger part knew it was for a greater cause. If she escaped and was able to complete her mission, the rogue island of Taipei would once again fall under China's protective arm.

"Stop fighting me, Shen Li," she said in an angry snarl. "We are leaving. Now."

A bright red mark rose angrily from the girl's cheek where her mother had struck her, but Shen Li bit her tongue and remained silent. Tan Lily knew her daughter didn't understand what was going on, and she would have to work to repair the damage she had caused. But it couldn't be helped. She needed to get them out before she could return to being the mother she had once been.

She turned back for the stairs, quickly bypassing the room where Margaret's body cooled in a pool of her own blood, and started down the steps two at a time. Shen Li lost her balance and fell, but Tan Lily held her upright and continued pulling her toward their freedom beyond the front door. "Mama...you're hurting..."

Before she could finish her thought, the front door burst open and Jax stumbled into the room with his gun drawn. He saw Tan Lily covered in blood, clutching her daughter's arm, and he quickly spun away to look for the threat. "Where is he? Where's Margaret?"

Jax took two more steps into the room and gestured for Tan Lily to move behind him. He incorrectly assumed the woman under his care was in danger. It was an assumption that would be his downfall.

Tan Lily quickly stepped behind Jax, then flung her daughter to the side. She grabbed a fistful of his hair and jerked his head back, then raised the knife and sliced it across the front of his neck. His skin split open and showered the air in crimson, but she didn't stop. She withdrew the blade and quickly stabbed upward into his lower back. Then she pulled it out and stabbed him again. And again.

He struggled against her and threw his weight back to knock her off-balance, but she clung to his hair and pulled him down on top of her. The impact knocked the wind out of her, but she was filled with a rage that couldn't be tamped. She shifted her grip on the blade and brought it around his body, pulling it into his abdomen with reckless abandon. Finally, his hand clamped down on her wrist and stopped her from removing the blade from his stomach. He coughed blood, but his grip was strong, and his body weighed heavily on her as she struggled to breathe.

Somewhere in the background, she heard her daughter screaming in terror. She heard a woman shouting in the distance. And she heard a dog snarling with unbridled anger.

57

Punky had crashed through the gate when she saw what remained of her car and Jax's Audi S3. They were both empty, which meant that Jax was probably in pursuit of the man who had shot her. But it also meant that Tan Lily was probably in the safe house protected only by Margaret and her dog.

To his credit, Camron hadn't said a word as the gate flew off its hinges and she pressed harder on the gas pedal to race down the narrow street toward the house. She had almost missed the turn and her tires dropped off the edge of the driveway into the grass, but she pushed onward to the front of the house.

She slammed on the brakes behind an empty Ford Raptor pickup truck and jumped from the Tahoe with Camron only half a step behind. She ached and felt light-headed, but the sudden scream of a little girl pierced through her fatigue and spurred her onward at a sprint.

"Punky, wait!" Camron yelled.

She ignored him. "Shen Li! I'm coming!"

All that mattered was getting inside and getting the little girl and her mother to safety. She reached the front steps and took them two at a time, launching herself up into the open front door. What waited beyond the threshold stunned her, and she froze with her gun in one hand and took in the scene.

Shen Li cowered against the wall at the foot of the stairs, screaming at the chaos unfolding in front of her. A bloody Tan Lily held a knife in one hand and shoved an unconscious Jax off her with the other. And Cher, Margaret's trusty Black Mouth Cur, raced down the stairs like a fur missile homed in on the woman she had come to rescue.

Without thinking, Punky lifted her gun and aimed at the dog but hesitated in pulling the trigger.

What's going on?

She looked at Jax and saw his gun drawn and the bright red gash across his throat where it had been slit open. She saw Cher's powerful mouth clamp down on Tan Lily's forearm and whip her head from side to side, ripping and tearing at the doctor's flesh as the knife fell from her grasp and clattered to the floor. She saw the little girl again, still screaming, and she lowered her gun and quickly scooped Shen Li up in her arms.

The girl flailed against her, but Punky only cared to get her away. The last thing Shen Li needed to see was a dog tearing her mother to pieces. She pressed Shen Li's head to her chest and spun for the door, brushing past Camron, who also had his gun drawn but stood motionless just outside the door.

"I've got you," Punky whispered.

A few minutes later, Camron came outside and walked over to where Punky had placed Shen Li in the back seat of the Tahoe. Flashing police lights reflected off the house and surrounding trees as the safe house was descended upon by a horde of local law enforcement officers who were responding to multiple reports of gunshots and a vehicular accident at the neighborhood's main gate.

"What a mess," he said.

Punky turned away from where Shen Li sat crying softly with a blanket wrapped around her and looked at her supervisor. The shock on his face said it all. "What's it like in there?"

He turned and looked at the handful of uniformed police officers who were questioning the Agency security personnel who had emerged from the woods west of the house not long after they arrived. What had started out as a tense standoff with the armed men as immediate suspects became a sharing of information between professionals who only wanted to understand what had taken place.

"The older woman—Margaret, you said—is dead. Her body is in the armory, the victim of multiple stab wounds." Camron's face paled as he struggled to compose himself. "I'm no expert with knives, but it looked like whoever killed her knew what they were doing."

The image of Tan Lily with the knife in her hand immediately flashed in Punky's mind.

"Jax is dead too," he added. "It doesn't make sense, but it looks like the doctor is the one who killed him."

She nodded. "Yeah, it does."

"What do you mean?"

Punky closed the door and sealed Shen Li inside, then took Camron by the arm and stepped away from the SUV and out of earshot. "I had it all wrong, Camron. I thought *SUBLIME* was the code name for a person who was after Tan Lily."

He squinted at her. "Who was after her, then?"

"That's the wrong question," she said, suddenly realizing just how foolish she had been.

"What's the right question?"

"Who was *SUBLIME*?"

A commotion near the front door caused them both to turn and see Tan Lily being escorted in handcuffs from the house by a pair of uniformed officers. "She was."

They both fell silent and watched the officers lead Tan Lily to a police cruiser parked in the driveway. It made sense now, though Punky still struggled to believe the enemy had been hiding right underneath her nose the whole time.

"So, who was the man who shot you?" Camron finally asked.

Punky shrugged. "I don't know, but I believe he was sent to make sure

Tan Lily activated the synthetic bioweapon. He wasn't sent to kill her. He was sent to rescue her."

The soft plodding of feet pulled her back from her brooding, and she looked down to see Cher limp next to her and press her bandaged body against her leg. Both ears drooped, and her tail hung in a characteristic display of sadness, but Punky reached down and scratched the top of the dog's head. She knew Cher had lost Margaret and knew she needed someone to shower her with love.

Punky squatted down to eye level with the dog. "You're a good girl, Cher. You made her proud."

The dog didn't lick her face or give any outward sign that she appreciated the praise, but Punky didn't mind. She knew it would take some time to heal from her wounds—both physical and emotional. As she stared into the dog's eyes, Punky suddenly had an idea.

She stood and walked to the Tahoe, then opened the back door where Shen Li sat curled up with her blanket. One of Cher's ears stood tall, and her tail started wagging when she recognized the little girl in the back seat. "Go on, Cher."

The cur needed no encouragement. She bounded up into the back seat and curled into a ball next to the little girl and rested her head in her lap. Shen Li bent over and gave Cher a hug, and Punky watched the two wounded children take comfort in each other.

"What about the bioweapon?" Camron asked.

Punky shook her head. Everything she had learned about synthetic bioweapons she had learned from the woman she now believed was a Chinese operative. If the USS *Ronald Reagan* really had been attacked with a bioweapon, the one person who she thought would be able to turn it off was probably the one person who could make it worse. "I don't know. Jax told me that the CIA believed Lisa Mourning had recovered intelligence that was vital to stopping the attack—"

"Did you say Lisa?"

Punky nodded. "She was the operations officer who went missing in Shanghai and—"

Camron interrupted her again. "Jax said something about recovering her intelligence."

She turned and looked up at him. "What? When?"

"After you were shot. He called and told me to deliver a message to you, but at the time I was more focused on the threat to Tan Lily and forgot he said he had recovered Lisa's intelligence."

They stared at each other for several minutes while puzzling over their next moves, then both seemed to come to the same conclusion. "It's in his car," Punky said.

Camron nodded. "I'll drive."

Punky closed the door with Shen Li and Cher still huddled together inside and climbed into the front passenger seat while Camron jogged around the front to the driver's side. If they were right, then maybe they could stop the bioweapon and save the lives of thousands of people on the *Reagan* and ten times that many on the island of Taiwan. Maybe the loss of Margaret and Jax wouldn't be in vain.

58

Andy sat up in bed and glanced at the vitals monitor beeping next to him. He still didn't understand the difference between systolic and diastolic, but over the last several hours, he had seen the numbers increase to what the corpsman told him was within a normal, healthy range.

"How are you feeling?" Doc asked when she walked into the room.

"Much better," he said. It was true. Compared to how he had felt since waking up with a debilitating headache and agonizing stomach cramps, his only real complaint was the restlessness he was beginning to feel cooped up in the hospital bed. "What did you give me?"

"Theophylline," she said.

He gave her a little shake of his head. "What?"

"It's a drug that's normally used for the treatment of chronic obstructive pulmonary disease."

Andy felt even more confused. "Isn't that something smokers get?"

Doc grinned and nodded. "It's also used to treat asthma, but that's not why we gave it to you."

Maybe he wasn't feeling that good after all. His brain hurt with trying to noodle the rationale for the ship's medical staff beginning intravenous injection of a drug he'd never heard of that was used to treat conditions he'd never had. He closed his eyes and leaned back into the inclined bed. "This is too much for me, Doc."

She rested a hand on his shoulder. "The reason we gave it to you—and everyone else on the ship—is because it was identified as the chemical switch that neutralized the effects of the bioweapon."

His eyes shot open. "Bioweapon?"

She nodded. "We learned that the *Reagan* was the target of a synthetic bioweapon attack and that the pathogen had been engineered with two switches—one that would make it more lethal, and one that effectively turned it off."

"How did you..."

"Don't ask, because they didn't tell me. All I can say is that theophylline was identified as the switch to turn it off, which is fortunate, because it is easily synthesized. When caffeine is metabolized in the liver, it is actually broken down into three metabolic dimethylxanthines—"

"I'm not really that interested, Doc."

She pursed her lips. "Fine. Let's just say we're lucky the solution was something so simple. With the pathogen rendered safe, you should be back to normal and can return to flight status in the next twenty-four hours."

It was the first bit of good news he had received since he had flown out to the ship from Iwakuni. Even though the last several days had been a blur, he already couldn't wait to strap into the pilot's seat of a C-2 Greyhound and launch off the pointy end of the ship and return to shore. Tom had told him that their skipper back in San Diego had called Jenn to tell her he had been infected, and he knew he had some work to do to put her mind at ease.

"Thanks, Doc."

"Sure thing," she said. "Just rest up."

Lieutenant Sierra "Doc" Crowe left Sickbay feeling like the deployment had turned a corner. What had started out as a months-long effort to go for as many back seat rides as possible quickly turned into a fight to save the ship from a mysterious illness. It had sapped her of her energy, especially when the other doctors and corpsmen also became sick, but she had taken some solace in knowing that her quick thinking had slowed the bioweapon long enough to find a solution.

"Salt tabs," she muttered, shaking her head.

Of all the things they could have done to respond to the rapidly spreading virus, it was her decision to begin administering doses of sodium chloride that had the greatest effect. Maybe it was seeing Andy thrashing in the bed from a seizure, but she was unwilling to allow her other patients to burn up until they suffered the same.

"Lieutenant Crowe," a voice called out.

Doc stopped and turned to see First Class Hospital Corpsman Diona Browne walking through the passageway from the enlisted mess. Doc had taken it particularly hard when Diona had fallen ill, and it brought a smile to her face to see the corpsman mobile again. "You're looking better."

"I feel better," she replied. "Just thankful it didn't get much worse."

"Me too."

"I heard they're going to start flight operations again."

She had heard the same thing and was just on her way to make her rounds between the squadrons and see about penciling herself in for a back seat ride or two. She was about to tell Diona as much when she noticed the mischievous look on the corpsman's face. "You know me too well," she said.

Diona grinned. "Enjoy your flight, ma'am. You've earned it."

An hour later, Doc glanced over the Super Hornet on the catapult next to them and watched as the yellow shirt gave the pilot the signal to take tension. The jet's nose squatted as the catapult shuttle tugged on the launch bar, and the pilot advanced his throttles to military thrust. The yellow shirt handed the jet off to the shooter sitting in the bubble between the two catapults, and she watched as the other jet's control surfaces moved in a flurry of activity. The pilot turned to look at the bubble and saluted the shooter hidden behind the thick green glass.

Within seconds, the catapult fired and pulled the Super Hornet from a dead stop to flying. The pilot immediately dipped his right wing in a jink to starboard while raising his gear and flaps. Doc took several deep breaths to prepare herself for their own launch that was to follow.

"Are you ready?" Colt Bancroft asked her over the intercom.

"All set," she replied, though the last time they had flown together, he had brought them back to the ship single engine. Not to mention the fact that he had just returned to the ship after ejecting from a jet he had allegedly depleted of gas.

As steam rose from the catapult track next to them, the yellow shirt turned toward their jet and prepared them to join the others in the sky above the *Reagan*. The yellow shirt again directed Colt to lower his launch bar and align it with the catapult shuttle, then had him add power as the sailors underneath attached a holdback bar to the nose gear. The reusable holdback bar involved collets and hydraulic fluid in a system that was a complete mystery to her. All she knew was that by design, it held the jet in place at full power but released it from bondage once the steam-powered shuttle began hurtling it down the flight deck.

That's when the fun began.

With the holdback bar in place and the launch bar lowered into the shuttle, Colt waited for the signal to take tension. Doc saw the yellow shirt hold two fists up on either side of him with bent elbows, then rotate his torso left and right before extending one arm up and one out toward the bow of the ship.

Here it comes, she thought.

When the yellow shirt raised his hand above his head and waggled his index and middle fingers, Colt pushed the throttles to the stops, and she felt their nose dip as the shuttle pulled the launch bar forward in preparation. Colt worked the control stick in a box pattern, then reached down for the launch bar switch before pressing on each rudder pedal. Even though Doc had never manipulated a single switch or control in the cockpit, she had flown enough in the back seat that she knew exactly what her pilot was doing.

Hand salute.

Colt saluted the shooter in the bubble, and Doc braced herself against the grab handle and waited for the catapult to fire.

Within seconds, she felt herself pushed back into the ejection seat as the Super Hornet raced toward the bow, and the deep blue water of the Pacific Ocean replaced the man-made world of haze-gray painted steel.

59

San Diego International Airport
San Diego, California
One month later

Punky sat behind the wheel of a boring government sedan and inched the car forward along the curb. She saw a police officer approaching to shoo them away, but she flashed her credentials and dissuaded him from bothering them. She glanced in the rearview mirror and grinned when she saw the nervous look on Jenn's face.

"Is this what you expected?"

Jenn turned from the window and made eye contact. "Not at all."

Punky had experienced her share of homecomings when her dad returned from deployments, but this one was unlike most. There wasn't a sea of people with mothers and fathers, husbands and wives, or children of all ages waiting patiently for their sailors to step ashore. There weren't women in beautiful dresses that conveyed either a sense of patriotic pride or a strong sexual desire. This one was a private affair for two people who had been through more than most.

Punky saw her reach down and rub her growing belly. "You look beautiful," she said.

Jenn glanced at her again and smiled. She wore a bright yellow form-fitting dress that ended just below her knees. Her red patent leather high heels were hidden from the California sun but matched her lipstick perfectly. Punky doubted they were the best shoes for a pregnant woman, but who was she to question what a woman waiting for her sailor chose to wear.

"Thank you," she said.

Punky grinned and nodded. "Andy's a lucky man."

In more ways than one, she thought.

If not for the intelligence Jenn had kept safe on her computer, the slow-burning virus that had spread across the USS *Ronald Reagan* might have succeeded in sidelining it during a Chinese invasion of Taiwan. If not for Andy getting sick early on, the carrier CO might not have ordered a quarantine that alerted Punky to the attack. There were so many what-ifs that kept her from simply enjoying the fact that the good guys had won—that freedom had again triumphed.

Punky glanced at her watch and mentally calculated how much longer they needed to wait. Andy's plane had touched down ten minutes earlier, and she suspected the C-2 pilot was just as eager to see his girlfriend as she was to see him. She glanced in the mirror and grinned when she saw Jenn nervously biting her lip.

"He'll be here soon," she said.

Jenn let out a little gasp, then the door flew open, and she jumped out in a hurricane of yellow. Punky craned her neck and watched the flight attendant weaving through a throng of deplaning passengers, homing in on her boyfriend like a heat-seeking missile. She saw Andy drop his olive drab seabag and lift his girlfriend into the air, kissing her and spinning her around with a look full of love in his eyes.

Her phone rang, and Punky answered it while watching Andy kneel to place his mouth on Jenn's growing belly. "Special Agent King," she said.

Jenn brought a hand to her mouth as if to stifle a cry that had been bottled inside, and Punky almost ignored the voice on the other end as she remembered what it had felt like to be reunited with a loved one. "Punky, it's Camron."

"What's going on, Camron?"

"There's something you should know."

The overwhelming sense of happiness that had consumed her suddenly vanished. "What?"

"A woman has come forward claiming to be Shen Li's grandmother."

"Her what?"

She felt her heart sink as she thought of the frightened little girl who had buried her head in her chest as a guard dog snarled and tore into her mother. She couldn't imagine what Shen Li was feeling without either of her parents—one who had died to prevent an attack engineered by the other.

"Her grandmother," Camron repeated.

"That's bullshit, Camron."

"I know it is," he said. "But the State Department received a formal request from the People's Republic of China to assist in reuniting the orphaned girl with family."

"Camron..."

"Which is why I'm calling you," he said. "If there is anybody who can sniff out the truth, it's you. If Tan Lily really is a Ministry of State Security operative, then there's a good chance the woman claiming to be Shen Li's grandmother is somehow connected to their network here."

"Where does she live?" Punky asked, feeling the familiar stir of excitement of a new investigation.

"In the Bay Area. The Willow Glen neighborhood of San Jose."

Punky turned and looked through the window to see Andy leading Jenn to the car. If she drove them to Jenn's place in Escondido and continued north, she could be in San Jose before dark. "I'll look into it," she said. "Send me an address."

Camron ended the call, and Punky turned as Andy opened the rear door.

"Welcome home, sailor."

60

San Jose, California

Punky sat behind the wheel of the borrowed Ford Fusion, lamenting the loss of not one but two marvels of automobile craftsmanship. First, her father's vintage Corvette Stingray had been destroyed in a crash while fleeing armed gunmen taking orders from China's Ministry of State Security. Then, her replacement—a brand-new Dodge Challenger Hellcat Redeye—had been destroyed when a Ministry assassin stole it after shooting her at point-blank range.

I need to find a new job.

She yawned and forced herself to stare at the screen broadcasting images of the mid-century house, one block over and adjacent to the neighborhood park. There hadn't been much activity since she'd arrived, and she was beginning to think it was a waste of her time driving all the way from San Diego with such little information.

But she had done a lot more with a lot less before. Sometimes a hunch was all it took.

Her cell phone rang, and she reached for the steering wheel to answer it when she remembered the government sedan didn't have the same bells and whistles as her damaged Challenger. Swallowing back a curse, she plucked the phone from her pocket and answered.

"Yeah?"

"How's it going up there?" Camron asked.

"It's not," she replied, then lifted her wrist to look at the time. "I've installed two pole-cameras, but I don't know how much longer I can sit here and observe the mundane goings-on of normal life in suburbia."

Her supervisor sighed, and she could tell he was working up to something. But before he got the chance, a pair of headlights swept across her parked car. She watched the older Jeep Cherokee pass, then turn the corner onto the target's block. On the computer monitor, she saw it come into view and stop in front of the target's house.

"Punky..."

"Hold up, Camron," she said. "Something's happening."

"What?"

She ignored the question and scrambled for the camera's controls resting atop fast-food wrappers crumpled up in the passenger seat. Putting her cell phone on speaker, she set it down in the center console's cupholder and panned and tilted the camera toward the Jeep.

"Talk to me, Punky."

She zoomed in on the Cherokee and focused on the driver's door. "Somebody just pulled up to the house," she said. "Blue Jeep Cherokee. Late nineties. Lifted with off-road tires and a roof rack."

"License plate?"

She panned the camera to the rear of the SUV, but a shrub at the park's southeastern corner blocked it entirely from view. "Not from this angle."

"What about stickers or decals?"

The driver's door opened, and she quickly focused on the man exiting the vehicle. Though the closest streetlamp was one house over on the corner, it cast enough of a glow that she could make out his features. "Hold on. The driver just exited. Male, white. Mid-twenties, about as tall as the Jeep, with a slim build."

"Doesn't sound like a Ministry guy to me," Camron said.

As she studied the man on the computer screen, she watched him walk around the Jeep's nose and approach the front door, kneeling next to a potted plant and tipping it slightly as if fishing for a spare key. "Well, he sure acts like he owns the place," she said.

Just as he set the plant back down, a light turned on over a pair of chairs on the front patio. He appeared startled but only stood tall and faced the door. He didn't shy away as if he had been caught red-handed trying to break in, and when the door opened, Punky zoomed in on the slight woman dressed in a simple robe.

"What's going on?"

"You know you can access the live stream on your own, right?"

She heard some rustling on the other end as Camron opened an application on his smart phone to receive the video her pole-cameras were broadcasting wirelessly. "Who's she?"

"The *grandmother*?" Punky replied with obvious sarcasm.

More rustling. "Okay. Her name is Fu Zan. Age fifty-eight, she and her husband, He Gang, a computer engineer with Adobe, immigrated from China a little over thirty years ago."

Punky saw the surprise on Fu Zan's face fade into happiness as she held her arms out and pulled the stranger on her patio in for a hug. "What the..."

"She definitely knows him," Camron said, stating the obvious.

"Yeah, well, who is he?"

Her phone crackled with static as Camron scrambled to come up with an answer. "The only information I have is on the two occupants of the house—Fu Zan and He Gang. I wonder..."

But Punky was tired of waiting. She set the camera's controls onto the seat next to her and pressed the button on the dash to start the anemic two-liter four-cylinder engine. It cranked over immediately with an unsatisfying purr.

Damn, I miss my Challenger.

"Shift to the other camera," Camron said.

"Hold your horses. I'm moving closer to get a shot of his license plate."

"Punky..."

But she ignored his plea. She put the car into gear and pulled away from the curb, rounding the same corner the Jeep had taken onto the target's street. She looked through her side window at the house just as Fu

Zan pulled the stranger inside and closed the front door. A moment later, the patio light winked off.

"They went inside," Punky said. "Stand by for the license plate."

She continued rolling forward on Cherry Avenue and plucked her cell phone from the cupholder, then opened the camera app and aimed it at the Cherokee's license plate. She snapped several pictures and dropped them into an open text message.

"They're coming your way," she said.

"Got them," Camron said a few seconds later. "Stand by."

She dropped her phone on the seat and rolled past the parked Cherokee to continue north. Though she was eager to learn the stranger's identity, she really didn't think it factored much into the reason she was there. She figured she had collected all the intelligence she would get that night and set her sights on the uncomfortable bed in her room at the Sonesta in Milpitas.

"Punky."

She yawned again and looked at the cars parked on the opposite side of the street, casually studying their makes and models as a car afficionado might do. But her fatigue evaporated in an instant. Tucked between two equally boring sedans was a European model with dark-tinted windows. Only the halo of light descending through the windshield and the subtle movement of a person in the passenger seat betrayed that it was occupied.

Her heart raced as she continued north. Without even looking, she knew the car was parked in the perfect spot to surveil the target's house, and she didn't believe in coincidences.

"Punky, you still there?"

She swallowed against the dryness in her mouth. "Yeah."

"The Jeep belongs to a US Marine," Camron said. "Corporal Adam Garett, an Aviation Logistics Information Management Systems Specialist —whatever that is—based down here at Miramar."

Punky glanced at the Mercedes sedan in her side-view mirror. "And we're not the only ones interested in him."

BOGEY SPADES:
BATTLE BORN #3

Enemies. Allies. It's hard to tell the difference when peace and world order hang in the balance.

Returning home a hero, TOPGUN pilot Colt Bancroft is called on to resurrect a Vietnam-era light attack squadron. Once soaring high, he finds himself on the dark side of special operations in a conflict he never saw coming. At its front lines, NCIS Special Agent Emmy "Punky" King is confronted with the timeless question—*is the enemy of her enemy her friend?*

As Colt and his band of Navy SEALs bring the *Black Ponies* of VAL-4 to the fight, Punky navigates the murky waters of international espionage and an uneasy alliance with a former adversary to uncover a new threat. At its heart is a weapon that could tilt the scales of global power. And the American Vice President is in the crosshairs.

In a world where every decision has repercussions and trust is a double-edged sword, Colt and Punky must forgive past transgressions and forge new alliances to confront an enemy who always seems one step ahead. In this high-stakes game: every choice counts, and the next move could redefine the future.

**Get your copy today at
severnriverbooks.com**

ACKNOWLEDGMENTS

They say you have your whole life to write your first book but only a year to write your second. In my case, I had even less than that. And it would not have been possible without the constant encouragement of my wife **Sarah**, and my three incredible children, **Tre**, **William**, and **Rebecca**. Thank you for believing in me and always supporting my dreams.

To my fellow authors who have offered their support from the beginning, I am truly humbled to be among your ranks. To **Brian Andrews**, **Don Bentley**, **Marc Cameron**, **Jack Carr**, **Simon Gervais**, **Mark Greaney**, **Chris Hauty**, **Josh Hood**, **Ward Larsen**, **David McCloskey**, **Taylor Moore**, **Ryan Steck**, **Connor Sullivan**, **A.J. Tata**, **Brad Taylor**, **Steve Urszenyi**, and **Jeff Wilson**, thank you for your friendship and words of encouragement.

To those who offered their critical eye to scenes in their areas of expertise, I can't thank you enough. Any mistakes in this novel are mine alone, but where I nailed it, the credit is yours. To **Layne Crowe**, **Charlie Mauzé**, **Del Roll**, and **J. Kenneth Wickiser**, thank you for ensuring this work of fiction contained at least a shred of realism.

To my amazingly talented super-agent, **John Talbot**, I am thankful for your patience and guidance as I navigate the publishing world. To **Andrew Watts**, **Cate Streissguth**, **Randall Klein**, **Kate Schomaker**, and the unsung heroes behind Severn River Publishing, thank you for giving me a home and helping to mold this story into a finished product I am incredibly proud of.

Lastly, to you, my readers. Thank you for continuing to give up your most precious commodity to spend time with Colt and Punky. I hope you enjoyed their adventure and look forward to the next one. I know I look forward to delivering it to you.

I'm out.
Farley

ABOUT THE AUTHOR

Jack Stewart grew up in Seattle, Washington and graduated from the U.S. Naval Academy before serving twenty-three years as a fighter pilot. During that time, he flew combat missions from three different aircraft carriers and deployed to Afghanistan as a member of an Air Force Tactical Air Control Party. His last deployment was with a joint special operations counter-terrorism task force in Africa.

Jack is a graduate of the U.S. Navy Fighter Weapons School (TOPGUN) and holds a Master of Science in Global Leadership from the University of San Diego. He is an airline pilot and has appeared as a military and commercial aviation expert on international cable news. He lives in Dallas, Texas with his wife and three children.

Sign up for Jack Stewart's reader list at
severnriverbooks.com